BRANCH

	DATE DUE	
	RECEIVED JUL 3 1998 By	

W9-CBX-131

The
Carringtons
of Helston

The Carringtons *of* Helston

Malcolm Macdonald

St. Martin's Press ≋ New York

Library of Congress Cataloging-in-Publication Data

Macdonald, Malcolm, 1932–
    The Carringtons of Helston / Malcolm Macdonald.
      p. cm.
    ISBN 0-312-18552-9
    I. Title.
PR6068.O827C37   1998
823'.914—dc21   98-14319
                                       CIP

First published in Great Britain by Judy Piatkus (Publishers) Ltd.

First U.S. Edition: June 1998

10 9 8 7 6 5 4 3 2 1

for

'Deirdre'

who turned out to be

Fiona

to our overwhelming joy

Contents

Part One

Helston station

The Enchanted Well

1   After Truthall Halt the branch line veers briefly northward, threading its way along the hillside among tiny, stone-hedged fields, meandering lanes, and wind-bowed copses. At the head of the valley it turns southeast again, leaps across a tall viaduct of Cornish granite, and completes its journey to Helston up a short and none-too-gentle slope, which always brings out a fine display of steam from the little saddle-tank engines that serve the line. From time to time the stolid square tower of Sithney church can be seen, a mile and more away, just breaking above the skyline of Sithney Common Hill.

"Is that it?" Leah asked the first time she noticed it, jabbing her gloved finger against the rain-streaked, smut-mottled window of their compartment. "Our church? Or it will be if we go ahead and buy this farm."

"We!" her brother echoed scornfully. "I like that! *You* won't be buying it." He looked to their father for support.

Their father raised a sympathetic eyebrow at his daughter. Since their mother's death in 1910, four years ago now, Leah had taken over the distaff side of the household, making all the decisions and undertaking all the public duties that would have fallen upon her mother. At eighteen it had seemed a heavy burden; now, at twenty-two, she shouldered it as if it had been hers from birth. He would never buy the Old Glebe Farm without her approval — and they all knew it. But William, two years younger than his sister, chafed at every show of her authority, no matter how slight or casual.

"I might, too," she said airily. "It depends on the price."

He did not rise to it. He was getting better at not rising to her more obvious provocations.

"Helston," their father said, leaning back from the other window to allow them a better view.

How often he had heard his old man speak of the little town, even though he, too, had never seen it; in fact, he had been passing on *his* old man's boyhood memories of the place, before he took the emigrant boat to America, back in the 1830s.

"I'm all discombobulated now, sir," William drawled. "Is Helston our old home town? Or is it Leedstown?"

Leah, who had noticed, since their arrival in Cornwall the previous week, how her brother's rather jocose Americanisms grated on local people, had to restrain herself from speaking out sharply. She, too, was getting much better at not rising to obvious provocations.

"A bit of both, son," their father replied. "Gran'pappy Carrington called himself 'William Carrington of Leedstown' when he first set foot in America. But he had all his schooling right there in Helston and did his early courting there, too. Or 'couranting' he called it. So I guess his heart was there."

"Home is where the heart is," Leah murmured. And though her gaze was on Helston still, her inner vision dwelled more fondly on a certain quiet street in far-away East Haven, Connecticut, where stood the dearest little clapboard house in the Cape Cod style ...

She closed her eyes then, to see it more clearly. *Oh, Tom,* she thought, holding her breath so that no sudden sigh might give her away, *will I ever see you again?*

"You okay, sis?"

She opened her eyes once more and found William grinning at her. He knew very well what had been going through her mind — and that the old man's talk of courting had provoked it. She lowered her eyes and waited for him to tease.

But no words came.

She glanced at him again and was met with an ambiguous expression — almost, one might say, a gaze of sympathy. She looked away hastily, having no means — that is, no experience — of dealing with such a novel emotion from him toward her.

"'Course, in those days," their father said, "his only way of getting about was on foot. They didn't even have bicycles. So 'home' was a few acres. But *our* home, I guess, will be the whole of Cornwall. Or West Penwith, anyway, when we get an auto."

"Where's West Penwith?" Leah asked.

"Clear to Land's End from here," he told her. "A couple o' dozen miles, mebbe."

"What sort of car are we gonna get ourselves, sir?" William asked eagerly.

Leah let their conversation drift off into the background as she turned her face to the grimy window once more. The train thundered over the viaduct and began its energetic final haul up to the station; it was only two coaches long, so each thrust of the pistons could be felt as a little nudge of the seat against her. They were like the nudges a parent might give a reluctant child: Go on! Go on! Go on!

Do I like this Cornwall? she asked herself, running her eye this way and that, tracing a path as random as the hedges and lanes out there.

Certainly the county was doing nothing to present itself in a good light on this particular day. February-filldyke, the nursery rhyme said, so the month knew how to behave. Today, a steady, almost invisible rain fell from a sky of uniform gray. Away to the west, crowning Trigonning Hill — the tallest in the district — one long streak of silver relieved that uniformity. But it was not wide enough to promise any improvement; it merely gleamed off every slate roof, every puddled byway, and each bare branch among the nearer trees, revealing something more profound than simple wetness. Soaking, sodden, sopping wetness. A wetness she could feel in her very bones, even here in the warmth of their first-class compartment. As if to confirm it, the cattle stood up to their bellies in mud, patiently steaming as they awaited their dole of hay.

Her dad once said Gran'pappy William told him he'd felt colder in Cornwall on a wet February day (just like today, in fact) than in New England at ten below. She thought of the crisp, snow-blanketed landscape they'd left behind them three weeks earlier and, this time, permitted herself a sigh. Never another summer on the remote, wild, untramelled foreshores of Cape Cod … never another motor ride upstate to picnic by the beaver lake above Bashbish Falls … never another Thanksgiving with all the …

Well, at least they *could* have Thanksgiving — anywhere in the world. Did they have turkeys in England? Never mind. They could get one shipped.

The train clattered beneath the bridge, just before the station, and the sudden noise jolted her out of her reverie. The brakes were already beginning to bite. *Baggage,* she thought automatically — and then remembered that today was just an outing, to look at this farm in Sithney. Their baggage was all at the White Hart in Redruth, only partly unpacked, waiting a permanent … yes, she'd soon have to start calling it 'home.'

Freed from responsibility for counting trunks and carpet bags and valises, she rose to her feet and punched her gloved fists alternately into their opposing palms, trying to get some warmth back into her fingers.

"There's our man, I guess." Her father had let down the window and, shielding his eye against smuts from the engine, was scanning the platform as they juddered to a halt. "Mister Coad?" he called. "Over here."

Steam from worn couplings rose around them as they stepped out of their carriage.

"Mister Carrington. I'm glad to make your acquaintance, sir." The auctioneer shook hands all round as the old man introduced his offspring. "I'm sorry Helston can't put on a better welcome." He shot an accusing glance at the rainclouds above, which had just opened in a new downpour.

Although the canopy protected them from direct assault, it could not shield them from that which splashed obliquely off the curved roofs of the carriages.

"It'll pass," Coad assured them. "At least, it did yesterday — eventually — and the day before. And the days before that. Shall we have a cup of tea while we wait?" He nodded toward the tea-room at the end of the building.

"What are all these?" William asked, tapping his cane on the nearer of two large stacks of crates, which impeded their progress along the platform.

"Winter greens, dead rabbits, daffodils ..." Coad said. "They'll all be in Covent Garden or Smithfield by this time tomorrow." He grinned. "If you think the price of land in these parts is outrageous, *there's* one explanation for it, right before your eyes." He jerked a thumb at the stacks of crates. "We can now get all our produce fresh into the London markets — within a day of harvesting, in fact."

"Well, I won't be *farming* the Old Glebe," John Carrington said. "As I explained in my letter, I want to make a garden of it. A garden on the grand scale ... a return to Eden, if that doesn't sound like blasphemy."

Coad went first through the tea-room door and held it ajar, first for them and then for a rather fussy, middle-aged couple who had been tormenting a porter all the way along the platform behind them.

"There's something in all of us that yearns for such a return," Coad said.

"I *beg* your pardon, sir?" the fussy gentleman exclaimed.

By gesture alone Coad managed to convey a petty apology to him, along with the explanation that he was actually talking to the Carringtons.

"Furriners!" he murmured as he joined the three Americans.

"Oh?" Leah was surprised. "They sounded very English to me. 'Veddy' English, as we say."

"Yes, they are."

"You call English people 'foreigners'?"

He chuckled. "You bet! — as you also say."

"What does that make *us,* then?" William asked.

"Oh, but you're Cornish, of course — by seed and breed. The Carringtons of Leedstown."

They stared at him in disbelief, suspecting a bit of salesman's persiflage. But he was clearly sincere.

The waitress interrupted at that moment to take their order — tea for four and toasted teacakes all round.

"You'll meet scores of people who still remember William Carrington of Leedstown," Coad said when she withdrew. "Not all of them kindly, I have to warn you. Celtic memories are long — as I'm sure you know. Even death will hardly make them fade." He smiled at each in turn, ending with his eyes on Leah.

She had taken an instant liking to him, not just because he was both presentable and easygoing but also because he had an air of culture about him. His demeanour suggested he was an auctioneer and realtor only to earn money for more important ends. Not 'realtor' — estate agent. Much grander-sounding.

"Oh?" Carrington had caught something in Coad's tone when he said that not all local people would remember his gran'pappy kindly. "Something I ought to know about?"

Coad stared briefly out of the window, marshalling his words. "I don't suppose William himself made too many enemies ..." he began.

"Hardly old enough," Carrington put in.

"Just so. But his family did, I'm afraid. There's one incident in particular that I have in mind, and it's pertinent to our present business. His uncle — who would be your great-great-uncle, sir — 'Honourable' Carrington ... his real name was Hannibal ..."

"Right." Carrington nodded.

"But schoolboy humour traded it for 'Honourable,' so it stuck to him for life. Anyway, he was a clerk to the Pallas venturers, who had a group of tin mines between Sithney and Carleen. I'll point them out to you. They're all abandoned now but that was their heyday. He lived in Sithney, not far from the Old Glebe, in fact. And he was one of the leading lights of the parish council. Indeed, he was its chairman in the year in question — the year of eighteen and forty — when the Old Glebe was declared redundant by the church and they put it up for sale. And Honourable Carrington insisted on a covenant to the title deeds, ensuring, in effect, that the farm never fell into the hands of dissenters and nonconformists. Of course, it has been voided since then, but it remained in force for about twenty years. No Methodists — primitive or otherwise — no Baptists, no Christadelphians ..."

"No Methodists!" Carrington exclaimed. "I can imagine how popular that must have been down here!"

"And the others I mentioned. There's a fair sprinkling hereabouts. But one family in particular took great offence at it — the Liddicoats. Staunch Methodists to the last man, woman, and child. They saw the covenant as a device to exclude them in particular. I think James Liddicoat, especially, was very keen to buy. And Honourable knew it. So of course Liddicoat took it personally. Who wouldn't!"

"But all that was more than sixty years back," Carrington protested. "D'you mean to say ..."

"Remember what I told you about Celtic memories?"

"Sixty years, though!" He shook his head in amazement.

"Is this James Liddicoat still alive, then?" Leah inquired.

Coad smiled as if he'd just been waiting for someone to ask it. "His son is. Clifford Liddicoat."

"Drop the other boot," William said. "He still lives in Sithney. Am I right?"

Coad nodded. "At Grankum Farm. The farm across the valley from the Old Glebe. In fact, he has the renting of the Old Glebe fields until Midsummer Day."

"Don't tell me!" Carrington exclaimed. "Now it's on the market again, he's interested."

Coad grinned. "You bet!" he said again.

2 They stood in a small group, leaning on the gate at the lower end of the cobbled yard of the Old Glebe. Ben Coad swept an arm across the western view from there. "When old William Carrington of Leedstown last set eyes on this," he said, "he'd have seen many more trees. The mines have pretty well denuded the landscape since then. The only surviving woodlands now are clustered around the big houses. Or they're preserved as game covert. Like that." He pointed to a sliver of the woods around Godolphin Hall on the Duke of Leeds's estate, which was just visible now that the rain had eased off. "Of course, Grankum Wood, just below us here, is too steep to farm."

"Oak?" John Carrington guessed from the bare trunks and branches.

Coad nodded. "And ash and hawthorn. There's an abandoned quarry down among them. Also a well, whose waters are said to be enchanted. They have magical powers."

"To cure what?" Leah asked.

"Loneliness, I suppose, Miss Carrington." He chuckled. "They say that if a spinster or bachelor has an eye on a possible partner and can induce him or her to drink of its waters without knowing it, love will follow almost instantaneously. But, against that, a couple of dozen families draw their daily water supply from that same spring, and there's no detectable increase in the infatuation rate of the two parishes."

She raised her binoculars to her eyes and surveyed the wood.

"It's near the upper end," he told her. "But I doubt you'll see it. It's below the flank of the hill from here."

"Are you married, Mister Coad?" Carrington asked with a twinkle in his eye.

"I have so far evaded ... I mean, I do not yet have that honour, sir," he replied.

"Then perhaps you will one day conduct the definitive experiment."

"Or be the victim of one," Leah added, lowering the glasses again and smiling sweetly at him.

Her eyes and Coad's dwelled in each other's for a moment. Then he said, "I walk in fear and dread already, sir."

"You mentioned two parishes?" she prompted.

"Ah, yes. Breage and Sithney." He pointed out the tower of Breage church on the skyline, a mile distant as the crow flies but almost twice as much on foot. It stood on the long southern flank of Trigonning Hill, which towered above the landscape. The narrow streak of brightness they had observed from the train had meanwhile expanded to fill half the sky.

Between the two parishes lay a Y-shaped valley, though from where they stood only the V-end of the 'Y' was visible. The Old Glebe was about halfway up the eastern arm of the 'V.' The ground between the two arms was not so high as where they stood so they were able to look obliquely down upon it — and to see over it to even more distant parishes, beyond Breage.

"What a curious mixture of landscapes," William remarked. "It's almost like a history diagram. I mean Grankum Wood, I guess, is the nearest thing to the primeval forest that once covered the whole of Cornwall. Right?"

Coad dipped his head.

"Then you've got all these lovely little patchwork fields with their stone walls all around ..."

"Hedges." Coad corrected him. "I know they *are* walls but we call them hedges in Cornwall. *English* people call them walls."

He made being *English* sound quite dreadful. Leah tried to imagine some remote part of America where people would talk of *Americans* with similar contempt; it was impossible. Except for an Indian reservation, maybe. Perhaps the Cornish were England's redskins?

"Okay, hedges," William continued. "Farms and fields and hedges — which is like Nature being *controlled* by us. Humans in control of Nature, right? Cooperating, you could say. But then you get *that!*" Like a courtroom lawyer producing some especially damning piece of evidence he waved his hand at the central portion of the scene before them. "Humans in contempt of Nature."

No one could disagree. A century and more of the steam engine, coupled with the skills of the Cornish miner, had produced a landscape of utter devastation: open quarries, mine buildings — all deserted and many already derelict — and heaps of poisonous spoil on which nothing would grow. 'Spoil' was the word for them all right.

Ben Coad reeled off some of the names, pointing each out as he went: "Wheal Fortune, Wheal Metal, Scott's, Wheal Vreah, Deepwork, Wheal Anchor …"

When they asked where all the wheels had gone he explained that a 'wheal' was a working or, specifically, a mine working.

"But so much waste rock!" Leah said. Once again she was surveying the scene through her binoculars. "Couldn't they have left it underground and just taken out the tin?"

He laughed. "I'm sure they'd love to be able to do that. But veins of tin ore are only *inches* wide at best. You'd have to train mice as miners. However, in some places the veins themselves are as close-packed as they are on a drunkard's nose. See Wheal Vor over there? By Godolphin Woods?"

"Where the entire hillside is covered with waste stone?" She passed the glasses, unasked, to her brother, who accepted them with pleased surprise.

"That's the place. The waste stone — *halvans* we call it — is all that's left now of the famous Great Lode of Wheal Vor. When it was fully mined out, about thirty years ago, the space it left was big enough to build two churches the size of Sithney's, one on top of the other!" He swept his hand once more across the scene. "It's five hundred acres of devastation now, but fifty years ago the land between here and Trigonning Hill was the richest thousand-acre spread on earth — richer than the Klondyke or California, richer than the Rand or any of the Australian goldfields."

"And where has it all gone?" Carrington asked, for they had seen little evidence of such wealth so far, and certainly not in the countryside immediately around them now.

"You're not the only Cornish people who'd like to know the answer to *that* question," he replied darkly. "Shall we look at the farmland while the rain holds off? Perhaps Miss Carrington would like to inspect the house meanwhile …"

"Not a bit! I came prepared, see?" Leah lifted the hem of her dress enough to show her toecaps. "Gum boots," she said.

"Ah, gum boots. Interesting. 'Wellingtons' we call them. I noticed a couple of spare pairs in the barn last time I was here — if either of you gentlemen are interested?"

The men decided their everyday boots would be stout enough if they kept to the less-wet parts of the land. The plan worked well enough except at the gates between fields, where Liddicoat's cattle had poached the land to a quagmire. There they had to hug one of the granite gateposts and inch their way around the strip of solid ground at its base.

"There's your southern neighbour," Coad said. "George Gosling of Trelissick." He pointed out the small group of trees among which nested the farmhouse.

"We should have saddled up those horses in the stables," Leah said, nudging her brother to return the binoculars. "Are they Mister Liddicoat's, too?"

"No, they belong to the rector, Reverend Langham. Despite his age, he's a keen member of the Fourborough, which is our local hunt, or one of them. The Cury is the other. Are any of you keen on hunting?"

"Not I!" William said at once.

"I am," Leah said. "As long as they don't catch too many foxes. I enjoy 'steeplechasing,' I think you call it? Why did you grin like that when I suggested saddling up those horses?"

Ben Coad was a little taken aback; he was not aware she had been watching him so closely. "Oh," he said diffidently, "nothing really. I showed an *American* over a farm the other side of Helston last week." He stressed the word as if to imply that they were not Americans, or not for the purposes of this particular story. "He told me about his 'spread' back home. He said he could saddle up in the morning and ride his horse all day and still not reach his boundary by sunset. Unfortunately I misunderstood him." His mischievous grin told them he had done no such thing. "I told him I'd owned a horse like that once. There was nothing to do but shoot it."

They were still chuckling when they reached the boundary of this particular spread — the stone hedge that separated the Old Glebe from Trelissick.

"Does this valley run all the way down to the ocean?" William asked as he followed its sweep with his eye.

"You could say so," Coad replied. "It curves round and joins up with the other one. Then they both broaden out and run down to Porthleven, which is behind this flank of the hill to our left, about a mile and a half away. Strictly speaking, it's not really ocean there, either. It's the English Channel. The ocean begins at Land's End."

"It all looks so rural," Leah said, "apart from the mines and the waste. You'd never think we were just over a mile from the ocean — or Channel."

"You can see it from the upstairs windows of the Old Glebe, though. With a good pair of glasses like those, you can even pick out the different kinds of ship — clippers, dreadnoughts, luggers, coasters ... It's a pretty busy horizon, you know. I'd guess there'd be at least one vessel in sight at any given moment, day or night."

While he spoke he was watching John Carrington's eyes traverse the fifty acres of the Old Glebe, back and forth, forth and back. "What d'you think of it so far, sir?" he asked at length.

"Morning sun," Carrington replied at once. "When there's any sun at all, that is — and we have yet to be convinced of that, I may say."

As if to answer him, a single narrow beam of sunlight poked through the clouds, over beyond Godolphin. Small as it was, it transformed the entire scene and lifted everyone's hopes of a brighter afternoon.

"What, may I ask, is the significance of morning sun, sir?" Coad asked next.

"I don't suppose it affects too many farm crops but a lot of garden plants that are allegedly damaged by frost are actually damaged by going straight from frost to full, early-morning sunlight. Still, that's not a point against it. We'd just have to be judicious in our planting."

"Which is Grankum Farm?" Leah asked, training her glasses up the valley once more.

"The one immediately above the wood," Ben Coad replied. "The house is bigger than it appears from here. There's a sort of annexe among the trees."

She only half heard him. Most of her attention was on a figure who had just emerged from among the trees Coad mentioned. It was Clifford Liddicoat, no doubt — their rival contender for the Old Glebe.

A tall, bareheaded man with a lithe spring in his step, he crossed the yard in a dozen easy strides and then vaulted the gate, pivoting with one hand on its topmost rail. It surprised her. Coad had said he was the son of that James Liddicoat who had been thwarted by Honourable Carrington's exclusion clause, sixty years back, so she had assumed he'd be much older — certainly too old to go vaulting gates one-handed. With that same agile step he strode halfway up the field, making for a calf lying among the rough tussocks of grass. It rose and trotted off as he drew near and this apparently satisfied him it needed no help. He stopped then and stared uncertainly about him — which was how he came to notice the party of four, standing at the farther end of the Old Glebe's fields.

Now that he was facing them Leah moved to the nearest gatepost and rested her glasses against its flank, to steady the view they provided. He stood like a colossus, feet apart, hands on hips, jacket open. His waistcoat buttons were out of step, she noticed, with a spare hole at the top and a spare button at the bottom. He was about her own age she guessed — lean, athletic, and devilish good looking, with his tight blond curls and his strong line of jaw.

He fished in one of his pockets and pulled out something dark and compact — a hipflask, she supposed, from the way he raised it at once to his lips.

Or no — not to his lips but to his eyes. He must have had her in clear focus by the time it dawned on her that he, too, was using a pair of binoculars.

Panic!

He must surely see her staring at him. True, his glasses were smaller and probably less powerful, but what did that matter over less than four hundred paces? Fortunately at that moment a bird of prey of some description — a peregrine, perhaps — rose from the hedge behind him and she gratefully followed its ascent with her glasses. Now he'd think that she'd been birding all along, not spying on him and his farm.

To complete the deception she passed the glasses to William again and pointed out the bird, which was now soaring high above them.

Coad and her father were already strolling back across the fields toward the farmhouse.

When her brother returned the glasses she risked a further peep, beginning high in the sky and slowly coming down, as if following some bird's descent. When she found him again, he was standing exactly as he had been a couple of minutes earlier — legs apart, glasses to his eyes, staring straight at her.

It pleased her far more than she could easily have explained.

Experimentally she raised a hand and waved it — not with the grand, semaphoring gestures she'd have made if neither had had binoculars, but with the hesitant, petite sort of greeting she might use across a room.

After a moment's hesitation he let go of his glasses with his right hand and responded with a breezy little salute, dipping his hand halfway and finishing with a flourish.

"What's this?" William asked.

"Oh, I'm just being friendly to our new neighbour," she replied offhandedly.

"Oh, so you've decided to buy, then!"

"Yes, I rather think I have," she said, still keeping the glasses to her eyes.

3   The Old Glebe had been built in early-Georgian times. In Cornwall, where builders' pattern books lingered on until no one could read them for thumbprints, the date meant that its style was from an even earlier monarchy: William and Mary. The Dutch influence was most obvious in the red-brick curlicues of the gable ends — a semicircular apex with little horizontal parapets on either side, yielding to concave quarter-circles down to the level of the gutters. It was pretty, but two centuries of Cornish weather had taken its toll of the brickwork, which was now spalled by frosts and cracked from movements of the roof timbers. The cracks had been repointed, along with the rest of the bricks, but their outlines were still alarmingly visible.

"That doesn't look too healthy," John Carrington commented as he surveyed the façade through binoculars. "I see several glass telltales there. When were they put in?"

"When they did the repointing — almost a year ago," Coad replied. "They were all still intact up to New Year's Day this year, which is when I last inspected them. So the movement is probably ancient. It's visible in photographs from the seventies, which I can show you back in the office."

Carrington's only reply was a sardonic grunt. He was laying the grounds for cheapening the price from the presently outrageous £600. "How old is the barn?" he asked.

"Medieval," Coad answered proudly. "It's the original tithe barn, built with a cruck frame, which you can see exposed in the end wall."

"That's where I'd be putting my glasshouses," Carrington murmured, more to himself than to them.

"Dad!" Leah was shocked. "You can't tear down a building that's stood for four hundred years!"

"Six hundred," Coad corrected her. "Possibly longer. It's about as old as the church building itself. Some of the timbers have the same carver's initials."

"There!" she said.

"If a building has outlived its time and utility, honey, there's no sense in preserving it." He turned to the estate agent. "Surely you agree, sir?"

"Well..." The man scratched the back of his neck awkwardly. "Six or seven hundred years is a long time."

"Long enough, I say. There's some sense in preserving royal palaces and town halls and other buildings of historical interest, but you start preserving stuff like that — old barns — and where do you stop? Factories? Those derelict mine buildings over there? Labourers' cottages? Pigsties? Why, you'd turn the whole of England into one great open-air museum. Life would be all pomp and no circumstance, to twist *Othello*. Is that what you want?"

Coad gave a baffled laugh. "Well, sir — to twist *Much Ado,* I can see a hobby horse — by daylight — so I'll say no more. Except for this: People might begin to think you more American than Cornish if you demolished such a fine old building."

Carrington had to accept that point — which, in any case, suited his purpose just as neatly. "Well," he sighed, "it reduces the value of the property to me. I hope that's understood."

Leah, who had seen that point even while Coad was still speaking, wondered why he had given the warning at all. Everyone knew that a realtor's business was to sell real estate. Whether the purchasers did popular or unpopular things after parting with their cash was none of his affair. So maybe 'estate agents' were subtly different from 'realtors,' after all.

Coad, too, was somewhat taken aback to realize he had spoken out so bluntly. The professional side of him was mildly annoyed, for obvious reasons; but the man himself, the private individual, was more than mildly surprised. It made him realize that, in the space of less than an hour, the Carringtons had come to mean much more to him than mere customers — or potential customers. If they did settle in the Helston area, he hoped to cultivate their friendship. He and the old fellow had 'clicked' from the first. And, to be sure, there was Miss Leah, too — charming, bright, open, capable, self-assured, and decidedly good looking. The boy also had his points, no doubt.

Coad could not deny that he would never have articulated such thoughts so forcefully, not even to himself, if he had not noticed how Miss Leah had kept her binoculars trained on young Harvey Liddicoat, across the valley at Grankum. For some reason he had omitted to mention that old Liddicoat had a son — two sons, in fact — when he had described the historical but still tender animosity between the two families, so Miss Leah had probably mistaken Harvey for his father, Clifford.

In short, the professional Coad, who was desperate to find at least one other interested buyer for the Old Glebe — to stop old Liddicoat from naming his own price — was at war with the private Coad, who was already lining up properties on the far side of Helston to tempt the Carringtons away from Sithney and the two young Liddicoat males.

"Well," he said genially in response to Carrington's latest comment, "I have even more attractive properties than this on my books at the moment. Over toward the Lizard. Good hunting country, too," he added by way of encouragement to Miss Leah.

But she pulled a face and said, "Lizard — what a name! I saw it on the map. It doesn't sound very … you know … attractive." She took the glasses from her father and inspected the patched-up cracks for herself.

"It means 'high field' in Cornish," he explained. "*Ard* is 'high' and *les* or *lis* is 'field' or 'enclosure'." He tried not to look at the line of her bosom, which her action had accentuated into a different sort of high enclosure.

"So," William put in, "instead of *les-ard* becoming 'Lizard' *ard-les* might have become 'Artless'!"

Coad laughed dutifully. "It would have been even more of a misnomer, sir," he replied. "Several artists have settled there, in fact. Some of considerable renown." He was about to qualify this rather bold assertion, admitting that the number was not as great as had settled in St Ives or Newlyn, when he noticed Miss Leah's interest prick up.

"Really?" she asked, letting the glasses fall to her breast. "Who, for example?"

"A Scotchman called Dougal MacKay?" He made a question of it, to suggest she'd surely heard the name. "Glasgow School?" He turned to the old fellow. "And the climate is even milder there than here, though it's only eight miles away. Water on all three sides, you see."

"I suppose you speak Cornish, do you, Mister Coad?" Carrington asked. He thought Coad was being rather clever, mentioning other properties instead of discussing the price of the Old Glebe.

The man shook his head. "The tongue itself is dead — has been for more than a century now. But dictionaries and texts have survived."

"What does Helston mean?" William asked.

Before Coad could reply they were distracted by the sound of an unoiled gate shrieking on rusted hinges. It was the gate at the lower end of the yard, where they had first stood and looked out over the hills and halvans to the west of Sithney. And there, silhouetted in the gap, stood what they took to be some species of wild man — tall, barrel-chested, gaitered like a bishop, and wearing over his head a four-bushel corn sack. He had tucked one of its closed corners into the other to make a kind of monkish cowl against the rain; but, there being no rain at that moment, he drew it off as he approached, revealing a mane of uncombed hair. Long but rather thinned by the years, it stood out in all directions, the way young children draw the rays of the sun on their older siblings' school slates. His face was grim and yet, looking at him closely, Leah could believe that a smile from him would be grimmer still.

"Mister Liddicoat!" Coad called out; his tone suggested that this was a pleasant surprise, indeed.

"Coad," was the dour reply. He did not take his eyes off John Carrington's face all the way up the yard. "Who's this-here, then?" he added as he reached their scattered circle.

"Cousin Jacks who've come back home," the man replied. Then, seeing no way of dodging the revelation, added, "Mister John Carrington."

The farmer bristled at the name, showing that Coad had been right when he warned them of the length of Celtic memories.

To Carrington he said, "This is Mister Clifford Liddicoat, who farms Grankum, across the valley."

In the corner of his eye he saw an *Aha!* light up Miss Leah's face and he knew she had earlier mistaken Harvey for his father. A moment later, when her father presented Liddicoat to her, she confirmed it, saying, "I believe I saw your son — or it could have been one of your labourers, maybe? — out in the fields just now, Mister Liddicoat."

Something in her words, or perhaps just in her tone, struck a chord in Liddicoat and made him change from whatever course he had intended to adopt in dealing with these interlopers, these competitors for a property he already regarded as his but for the ink on the deed. He was shaking her hand with perfunctory speed, and would surely have let go a second later, when her words penetrated the hairy thickets that sprang from his ears and made him slow down. He kept her hand between his but held it still, pumping it up and down very occasionally, as he stared deep into her eyes. The effect on her was hypnotic.

"Seen 'n, did 'ee?" he asked.

"Quite clearly. Through these binoculars." She patted them with her free hand.

He glanced at them and then looked her up and down slowly. She could not remember being subjected to so blatant an appraisal before.

"'Es," he said at last and in a tone of evident approval. Then, turning to shake William by the hand, he said, casually, "Fond of farming, then, are 'ee, young master?"

"I a farmer? Jee-willikin, *no,* sir! True's preachin' I'm not."

Still holding William's hand he stared into his face, hoping to embarrass him into saying more.

In the end his father spoke. "The boy's interested in mining, Mister Liddicoat — like his great-gran'pappy, you know?"

Ponderously the farmer let go of the son's hand as he turned to face his informant. "That'd be William Carrington of Leedstown, I daresay?" he commented evenly.

"The same, sir. And I gather your family has no cause to remember him — or my great-uncle Honourable — with any particular affection."

The man stared at him in amazement. Directness does not come easy to any Celt.

"See here!" Carrington went on. "No sense in beating about the bush. If apologies might serve a purpose, I'd tender a whole book of etiquette this very minute. But the fact that we're both interested in buying this place shouldn't ..."

"Me?" Liddicoat was scandalized. "Who says I be interested?" Carrington glanced at Coad.

"Aha!" the farmer exclaimed. "Told 'ee I was interested, did 'e? Well, I aren't. So there!" He challenged Coad to dispute the assertion and, when the man said nothing, added, "I told 'n if no one else *wanted* the place, I'd take it off his hands. More out of kindness than good sense ..."

"Mister Liddicoat is a noted local philanthropist," Coad put in, absolutely straight-faced.

The man looked daggers at him. "'E've been on the market more'n a year now," he said.

Coad poured on the salt and rubbed it in: "And Mister Liddicoat must be telling the truth when he declares himself uninterested in the property — he has let so many chances slip by him, to put in his bid."

The man's lips vanished inward. Deep, weather-etched cracks in his skin marked the remnant furrow. "The place is haunted," he said angrily.

Coad folded his arms, as men do when bracing into the wind. "Haunted with the spirits of men who failed to bid for it in time," he said evenly.

Carrington decided to put his oar in then. "I'm not at all certain I like the place, Coad," he said. "I prefer the sound of those properties you mentioned — on the Lizard, despite my daughter's aversion to the name."

This did not suit the auctioneer's tactics at all, so, while he still had some slight advantage of the farmer's stubbornness, he challenged the man: "Can I take it those are your last words, then, Mister Liddicoat? In no circumstances are you interested in buying the Old Glebe?"

Liddicoat reined in his anger at that, annoyed he had let it gallop him so far from the path of his own best welfare. "I'm interested in *any* property — at the right price. But six hundred pounds is daylight robbery."

Carrington cleared his throat with a chuckle. "The more I hear of you, Mister Liddicoat," he said, "the more I believe you to be the most sensible man in the whole of Cornwall. Six hundred pounds *is* daylight robbery. I never heard a sentiment with which I could agree more wholeheartedly."

The auctioneer stood his ground and beamed at them — a lighthouse that had withstood many a gale from this particular quarter. "Those are my instructions, gentlemen, and I have no power to vary them — nor inclination to, either. We will surely get our price in the end."

"But how long will you wait meanwhile?" Carrington asked.

"As long as it takes. The property is in the estate of a minor, who will have no need to realize its value for many years yet — if ever. The trustees are happy enough with the existing rents, I gather. In short, six hundred is both the asking price and the sticking point." He turned exclusively to Carrington. "Shall we go inside, sir? I think the interior may improve your opinion of the Old Glebe — as a man of taste and refinement. It is one of the few houses in the area that is *fitting* for a gentleman." He studiously avoided Liddicoat's eye.

The tactic bore fruit. The farmer nodded curtly to each and stalked off the way he had come. After a dozen paces he turned and shouted angrily at Coad: "You do think I can't pay six hundred, do 'ee?"

Coad bet everything on one final gamble. "On the contrary, Mister Liddicoat. I know full well you can. But I'm equally sure you won't."

"How?" the man asked — which, in Cornwall, means 'why?'.

"Because it's not a house in which *you* would feel comfortable."

If looks could kill, there would have been three witnesses to murder at the Old Glebe that morning.

"I think you've lost one party to this sale, Mister Coad," Carrington murmured as they watched the man stamp his way back to the creaking gate.

"We'll see about that," the agent replied, with more confidence than he actually felt. He took out the key and offered it to Carrington, as if to suggest he was already the proprietor.

"I have to tell you," Carrington said, "that the thought of making an enemy of such a neighbour as that, gives me a mighty disinclination to make any offer at all."

But Leah, who was watching the old farmer through her binoculars, was of a different opinion. Halfway down the field, just before his head vanished from view, he turned and stared at them. He was obviously not aware she was using her glasses again for, instead of the expected scowl on his face, she saw a self-satisfied grin — as if he thought he had carried off some triumph from their encounter. Friend or foe, she thought, he would make a most interesting neighbour. And anyway, what could he actually *do* that might harm them?

4 The house had been untenanted for more than three years and, what with the scandalous price of servants, even on board wages, it had been left unoccupied, too — a fate that had overtaken many houses of late, including mansions far grander than the Old Glebe. So Coad's description of it as a 'gentleman's house' needed to be taken along with liberal doses of imagination. Rooks had fallen down at least two of the chimneys, dislodging volumes of soot that carpeted the floor and half buried their decomposed and mummified bodies. Even the rats had shunned them, though they seemed to have chewed at almost everything else in sight. And, most horrid of all in Leah's opinion, a colony of some fifteen bats was hibernating in the passage outside the scullery door, which she was exploring on her own.

She fled in a panic to rejoin the others, took a wrong turning, and almost fell into an earth closet at the opposite end of the passage. She wrinkled her nose at it for someone had certainly been making use of the convenience, it being easily accessible from the side yard. She took a grip on herself and, containing her fear of those squeaky, flea-ridden balls of flying fur, found her way back into the main part of the house. She joined the others as they were making their way up the servants' stair.

"Watch out for bats," she told William, clutching her bonnet tightly around her hair.

"What's wrong with bats?" he asked with tendentious, manly scorn. "Lovely little velvety creatures."

Ignoring him, she turned to Coad and asked if the house was on town water; earth closets were intolerably primitive to her.

"Mains water?" he replied. "It's promised for this year, for the whole of Sithney, that is. There's electricity in the village already, from the Helston Power Company, but the Old Glebe isn't yet connected. You could site a septic tank ... you know what I mean?"

"Yes," Carrington said. "Americans call it that, too — in mixed company."

"You could site one just to the left of that gate at the bottom of the yard. I don't suppose gas will ever come out this far, but there's an ironfounder in Helston called Toy who makes excellent cooking ranges. They heat water, too — all you could want."

"And how about steam heat?" William asked. "For the rooms and passages, you know. Do you have steam heat here?"

Coad shook his head. "I've seen it in hospitals and one or two large public buildings. But really, you know, I think our winters here must be much milder than yours. There are very few days in a year when a simple coal fire would be inadequate. You could count them on those fingers. And that's the truth." He held up one hand, noticed a tear in his glove, and turned it quickly round.

He saw Leah grinning at him and smiled ruefully back.

"It is a truth universally acknowledged ..." she murmured to him as they passed into the first of the servants' rooms.

He looked at the hole in his glove, taking no care to hide it now, and added, "... that a bachelor with holes in his clothes must be in need of a wife? Yes indeed, Miss Carrington."

"How many servants board in?" Carrington asked. "I mean how many used to?"

"In the good old days? When the Daveys were here, which was around the time of the Boer War, there were eight maids, a butler, housekeeper, valet-cum-coachman, cook, three living-out kitchen and scullery maids, four in the stables, a gardener, and a boy. And anything from eight to twenty farm labourers, depending on the season."

"Why, this house must have been quite a little village in itself!" Carrington remarked.

Coad looked about the tiny room with its low-hung ceiling and said, almost apologetically, "They got four maids into this room and four next door. But girls wouldn't put up with such conditions nowadays."

"But the Boer War ..." William began. "I mean, that was only, what? Ten years back?"

Coad agreed. "Yet it seems much longer. A whole generation, almost. I don't know what people thought about it in America, but here ..."

"Oh," Carrington replied, "we ... that is, *they* ... thought it an absolute scandal. Naked English imperialism ... which is understandable when you remember the history of England's involvement with America."

"There were plenty of the same mind in England, too," Coad said. "There were disturbances in every town. It almost brought about a second civil war. Neighbours who'd lived together amicably for years were suddenly at daggers drawn — especially down here in Cornwall, where the Liberal-nonconformist traditions are so strong. And it's still going on, too. Newcomers to the county join this or that social circle according to where they stand on the Boer question."

"And the two don't mix? Never?"

"Not socially. Of course, pros and antis work side by side on charity committees, the Red Cross, the RNLI, and so on. And they obviously have to mingle at big social occasions — Helston Furry Dance, the church fête, and events like that. But that's the limit. A stiff nod of the head is all the recognition they'll give each other in the street."

"Extraordinary!"

"It even divided families. Take Clifford Liddicoat just now. His brother, Frank Liddicoat, who's an auctioneer in Camborne, hasn't spoken to him in years. Come to that, I've only just patched up relations with my own father." He frowned. "How did we get on to this? Oh yes! Servants and changes in attitudes and so on. It seems that a vast social upheaval of that kind brings other, unexpected changes in its wake. The sight of the ruling class tearing itself to shreds gave the servant class ideas, too." He laughed. "And to think that, by fighting the Boer and the Zulu for four years, we produced a new generation of servant girls who will refuse to sleep four-to-a-room when the room is the size of this one!"

"It'll hardly matter in our case." Leah looked at her father. "I don't suppose *we* will be employing a household on anything like that grand scale."

The old man nodded. Then, to Coad, he added, "It's not that we couldn't afford it, mind, and nor are we close-fisted. It's just not our style. I'm here to create a wonderful garden. He's here to study mine engineering." He nodded at William. "And she's to make a good match and raise a new dynasty."

He didn't even glance at his daughter. But Coad did. And the fleeting annoyance he saw in her eyes made him realize that her notions did not entirely coincide with her father's.

5 The Carringtons were so taken with the Helston area that they moved to the Angel Hôtel and set about inspecting several other houses, both in the town itself and farther afield. Their choice was plentiful because the collapse of tin mining had left many once-rich families with establishments no longer suited to their incomes. Only a handful of mines were left working now — near Land's End, at Porkellis, and in the Camborne — Redruth area. There were none at all in that part of the country which Coad had called the richest thousand acres in the world, once upon a time. At several of those fine houses they came within an ace of making a firm offer, but the same thing always held them back: their memory of the Old Glebe at Sithney.

Its grip on their imaginations was hard to explain. The house needed considerable work before it would be habitable, and the fact that a third of its acreage faced slightly north of west made it less attractive to John Carrington as a potential garden. As for his two children, there were several other suitable houses, nearer not only to Helston but also to other young people — which ought to have commended them more to Leah and her brother. And yet all three Carringtons felt their preference drawn to the Old Glebe instead, though not always for identical reasons.

For William, it was the landscape itself and those elements he had noticed on their visit to Sithney — the rich and contradictory mixture of ancient and modern, the struggle between the despoiled earth and that inexorable cleansing power of nature which was already showing its fringes and would one day reclaim its very heart.

This subtle fascination drew him back, alone, one afternoon toward the end of that same February. His father and sister were intending to visit yet another house, over near Gweek, which lies at the head of the Helford River estuary on the Falmouth side of Helston. William had long since tired of these inspections and, in any case, he felt in his bones that they, too, had already decided on the Old Glebe and were simply being prudent New Englanders in looking at other possible homes. So he cried off joining them and, while they boarded the horse-drawn bus for Gweek, he took one of the new motor charabancs travelling in the opposite direction, toward Penzance.

He sat behind Billy Trim, the driver, and marvelled at the skill with which he changed gears, hardly ever making a clash. It was especially noticeable at the start of the journey from Helston, where the road ran pretty well level through the market at St Johns, past the gasworks and the yards of the quaintly named Kernow & Daughter; but then, at the bottom of Sithney Common Hill, it suddenly rose at an angle that had defeated many a horse and cart down the years.

Billy Trim went down through the gearbox like a maestro — click, snick, slick! But the racket from the motor itself was quite another matter. Even in bottom gear, the cogs groaned like the damned and clouds of blue-white smoke belched from the exhaust. Old Frank Trevose, the miller, came out of his store and stood in the thick of it, provocatively holding his nose and flapping his flour-sack apron uselessly at the fumes.

"That's another letter to the *Helston Vindicator*," Trim said over his shoulder. "How he don't just shut his doors till 'tis gone away, I don't know. Th'ole fool!"

"In America they make the exhaust tubes point at the sky," William told him.

"We'd have the bird lovers writing in then," Trim said. "Different class of letter but the same old complaint. Some people don't want progress at no price. Old Trevose has forgotten the number of horses he's seen put out of their misery, right there where he's standing now. Terrible sights. I've seen the blood running down that hill in rivers. People do forget, see?"

"It is a very steep hill, that bit," William agreed.

" 'Tis often worse going down. 'Specially on a frosty day. The sun don't hardly ever reach there and I seen horses slip going down and the cart run on and break the shafts and roll over them. Terrible sights." His eyes gleamed as he repeated himself: "Blood everywhere. People do forget, see?"

The bus reached the point where the steepest part of the hill gave way to something gentler. He moved up a gear or two, with the same enviable skill, and advanced the ignition a couple of clicks; the belching fumes turned thinner and paler. All the while he kept a nervous eye on the thermometer, out there on top of the radiator filler cap.

"You from North Cornwall, are you?" Trim asked. "You don't talk like we round here."

"I grew up in America," William explained. He went on to introduce himself properly, which was when he learned Billy Trim's name and parish, too — Godolphin, which stands at the northern end of Trigonning Hill. The man added that the village was named after the Godolphin family, great courtiers in the days of Jacobites and Williamites. He added that the Angel Hôtel, from where the buses departed, had once been the Godolphins' town house. "You interested in history, are you?" he asked.

William replied tactfully that he hoped to learn the English slant on things now that they were going to live here.

"Ah, the English!" Trim mused. "We've seen bloody times down here on their account."

The name of Godolphin reminded William that Coad had pointed out the woodlands of the Hall, on the skyline as seen from the Old Glebe. "Godolphin's near where I'm headed today," he said. "I want to walk through all that old mining country between Sithney and Carleen. Carnmeal Downs, it's called on the map. Where's the nearest you go to that?"

"The stop gate," Trim replied. "That's where they belonged to take the tolls, backalong in the good old turnpike days. I'll set you down there."

Three Jersey cows, which had been standing placidly against the hedge on the upper side of the road, suddenly panicked as the bus drew level and ran off, kicking wildly, their udders flapping like laundry in a gale.

"At least they can't write letters to the papers," William said.

"The farmers can, though," Trim answered morosely. "You related to Harold Carrington of Releath, then, are you?"

"I don't know. I suppose all Cornish Carringtons must be related, if you go far enough back. We must call on him."

The driver chuckled grimly. "You'll need one of they ouija boards, then. He's in his box in Wendron churchyard now. But his daughter, Gwen, she married Hugh Thomas of Trenear. She'd tell you, I daresay."

William stored the names in memory and then watched the man closely for any reaction as he said, "I'm directly descended from William Carrington of Leedstown — I was named for him, in fact."

But Trim just shook his head. "I never heard tell of he. A Cousin Jack, was he?"

William obliged with a potted family history, which prompted the further question: "Just over here on a visit, are you?" — which led to a few more revelations. However, William was careful to say nothing of the old enmity between the Carringtons and the Liddicoats. He wanted to know how widespread the knowledge of it was in the immediate neighbourhood. After all, Godolphin was only three miles or so from Sithney, so, if Trim knew nothing of it, the feud could hardly be a living issue for anyone but the Liddicoats themselves.

He came as close as he dared by letting slip that they were possibly interested in buying the Old Glebe. When he saw the sudden interest in the driver's face, he supposed his words had provoked a memory of the Liddicoat — Carrington story at last. But it was not so.

"The haunted house!" Trim said with ghoulish glee. "Who's got the sale of that ole place — Coad, is it? I'll be he never told you 'tis haunted!"

"Really?" William laughed dismissively. "By what, may I ask? Or by whom?"

" 'Tisn't no laughing matter, young feller," the other said in a slow, lugubrious manner.

"If it's haunted by anything, it's by the spirits of all those birds that fell down the chimneys and died trying to get back out."

"Ah! Not the house. I'm not talking about the house. The house isn't haunted, as such. 'Tweren't even built when the murder happened, which was in that ole barn. Been inside there, have you? The ole tithe barn."

"I know the one. Yes, we had a quick look inside, but ..."

"That's all you'd want, too — a quick look." With a sigh and a shake of his head he implied that even so brief a contact with the ghost that haunted the place was perilous.

They had reached the top of Sithney Common Hill by now and Sithney church tower itself was in sight — also the chimney-pots of the Old Glebe and the ridge tiles of the allegedly haunted tithe barn. Billy Trim wagged a finger in their direction before slipping into top gear and advancing the ignition fully. The motor responded with a satisfactory backfire that sent up flocks of gulls and rooks from the neighbouring fields. The thermometer steadied and from there on began to fall. "Stay clear of there after night has fallen, young fellow," he warned, "if you do value your peace of mind."

"At least tell me the story," William said, doing his best to conceal his incredulity.

The man cleared his throat impressively and resettled himself in his seat. "Ever see that play, *Murder in the Red Barn,* did you?" he asked.

"The old Maria Marten melodrama? Yes, I saw that in summer stock at …"

" 'Tisn't no melodrama, boy. That's a true story, that is. Maria Marten was as real and 'live as what you and me are. So was her betrayer and murderer, a feller called Corder, the squire's son. And 'twas the same story in the Old Glebe, backalong in the days of Oliver Cromwell."

William frowned. "You mean the Maria Marten business really happened down here in Cornwall?"

"No," Trim said patiently. "Same story, different names. The maid's name was Catherine. Catherine Geach. That's an old Cornish name, Geach. You'll find her grave in Sithney church-yard, near the west door. And there's a memorial on the wall inside, too. 'Foully murdered,' it do say. Anyway, her father was land agent to the first Earl of Godolphin in the times after Oliver Cromwell. He belonged to live in Sithney, but the house has now gone."

They stopped to pick up passengers from Antron, and, of course, to exchange the gossip of the day; so it was several minutes before the driver resumed his tale. And then, realizing that the stop gate was now less than a mile away, he reluctantly reduced it to its barest bones:

Catherine Geach, daughter of Edward Geach of Sithney, was, in her twentieth year, courted, deceived, and ruined by the son of the rector, who, when the baby was almost come to term, ripped it from her living womb and so murdered her. And this 'murder most foul' had taken place in the grounds of the Old Glebe, under the roof of the even older tithe barn. Several doctors declared the young man insane but the wrath of the mob was such that they broke into the Helston jail, whipped him at the tail of a cart all the way back to the very scene of his crime, and there killed him by the same barbarous means — that is, by docking his genitals and opening his belly while he hung by the neck from a beam.

"And at times," Trim concluded with mournful glee, "when the wind do howl among the tops of the trees, and the storms do lift the seas above the cliffs down to Porthleven, they belong to pick their old quarrel all over again — he and she. He do curse she to the blackest pits of hell. And she do scream again as he do rip her open and take two lives with a single cut. So just you mind you stay snug and warm indoors on stormy nights, young fellow." He raised his voice and shouted out the impending stop: "Roseladden!" Then, to William again: "Now this here's the stop gate. See the cottage, there? That's the old tollkeeper's. And the road you do want, up to Wheal Fortune, is right beside of it."

And what was the wretched youth's name? William wondered.

The answer, spoken over the constant roar of the engine and the sudden screech of the brakes, gave him quite a start.

"Did you say Liddicoat?" he asked in amazement as they lurched to a halt. "Are you sure of that?"

"No, not Liddicoat," came the reply. "Lidgeycot. John Lidgeycot. That's another old Cornish name. There's a place called Lidgey, up Saint Gluvias, on the far side of Truro." Then another thought struck him. "Though, now you do mention it, there *is* a Liddicoat living to this day in Sithney parish. I never thought of that, afore. Clifford Liddicoat. Farms over to Grankum. He'd be neighbour to you if you do buy the Old Glebe. Liddicoat ... Lidgeycot. We-ell! I wonder?"

"Food for thought," William agreed as he closed the charabanc door and waved farewell. He could not, however, imagine what bearing a murder committed over two centuries ago might have on the present day, even if this John Lidgeycot proved to be a direct forebear of the Liddicoats of Grankum.

He heard the exhaust roar deepen as the driver retarded the ignition to pull away up the hill to Breage. The old toll-keeper's cottage was just about the tiniest dwelling he had ever seen — tiny even by Cornish standards. An old crone stood within, leaning on the half door, smoking a clay pipe. If she stretched one foot out behind her, he thought, she could probably touch the back wall with it.

"How are 'ee keepin', my lover?" she called out cheerily as he strode back down the road toward her. "You goin' up Wheal Fortune, are 'ee?"

He glanced at his map, the Ordnance Survey's geological survey of the area. "I'm going past it and on over Carnmeal Downs to Carleen. Why? May I carry a message for you?"

A 'message' to her was what 'messenger boys' delivered by bicycle from butchers, grocers, and other tradesmen. So, delighted in her misunderstanding of his offer, she said, "Why, 'es. Bring I a quarter-pound o' butter and two eggs back from Wheal Fortune Farm if you mind to. That's Mrs Rogers up there. Tell she 'tis for Mrs Oliver down stop gate. And I'll pay she when me Lloyd-George do come at the end of the week."

Willy-nilly, he had to accept.

"Where you from then?" she asked as he passed her door. "You aren't from round here."

So there went another five minutes while various genealogies were sorted out, followed by a more worthwhile conversation (to William) in which she described the scene of industry this tranquil valley had been in her girlhood. Then the little stream beside her cottage, which ran only a mile and a half, from an adit in Wheal Vor to the sea at Porthleven, was so rich in tin 'waste' that at least a dozen people made a living vanning the metal from the man-made sand it bore toward the sea.

Vanning.

He stored the word away. Separating grains of metal ore from ordinary sand, presumably by some water-washing process. Cornish. Could be dialect for 'fanning'? Or a corruption of 'panning,' perhaps?

"A thousand souls once lived 'tween here and Carleen, my lover," she said. "Now there aren't but two dozen. See that field there?" She pointed across the road. "There was a mine there — the Hanson Mine. And in the next field there. Antron Consols. And another one up the hill here. Wheal Rib. Yet you could search a year and not find a trace of them now. All gone. And the men as worked them. Your grandfather, maybe."

When she came out of her cottage to show him where Roseladden Stamps had stood, he saw she was barefoot and wearing flour sacks for a skirt.

"There now!" She pointed to a vast expanse of gray sand in which nothing seemed willing to grow — which was a decided contrast to the rich, fertile green of the rest of the valley, including the fields where she said the mines had once stood. "When they stamps was roaring away, full blast, you'd sit in that cottage and fear for the slates on the roof. Yet she've stood the test of time and they haven't. Not a splinter left. But there's another set still standing up Wheal Fortune, if you mind to see it — stamps, buddles, and vanning floors, just like the ones as was here, backalong."

"I certainly will." He stared back at the fields across the road. "Were there no buildings? No steam engines? How did they drain them? We're only ... what? Ten, twenty feet above sea level here?"

She shook her head. "No need. They never went down, see? But flat." She moved her hand horizontally. "Straight into the hill, following the lode. Not like the mines where you'm going, round Carnmeal. Now they went down *hundreds* of feet below sea level. Wheal Vor was the deepest. My father told me they had a Cornish engine there could lift ten ton o' water each stroke. Her cylinder was over a hundred inches across. And afore they put her in steam, eight gentlemen dined at a table inside her — there now! That's as true as we're standing here. 'Course, they'm all flooded now, they mines. Filled up to the adit — which is where this here stream do come out, up by Carleen Flow. Beyond Scott's Mine. If you do want to see good old granite buildings and fancy-brick chimbleys, that's the best you'll find in this valley — Scott's."

He spoke a little longer with old Mrs Oliver, asking her about the other ruined mines he'd be seeing up on Carnmeal Downs, but she knew nothing of the technical details that interested him. All she could recall were fantastical tales. For instance, she said that when the old mines were exhausted, their passages and adits were all interconnected — which would be a natural consequence of removing the ore, of course; the fantastical part came when she said that the old miners used to get drunk and bet each other on which champion could get from, for instance, the ten-fathom stope in Wheal Fortune to the abandoned crosscut, three fathoms below grass at Pallas Consols. And, she said, they would then run two or three miles underground, leaping narrow chasms several hundred feet deep at times — all drunk as lords and with nothing to show the way but a lighted tallow candle in their helmets (or 'hemlets,' as she called them).

He laughed in dutiful amazement, shook his head at the folly and courage of the human race, and bade her farewell as he set off along the goodish macadam road that ran up the valley beside the stream.

"Doan 'ee forget my messages," she called after him.

It was a moment or two before he recalled the butter and eggs. "Right!" He waved back to her and promptly forgot them yet again.

6 A short way up the road he passed a small quarry, abandoned for some years and already partly overgrown. And there he became aware for the first time that the rock strata in Cornwall do not, as in most parts of the world, lie one upon another in neat, more-or-less horizontal bands. Strata there were, all right — of quartz and shale and a crumbly sort of mudstone full of iridescent flakes that suggested mineral wealth to his as yet untrained eye — but they were closer to vertical than horizontal. Ten degrees off the perpendicular, he guessed. But what titanic forces could have lifted the earth's crust like that and left it in such disarray? It was surely beyond the reach of man's most fevered imagination. Yet there they stood, those wrenched-up layers, so calm and still now, damp with winter and caged behind tendrils of briar and traveller's joy. The deep tranquillity made their violent origins even harder to imagine.

Only the promise of even greater geological marvels ahead let him tear himself away from the spot. A hundred paces later the road crossed the stream and continued on, now along its eastern bank. He squatted on the bridge and stared into the rippling water, a mere two feet beneath his boots. The brook itself was only three feet wide and no more than a foot deep; he estimated it passed about thirty thousand gallons an hour — American gallons, of course. That would be ... his eyes vanished inside their sockets as he did a swift calculation ... twenty-four thousand imperial gallons. He must get used to thinking that way now. He dipped his hand into the water and lifted a fistful of sand. My, but it was heavy! Heavier than just any old wet sand. Perhaps one man could still make a living out of this brook — where twelve had once thrived?

He swilled it away again, rose, and resumed his walk. The valley sides were now closing in. They had been two or three hundred paces apart at the stop gate; but here the gap was a mere twenty, and the slopes were almost too precipitous to till — though the farmers on either side were obviously managing it. This was that part of the valley which had lain just out of sight from the end field of the Old Glebe on the first day they had visited it. So the farm to his right, he guessed, would be Trelissick, farmed by George Gosling. He wondered if that was the man himself, with a turnip-lifting gang in one of the top fields.

A moment later his guess was confirmed when he reached the point of division of the Y-shaped valley. The eastern branch, which ran round to Grankum, opened up to his right and the Old Glebe itself came briefly into view. From this vantage the old tithe barn obscured half the house. Only then did he recall the strange tale the bus driver had told him; he had put it from his mind the moment the serious — that is, geological — business of the day had begun. But now, what with the old barn so prominently silhouetted on the distant skyline and with Billy Trim's tale still fresh enough to curdle the blood, he found it less easy to forget a second time.

Here, too, the road turned right and led steeply, tortuously uphill, toward the northeast, as if heading for Grankum. Halfway up this rise he came to another road, which led off to his left, continuing along the western branch of the valley. He hesitated, not knowing which to take. Had he bothered to unfold his map again, he would have seen that the winding road on which he stood turned right, then left, then right again ... and so up to the farm at Wheal Fortune, which was his immediate destination.

Instead, he guessed that the branch road, which led along the western valley — though now some fifty feet above the level of the stream — was the one to take him there.

And so it did, in a way — that is, it took him to Wheal Fortune but not to the farm. Instead, it led to the abandoned workings of one of the most extraordinary tin mines in the country — indeed, in the world. He got the first intimations of it when he was about five hundred paces from the parting of the two roads, where he came to a stone-lined water course cut into the side of the valley. It was filled with running water, which poured in a smooth green arc over the top of the wooden sluice that barred its end. It was a recently made sluice, too, with the wood still pale and fresh. From there the water splashed and complained down a rocky gully it had eaten for itself in the hillside and eventually joined the stream below.

Indeed, it *was* the stream below, for, although the track of the ancient watercourse was still visible among the reeds and tussocks of marram grass upstream from that junction, William could see, even from a distance, that little water now flowed along it. And from this he guessed that somewhere farther up the valley — half a mile or so farther on and round the bend, to judge by the shallow slope of the valley floor — that same stream had been diverted out of its ancient course and forced along this man-made conduit instead — probably to power those stamps Mrs Oliver had mentioned. With renewed eagerness he set off up the path beside the conduit; once it had been a road as wide as the one he had just left, but already the brambles and bracken were reclaiming it for the great green world.

Excited as he was, though, he could not now forget the old tithe barn and its grisly history. He had, in fact, done more than just poke his nose inside the door, as he had claimed when talking to Trim; he had wandered all over it and climbed a stack of straw bales to take a closer look at the old mortice-and-peg joints of the timber frame. But of unquiet spirits and foul deeds he had felt not the slightest intimation. Of course, any old building must have been a silent witness to the whole gamut of human activities and emotions. And he had, indeed, tried to imagine the harvest suppers, the bucolic dances, the romantic assignations, the fist fights, and the conspiracies that must surely have taken place in so venerable a building. And, to be sure, some vaguely nostalgic whiff of them had stirred his senses — enough to amuse the rationalist young man within. But nothing had hinted at the agonies and bestialities of the Geach-Lidgeycot saga, so that same rationalist young man decided to pooh-pooh the whole tale, taking it to be a feverish embroidery of some very commonplace little murder and a subsequent act of revenge.

Unfortunately, as in all of us, his rationalism was not large enough to light his soul entirely, and its darker corners remained filled with an uneasiness that, he knew, would not go away until he had followed up the bus driver's tale and laid it to rest — or, of course, confirmed it.

"Concentrate now!" he urged himself aloud. "Mines. Minerals. Geology. Metamorphic rocks."

"Aaaieee!" came a scream from somewhere up ahead. A man's voice, he thought.

The hair stiffened on the back of his neck and a shiver ran from his scalp to the soles of his feet, for there was no one in sight, though the caller was clearly in some distress. He opened his mouth to shout back, but no sound came. His tongue was dry and he began to shiver with fear.

This is stupid! he told himself. *You're letting your imagination run away with itself — just because of some idiotic tale told by a ...*

"Hallo?" The cry came again, and this time a note of inquiry was laid over the distress. And it was definitely a man's.

William found his tongue at last. "Hallo?" he called back. "I'm coming."

"Quick! For pity's sake!"

The voice was now clearly coming from beyond a little spur that projected from the slope on his side of the valley. In fact, as he reached the foot of it, he realized it was not a natural feature at all but was composed of rubble, the waste of some mine, no doubt. Loose rock and shale skittered away beneath his boots as he clambered up its steeply sloping side. And, as he gained the crest, he almost tripped over the rails of a narrow dram line running out, not from a mine but from a quarry about twenty times larger than the one he had seen earlier on that walk.

But he had little time to examine it for there, in a sort of amphitheatre of rock and waste below him, stood the stamps Mrs Oliver had mentioned — six wrought-iron pounding heads, each of which must weigh a couple of hundredweight. They were held on stout wooden rods the thickness of telegraph poles, and, when the machine was working, they would be raised by eight-inch cams fixed to a drive train that was ultimately powered by an overshot wheel in the diverted stream. Fortunately it was not turning at that moment because, as William saw at once, the distressed caller, a young man of about his own age, was lying awkwardly across a stretch of smooth concrete on the downstream side of the stamps with one of his legs trapped beneath the nearest of those massive pounding heads.

"Hold on!" William called out, somewhat redundantly, as he ran along the dram line to a point where any stones he might dislodge in his descent would not fall upon the young man — and he dislodged plenty, and severely risked his own safety, as he leaped and slid down to the level of the stamps. Once there, he ran back to help the man.

"There's a crowbar against the wall behind you," the fellow called out. "You won't lift it by hand. Hurry!"

In turning round to seek the tool William's eye fell on the waterwheel and drive train, part of which was secured on the wall where the crowbar lay. He glanced back at the stamps and saw that the head nearest the top of its lift (and therefore due to fall next in sequence) was the third one away from the trapped victim. The fourth one away would be next, then the fifth and final one — by which time the one trapping the young man's leg ought to be raised halfway up its lift.

"What if I just turn this?" he suggested, grasping the largest of the cogwheels. "Keep your hands clear of the one that's just about to fall."

"Oh, thanks for that warning!" The fellow laughed. "Go on — good thinking!"

Gingerly William tugged at the wheel. There was a squeak from one of the centre cams and then the head it was lifting fell off the end and crashed to the bed with a ringing clangour.

"Jee-hoshephat!" William exclaimed. He remembered what Mrs Oliver had said about fearing for the house when the Roseladden stamps were in operation. "Can you feel any movement yet?"

"I'm not sure I'm going to *feel* anything," was the glum reply. "But go on."

There were more screeches from the next cam as the head it was lifting came near the trip point.

"It *is* moving, by George!" the man cried out joyfully. "And I *can* feel it, too!"

"Can you move the leg itself?"

"Not yet. Go on."

The fall of the next head was just as loud, but somehow less startling now that William knew what to expect.

"Another turn will do it," the man called out. "Keep going!"

One full turn of the big cogwheel turned the camshaft a mere ten degrees, which brought the final head to the point where it was about to be tripped. And the first head, the one pinning the young man down, would be next. William decided to leave that much margin of safety between such a catastrophe and the present state of the machine. "Can you move it now?" he asked, walking swiftly to where the other lay.

"Maybe. If you could just pull some rock out from under it?" the man suggested.

William squatted beside the stamps and saw that the wounded leg was half buried among crushed rock. It was curious because the bed beneath the other stamps was entirely free from rock — hence the ringing clang the heads had made when they fell. He scrabbled some of the fragments away until the leg was low enough to pull out from under the suspended head without scraping on it, but still he continued until all the fragments were gone and the bed was smooth from end to end.

Wincing, the man scooped them into a pile, as if they had some sentimental value for him.

"Now!" William said, changing his position to where he could get a hand to the leg both above and below the injury. "I hope this doesn't hurt too much. I'm going to try to pull it out evenly this way, toward me. I suggest you don't try to do anything yourself — in case the foot is no longer joined to ... well, you know what I mean."

"Cheerful bugger, aren't you!" the other exclaimed.

William hesitated a moment and glanced at him. "You're saying it's not as serious as it seemed before? Actually, there's no blood visible."

"Well, it doesn't feel so painful now the pressure's off. More numb than anything."

"Okay. Well — here goes!" Privately, William thought that numbness might not be such a good sign but, having already been accused of 'cheerfulness,' he held his tongue. However, when he slowly withdrew the leg and foot from beneath the overhanging head, inch by slow inch, he could feel that the whole limb moved as one. So, though the bone might well be fractured, it certainly was not broken in two.

He said as much to the fellow and added, "That rock probably saved it from being crushed completely. How did it happen?"

The man pulled a face and raised himself on one elbow, reaching out the other arm for William to help him sit right up.

"Whoa-back!" William cautioned him. "Let's just see how bad it really is first. Can you move your toes?"

He gripped the man's boot over the top of his instep. A moment later he felt sinews flexing beneath the stout leather — and heard an *ouch!* from the man himself. "Good!" he said. "Nerves intact and no bleeding. Can I take off your gaiters and look at the skin? The name's Carrington, by the way. William Carrington." He reached out a hand.

The other gripped it as best he could. "I guessed as much from the accent," he said. "And I'm Nicholas Liddicoat. I think you've met my father."

"To put it mildly," William replied as he set about easing the gaiter buttons out of their eyes. "And I think I saw your brother through a pair of binoculars on that same day. Sorry!" he added as Liddicoat winced. "Tell me how it happened — take your mind off what I'm doing."

"My brother saw your sister, too," the fellow replied. "You're not the only one with binoculars, you know. He's hardly stopped talking about her since. Says she's the most beautiful creature ever to flutter down gently to earth."

William grunted. "He must have been looking through the wrong end, then." He freed the last of the buttons and eased the gaiter off. It was stiff with age and want of greasing. When he tapped it with his knuckles it rang like thin plywood. "That might yet prove to have been the saving of your leg," he said as he began to ease up the knickerbocker leg. "You didn't say how it happened?"

Liddicoat pulled the same self-deprecating face as before. "I noticed that head was almost off its cam, so I put a bit of rock under it and tried to shake it off. I just wanted to see what damage it could do — to the rock, I mean. But it wouldn't drop. So I shook harder ... slipped ... got one leg under ... the other leg hit the side-stay there ... and bang! Down she came." After a pause he added, "Grin away! I agree."

"I wasn't grinning *at* you, Liddicoat, but at the thought that it could so easily have happened to me if you hadn't got here first. It sounds pretty much the damfool-numskull sort of thing I might try."

"Well, thanks for the rescue, anyway." Liddicoat managed to sit up on his own now, the better to see his leg for himself. "What does Doctor Carrington say?"

Now that the gaiter was off, the potential swelling became actual and, even as they watched, the inward side of his shinbone swelled until it looked as if a smallish tennis ball had materialized under his skin.

"I think that if you could stand soaking this in water for ten minutes or so, while I go up to the farm and borrow or fashion a crutch out of something, that bruise might last only two months instead of four. If you leaned on me, d'you think you could hobble over to the stream?"

Five minutes later, with his 'thornproof' tweeds torn in several little triangles, he trotted into the yard at Wheal Fortune, where he found Jethro Rogers, the farmer, turning the handle of a mangle-worzel cutter while one of his labourers topped and tailed mangles and turnips and threw them into the hopper. The mushy-sickly smell from the chopped roots told him where the taint he had noticed in his breakfast milk this past week had come from.

When he explained what had happened Rogers turned to the labourer and crowed: "Jarge! What did I tell 'ee? Gusson now, boy — go get 'n!"

And when 'Jarge' limped away, William saw he was wearing an almost circular boot, more suited to the hoof of a large shire horse than to a human foot. The farmer explained that the man had been badly trampled by a horse two years back, and that while it was mending — even though in a badly deformed shape — he had hobbled around the farm on a crutch. "And only yesterday we looked at 'n, in the rafters in the cowshouse, and

Jarge said to throw 'n away, but I said we'd have need of 'n agin, soon 'nuff. So there now!" He took the crutch from Jarge, who returned as if on cue, and presented it to William like a trophy. "Go on down and see if Liddicoat can walk with that. Us'll follow with a stretcher in case he can't."

William set off without arguing, though he was sure no stretcher bearers would ever make it through the thickets that had delayed him on the way up. At the yard gate he turned and called out, "If you hear me whistle" — he put his little fingers to his tongue and gave an ear-splitting example — "you needn't bother to come."

Rogers waved back. "Kettle's boiling, anyway," he called out in reply.

On making his way back down the slope, William noticed a well-worn path leading obliquely across the direct line to the stamps and, by following its zigzag trail, he came unhindered to the spot in half the time.

"I think it's fractured, all right," Liddicoat called out cheerfully as soon as he caught sight of his rescuer returning. "But thankfully not broken."

To prove it, he swirled his leg about in the water when William drew close enough to see. "Hurts like hell but shows no tendency to float away on its own," he added. "I say! Is that one of Jarge's old crutches?"

"Think you can manage it? That bruise has gone down quite a bit. Perhaps you ought to bathe it longer yet?"

"If I do, I think my leg will freeze and drop off. Help us up, there's a good chap."

In looking round to check that nothing of value was being accidentally left behind in all the excitement, William noticed that the little pile of crushed rock by the offending stamp had been cleared away — the pile young Liddicoat had so carefully scraped together earlier.

"What now?" the man asked with jocular weariness, suggesting that William was the world's fussiest.

Behind it, however, William thought he detected a note of genuine anxiety. But for that, he would have said straight out, 'You've cleared all the crushed rock away.' Instead, he replied, "I thought I had a map with me. Didn't I?"

"This?" Liddicoat tugged at the edge that protruded from his, William's own, pocket.

William thumped his forehead with the butt of his hand and, carrying one of Liddicoat's boots, walked on his downhill side, ready to buttress him in case he fell.

After a few paces he was satisfied Liddicoat would make it all the way on his crutch, so he gave the promised whistle, which he then explained to the man.

"Seriously," the fellow replied, "I am more grateful than I can say …"

"Stow it, you oaf!" William had read enough English school yarns to know the right words for such embarrassing moments.

"No. If you hadn't happened along just when you did, it could have been pretty nasty."

"Why were you trying to crush the rock anyway — if I may ask? You've lived here all your life, surely?"

"Yes?" Liddicoat made a question of the word, implying he didn't see that the point had any relevance.

"Well, judging by their condition, those stamps have been working until very recently. You must have watched them many a time. With me, it would have been out of curiosity — to see how well they crushed the stone."

"Oh, well … I suppose it was just the sight of that thing, hanging there by the thickness of a hair. I mean …" Inspiration struck him and he gushed suddenly: "Any child could have wandered down there and been maimed for life. Or even killed, my God."

It sounded a pretty thin sort of excuse but William pretended to accept this 'logic.'

Then, apropos nothing, Liddicoat added: "I only put the stone there to cushion its drop."

Now it sounded thinner than ever but William did not press the point. Instead he resolved to be assiduous in his study of Cornish mineralogy — and then to return here to see what had excited young Liddicoat into making such a stupid blunder.

7 That evening at the Angel, when the Carringtons assembled for dinner, the old man and Leah announced that they had finally settled on — and would soon settle in — the Old Glebe. "Not without some degree of reluctance," John Carrington added. "I don't know what it is about that place. Maybe it's just because we saw it first and it stole our hearts away ..."

"I just felt we belonged there in a way I haven't felt in any other house we've seen," Leah put in. "It felt like ... I don't know — somewhere we once lived and have forgotten about. I mean, if we looked through the old deeds and saw the name Carrington there, it wouldn't surprise me."

After a brief silence her father turned to William and said, "You're mighty quiet on the subject, my boy."

He cleared his throat awkwardly. "I wonder if the two of you will still feel so all kiln-fired enthusiastic when I tell you the tale I heard this morning."

The serving maid came to their table, picked up the butter dish, sniffed it, put it back, and called out, "No. This one's all right, Martha."

William stared at the butter and said, "Shoot! I forgot."

"What?" Leah asked impatiently.

"I promised Mrs Oliver I'd ... oh, never mind. I'll take her some butter and eggs myself tomorrow."

"Hark at the big butter-and-egg man!" Leah said to her father, jerking her head toward her brother.

The old man did not think it quite so amusing. "Son," he said, "I hope you aren't going around the district giving out the impression that *I* am a big butter-and-egg man. Everyone here thinks all Americans are dollar millionaires and good-sense paupers. I've been very careful to ..."

"It's nothing like that," the young man said wearily, and with a baleful look at his sister. "Anyway, suppose I was to tell you a foul murder was once committed in ..."

"Whoa-back!" his father interrupted. "One thing at a time. What is it with butter and eggs, anyway?"

"Nothing!" William sank his head in his hands. "I asked an old lady, a Mrs Oliver, the way to Wheal Fortune, meaning the mine, and she thought I meant the farm of the same name. Anyway, it didn't matter, because they're cheek-by-jowl. And she mentioned the farmer's wife's name, Mrs Rogers. And I asked if I could carry any message. And it seems that 'message' down here is like 'errand' — so ..."

"What has this got to do with murder?" Leah asked.

"Nix. But I was told to take one thing at a time."

"And you're not even making sense of that," his father said.

William let out a short, hopeless sigh and said, "No."

"Well?" Leah asked after another short silence.

"It doesn't matter. It was all probably hokum, anyway."

"What was?"

He sat up, squared his shoulders, gave them a rather brittle smile, and said, "I had a splendid day, thank you. I saw an abandoned mine where the tin lode was so rich they *quarried* it. I heaved rocks down abandoned shafts and heard reverberations and splashes that would chill your blood. I saw a mine chimney with the fanciest brickwork. And there's enough abandoned plant and machinery out there to make you think an overnight plague swept through the place."

"All very productive, I'm sure," Leah commented, being envious of her brother's freedom to roam where he liked.

A splendid steak-and-kidney pie rescued them from further profitless discussion; but when they pushed their empty plates away, the awkward silences returned. At length William announced that he had no stomach for pudding and begged permission to leave them. "I'll just go for a stroll down to the bowling green and back and then turn in," he said. "I must have walked miles today."

It was, indeed, true that he had no stomach for the pudding for he had eaten so many pieces of Mrs Rogers's 'fuggan' — a sort of lard-rich plum bun — while she put cold compresses on young Liddicoat's damaged foot. And oh! the things he'd heard — the things he could have told his father and sister if they didn't keep putting him down like this!

His father, misunderstanding his son yet again, followed him out to the passage where he gave him a sovereign. "Don't do anything I wouldn't do," he said with a wink.

William was too astonished to make any reply, other than to stammer his embarrassed thanks — an embarrassment his father, yet again, misunderstood. "We've all been there, son," he said as he went back to rejoin his daughter.

"I worry about him," she said as her father resumed his seat. "D'you think his brain is going soft or something?"

The old man, still believing he knew precisely what was distracting his son — and knowing he could not possibly discuss it with Leah — dismissed the idea. "He got good grades at school," he said. "And the Camborne School of Mines seems keen enough to accept him."

"But he's so scatterbrained, Pa. He can't even retell a simple story or stick to a single train of thought."

"Maybe he's got other things on his mind."

"I'd like to know what!"

Carrington cleared his throat. "It's different for you and me, honey. I've made my way in the world." He grinned and lowered his voice. "Tell it not in Gath but I've got all the butter and eggs we'll ever need. And as for you, well, a woman's place is the same in the Old World as it is in the New. But young William is still a little fish in a big pond — and a *new* pond, too. Don't let's forget that. Old World, maybe, but new challenges, new rules. And he's competing against people who grew up here, who know it all in their very bones. Indeed, it would be surprising, not to say alarming, if he weren't a little … unsettled, shall we call it?"

He smiled with relief, thinking he had buried *that* subject most satisfactorily. He thought of his son, out there somewhere, going through the 'Hallo, Charley — looking for a bit of fun?' ritual with some pretty little drab under a street lamp, and felt a twinge of envy himself.

Leah, who had a puritan distaste for wasted food, eschewed the 'polite' habit of always leaving a morsel on the plate. She swallowed the last mouthful of a rather stodgy plum pudding. Then, as if asking the most casual of questions, said, "I wonder if they take women at the Camborne School of Mines?"

Her father laughed. "No such luck for young William, I fear. He'll have to sail on wider seas to find his bride to be."

But his smile vanished when she responded, "Actually, Pa, I wasn't thinking of him."

He frowned. "Who, then?"

"Me."

He laughed again, though not quite so wholeheartedly as before, she noticed.

"I'm serious," she persisted.

"Yes, honey. So is measles, but it passes."

"Why shouldn't I have the same chance as William?"

He looked about the room as if he hoped for rescue from some quarter. "The answer's too obvious even to need stating," he replied.

"Those gardens we saw this afternoon," she said.

"What about them?"

"Mrs Scawen made those terraces herself. She blasted them with dynamite out of bare cliff."

"Not herself."

"Pardon me but she did. Mrs Curnow told me — while you were talking to Mister Petifer, I think. She said Jane Scawen was the first person, man or woman, to use dynamite in Cornwall. She learned dynamiting in Camborne solely in order to ..."

"At the School of Mines?"

Leah hesitated. "Well, that was implied."

He smiled dismissively. "Maybe one of the instructors there taught her privately. She was a rich lady even then by all accounts, so that's possible. But as for lady pupils at the school itself ... ha!" He raised his hands as if inviting laughter to fall from heaven. "Where would be the point of allowing them in, anyway? Women aren't allowed to work down mines in these enlightened days."

"If I learned dynamiting, I could help you terrace the fields at the Old Glebe."

He reached across and patted her hand. "At least you tried, honey," he said soothingly. "You've got spirit. I'll yield to none in my admiration of you for that. But dynamite will not be necessary at the Old Glebe — except maybe to get rid of that ugly old barn. For the rest, a gentle steam shovel and good old elbow grease will accomplish all the landscaping I intend doing, thank you very much."

At least I tried! Leah echoed the words angrily in her mind. *Well, Pa — don't imagine I'm giving up this easily.* But she smiled sweetly as she said, "Tell me about them — your plans — now that we've decided at last. We have decided, haven't we?"

"One hundred per cent," he replied.

8 William seethed with frustration as he set out into the Helston night. Why did they never let him get out more than half a sentence before they jumped down his throat like that? Well, it was their loss. They'd chosen ignorance and now they'd have to suffer for it. A smile returned to his face as he thought of one item of ignorance for which they probably *would* pay, and in extreme discomfort.

When he'd mentioned Coad's romantic tale about the love-potion powers of the Grankum well, young Liddicoat and the Rogerses had almost burst a blood vessel laughing; and later, after they had left the farm, Liddicoat had explained: "It's beautiful, clear, tasty water," he said, "and people who've drunk it all their lives aren't affected by it. But the first few times that newcomers drink it, until they're accustomed, well, it's better than epsom salts, cascara, and the number nines all rolled into one. In short, it gives you the backdoor trots."

Well, let them find out the hard way now — then they'd be smiling on the other sides of their faces!

He was halfway down Coinagehall Street before he realized what his father had been talking about. 'Don't do anything I wouldn't do'! My God, he meant *that!* The very thought of it stopped him in his tracks. He felt his face flush with embarrassment and was glad of the darkness, which the flickering gas lamps barely penetrated. Unfortunately that same darkness prevented the man behind him from noticing that he had stopped. His eyes were not yet accustomed to the dark for he had only just emerged from the house that fronted the footpath. The resulting collision almost sent both of them into the Helston River — which was a rather grand name for the insignificant brook that ran in open granite kennels on either side of the street. In the ensuing dustings-down and hearty apologies, the stranger heard the American accent and said, "Have I the honour of bumping into Mister Carrington, then?"

William replied that he didn't know so much about the honour but the rest of the surmise was true.

"And is it Carrington *père* or Carrington *fils?* Forgive me — and allow me to present myself. Frank Kernow — your servant."

"William Carrington — yours."

As they shook hands, William glanced up at the darkened window of the house the man had just vacated and saw there, in black-edged letters of gold: *Francis Kernow, Solicitor and Commissioner for Oaths.* "The lawyer!" he said, as if he'd already heard of him from half a dozen sources.

Kernow laughed. "Well observed, young man! May I buy you a drink to show there are no hard feelings? Have you dined, by the way?"

"Just. But let me do the buying. After all, I was the one who stopped so abruptly."

"The night is yet young. We'll *both* buy," the other decided, putting a hand to William's shoulder and propelling him toward the saloon-bar door of the Blue Anchor. "Me first. Age before beauty, as they say."

Kernow's youthful voice and manner had led William to believe the lawyer was joking, that he was at most two or three years older — which he would have had to be in order to qualify. But when they reached the lighted passage of the inn he saw that the man must be in his early thirties.

"Whisky?" Kernow suggested. "No bourbon or rye, I'm afraid, but they do Scotch or Irish."

"Jee willikin!" William had never tasted either and said so. Indeed, he had only once tasted rye — an occasion that nobody cared to mention nowadays.

"Irish," Kernow decided. "It's smoother. They distil it twice, you know. The Scotch only distil once." He held up two fingers to the barmaid and nodded. "Let's go and sit over there."

He led William to a table for two in the inglenook, where he stretched his hands gratefully toward the fire. "Glorious!" he exclaimed. "I sometimes think Scrooge could return and live happily in my office — except that in my case it's the clerk who dictates to the master. My clerk cannot abide a warm room. Indeed, he cannot abide a cold one, either, but must have it as frigid as the North Pole."

"And if you ignore him and stoke up the fire?"

"He falls asleep and blames me."

The barmaid brought their whiskies and did not wait for payment, from which William assumed his companion had an account there.

"Did that brother of yours get his back-pay yet?" Kernow called after her.

She turned and smiled. "All thanks to you, Mister Kernow," she said.

He waved away her gratitude. "It was pure pleasure, Eileen." He pushed William's glass a token inch across the little table. "Cheerioh, me dearioh!"

"Cheer-ho!" William took a sip and gasped at the fiery bite of it. And this was supposed to be the *milder* of the two whiskies?

"Tell me true, now," Kernow went on. "Had you really heard of me before our fortuitous meeting outside just now?"

William wondered what was 'fortuitous' about it but he replied, diplomatically, "Kernow's quite an important name in Helston — so I gather."

"Ah! You're thinking of Giles Curnow, no doubt. But he spells his name quite differently."

He was about to spell it when William answered, "No, I was thinking of Kernow and Daughter, actually. I've noticed the shingle several times."

"Yes," the other snapped. "One can hardly avoid it."

"I saw it from the bus this morning. Are you related to them, by any chance?"

"The 'Kernow' is my father and the 'Daughter' is thus my sister. Let's speak of something more congenial."

"Than sisters?" William responded. "Hear hear! I'll gladly drink to that!"

"Oh?" Kernow raised an interested eyebrow. "Is yours older or younger?"

"Older, by two years."

"Mine's younger by one. Makes no difference, I suppose. They're all as fickle as opal. You help them all you can. You put your life and career in the balance. And what do they do — once they've got what they want? Turn round and kick you in the teeth! Don't tell me." He laughed to show that his vehemence was largely theatrical. "Actually, *do* tell me! A misery shared ... you know."

William sighed. "Everything was fine between us — give or take the odd attempted murder — until our mother died. Almost four years ago now. And since then Leah, that's my sister ..."

"Yes, I've heard of her. Come to think of it, I'm almost sure I've seen her — now I know who *you* are. Short, dark, curly hair? Petite? And strikingly good-looking?"

"Matter of opinion," William said coldly. "Anyway, she's assumed the maternal mantle with a vengeance." He took another sip and again gasped at the sting in it.

"I wish whisky still did that to me," Kernow said as he matched him, sip for sip.

"I can't help it that I enjoy freedoms she doesn't," William complained. "I didn't make the world the way it is."

"Oh, familiar ground!" Kernow exclaimed. "You know my sister is the founder and owner of the local electricity company? Did you ever hear of such a thing? A woman! She did it entirely to spite our father, who only wanted her to behave like every other sensible girl in the land and make a good marriage. *She* chose electricity because *he* owned the local gas company! Pure spite, as I said. And who helped her? Who did all the legal spadework and got in the subscriptions?" He tapped his breastbone. "Juggins here! And would you like to see my shares in the company today?" He reached forth an empty hand, palm up. "There they are — count 'em!"

"I say! Hard cheese!" William drew once again on the schoolboy yarns.

Both men stared at the flames in an easy, ruminative silence, which was punctuated only by sips and William's gasps at the spirituous afterburn.

"You're buying a house in the district," Kernow prompted, not making a question of it.

"The Old Glebe in Sithney," William vouchsafed. "They've made their minds up today. They went to see a house in Gweek and decided against it. And that was the last of the other possibles. So the Old Glebe it is."

"You don't sound too keen."

"Oh, I'm keen enough. It's very handy for me. I'm going to the Camborne School of Mines, you see."

Kernow nodded.

William continued, "Is it true there was once a rather gruesome murder there? I was told something of the sort this morning. They say a John Lidgeycot seduced and then murdered a girl called Catherine Geach in the old tithe barn."

Kernow nodded. "True enough — though I doubt it was as grisly as the popular tongue has since made it."

"They say the old barn is haunted."

The other laughed. "But surely you don't believe in such rubbish! Haunted, indeed! It's strange — there's a murder in Cornwall almost every week. Certainly one a month. In short, there have been at least two *thousand* murders down here since that particular one. So what makes it special? Why does only Catherine whatsername's ghost haunt her place of death? Where are the rest of those two thousand victims? I have no patience with it." He chuckled. "Mind you, as a bargaining point to abate the price ... *then* I believe! Whoever your lawyer is, he should certainly make a strong point of it."

"Yes," William said decisively. "You're right. That's the way to approach it."

"Who is your lawyer, by the way?"

William shrugged. "I don't believe we have one yet. When the time comes, my father will probably seek Coad's advice — the estate agent, you know."

"Oh, I know young Coad!" the lawyer said heavily. "Did he think to tell you about the bad blood between the Carringtons and the Liddicoats?"

"Oh, yes — even before he showed us the house."

"Did he, now!" The answer clearly surprised Kernow but he recovered swiftly. "He must have had some other property he preferred to sell you."

"Or he fell in love at first sight with my sister, and didn't want her to think ill of him if we bought the place and only *then* learned of it."

"You're a shrewd fellow, aren't you!" Kernow eyed him with approval. "Did Coad tell you about the ghosts, too?"

William shook his head. "Perhaps he didn't want to appear ridiculous. Look how scornful *you* were just now."

"True." The lawyer nodded. "But someone has obviously told you. What do your father and sister think about it?"

"That's the trouble." He sighed. "I'm the only one who's heard the tale. I tried to tell them tonight — I mean, I only heard it myself this morning — so I tried to tell them tonight and they both ... I don't know ... made it impossible."

"Sat on you?"

"Yes! A very good way of putting it. They utterly squashed me." He looked at his companion's glass. "I say. You've finished your drink."

"So have you."

William held up his own glass and stared at it in surprise. "So I have! Let me do the honours this time."

Kernow raised his hand again and, when Eileen came over, William handed her his sovereign and said, "You may serve me the same again, miss."

"Similar," the woman said with a grin at Kernow.

"She's passing on my pedantry, I'm afraid, old chap," the lawyer said. "It can't be the *same* again because we've already drunk it."

"Same *substance,*" William objected.

"Ah, now we're into theology — how much does the deity weigh before and after all those millions of people eat and drink Him at the Communion table?"

William decided he wasn't getting light-headed; it was just an effect of Kernow's strangely haphazard conversation.

"And why aren't the mines haunted?" the man continued. "You wouldn't believe the number of disasters there have been in that area. You go up Trigonning Hill and look down on it and you'd think it's all solid land. Not a bit! It's riddled with great empty spaces beneath the surface. And almost every one of them has been the scene of some disaster or other — some within living memory. Carnmeal Downs should be 'standing room only' for spectres and elementals."

Like so many of the lawyer's comments, this did not seem to invite further development. How they train to be judges, William supposed — sprinkle an air of finality over everything.

Eileen returned with their whiskies. "And nineteen shillings," she said as she handed William his change. He wondered whether it was gentlemanly to count it and decided it probably wasn't; so he mentally photographed it as he slipped it into his pocket. "We won't be able to move into the Old Glebe at once," he said as he totted up the coins in his mind. "So I suppose we'll be at the Angel for most of the spring. Cheer-ho!" The whisky hardly burned now.

"Cheers!" Kernow looked thoughtful. "I wonder ..."

"What?"

"That never occurred to me. Is there a lot that needs doing out there?"

"By the time my sister has finished drawing up her wishing list, yes!"

"Well, it so happens that I own an apartment house down in Cross Street, Helston's most salubrious suburb — if a single street can be called a suburb. It was once a gentleman's town house but it was divided into four very pleasant apartments about twenty years ago. And, it so happens, one of my tenants is leaving at the end of next week. I wonder — d'you think your father and sister might be interested?"

"I'm sure they will be. I'll ask them."

"May I ask you something?" He raised his glass and toasted the young man silently.

"Fire away!" William raised his glass in response.

"Can you tell me what coins you have in your pocket?"

"Easily." William laughed. "Why?"

"I'm just curious about people. Did you actually count it that quickly, in the blink of an eye, or are you so rich you don't bother with such trifles?"

"I'm certainly not rich," he replied vehemently. "I only got given that sovereign because my father supposed ..." His voice trailed off in embarrassment. "Anyway, Eileen gave me six half-crowns, two florins, a sixpence, a threepenny bit, and three pennies. Nineteen shillings, I believe?"

"Bravo!" Kernow was genuinely impressed.

They sipped in easy silence awhile, smiling into the flames, crossing and uncrossing their ankles, watching the steam curl off the soles of their boots.

"So!" Kernow said at length. "Your father must imagine Helston boasts some exquisite courtesans if he gave you a whole pound for that special purpose. A shilling would easily get most of 'em. Still, since it's now paying for a much more reliable pleasure" — he held up his almost empty glass — "we ought to drink an appropriate toast, eh? So here's to both ends of the corset!"

They laughed and drained their glasses.

"One more for the road, eh?" Kernow said, clapping and rubbing his hands. "On such a bitterly mild night as this I think we deserve it."

9 Frank Kernow pulled his gig into the stable yard of the Angel. He had raised the hood just in case anyone might be around, even at that late hour, and might notice the young man sprawling unconscious in the body of the vehicle. But only a single light burned in the empty yard. The stable lads, kitchen staff, and sundry loafers and scroungers had all gone. One lone scullerymaid was finishing up for the night, down on her knees, scrubbing the floor. She rose painfully to see who the visitor might be and buried her hands in her armpits, partly to thaw her fingers, but mostly out of shame for their soda-cracked, water-wrinkled skin. "Sir?" she said. Then, as he stepped beneath that single lamp, "Oh, 'tis you, Mister Kernow."

" 'Tis me, Mary. And here's a penny for you if you'll slip upstairs without alerting anybody and let Mister Carrington know he's wanted down here. D'you think you can do that?"

"And if 'e do ask why, sir?"

Kernow smiled. "I'm sure he'll guess why. Cut along now, there's a good girl."

She certainly earned her penny for, within a remarkably short time, she returned with a half-anxious, half-angry John Carrington in tow.

"Permit me — Frank Kernow, sir." The lawyer extended a hand. "At your service."

When he learned why he had been summoned in such secrecy, Carrington gave the girl sixpence and said, "Not a word about this to anyone, eh?"

Between them, and in silence, they got the stupefied William up the back stairs to his room, where they removed his boots and tie and left him to sleep it off.

"May I offer you a nightcap, sir?" Carrington asked the lawyer. "I'm sure mine host has not yet retired for the night."

"That's remarkably civil of you, sir," he replied.

"Not at all — the very least I could do in the circumstances. I hope you've not been put to any, er, financial ..."

"Not a bit. But a modest glass of mild ale would be most acceptable. I'm delighted to make your acquaintance, anyway. I'm only sorry the circumstances are so disagreeable."

"I hoped the boy would have learned his lesson after the last little episode, back in the States," Carrington said as they made their way down to the landlord's quarters. "Apparently not. Did you find him in that condition or what?"

Walter Blackwell had been proprietor and landlord of the Angel too long to show his true feelings at having to reopen the bar so late at night, but he returned to his bed nonetheless and left the two men to their ale when they assured him they would not require a refill.

"You asked how I found him, Mister Carrington," Kernow said as they settled by the embers of the fire. "In fact, we bumped into each other — quite literally — in the dark. I, being mostly at fault, invited him to a convivial jar at the Blue Anchor, which was at hand, and, well ... I chiefly blame myself for his condition. He did not, in fact, drink very much. I suspect he has no head for it, that's all."

"He has no head for *anything,* it seems to me," Carrington said. "I hope he pulled his weight tonight — paid his way? He had the resources. I made sure of that before he went out." With a cautious glance at his companion he added, "Though it was not to finance a drunken spree, I may say."

The lawyer ostentatiously hid a smile behind his hand.

"Told you about it, did he?" Carrington asked.

"In a way, sir. I don't believe he quite understood the impulse behind your splendid generosity. At least, not at once."

"Impulse, eh! I don't believe that critter *has* any impulses — except to stun himself with hard liquor. But what can *I* do, except keep him short of the price of a drink? Which is no answer at all. May I ask if you're married, Mister Kernow?"

"I've successfully evaded my responsibilities in that line. So far, anyway." He smirked.

"It seems to be quite a general custom down here. Coad said almost the identical words. Anyway, you'll see the difficulties when you have to raise a boy of William's age — larn him the facts of life, as we say. It's hard for a father to maintain a scrupulous respect for morality while, at the same time, recognizing that young men are full of wild oats. And wild oats demand to be sown *somewhere* — and with as little damage to decent society as possible." He smiled gloomily and added, *"Some* young men, anyway."

"Oh, I'm sure your son is ... how may I put it? Not *different* from others in that respect, sir."

Carrington glanced up hopefully. "You have evidence of it, sir? I have no wish to pry into the details of your evening together, but I don't mind telling you I have often worried on that score."

Kernow shrugged. "I confess I have no direct evidence, Mister Carrington. We spent our evening in light, convivial conversation around the fire at the Blue Anchor. His collapse into his present condition was quite sudden. However, to address your fears, there is one infallible way to set them at rest."

"Yes," Carrington mused as he scratched the day's stubble on his chin. "It's what my own father did, after all. But he took me to a sporting house in another town. In another state, in fact. But where's the equivalent here? Is Falmouth far enough away? Will an American accent mark me out there, and so bring the tale back here? Do I have to go as far as Plymouth, then? And how can I possibly leave my daughter unguarded here?" He chuckled. "I could hardly take her with us! And what reason would I give her?"

Kernow looked up sharply. "She would require *reasons?*"

"Yes, siree!" The other shrugged hopelessly. "American girls are, well, American girls."

"Well," the lawyer said soothingly, "Cornish ones are little better these days. Ask my father — no one knows it better than *that* poor man!"

"The 'Kernow' of 'Kernow and Daughter'? It is an eye-catching shingle. Yes, I've heard the story. And so has Leah, *my* daughter. She's avid to meet your sister." He sighed.

Frank Kernow thought it significant that, while the son had known nothing of Jessie Kernow's waywardness, his father and sister had not only heard of it but had obviously discussed it, too. "That would be very easy to arrange," he said lightly. "Or *not* to arrange, just as you wish!"

Carrington dipped his head in gratitude but soon was gloomy again. "As to the other little matter, Mister Kernow, may I ask what you would advise?"

The man bit his lips and licked them nervously. "I hesitate to trespass upon an acquaintance so brief and fragile, sir ..." he said diffidently.

"Oh, come!" Carrington broke in with bluff embarrassment. "Brief, I grant, but fragile? Surely not. I'm a man of the world, sir, used to dealing with all sorts and conditions of men, both socially and in the way of business. And I pride myself on being able to judge a man by more than the cut of his cloth and the superiority of his sentiments. And at the risk of embarrassing you, Mister Kernow, I'd say you're no 'squirtish sort of a feller,' as we say. I'll stake my veracity on it. Come to think of it, I'll be in need of a good lawyer soon enough. Is there a page for me in your books?"

Kernow raised his glass and smiled. "Mum's the word," he said. "It's not the custom here to discuss business in a bar — except for the one marked 'private bar' — I'm sure you're unaware of that. But if you'll call upon me at my office tomorrow, we may happily conclude the business. And as to the other little matter — the sowing of wild oats …"

"Yes?"

"Would you think me presumptuous if I volunteered my services … mind you, I do not speak of service in a professional sense …"

"More in a veterinary sense, what?" Carrington guffawed.

"Quite. Yes, very good — I must remember that."

"I would be indebted to you for ever, man. You do see my predicament, I hope."

"I do indeed, sir. And in stating it you reveal yourself to be a man of infinite refinement. As for me, while I do not frequent such houses as you mentioned …"

"Oh, well, in that case, look here …" His voice trailed off as the lawyer raised his hand.

"The fact is, I have made my own private arrangements with one particular young female — I mention it merely to reassure you that I am not 'different' in that sense you employed earlier." He snickered. "I may have my own wild oats to sow, like any man, but they are not *Oscar* Wilde oats!"

"Good! Good!" Carrington rubbed his hands. "And *I* must remember that one."

"However, like all lawyers with a courtroom practice, I am inevitably kept informed of goings-on among the *demi-monde*. And I think you may safely leave me to guide your son in his ventures into this particular *passage* of life."

10 Leah and her father descended from the bus at the Sithney turn, just over the brow of Sithney Common Hill. He carried a postman's satchel filled with notebooks, measuring tape, binoculars, and a packed lunch, for they intended spending the best part of the day at the Old Glebe.

They watched the vehicle draw away, looked at each other, and smiled a slightly baffled smile. "What a preposterous tale, eh!" Carrington said.

In the corner of her eye Leah caught sight of a plume of smoke and steam away on the northwestern skyline, beyond Mellangoose. "There goes William's train to Camborne," she said. "I wonder what sort of day he'll have?"

Her father grunted but said nothing. The train vanished between the high banks before Truthall Halt.

"I'd hate to join a course that had already been running half a year," she said. "But they seem to think he'll have no difficulty catching up."

He sighed. "They see things in that boy which certainly escape us." Turning again to watch the departing bus, he went on, "What did you make of that driver's tale?"

"Ghosts? Ha!" She took his arm and started to cross the road. "Come on — this sun may not last."

"No, but the fact that he told that same tale to William — and the boy didn't even mention it to us. And then that business Coad told us yesterday — about how William rescued the Liddicoat lad from being trapped in some old mining machinery. Two dramatic happenings in one day — and yet what did *he* think was the most important thing to tell us about? Remember? Some garbled tale about an old woman and forgetting her butter and eggs!"

"And a mine chimney with some fancy brickwork." Leah sighed, too. "I do see what you mean."

"So where is this smart-as-a-lick-o'-paint young man Coad and Kernow claim to see in him — not to mention the absolute genius they found in him at the Camborne School of Mines? It beats me." He grunted and shook his head, the way a dog shakes off water. "Anyway, what about our bus-driver's tale?"

His tone was less scornful now. "You don't set much store by g-g-ghosts?"

"Do you?" She was surprised.

"I don't know," he replied awkwardly. "Somehow, it's much easier to believe such things when you know the building is at least five hundred years old. I took against it from the start."

She chuckled. "That's only because it's standing on the best site for your beloved glasshouse. Anyway, we won't be able to do a thing there for months and months yet — not until the place is ours."

"Can you believe that? The church has owned it since time immemorial — or until a couple of generations back — and yet it's going to take Kernow *two months* to do all these *searches!* Just to establish clear title 'in fee simple' and to make sure it's not encumbered with liens and mortgages. I'll bet the fee will be anything *but* simple! And then, Kernow says, if, one week after buying the place, we decided to sell it again, the new purchaser's lawyer would have to go through the whole idiotic business all over again! 'I don't know how they manage in the States,' I told him, 'but I do know that if any lawyer took the best part of two months to convey a piece of real estate, he'd be run out of town.' Times like this I'm happier to be American than Cornish. I'm sure he thinks we're the most impatient people ever."

At the next bend in the road, where it forked to the right for Sithney and to the left for Breage, a rather fine two-storey house came into view. They paused a moment to admire it. "Parc-an-Ython," Carrington said. "According to Kernow, Mrs Vosper Scawen used to live there — that woman who dynamited those gardens out of the cliffs at Helford. She lived there before she married Scawen."

"Oh?" Leah looked at it with renewed interest. "I thought she lived out in that big house we saw beyond Breage — Montpelier, was it?"

"Sure. That was before her father died — back in the eighteen-fifties. She was unmarried then and, of course, having inherited his considerable fortune, she could not possibly live there unchaperoned. So the mistress of Parc-an-Ython — whose name I've forgotten — gathered her under her wing."

They took the Sithney turn and halted again, briefly, as they passed the house. "Bricks and mortar don't care about us at all, do they," Leah mused aloud. "Think of all the arguments that must have gone on under that roof. And the murders in the old tithe barn, too. All those overwhelming emotions! Yet how serene both buildings are now!"

"Arguments?" her father echoed, frowning at Parc-an-Ython as if he had missed something.

"Well — use your imagination. A rich young heiress with the world at her feet — a woman of some spirit, quite obviously — and a fussy old chaperon telling her she couldn't do this and mustn't do that and 'no, dear, it would be utterly reckless to have *two* dances with young so-and-so' ... All I can say is thank heavens *we* live in this much more enlightened age!"

"Er ... yes." Her father cleared his throat uncomfortably as they walked on. Then, hoping to get back on safer ground, he said, "D'you know, even *after* we've signed the contract — which has all the outward appearances of a legally binding document — it turns out to be no such thing. Either party can withdraw right up to the moment of the sale. Kernow cheerfully agrees that 'something ought to be done about it,' but it would probably take five years of parliamentary time — and since they're all lawyers up there, anyway, they have no interest in changing a law that lines their pockets so warmly."

"Well, at least we have 'reasonable access' to the property for our architect, builder, surveyor, and so on. Did Mister Kernow get the surveyor's report back yet?"

"Oh, yes. I forgot to tell you amid all the excitement of getting William off to college. The cracks are nothing to worry about. They're almost as old as the building itself. They used green timbers, apparently, because the navy took all the seasoned oak. You just can't get away from history, here!"

"It's not subsidence?"

He shook his head. "There are no mine workings under the property, except for the corner of one field down near Grankum Wood ..."

"Oh! Speaking of the wood — may we go down there today? If it doesn't rain?"

"We'll see. What do you think of young Kernow, by the way?"

"We could eat our sandwiches down there perhaps — and drink the water from this well, which is supposed to bring on attacks of love at first sight."

Her father shifted the satchel onto his other shoulder but said nothing. She knew he was waiting for an answer to his question. "Kernow's probably a good lawyer," she said carefully. "He would need to be. There's so much competition in Helston. The town's crawling with them. I don't think a bad one would survive. So he must be quite good."

"Well, thank you, honey, but you know that's not what I meant. I can make up my own mind about him as a lawyer."

"As a man, then? Well, I guess I'd trust him as long as he stayed in plain view. I sure would like to meet his sister, though — Mrs Trelawney. Did you ask him?"

"What about Coad, then?"

Now she held her silence until he was forced to say, "Mrs Trelawney is away with her husband, visiting his people in Leeds. Kernow says she goes up there every now and then to mend their generators but I think that's just a family joke. So what about Coad — and I don't mean as an estate agent?"

"He's amiable ... enjoyable to talk with ... well read. What more can I say? He'll make some lucky girl an admirable husband one day, I guess."

"And do you also guess that the lucky girl has a name?"

"Pa — stop it! I am not on the *qui vive* for a beau right now. Much less a husband. I'll find one when I'm good and ready. And he'll probably be someone we haven't even cast eyes on yet." She took his arm again, briefly, and squeezed it. "I know I'm getting awful long in the tooth but ... patience, huh?"

Shortly after that they entered Sithney itself. The road through the village followed a tight oxbow loop, making an almost complete circuit of the church and the new glebe house. At the bottom end of the loop, in the middle of the village, a macadamized farm track led slightly downhill to the Old Glebe — and then swung right to join up with the Carleen road. The junction itself was called Boase's Burnthouse, presumably because a house belonging to one Boase was burned down there once upon a time. However, all trace of it had long since gone.

"Now in *that* house," Carrington said as they passed a dainty little cottage with roses — at present flowerless — rambling around the porch, "there once lived a widow woman. She was the wife of a penniless nobleman who died and left her with nothing in the bank and four nubile daughters in need of husbands. And she managed it! And — tarnation! — I've forgotten *her* name, too."

Leah chuckled. "How d'you know these things anyway?"

"I asked Coad. I figured that, since we're going to settle here, we might as well know the recent history and background of the parish. I hate walking past a place and seeing just a heap of stone and mortar, don't you? That's why graveyards are so dismal. It's not the thought of death — which we know very well is inevitable — but all the histories that died with them. All the stories we'll never know."

Leah's immediate thought was that her father had acquired these sentiments in conversation with some woman; they seemed too feminine for him to have arrived at them spontaneously. Then she realized that, even so, he was not wearing them as he might wear a woman's dress for a masquerade. He truly meant what he had said. Was he, in fact, revealing a part of his nature he had been concealing all these years?

"Doesn't it bother you?" he asked.

She decided not to agree too readily, to make him talk about it and, perhaps, reveal more. "Not until now," she said.

"When you see a gravestone, d'you just say, 'Oh, that's the site of a mouldering corpse.'? You've never yearned to know their histories?"

"If I want histories, I can always read Sir Walter Scott. Or Charles Reade. Or Jane Austen — if it's a woman troubled by unmarried daughters."

"But that's not *real!*" He hammered his brow at the seeming impossibility of making her understand his point. "I'm talking about *real* stories. Stories with no contrived endings — they just stop when the grim reaper reaps. But the loose ends trail on in the flowing river of time until they snag on other people's lives. Get woven in. Into yours and mine, now we're going to live down here. Don't you realize we're going to get caught up in all sorts of loose ends of dead lives — things we don't even know about. Come on, Leah! You're not so detached you can't follow me here."

She was amazed. With every word he revealed a man she had not met before. If a stranger had asked her to describe her father, she'd have said he was a no-nonsense man of business who, whether or not he had been born with more than his share

of down-to-earth common sense, had certainly acquired it in his dealings with his fellow man. But on the question of his imagination — certainly of the sort of imagination he was now revealing — she would have passed rather than rate him low.

"You should make them up, Pa," she said. "All these unknown or elusive stories — just invent them. Show Scott and Jane Austen where they go wrong!"

"You still don't understand," he said in disappointment. "Think of the tale Coad told us the day we arrived. If he'd kept his mouth shut, we'd have behaved very differently when old Liddicoat came charging across the valley. But because we *did* know, even as he came striding up the field, all sorts of cogs and gears in our brains were going clickety-click! And when he started speaking, we knew exactly what was behind it all. *That's* what I'm talking about. These people who've lived here all their lives — they see each other and little cogs go clickety-click! inside their brains all the time. And when any one of them opens his mouth, everyone else knows what's behind it. But we won't. That's what we're missing. That's why I want to know all these human histories. It has nothing to do with Sir Walter Scott and Jane Austen. Now d'you see?"

She did, of course. But what he had just said did not sit quite square with his interest in the prenuptial life of Mrs Scawen and in the fate of the anonymous widow and her four undowried daughters. That was in a different category to the history of ill-will between the Carringtons and the Liddicoats. She suspected her father was now cloaking a curiosity that was essentially romantic and feminine in justifications more utilitarian and masculine. But was he aware of it?

"You do see," he said, taking her silence for agreement. He held the garden gate of the Old Glebe open for her; it squeaked and fell off one of its hinges. "Good start!" he commented.

"I see a difference between the Liddicoat feud and the widow-with-four-daughters tale," she said. "In terms of value to us."

But he was not to be drawn again. "If you ain't the most cantankarest female!" he exclaimed. "It's like picking houses — or stocks — or hiring hands. Until you've looked them *all* over, you can't talk 'in terms of value to us'!"

"The same with husbands, I guess," she added lightly.

"Hmph!" was all he said to that.

11 With New England thoroughness they measured and remeasured every room in the Old Glebe, and not just the principal dimensions but into every niche and alcove, too. They also compared the two main diagonals, to check that the rooms were square. Only one was — the room where four maidservants had once been crammed. "So their accuracy here was probably an accident," Carrington said.

"Coad told me that Truro Cathedral, which was built in living memory, is twenty feet shorter at one end than the other — which was deliberate, because that's the way they used to build back in medieval days. Just by eye."

"That man!" Her father shook his head admiringly. "He comes up with the excuses before we've even lodged the complaints! I'll bet he knew we were going to find everything here out of plumb."

"Does it make the building less safe?"

"No. Just more ... more ..." He hunted for a word and settled on, "... *quaint.*"

She sniffed the air. "I'll tell you this — after only a morning with the windows open and the sun pouring in, it sure smells a lot less musty. Can we go down Grankum Wood to eat?"

"'Go down Grankum Wood'!" he echoed in amusement. "You're starting to talk like a local, my girl."

"'Es!" she replied, relishing her talent for mimicry. "Proper job, my 'ansum! Can us?"

He laughed. "I guess so. And when we come back we'll discover if it really does smell less musty or if we've just gotten used to it."

He emptied the satchel of everything but the two packed lunches, which were wrapped in greaseproof paper and tied with thin white string in such a way as to furnish a small carrying loop. When Leah pointed this out, he left the bag, too, and they sauntered out into the back garden, each dangling lunch from one crooked finger.

The first thing they saw, naturally, was the old tithe barn, which almost dwarfed the house. Their eyes met and a wordless question flashed between them.

"Why not?" Carrington said, turning his steps toward the barn door.

But disappointment faced them when they arrived at its threshold, for a new galvanized padlock secured the bolt.

"Liddicoat doesn't trust us, it seems," he commented.

But Leah discovered that by lifting the padlock up and pressing it flat against the door, she could ease the crook-end of the bolt past it. "The old boat house for the Yale Rowing Club was like that," she remarked.

"Oh?" His tone begged her to tell him more — until he recalled that Tom O'Leary had been a leading light of that club. Then his repeated, "Oh!" closed off further discussion. Before they left East Haven he'd had enough of Tom-O'Leary-this and Tom-O'Leary-that to last a good while yet.

But when he saw the sadness in his daughter's eyes as she stood there, absently holding the padlock and staring through it at infinity, he could not help giving her arm a little squeeze and asking, "How is it now?"

She came back to the present moment with a little start. "Oh," she said. "Not so bad, I guess."

She opened the bolt to the full and pulled at the door with the toe of her boot. "Who's going to brave it first?"

Chuckling, he stepped past her into the gloom.

Dust motes hung in the shafts of sunlight that fell aslant the lofts and ladders, mocking the insignificant hoards of hay and straw they held. Leah followed her father and then overtook him, arriving at the heart of the barn first. Birds fluttered up in panic — two pigeons at one end and a jackdaw at the other. As her eyes grew accustomed to the gloom, she noticed an unflustered barn owl squatting on the wall plate above the door.

"Could that be the beam they hanged him from?" Carrington asked, pointing to the central rafter and prodding the air beneath it as a blind man in a forest might test the way before him. "Was this the space that once caged his insane but dying presence?" Then, assuming a comic-sepulchral voice, he boomed: "O, unquiet spirit of John Lidgeycot, if such thou art, I charge thee! Come forth and ..."

"Pop!" Leah shrieked in horror.

"Ha!" he cackled and stabbed an accusing finger toward her. "So you *do* believe after all! Where's your fine skepticism now!"

Realizing he had just been trying to trap her she was quick witted enough to keep the look of horror on her face and whisper, "No! No! Look behind you!"

The blood drained from his face as he spun round and saw ... nothing!

Now it was her bright, mocking laughter that turned the tables on him.

"Okay!" He held up his hands in surrender but added in a steely voice: "Even so, I guess that, skeptics or not, neither of us is going to volunteer to come out here upon a midnight hour if the fire needs another log!"

They stood there a moment in silence, trying to feel any sort of presence or atmosphere that could be called supernatural — an unprovoked tingling of the skin, the stirring of hair roots in the scalp, a vague frisson up and down the spine. But nothing of that sort lingered in the quiet air; no host of phantom listeners, ready to oblige.

"I guess we're not such stuff as hauntings are made on," Leah said at last. "Also, I'm starving."

He looked up into the ancient rafters, shook his head sadly, and said, "What on earth are we going to do with all this useless empty space?"

As they reached the door he took two old horse blankets from a peg beside it.

Outside again she reversed the trick with the lock. Her father stared at the result in amazement. "You'd swear that was impossible," he said.

In the gateway at the bottom of the yard they paused again, this time to take in the panorama. It was the same half-wild, half-polluted landscape as before but now it was made cheerful by the sun.

"D'you think we could have inherited some memory of this scene, Pa?" Leah asked.

"Why, honey?"

"Because it looks so familiar. Even that first day it looked like something I'd seen once, long ago, and forgotten. Didn't you feel it, too?"

"Mm-hmm," he agreed vaguely. "But then Coad had already told us that tale about the place."

"How would that make a difference?"

"Well, we knew the Carringtons — or one of us — had been remarkably possessive about the Old Glebe, even before we set eyes on it. Coad made sure of that!"

"You think it was deliberate?"

"I'd take a note on it." He chuckled. "Smart fellow, Coad."

"Okay, Pa," she said wearily. "I hear you." She set off into the field, forcing him to follow.

"A woman's no different from any other female in creation," he said. "They all want a good, secure nest for their cubs."

She halted and turned to face him. "And you?" she asked. "What do you want?"

"By happy coincidence, my dear, men also want a good, secure nest ..."

"No. *You!* Just you. What do *you* want?"

"To see William launched into life and you secure in *your* nest, of course."

"Right!" she exclaimed, as if he had fallen into her trap. "And what then?"

"What d'you mean — then?"

"I mean *then!* Look at that house!" She spun him by the shoulders and spoke to the back of his head. "Look at the size of it! With William gone and me gone ... just you and the help rattling around inside there. What d'you want then?"

He faced her again, frowning in bewilderment. "Are you saying we shouldn't buy the place after all?"

"Of course not!" She set off once more for Grankum Wood, whose uphill margin was now a mere hundred paces distant. "What I *am* saying is that sauce for the gander is sauce for the goose. If *this* gander has to be looking out for a goose to nest with, then there's another goose, not a thousand miles from here, who ought to be thinking of a gander to share *that* huge nest with him." She jerked a thumb back toward the Old Glebe.

"Ho-ho-ho!" he responded with ironic joviality. "I see your game, young miss. Every time I mention husbands from now on, you'll respond with talk of wives, for my benefit — yeah?"

"Don't you think it's a point worth considering?"

"Sure," he replied complacently. "And I have, too, considered it — so there!"

It was her turn for bewilderment. "Who?" she asked, cudgelling her brains for one likely name.

"Not in particular, my dear, but in general. The obvious thing to do is to hire a housekeeper."

They had reached the fringe of the wood by now. Its beauty and stillness silenced them, held them in awe. Spring was still some way off, yet all the buds were there, tight on their twigs and branches — minute pinholes of green that combined to lend a subliminal shimmer to the scene, a greenness that trembled at the very threshold of being. Just for a moment they had an intimation of some mighty force in the dark earth underfoot, stirring itself, reaching up into the lichen-mottled trunks all about them, building up the pressures that would, one day soon, erupt in a riot of new foliage.

"No birds sing," she whispered.

"Midday," he replied.

Rooks cawed far off, in the elms around the church and the Old Glebe.

He sniffed the air. "Fox," he said. "D'you get it, too?"

She moved upwind of him and said, "Oh, yes!"

They tried to follow it but lost the line within very few paces.

But the spell of the woods was broken and Leah returned to their earlier conversation. "Why is hiring a housekeeper so obvious?" she asked.

"Because a wife can say, 'Go back outside and wipe those boots this minute!' and you've got to knuckle under. But a housekeeper …"

She interrupted, continuing his sentence for him: "… will tell you if you're going to walk mud all over the house like that, she'll want better wages!"

"Right, honey," he said. "My train of thought exactly!"

"Oh." She felt deflated.

"Only a fool hires a woman," he went on. "It's smarter to hire her husband — then you get her labour for free!"

"Good luck!" she said, abandoning any attempt to speak seriously with him on this particular topic. At least he'd know what to expect in future, any time he started in on his hobby horse about her finding a husband.

The slope of the valley grew steeper as it neared the bottom and it was soon impossible to go directly down. Instead, the hillside was criss-crossed by a maze of narrow paths that alternated between horizontal and gently sloping. Leah picked one a yard uphill from his, which brought their heads almost on a par.

She was now the same height as her mother had been. Their similarity, which was less obvious when she stood at her normal height, eight or nine inches below his eyeline, brought a sharp pang to his chest — so much so that he had to pause awhile and pretend he was out of breath.

She relieved him of the horse blankets and continued along the path. "There's the enchanted well," she cried out when she had gone a couple of dozen paces. Then, "It's not a well at all. It's a three-sided cutting into the rock. With a shallow pool at the bottom. I could walk right into it from here."

"Man made?" he asked, coming to join her. "Yep!" he answered himself, running an appreciative hand up the smooth-carved walls. "Looks like good water, too. Silvery and clear. Must be a spring."

"It's all we have for drinking right now," she said. "Are you going to risk its enchantment?"

"Risk?" he asked.

"Well, some hideous old crone might come along right after you've drunk your fill — and it'd be love at first sight!"

"Oh, that old tale!" he replied wearily. "Hand me one of those blankets."

He passed her his cap in return and, holding back his forelock in one hand, knelt and slaked his thirst. If he had not just seen her likeness to his late wife, he would have joshed with her on rising — pretending to have fallen under the spell of the waters and with her as the object.

And she, being his daughter, would have played the same joke on him after she had drunk her fill — if they hadn't heard the sounds of someone approaching.

They moved back onto the path and saw him at once — a good-looking young man, dark-haired and wiry, striding with easy grace along well-known paths, making no effort at silence. When he saw that they had noticed him he stopped, being still twenty or more paces away. "Mister Carrington?" he called out. "And Miss Carrington?"

"The same," her father called back. "Have we met?"

The fellow resumed his approach. "I've met your son, sir," he replied. "In fact, he saved me from a most unpleasant situation

— involving an encounter with some abandoned mining machinery over at Wheal Fortune, in which I had come off second-best. Nicholas Liddicoat," he added, being now close enough to offer his hand.

But Carrington could hardly take his eyes off Leah — and from the light that danced in her eyes he was almost ready to swear there was something in that old wives' tale after all.

12 He had two bloodied rabbits and a pheasant dangling from his belt. Slung over one shoulder was a short bow; over the other, a quiver with half a dozen arrows; he divested himself of both and laid them carefully on the ground beside him. John Carrington looked on with amusement. "If you hadn't told us your name, young man," he said, "I'd have guessed at Robin Hood."

Nicholas Liddicoat shook his head solemnly. "Robin Hood used the long bow," he replied.

"Sure." Carrington could not tell whether he was making a straight-faced joke or a serious point.

"Also Robin Hood is dead," Leah put in, as solemnly as the young man.

"Ah!" His tone suggested he could say a great deal more on that particular subject.

"Have you eaten, Mister Liddicoat?" Carrington asked. "May we invite you to share our humble ..."

"I have eaten, thank you."

"Then you don't object if we ..."

"Please do! Did William tell you about our meeting?"

"He saved your life — at least, that's the way they're telling it all over Helston."

Liddicoat laughed at the exaggeration. "I bruised my leg, that's all. However, he certainly saved me a great deal of discomfort and boredom. I could have been trapped there for days. In which case, come to think of it, he would have saved my life. Did he say that?"

Father and daughter munched their sandwiches and exchanged awkward glances, aware that, between them, they had perhaps not given William much chance to account for his day.

"He's not usually the most communicative of persons. Not to us." Carrington explained.

"Really?" Liddicoat was surprised. "Oh, well." He nodded toward the Grankum well. "Did he tell you about the danger that lurks in those waters?" He grinned knowingly.

"Coad told us," Leah said. "The very first day we came here." She spoke coolly, not wishing him to get any ideas.

"Ah," he replied. His eyes did a quick scan of their meagre rations. "And yet I see no flask of water, no pop, no ginger beer? Did you risk a drink despite the warning?" He grinned again.

The nerve of the man! Leah thought. He must imagine that, just because he was pretty good-looking (she could not deny him that), he could hang around the spring, posing as Robin Hood, and bamboozle credulous damsels with that old wives' tale! Who did he think she was? "We don't believe *everything* we hear, Mister Liddicoat," she said loftily.

His grin only broadened. "Faith is not necessary in this case," he told her. "It's a simple physiological reaction. You don't feel anything yet?"

For brazen effrontery, this took the gold medal. She replied in her coldest, most off-putting tone, "I believe my constitution is proof against whatever *spell*" — she spoke the word with contempt — "those waters may cast upon me."

"Amen to that, Miss Carrington," he said sympathetically. "I trust it is so. And for you, too, Mister Carrington."

"I?" he responded with surprise, looking around for a female object of this supposed witchcraft. "I feel quite safe so far." Then, wishing to change the subject, he went on, "Tell me, why did you say 'Ah' in that tone just now — when my daughter pointed out that Robin Hood is dead? Were you going to tell us that death does not stop the unquiet spirit from roaming abroad in these parts? Because, if so, we've heard *that* old tale, too."

Liddicoat, thinking that the sight of his bloody trophies was putting Miss Carrington off and making her so snooty, hid them behind a clump of wild garlic. At the same time he replied, "So William told me. But I don't believe in anything supernatural like that, do you?" Being turned away from them, he did not catch their mystified expressions. "This is a rational universe, in my book. Ghouls and spectres belong to the age of, well, of Robin Hood, I suppose."

Leah was now convinced he was that shallow sort of young man who talked in scribble, saying the first thing that came into his head — and no doubt thinking it mighty clever because it came from *his* head.

"And what of chalybeate waters that act as love potions?" Carrington teased him.

He flapped his hand as if wafting the thought into oblivion. "You heard that old tale, too, did you? Love at first sight! Well, I've drunk from that well since childhood and, I can assure you, it never had *that* effect on me."

"I wouldn't be so sure," Leah said acidly. "I noticed just now, when I drank from it myself, that the first living creature I saw — reflected in the surface, of course — was myself!"

Their eyes met and locked. It took him a second or so to grasp her meaning. Then his face darkened with anger. "Then you *do* believe that old nonsense," he said. "Well, it puts you on a par with most of the women hereabouts. And now they clamour for the vote! Hah!"

Leah was momentarily speechless. Her jaw clamped so tight it hurt the muscles at her temples; her nostrils flared as she drew a deep breath to reply.

"Now, now ..." her father began, but he had left his intervention too late.

"We have the vote in Spain," she said. "In Norway. In Australia. In New Zealand. And in at least three states of America. And — it may interest you to know, Mister Liddicoat — in none of these enlightened places has the world come crashing down around men's ears."

"Yet," he replied calmly. "You are obviously a bit of a suffragist yourself, Miss Carrington."

Her father moved his hand up and down as if seeking to cut the invisible rays of hostility that flashed between them. "Come, come!" he exclaimed. "Young man, you have catapulted yourself into tiger country."

"What d'you mean 'yet'?" Leah asked. "D'you mean the world *will* come to an end in those places — and any others that may follow?"

"Absolutely!" He chuckled happily, the way a teacher might chuckle when a dim pupil grasps a difficult point at last. "The world as *I* know it, anyway."

"Aha! Aha!" she crowed. "There we have it! The world as *you* know it."

"You'll get on famously with my brother Harvey," he told her. "He was arrested, along with a whole gaggle of the shrieking sisterhood, in Camborne last year."

"In that case, I think I will," she said.

"I'm quite sure of it!" He laughed sarcastically. "His head's 'crammed with louch,' too — as we say."

"May I ask …" Carrington tried again.

"I like him better by the minute," Leah said.

"He'll be delighted to hear that, Miss Carrington. He already feels pretty *hurrisome* about you — there's another Cornish word for you." He turned to her father. "I'm sorry, sir. You were interrupted just now."

Carrington sighed. "I merely wished to ask if you had any particular reason for stopping and talking with us?"

"Oh. Just to be neighbourly, actually." The young fellow laughed at the incongruity of the remark. "To be precise, I hoped to discover if we *were* neighbours. Or are about to become neighbours, sir."

"In other words, spying for your father!" Leah suggested.

"He'd like to see *that* day!" was the enigmatic reply.

"Well, let me *spy* in my own behalf." Carrington hoped his humour would rob the word of its sting. "Is your father intending to put in a bid on the Old Glebe? Coad is rather surprised not to have heard from him already."

"Surprised and disappointed, I imagine," Liddicoat said.

"So he won't be bidding? I'll be frank with you, young man. We *have* put in a bid, and it has been accepted — though, as I've also learned, it means nothing in law. Another, higher, bid could be entered even now, and we'd be right back where we started." He paused and waited for a reply.

Liddicoat squirmed a little before he responded. "Let's just say that my father is, after all, a farmer."

"Meaning?"

"Meaning he's quite happy to sow seed in the fall and see no result until next spring. I also intended — whether we are to be neighbours or not — to offer to take you over the old mines, show you the things I showed William last week. I suppose he told you about that?"

It was their turn to squirm — again. "As I said, he's not the world's leading conversationalist," Carrington responded.

"Yes," Liddicoat went on. "That surprised me the first time you said it."

The implication that it no longer surprised him, now that he had met them and got to know them slightly, was not lost on either father or daughter. To Leah it was just one more example of the fellow's arrogance; she just wished he'd go away. But her father took it in quite the opposite spirit. The jibe made him eager to continue in young Liddicoat's company, if only to show him how wrong he was.

"Why, that's mighty civil of you, sir. Isn't it, Leah. We'll be happy to accept."

Liddicoat grinned triumphantly at her. She knew what he was thinking — the fiery suffragist was being forced to submit to the patriarch's will. There was no warmth, no spark of friendship, in that smile at all.

Actually, come to think of it, that was what made the suggestion at all acceptable. If she'd thought for one moment that he was truly aiming at a friendship with her, she'd have risen without a word and left them to it. Even so, she did not yield without a protest. "We left the house unlocked," she reminded her father.

"Grankum Farm has no locks," Liddicoat put in. "I don't think any house does in these parts."

"Besides," Carrington said, "what's there to steal?"

Liddicoat strung his game from an overhanging branch, beyond the reach of foxes, and rested his bow and quiver against the tree itself. The other two stuffed the paper wrappings and string down a rabbit hole and prepared to follow young Liddicoat on his tour of discovery.

"One more sip before we set off?" he suggested mischievously as they passed the entrance to the well.

"I will!" Leah could not resist the challenge.

"Good," he said as she emerged from the narrow cleft again, wiping her lips.

"Why so?" she asked.

"I'm keen to see this constitution in action — the one that can withstand the effects of Grankum's 'chalybeate waters'." He smiled at Carrington as he quoted the words. "You'll be the first in my experience, let me say."

"Such airs!" she said, pushing past him. "Are we going that way?" She pointed down the valley.

"Anywhere that's close to a hedge," he replied. "Such would be my recommendation, anyway. Right along the floor of the valley to the end of the wood."

"There's no such thing as poison ivy in Cornwall, is that right?" Carrington asked nervously.

"Only stinging nettles," he replied.

"Yeah, we learned about stinging nettles — the hard way."

The trickle of water that spilled over the basin of the well joined a small brook that drained the upper part of the Grankum valley. Paths led downstream along either bank.

"If we cross up here, we won't have to leap across it lower down," he added. "You'd not want to do too much leaping for the next day or so."

"This stream looks man-made," Carrington commented as he helped Leah cross to the path on the farther bank.

"Man-improved," Liddicoat agreed. "In my grandfather's time, the area where we were just sitting was one big marsh. When they started quarrying stone there — did you see the quarry up there?"

"We glimpsed it."

"That was when they dug this deep channel for the stream — and hewed out the sides of the well."

Walking in single file and picking their way carefully among brambles and fallen branches made conversation difficult. Mostly they listened to a monologue from young Liddicoat — pointing out a spot where they would see orchids later in the year, describing the 'one carpet of blue' that covered the ground in bluebell time, warning them of a badger's 'set' — a word new to them, meaning 'earth.'

"D'you say 'set' for foxes, too?" Leah asked.

"No — it's 'den' for foxes. 'Form' for hares. 'Burrow' for rabbits. 'Nest' for birds …"

"Yes. Thank you, Mister Liddicoat. I didn't want the whole encyclopedia. I only asked about foxes."

He could not do the simplest thing, it seemed, without trying to annoy her. It even annoyed her that she had let him go ahead because it would allow him to imagine her eyes were upon him all the way. But when she tried ostentatiously looking to one side or the other, just in case he should turn round to check, she ran into trees and stumbled over roots. She thought of sidling past him on one of his frequent lecture-stops but then, she realized, she'd be giving him the chance to ogle her from behind. So, that wouldn't do, either. Therefore, whenever the path divided into two or three parallel trails, she chose one that would bring her abreast of him, where she could look ahead without letting him think she had eyes for him.

Chalybeate waters, indeed!

A similar dilemma occurred at the end of the wood, where they were obliged to leap from the top of a stone hedge down into a field, about a hundred paces from the very bottom of the valley. The drop was a mere thirty inches, which she would normally have done without a pause; but here, near the foot of the valley, the field sloped at a giddy angle and she was afraid of turning her ankle. Only the thought that she would then have to rely on his support until they came to the nearest dwelling made her steel herself to accept his outstretched hands. He clasped her by the waist and, with what seemed like no effort at all, lifted her down to the grass.

"Thistledown!" he said, not letting go of her waist. "May I call you Thistle?"

Behind her she heard her father laugh. "Hang me if that ain't *le mot juste,* young feller!" he said. "Come on, daughter — what d'you say to that?"

Fastidiously she peeled his hands away, saying, "If he calls me Thistle, I'll call him Nark — short for Narcissus."

The reference to the youth in the Greek legend who fell in love with his own reflection in a pool of water and pined away at his unattainability was not lost on him, coming as it did on the heels of her jibe about his drinking at the Grankum well. "I reckon Miss Carrington knows best," he said quietly. "Well now!" He pointed along the valley. "We can go that way and pick up the path William took last week. Or we can go arrow-flight, straight up the hill here, over the brow, and down to where he found me." He indicated the land rearing above them to their right.

Carrington stared up the punishing slope and echoed him ironically. "Arrow flight! I'm for the horizontal walk. It may be longer but it looks lovelier."

They went diagonally down to the very bottom of the valley. There at last they were able to amble side by side. The jests about Thistle and Narcissus, barbed though they were, had eased the tension a little — enough to let Leah ask, in a most reasonable tone, "Why d'you say that women's suffrage will end the world as you know it, Mister Liddicoat?"

He chuckled defensively. "D'you want a long argument or a short one? We've time enough for both."

"I don't wish for an argument at all," she replied. "But I suspect that, even with all eternity before us, I should never find reasons enough to change *your* mind."

"Any more than you'd find herrings enough to feed us in the middle of the Sahara."

"You imply there are none."

John Carrington, who knew everything his daughter might say on this topic, listened with only half an ear. He spent most of his time gazing into the fields at their left — the Old Glebe lands — daydreaming their conversion into one of the great gardens of Cornwall. Exotic trees that would not break the skyline until his grandson was an old man waved their fronds in his mind's eye and gladdened his heart.

"I *assert* there are none, Miss Carrington," Liddicoat told her. "And it is not open to question, either, since all I assert is that *my* world, or the world as *I* know it, would be changed for ever by the granting of female suffrage. Who can gainsay it?"

"And what is so wonderful about your world — if I am not guilty of *lèse majesté* in asking?"

He marshalled his thoughts before responding. "If it were merely a matter of granting the vote, I'd yield it this minute. Gladly. For me, that's not the problem."

"Problem?"

"Threat, then. If women ever get the vote — which will be over my dead body, let me say — it won't take them long to discover what men discovered when manhood franchise was granted back in ... eighteen ... whenever it was ..."

He looked to see if she would jeer at his ignorance.

She kept her eyes fixed on the path ahead.

"So there are some things that even you don't know!" he remarked. "Interesting!"

"Eighteen eighty-four," she said flatly.

"I shouldn't have asked." He sighed.

"You didn't ask. You jeered."

"I shouldn't have jeered."

"Quite. What did men discover back then, anyway?"

"Not all men. Just those without economic power. They discovered how useless political power is without economic power to back it."

"Ah — and you're afraid that disillusioned women will start demanding economic power, too?"

"You know very well they will. *I* certainly would — and I don't think I'm any brighter than most of you lot."

"And what about fairness?"

"What about it?"

They had arrived at a gate. The next field marked the lower end of the Grankum valley, where it curved round to their right and joined the valley William had followed up from the stop gate. It was well stocked with cows, some too close for Leah's liking. "Do they …?" She hesitated.

"Bite?" he suggested.

"No!" She withered him with a glance. "But they won't charge us or something? Their horns look fearsome."

"The breed is called dairy shorthorn, funnily enough."

"They may be short but they look wickedly sharp to me." She turned to her father. "What about changing our mind and going up the hill?"

He smiled tolerantly and opened the gate. "They won't dare harm either of us, honey," he said, winking at Liddicoat to show who 'us' included. "Not with you here to protect us."

Half angry, half terrified still, she followed them through and, taking her father's left arm, placed him firmly between her and the bulk of the herd. And as a shield against stragglers on her other side, she walked rather closer to young Liddicoat than she would normally have wished.

"What about fairness?" he asked again as soon as their walk was resumed.

This time she saw to it that they marched rather than ambled.

"You imply that men have all the economic power," she said. "Don't you think it would be only fair to share it?"

"Yes," he replied.

"Well, then!" she said. "Why not do it?"

"Because fairness doesn't come into it. If we all went around being *fair,* civilization would grind to a halt."

"Oh!" she exclaimed. "'You're just enjoying being perverse for the sake of it. I'm sorry I started this."

"I'm not," he went on in that same infuriatingly 'reasonable' tone. "I'm neither sorry you started it nor am I simply enjoying being perverse. Look — my family owns Grankum Farm. Yours owns the Old Glebe — or soon will. I could introduce you to a hundred people, living in this very parish, who think that arrangement is most *un*fair. And they're very probably right. Follow the history of ownership back to its roots — in time immemorial, I mean — and you'll find it was almost always taken at the point of a sword. What we call theft nowadays. Just imagine for a moment that you own the Old Glebe. It's yours — freehold. You can do anything you like with it. What does your sense of *fairness* tell you to do?"

Angrily she probed this argument for weaknesses. It must have some, but none was immediately apparent — which merely angered her more.

"See?" he concluded calmly. "That's why people like me — men — will never give you the vote if we can avoid it. Most of us have only a fraction of the economic power we feel entitled to. So we're never going to dilute our share by heeding your cries of 'Fair Play!' And such cries would follow the suffrage as sure as moon follows sun."

"Well," she replied, wishing she could find something more crushing to say. "We must just agree to differ on the topic. That's all. One day the constitution will be amended and we *will* get the vote."

"Talking of constitutions, how is yours holding out?"

She did not deign to reply.

Half an hour later he repeated the question, after he had shown them the stamps and explained how William had 'saved his life.' She answered him with the same withering glance — except that, this time, she was showing distinct signs of uneasiness. So was her father.

He showed them all over the old mine workings, then, beginning with the quarry at Wheal Fortune where the stamps stood abandoned. "Wheal means 'mine'," he said. "But here the different veins of the lode were so tight-packed — and so close to the surface — that the workings collapsed into each other and turned into this quarry." He waved a hand at the fractured stone walls all around.

"That tunnel I can see up ahead," Leah said awkwardly. "Is it, er, still in use?"

"Only by bats," he assured her. "It's an adit, actually."

"Bats?" She cried out in dismay. "Well, what about the other one? Is that an adit, too?"

"Why?" He guessed, of course, but he wasn't going to show any sympathy, not after all her boasting.

"Oh …" She flushed with embarrassment. "I find I need to … to pay a call of nature."

He waved toward the second adit, whose mouth was about seven feet high by three feet wide. "That only goes in about six yards. They started to …"

"No bats?" she asked urgently, already walking in that direction. "You promise?"

"No bats. I'll wait back there by the stamps."

"Actually, young fellow," her father said apologetically, tearing up handfuls of dry grass as he spoke. "I'm in a similar predicament. The summer scour. There must have been something in those sandwiches. I'll see you by the stamps, too."

While he stood by the old machinery, Nicholas Liddicoat ran his mind back to that odd remark: 'Must be something in the sandwiches.' Surely, if they knew all about the aperient power of the water in Grankum well, they had no need to suspect the sandwiches? Therefore they did *not* know about it. Not at all. Therefore … and therefore …

And so, step by logical step — for, as he had told them, his was a rational world — he worked out that while he had been referring to the aperient influence of the water upon the bowels, the Carringtons had been talking about … something quite different. About what?

He began to laugh.

About the old wives' tale of falling in love at first sight! Even more confusingly, they had assumed *he* was talking about that old legend, too.

And so he understood very well why Leah was so affronted to find him laughing his head off when she rejoined him at the stamps. But that only made it worse.

13   The signing of the contract to buy the Old Glebe might have had little legal standing but it was an adequate sign to local society that the Carringtons were now committed to the district. It was therefore time for that same local society to determine their fitness as new members. The newcomers had already leaped one hurdle: John Carrington was clearly well-to-do. And any rich man with a young bachelor son and a nubile spinster daughter would be welcome in a society brought to the verge of ruin, first by the collapse of tin mining, then, more recently, by a decade of agricultural depression.

But old ways die hard in old country towns. It was rumoured that Carrington's father had made his fortune in something called 'hog trading' in Chicago and that Carrington himself had worked in the business until he was fortyish. It did not sound too auspicious. However, no one was sure whether the American 'hog' meant exactly the same as the English 'pig.' And then there was that other word, 'trading' — had it been respectably wholesale or undesirably retail?

Fenella Compton, who dabbled in oils, knew that the best brushes were made of hog bristle, which proved, she said, that the hog trade had a genteel side to it and so they should give Mr Carrington the benefit of the doubt. She was not alone in profound commentary of that sort. But the acknowledged authority in this particular field had to be Jimmy Troy, himself an American, and rich, and the third-generation descendant of a Cousin Jack. His wife, Elizabeth, was the heiress of the Pallas estate, one of the biggest in West Penwith; so the word of either would count for something. And Jimmy Troy's word was that hog trading at the Carrington level involved tens if not hundreds of thousands of carcases. So it was all paperwork — and thus eminently respectable.

He was one of the first to call on his compatriot, who was his junior by a mere six years. The leaders of local society imagined it was to appraise him; in fact, Troy's purpose was to *apprise* him of the forthcoming ordeal of Trial by Scrutiny and Sneer, which he, too, had once endured, back in the nineties. His method of 'calling' was hardly orthodox, except by the mores of that commercial society in which both men had been raised. Troy walked straight up to him in the saloon bar at the Angel, slapped him on the back, gave out his own name, and proffered a Havana cigar. His accent revealed his origins and so, within minutes, they were agreeing about English beer, crazy plumbing, and lunatic systems of property conveyance.

When Troy got round to his warning, Carrington took it with a laugh. "I'm well used to that, ol' feller," he said. "America isn't so different. Why, I've known men whose fathers made a fortune selling bad whiskey to Injuns yet their wives would claim to sniff pork when they just heard my voice in the next room. Society cultivates and refines, they say. Well, I'm just amazed at the speed of the operation."

Jimmy chuckled. "Yessirree! We sure do things quicker in America. Here in Cornwall, if your ancestor was a farmhand, it takes at least three generations to forget him. But in New York the putting-on of mourning is an universal way to forget an inconvenient ancestor. And in Pittsburgh they go one better. Why, I knew ancestors who were still slaving daily at the board of trade, but who were already completely forgotten by their own sons and daughters across the river in Allegheny. By the way, a 'board of trade' is called a 'commodity exchange' over here. But I wouldn't bother to translate. 'Board of trade' sounds much more respectable." He winked.

The two men, starting with so much in common, got on famously. As John told his daughter later that evening, "I took to him like a Yankee takes to pie, honey. Anyway, the long and short of it is that he and his wife, Elizabeth, are hiring the old Coinage Hall for the night, just up the street here, and giving a ball to welcome us and introduce us to local society. Isn't that swell of them?"

"When?" Leah asked.

"Oh, he didn't say exactly. Sometime next week, I guess."

"Next *week?*" she echoed in horror. "But I haven't a thing to wear. Oh, my lord!"

"Nothing to wear?" he protested. "You have trunks full of gowns you haven't even opened yet."

"Yes, and all in last year's American fashions — or older. Very appropriate!"

"Well, why did we bring them at all?"

"It's only *four* ballgowns, Pa. You make it sound like ..."

"Correction! Why did we bring even four ballgowns if not one of them is good enough?"

Having no answer to that, Leah simply stared balefully at him and told him he didn't understand.

"Can't one of them be made over?" he asked. "Your mother was a regular dab at that."

"There won't be time to do anything else, will there!" she replied angrily. "I do think he could give us a bit more notice."

Elizabeth Troy agreed but, since Jimmy had gone directly to the town clerk's office and hired the hall for the following Friday, the 20th of March, which was a week to the day after his conversation with John Carrington, there was nothing she could do about it. She accordingly left her card at the Angel, desiring Leah to call on her at Pallas Home Farm at her earliest convenience. Her telephone number — Tregathennan 1 — was scribbled on the back of the card, so Leah called her and arranged to take tea that very afternoon. She was to catch the early-afternoon train to Pallas Halt, which was the next stop beyond Truthall, where Mrs Troy would meet her. She was also to bring one or more of the ballgowns, suitable for alteration, and Mrs Troy would see what her maids and 'a little lady she knew' could manage between them.

It was all very bewildering to Leah, who had so far received no more than the usual courtesies due to a visitor, a mere tourist. That is, people she had met casually in shops and tea-rooms were friendly and interested; but the friendliness stopped short of friendship and the interest ceased at their parting. An intimate meeting like this one with Elizabeth Troy, in her own home, too, had never before been suggested. She just prayed she would do nothing, even inadvertently, to start a bad report circulating in the district. At times like this, as she prepared herself for that teatime ordeal, she missed her mother more keenly than ever.

She spread out her four ballgowns and stared at them ruefully. Even for East Haven they were out of date. She knew very well why she had insisted on bringing them, just these four — because at one time or another Tom O'Leary had danced with her while she had been wearing them. That one at the sopho-mores' ball, that one for inauguration, that one last Thanksgiving, and that one ... she couldn't remember. But he had touched them all. She lifted one, of pink bolting cloth over black and gold brocade, and pressed it to her cheek, choosing the part that would have covered the small of her back, where his hand had rested.

Oh, Tom ... She surrendered to a dear and familiar yearning. But she had to shake her head and throw the dress back on her bed before it brought on real tears, which would leave her looking a sight.

Why all this fuss about a pip-squeak ball in a boondock town like ... no, she mustn't start thinking like that. People are people the world over. The same value everywhere. But why all the fuss about the eligible young men who would be introduced to her ... when there was only one truly eligible young man in all the world? No question of same value there.

She returned to the practical business of discarding the gowns that might prove least adaptable to the prevailing fashion. In the end, curiously enough, she picked the oldest, the one that had started life as her mother's, back in those prehistoric days when they still wore bustles — all of ten years ago! Since the banish-the-bustle revolution came in, the only real change had been in the position of the waistline, which had now crept up almost to where it had been in the days of the American Revolution, right up under the bosom. This particular ballgown, made of blue, watered-silk, had no waist at all; so a band, suggestive of a waist, could be sewn in at any level. And with as many, or as few, tucks and folds as fashion now required. Even so, and despite such practical considerations, she knew she really picked it because its elegantly faded blue, with just a hint of green, would bring out the dark blue of her eyes perfectly. And while these part-vain, part-practical thoughts milled around in her mind, a nagging little doubt crept in at the edge — harking back to her undiminished love for Tom O'Leary.

Since it was highly unlikely they would ever meet again, why did she, who had always been praised for her robust practicality and good sense, continue to hanker after him? Could it be a convenient way of shutting out thoughts of Coad and Kernow and Harvey Liddicoat — not to mention all those yet unknown young men whom Mrs Troy was about to add to her dance programme? And even Nicholas Liddicoat, perhaps? No. She had to laugh at that. Nark Liddicoat (as she now called him on those few — those very, very few — occasions when thoughts of him flitted across her mind) needed no phantom beau to keep him at bay; his own odious personality was quite sufficient for *that* task!

In the end she decided that, whether her feelings for Tom were a true embodiment of undying love, or were a convenient 'hedge,' as her father would say, against a precipitate romance on this side of the Atlantic, they had their practical uses in her life; and for that reason, if no other, she would do nothing to dispel them.

In good heart, therefore, she took the train from Helston and, thirteen minutes later, alighted at Pallas Halt. The single platform stood in a shallow cutting on the slope of Tregathennan Hill, a near-rival to mighty Trigonning, on the skyline to the west. Her first impression, as the train pulled away in swirls of leaking steam, was that she had got off at the wrong place. Only the word PALLAS in flaking paint on a rickety old board reassured her it was not so. But the platform was a mere ten paces long, which was hardly the length of a single carriage, and there was not even the most rudimentary shelter against the elements.

A cow, which had been standing with its head over the hedge, chewing the cud and staring impassively at the little branch-line train, suddenly seemed to notice her. It threw up its head in fright and galloped away down the field. Elizabeth Troy appeared at the top of the embankment at that same moment and said as she walked down the gravel path, "It probably never saw a human being alighting here, you know. Usually the only things that get on and off are our milk churns. You must be Miss Carrington. I'm Elizabeth Troy. How'd'you do? And welcome to Pallas." She waved her hand vaguely about. "Such as it is!"

Leah shook the proferred hand and bobbed a curtsey.

"My, my!" Elizabeth said, slightly embarrassed. "There's really no need for that."

To be honest, Leah was a little disappointed in Mrs Troy's appearance. She owned one of the biggest farms in West Penwith, if not the biggest, and was certainly the doyenne of local society. Yet here she was in boots and gaiters, a plain dress of dark gray denim that didn't reach her ankles even, a tweed hacking jacket, and an alpine sort of trilby hat with a pheasant feather stuck in its band. She wasn't even wearing gloves! Against that, however, she had the most wonderful auburn hair, silky and lustrous, and plaited in a single long tail; also the merriest eyes, light brown in colour and brimming with promises of fun and secrets to share. And her complexion would be the envy of a woman half her age — which Leah (who *was* that woman and did, indeed, envy it) guessed to be forty-five-ish.

The road was little more than one carriage wide, moist at its verges, dry and dusty along the middle. It rolled over the smaller ridges and meandered around the larger ones skirting the flank of Tregathennan. The high stony hedges on either side often shut out the view, lending their walk an air of privacy.

"It's very good of you to spare me your time, Mrs Troy," Leah began.

"Not at all. Forgive my appearance, by the way. Saturday is my day to share the milking — which is also a way of keeping a check on my herdsmen without making it too obvious. Have you ever milked a cow?"

Leah shook her head in amazement. In every way Mrs Troy was turning out to be the opposite of the sort of woman she had expected to find. Her own fears of proving socially inadequate were evaporating fast, only to be replaced by fears of a subtler nature — the fear of being dull, of seeming too conventional.

"You might have a try later," Mrs Troy said. "It's not too difficult. I can lend you some suitable clothes." She stopped and stood alongside Leah, measuring herself by eye. "Give or take an inch, we're pretty well matched," she said. "You could look through my ballgowns, if you prefer. It might save a lot of panic-work on yours."

Leah, now eager not to appear conventional, said, "May I ask, Mrs Troy — are you a suffragist?"

The woman chuckled as they walked on. "You mean, do I go around slashing pictures of nude women in public galleries?" Mary Richardson's notorious axe-job in the National Gallery, on the Rokeby Venus by Velasquez, had occurred the previous Tuesday, four days earlier, and was naturally on everyone's lips. "I don't think I'd have the courage for that," she concluded. "Would you?"

Leah had at first deplored the action, but the sneers and contempt of the men around her, and the vicious tone taken by the newspapers, had led her to defend it as, at worst, noble but misguided. Now she did not know what to say. So, when an apposite thought popped into her head, she spoke it without pausing to think where it might have come from. She said, "I salute Polly Dick" — Miss Richardson's nickname — "but I think political power on its own will prove a delusion to women."

Mrs Troy stopped again, this time to stare at her in frank admiration. "How extraordinary!" she exclaimed. "May I ask how old you are?"

"Twenty-two," Leah replied, pleased to have excited this admiration but annoyed, too, for — of course — she now remembered from whose odious lips she had recently heard these sentiments.

"I share your opinion precisely," Mrs Troy said. "But then I was married to a member of parliament for several years — my second husband. In fact, he still is our local MP. But I had to observe the Westminster Follies at close hand for some time before I reached that same conclusion. Is it your own? How did you come by it?"

Leah pursed her lips.

"I'm sorry," Mrs Troy began.

"I'm annoyed with myself," Leah told her. "For speaking without thinking. I suppose it *is* my opinion, but I heard it from a person I despise so heartily that I still feel it to be tainted."

"Ah, yes! I often had the same difficulty with the opinions of my second husband, whom I, too, despised most heartily. Alas, he was often right, though." She smiled engagingly. "Isn't it *maddening* when that happens? Who, may I ask … oh, dear, I seem to be presuming rather a lot upon an acquaintance that has hardly yet …"

"Nicholas Liddicoat," Leah said — and from her tone of voice there was no doubting the depth of her dislike. Nor its length and its breadth, either.

"Mmm," was all the other replied to that. Then she said, "Here, let me take your valise a while."

After a polite struggle they agreed to take a handle each — a symbolic linking that somehow made possible a greater intimacy than so brief an acquaintance might otherwise sanction.

"Is that *your* opinion of Nicholas Liddicoat?" Leah asked. "Just 'mmm'?"

"Oh dear!" Mrs Troy sighed. "I asked for it, I suppose. I know exactly what infuriates you about that arrogant, opinionated, pig-headed, contemptible young man. Many's the time I have only just managed to stop myself from sending for an axe to sink between those supercilious eyes. And yet … and yet …"

"Yes?" Leah prompted eagerly.

"Well, loath though I am to admit it, he is one of the few men I know who will argue with a woman and take her seriously. True, his arguments themselves are odious in the extreme, but he expects you to refute them if you can, and to do so as robustly as he advances them. And he does *listen!*" Her laughter was more baffled than amused. "Perhaps that's the most annoying thing about him. Other men − who may be much 'nicer' in the conventional sense − politer, more considerate, et cetera − argue with one hand ostentatiously tied behind their backs, if you see what I mean. They sort of verbally pat us on the heads, as if to say that any *real* display of their mighty intellects would pass right over us. So they say yes and we 'may be right' and 'there's something in that' and you know they're really thinking 'poor, dear, muddled, creatures but God bless 'em all the same!' − d'you know what I mean, my dear?"

"Only too well!" Leah replied.

"But not Mister Liddicoat the younger − alas." After a brief silence she murmured, "I wonder?" and fell silent again.

"What?" Leah asked.

"Tell me, what is it about him that infuriates you? Precisely."

"Precisely?" Leah echoed, as if that were a tall order. "All the things you said, I suppose. Arrogance …"

"Yes," Mrs Troy interrupted. "But what is the precise nature of that arrogance?"

Again Leah hesitated. Her companion, who had a shrewd idea what the difficulty might be, said − as if changing the subject − "Suppose he were to lose his heart!" From the way Leah's eyes suddenly fixed upon her she knew she had struck a chord. "I don't just mean lose his heart. I mean lose it *utterly*. Become besotted … possessed … head-over-heels! Not able to eat or sleep! Be turned into a 'wretched wight, alone and palely loitering'! Wouldn't that fetch him down off his high horse! And wouldn't it be a sight worth seeing?"

"Yes!" Leah gasped, not realizing until then that she had been holding her breath with excitement at the thoughts and images Mrs Troy had been conjuring up. "You've put your finger on it. Ever since I met him — which was only last Tuesday, actually — the same day as the Rokeby Venus attack, funnily enough! — ever since then I've been thinking he was filled with contempt for me. I mean for women in general. But actually, it's not quite that, is it. He's contemptuous of the notion that he might one day be bewitched by one of us. He's so *sure* he's immune." She gave a deep sigh of satisfaction. "Oh, yes! It *would* be a sight worth seeing."

Their eyes met. A silent proposition flashed between them.

"Well," Mrs Troy said, *"I'm* a little long in the tooth for that sort of thing. Besides, I'm rather satisfied with my present husband, even though I've had him for nearly twenty years now. I'm thinking of keeping him, anyway."

Challenged, Leah, who enjoyed the fantasy far more than the prospect of its realization, said, "I don't know ..."

"Afraid it might backfire? That you might suffer the fate intended for our victim?"

"Never!" Her eyes flashed.

"Well then!" Mrs Troy said.

14 No more was said about Nicholas Liddicoat for the time being. The notion floated by Elizabeth Troy and half taken up by Leah sank into a kind of limbo, neither pleasant fantasy nor fully hatched plot. Their conversation turned to other things. After a time Leah began speaking of her father's impossible desire to know the history every stone would speak if only it had the power of utterance. The notion seemed to fascinate Elizabeth Troy. They happened to be approaching the derelict gate lodge of Pallas House at the time.

"I think I know what he means," she said. "I remember feeling it myself when I first came to Cornwall. Walking along this very lane, in fact!"

"Aren't you Cornish, then?" Leah asked in surprise.

She shook her head and smiled. "I'll be a furriner till the day I die, my dear. I only *married* a Cornishman — the man who owned this estate." She waved vaguely at the trees to their right. "You'll already be considered more Cornish than me. My present husband, who's as Yankee as they come, is much more accepted then me — because his grandfather was Cornish. Don't ask me to explain the Celtic mind to you — just take it that it's so. Besides, I've ruffled too many feathers..." Her voice trailed off as if she would like to say more.

Leah gave a little tug at her handle of the valise, hinting that she wanted to change hands.

But Mrs Troy had stopped and was staring at the roofless gate lodge. "If stones could speak, eh? Zakky Gilbert — the man who built those stones into a wall — was sacked from the Clowance estate for being *too* good. True! He was on piecework and they said he was earning too much money. So I snapped him up and put him to work here. I didn't care how much he earned as long as he truly earned it — which he did. You never saw such a worker. Now he's one of the biggest highway contractors in Cornwall. Now *there's* a story to gladden a Yankee heart!" Her tone was merry but a sadness crept into her eyes as she went on. "And when that lodge was finished, my mother moved into it, God rest her, and she went about the county stealing silver and knicknacks from friends' houses — which I had to return in great embarrassment. Oh, yes — these stones could regale him for many an hour!" She laughed as she added, "And bore him to tears, I'm sure."

"No!" Leah said fervently. It was the first moment she truly understood her father's fascination for such gossip. Coad's stories and Kernow's had seemed as unreal as any 'true' story told at second hand. But Mrs Troy was not just telling a tale for the sake of it, she was reliving it, too — and making it seem like hers, even when it wasn't.

"D'you want to know the *most* astonishing thing that happened along here — that *I* know of, anyway? You've seen these brewers' drays going around with 'Rosewarne Ales' on their sides? Of course you have. Well, that huge firm was founded more than sixty years ago by a certain Johanna Rosewarne, who started brewing in an outhouse up in Ashton — the far side of Breage from here. She did it to make a living when no one else would give her work. And the reason they wouldn't give her work was that she'd had a baby out of wedlock. And that baby

— a little girl she called Hannah — was born in this very lane, just a couple of hundred yards from here — in a howling gale with the rain falling in stair rods. I'll show you when we pass it."

"Is she still alive? Hardly." Leah set down the valise at last and stared into the tree-girt gloom that had once been a gravelled front drive.

Mrs Troy laughed. "Yes, you *are* Cornish — asking questions and answering them like that. Hannah is still alive — getting on for seventy now. She married into the Fox clan, who own the Falmouth shipyards. If you're ever over there and you see a Rolls-Royce landaulet with a little old lady in the back, you can smile to yourself and say, 'I know the ditch where you were born -- you grand old thing!'" She laughed at her own fantasy. "But how will it profit your father to know these things?"

"I don't know. I don't really understand it — not in his case. I mean, I understand the desire to know all this gossip but not why *he* feels it."

Mrs Troy followed her gaze into the gloom beyond the gateless gateway. "Would you like to see the house into which I was married? Pallas House. It's a ruin now, like this lodge. But *there* are some stones that could talk, for those with ears to listen. Leave the bag there. No harm'll come to it."

Leah bit her lip uncertainly. "We mustn't forget my ballgown ..." she said hesitantly.

"I've got lashings," Mrs Troy said. "Don't worry." She looked at her quizzically. "You're a bit of a puritan in matters of duty and pleasure, aren't you. Now that's *not* Cornish!"

"Really?" Leah closed the small gap between them and they set off along what had once been the drive, leading a serpentine trail through ten acres of fox covert to Pallas House. "I thought nonconformism held great sway down here. That's the puritan tradition, surely?"

"It's like the safety valve on a Cornish steam engine. Beneath that tight, iron-banded exterior you've no idea what passions are stirring the Celtic spirit. They're like the Irish — the other branch of the Celts. On the outside it's all humble submission to religious authority. But inside they're seething with fervour and wild emotions of every kind. Especially where land is concerned. You tell your father to keep a sharp eye out for the Liddicoats — especially the old man, Clifford. His family have had their hearts set on that place for ... well, at least a hundred years. Ever since they farmed at Grankum."

After a pause Leah said, "It's no use warning my father about threats like that. They only make him more stubborn. I mean, we do *like* the Old Glebe, but we saw lots of other places where we'd have been equally happy ..."

"Yes, I'm afraid there *are* rather a lot of them on the market just at present!"

"But I think he took the Old Glebe *because* of the threat, not in spite of it."

"He's a Celt, then," Mrs Troy said firmly. A moment later she clutched at Leah's arm and froze in what looked like horror.

Leah followed her gaze, which was fixed on the path ahead of them, but she saw nothing, apart from some fairly recent horse droppings. "What?" she asked.

Mrs Troy shook herself and relaxed, but not enough to let go completely. "Extraordinary," she murmured. "D'you ever get that feeling called *déjà vu* — where you're convinced that everything you're experiencing has happened before?"

"Yes?"

"Well, the really odd thing about it this time is that I *know* this has happened before — finding horse apples here in the drive — exactly here. And I know exactly when it happened, too — a day I'll never forget — the day of my first arriving at this house. That was in the September of eighteen eighty-nine. I'm hopeless at sums. What's that?"

"Getting on for twenty-five years ago," Leah said at once — and thus realized that Mrs Troy must have gone through her first two husbands in five years or less.

"Don't think me silly, dear." She let go of Leah's arm at last. "But would you mind going up to that ridge and seeing if the house truly is derelict — you'll see it in the hollow below you. I just get these premonitions sometimes."

The ridge was a mere twenty paces away and Leah was there almost before the woman had finished speaking.

The house was derelict, all right. It must have been beautiful in its day — plain, simple Georgian, a style just coming back into vogue. Like high waistlines, indeed. That connection had never occurred to her, oddly enough.

"Well?" Mrs Troy prompted.

"I'll bet it was beautiful," she said, returning to the drive. "Why did you never rebuild it? I presume it was fire?"

"Too many cross-currents. Too many ghosts."

Leah knew the woman was staring at her, to see if the word had any effect. She steeled herself and suppressed the obvious response. "Funnily enough," she said, "going back to the Liddicoats, my father asked Nicholas Liddicoat directly if *his* father intended any mischief to us if we bought the Old Glebe."

"And?"

"Well, it was quite strange. He got very uncomfortable. He wouldn't say yes and he wouldn't say no. When we pressed him, all he said was, 'He's a farmer'!"

"Meaning?"

"That's what my father asked. And Liddicoat said it meant he was used to sowing his seed in the fall and seeing nothing happen until the spring."

"Playing a waiting game, as they say."

"Yes," Leah agreed. "But waiting for what? For an earthquake to move the Old Glebe bodily onto Grankum?"

Mrs Troy made no reply but sank into thought for the next hundred yards or so, until another bend in the drive, or ex-drive, brought them below the ridge and in sight of the elegant ruins once again. Then she said, "Are you going to inherit the farm or your brother? I'm sorry. That sounds brutal, put like that. Of course, we hope it'll be a long time yet — but that's what we're talking about, isn't it: waiting a long time!"

Leah half glimpsed the conclusion of this train of thought. "You mean ..." she said, hoping to prompt Mrs Troy to spell it out. "Oh, but it won't be a farm by then. My father has plans for a garden to rival Trengwainton."

But Mrs Troy waved away the objection. "Trengwainton could be turned back into farmland inside a year, trees and all. How does your father intend to leave it? Tell me it's none of my business if you wish."

"No, no. He's going to leave it to me, I think. And the money and stocks and things to William. But he might marry again — which would change everything. I've tried suggesting it to him — remarriage, I mean. After all, it's more than four years since our mother died. Or even just hiring a housekeeper because ... you know ... I've got my own life to lead — which he doesn't

seem to appreciate yet. But anyway, that's the present arrangement. House and land to me, the rest to William. Why?"

"And might he have told anyone of it?"

Leah had to concede the possibility. "It's not a secret. He's
almost certainly told lawyer Kernow because of having to make
a new will. An American will cannot dispose of English property.
Not in an English court, anyway. He probably told Coad, too."

"So it's not hard to see how such a story could have reached
Clifford Liddicoat's ears. And he has two bachelor sons — two
arrows to the bow. And you're an only daughter and an heiress
— just one target to aim at. Now *that* fits in pretty well with the
idea of a waiting game, wouldn't you say?"

15 In open countryside Leah's mild unease about cows
would lead her to take long detours through empty
fields rather than risk a shorter walk across one with a herd in it.
At close quarters, however, that same unease grew into something like terror. The creatures seemed so much bigger when
they stood only a yard or two away. Out in the open you might
even admit there was something appealing in their eyes, so
large and dark and uncomplaining; but here in the gloom of the
cowshouse they seemed black, watchful, and menacing. How
Mrs Troy could serve such an elegant tea and converse in such
civilized tones and then immediately transform herself into a
blustering milkmaid, hollering at the cows, getting them into
their stalls with knee-thrusts and elbow-jabs that would fell a
heavyweight wrestler was beyond comprehension. Half excited
and half repelled, and still wholly terrified, Leah shrank against
the milking parlour wall and watched.

The parlour had only four stalls, divided into two pairs by a
low brick wall, to which the two middle cows were tethered. A
narrow passage ran the full length of the back of the parlour,
along which a milkmaid — a real everyday one called Martha —
carried hay and chopped roots to each cow as it came in. She
then took up her pail and joined Mrs Troy at the business end of
a cow — not the same one, of course — and soon the jets of
steamy-hot milk were pouring in a continuous stream. The
sound of it was high and tinkly when the pail was empty but, pull

by pull, it turned to a rich foamy thud as it slowly filled up toward the brim.

So that was the system; Leah watched with interest despite herself. There were always two cows feeding while they waited to be milked and two others finishing off their feed while Mrs Troy and Martha milked them. Leah worked out that, since there were still sixteen milkers out in the yard, the parlour would see five complete changes of the four before this ordeal was over. Her heart fell when she realized that, at the present rate of progress, it would take almost an hour and a half. Ninety minutes, trapped in this dangerous purgatory among huge, unsteady beasts with shiny black tips to their horns — beasts that slithered and stumbled over cobbles and concrete in their eagerness to get at their food. It was ghastly. Not even the thought of the beautiful ballgown in blue watered silk and the jewelled wrap in sea-green satin could compensate for *this!* Not even when she remembered that Mrs Troy had told her it was hers to keep.

It did not take Leah long to realize that the safest place in the parlour was in the feeding passage at the back, where only a cow with the blood of a mountain goat would dream of trying to go. The decision to suggest it to Mrs Troy — that she should be allowed to take over Martha's feeding chores — came right after one of the cows had lifted her tail and, coincidentally, coughed. The product of these activities only just missed Leah, though she was standing almost ten feet away; a large greeny-brown blob slithering down the limewashed wall at her side showed her what she had so narrowly avoided.

The laughter of the other two suggested it would have been even louder had the cow's aim been more accurate — which at last emboldened Leah to make her suggestion.

"They don't all get the same ration of roots," Mrs Troy warned her. "The heaviest yielders get more. I'll tell you how many scoops for each one as she comes in. But you càn shake out the hay ad lib."

Leah's sense of relief was enormous. Safe behind the barriers of the mangers she could afford to relax and observe. She had to get at least one scoop of roots into the manger before the next cow came in, because the first thing it did was put its head down into the trough — and that gave Martha or Mrs Troy the chance to close the wooden vee-shaped structure that secured the cow by the head while it was being milked. The vee, when closed, was wide enough to leave the neck free but too narrow to allow the head to get out, especially with the span of those wicked-looking horns.

She noticed how they treated each cow as an individual, and not just in the matter of food. One liked to have her ears tickled and stroked as soon as she was in her stall. "It do help she to let down 'er milk, see?" Martha said. Another, for the same reason, preferred to have the point of the drover's stick rubbed up and down beside her spine with enough pressure to have made any human beg for mercy. Others would have none of these inducements but would let down their milk *too* early — at the first touch of the warm water in which their udders were cleaned immediately before milking.

Then even Mrs Troy would shriek, "Not yet! Not yet, you heller!" and smile at the shock on Leah's face. "It's the only language they understand, I'm afraid," she added.

Every now and then Martha would slip into song — the same song, so that by the end of the milking, Leah knew it off pat:

As I went walking to London town
I met a young man who was singing a song.
And although 'e was singing, 'e wished 'isself dead.
You could tell by 'is faace that 'e wanted for bread.
Cold blew the blast, down come the snaw.
No plaace to shelter, no plaace to go.
No mother to guide 'im, no friend to turn to.
Cast out upon the wide world was Poor Old Joe!

"Don't you know any others?" she asked the woman after the tenth recital of this dirge.

"Only sad ones, my lover," the woman replied.

"It's Saturday," Mrs Troy explained. "There's a different song for each day. The cows like strict routines, so if you want to hear the others, you'll have to come back."

"Thanks," Leah said, insincerely heartfelt.

As cow followed cow into the stalls, she gradually conquered her fear, or the worst of it — sufficiently, at least, for her to bend down and give the beast a few hesitant pats, or a rub between the ears, or even, on the one at the end, beside the gangway leading to the feeding passage, a stroke up and down the spine with a stick.

"That's the idea," Mrs Troy said encouragingly. Then she undid all Leah's progress by adding, "Actually, this one's a bit of a kicker." She broke off and yelled "No!" at the cow in a tone that would have made even a guardsman take notice. Then, gentle again, "Would you mind just lifting her tail onto her back? Like this."

She put the milking pail beyond reach of the creature's kick and, standing up, grasped the tail about fifteen inches down. Then she brought her hand round and up, resting it on the spine, which bent the tail a full half circle. "No tighter than that," she said, "or it will hurt her."

Swallowing her distaste as best she could, Leah grasped the thick, hairy, gristly *thing,* which did not feel truly alive, and said, "What does that do?"

"It keeps her legs where I want them. If she lifts one to kick, her tail *will* hurt. You know the motto with cows?"

"No?"

"Cows may be dumb, but they're not stupid. Isn't that right, Blackeye?" She butted the cow's flank with her head. The cow went on munching her roots with that peculiar, rotatory motion of the jaws.

The milk thundered, thick and creamy, into the pail and Martha's voice rose among the rafters yet again: "As I went walking to London town ..."

And for the first time that afternoon Leah, in absolute control of Blackeye's movements, felt that here was something she might even get to enjoy.

But her flimsy confidence was shaken yet again when Mrs Troy said, as she came to wash the last cow of the day, "D'you want to go home and *really* surprise them all? Tell them you've milked a cow and there's nothing to it?"

When the challenge was posed in such terms, how could Leah possibly refuse!

All the same she approached the hind quarters of the animal with great reluctance.

"Old Celandine's the mother of the herd," Mrs Troy said encouragingly. "And grandmother. She wouldn't kick out if you had nails like a Chinese mandarin. Give her a little scratch in the small of her back."

Celandine stirred as Leah obeyed. The parlour door creaked — or so she imagined; but when she looked she saw it was still closed. "What was that?" she asked.

"Rheumatics," Mrs Troy told her.

"In cows?" Leah stared in amazement at the bony knobs beneath her fingers.

"It happens to us all, my dear. That's enough mollycoddling — or Celandine-coddling. Sit down on the stool, make a valley of your skirt between your knees, and stick this pail there."

Keeping a wary eye on the nearer hind leg, Leah did as she was bid and then reached a tentative hand toward the nearest teat. She wished now that she'd volunteered to milk one of the heifers, who had small, neat udders and smooth pink teats. Celandine, a veteran of seventeen calves and an equal number of lactations, had warty old things made even less inviting by huge melanic freckles the size of a half-crown. "You're sure she won't kick?"

"Well, as the horse dealer said when the farmer came back and complained that the mare died as soon as he got her home, 'She never done that before'!" And with that reassurance she squatted beside Leah and reached her left hand past her to grab the hind teat. "Like this," she said, nipping it high up between her thumb and the ball of her index finger. "The teat is full of little channels down which the milk flows. They're full of milk now, so trap it at the top to stop it all flowing back up into the udder when you squeeze. And then squeeze from the top down. No — don't pull. That makes them uncomfortable. Squeeze progressively from the top down. D'you know the names of fingers? Start with Minnie Milton, then Long Lauder, Davy Gravy, and end with Little Dido Bone. There!" she exclaimed with delight as, both from her teat and from Leah's, two thick jets of milk went pinging against the silver bottom of the pail.

Leah laughed with incredulous delight and made to stand up again, glad beyond measure that it was all over.

"What are you doing?" Mrs Troy asked.

"Well, I've done it. I got milk from a cow!"

"And now you'll finish the job," the other commanded with jocular severity. "It's not everybody who can do what you've just done — and at the very first squeeze, too — so you just sit down and make a proper job of it." Her vowels broadened as she added, "Praaper jaab, as we do say."

Leah steeled herself to resume her position on the stool and reach again for one of those repulsive teats. But the reward of a rich stream of milk was more than recompense for that unpleasantness and soon the warts felt like old friends as she squeezed away.

"Now try with both hands," Mrs Troy advised. "Alternately, the way you saw us doing it."

Leah amazed herself. Celandine's teats were so old and slack — and thus so copious — that it took a full second to squeeze each one empty, during which time the other refilled itself to capacity, too. So, by slightly overlapping her squeezes, she was able to make the milk fill the pail in what sounded like a single, unbroken jet, tinkling at first but soon thundering into a creamy froth that swiftly filled it.

When the froth rose to the level of the brim, the actual milk about three-quarters filled the pail. Then, though the cow still had some milk left to yield, Leah rose without bidding and, as she had seen the others do, carried the heavy pail across to the diary. This little ante-room was built 'foreanenst' the cowshouse (as she had heard Coad describe a lean-to) and was reached by a door at the start of the gangway to the feeding passage. There she tipped it slowly into a big, wide tundish, or funnel, as she would have called it. It had a muslin filter over the hole at the bottom — 'to keep back the horns and tails,' as the joke went.

"Well done!" Mrs Troy said as she returned. "Shall I just finish her off?"

"Not by a jugful — nothing doing!" Leah squeezed her hostess aside and sat down with as much eagerness as she had earlier shown reluctance for the selfsame task. After a while she broke spontaneously into song — "The lambs on the green hills they sport and they play-ay ..." Its elegaic rhythm fitted well with the pace of her work.

As the flow of milk began to dwindle she started giving the udder a light upward prod, first with one hand, then with the other, every fourth or fifth squeeze.

"Who taught you that?" Mrs Troy asked admiringly.

"An old Irish maid we had back in East Haven."

"No! I mean who taught you to pummel the udder like that when the flow starts to die?"

"Oh, you did. I watched you. And Martha."

"You're a quick study, Miss Carrington. You know why we do that? Because it's the way a calf will persuade its mother to let down her milk when it wants to suckle. You may think there's nothing more unnatural than modern farming — yet we always try to work *with* nature wherever we can."

What with these and other excitements Leah missed the evening train home, so Mrs Troy drove her back to Helston in her car — an experience, Leah later said, she would not repeat even if the alternative were to pass the entire night in a field full of cows and every one a bull. The car was sound enough — a six-cylinder Thorneycroft of 45 h.p. only three years old — but its driver seemed to think it should spend as much time as possible with all four wheels in the air. Also that it would be a kindness to the parish hedgecutters to do half their work for them. They came to a screeching, skidding halt outside the Angel and, if it had not been for the granite cover to the kerbside river at that point, to allow coaches to get to the stable yard, she would surely have ended with one wheel down in the water.

It had obviously happened on previous occasions because, as they descended, Mrs Troy looked at the nearside front wheel, saw it was mere inches from disaster, and said blithely, "Not this time — jolly good!"

"You drive with great ... er, sort of ..." Leah wished she had not started the sentence.

"With great panache?" Mrs Troy rescued her. "I know. You're not the first to say so. I took to it like you took to milking — immediately. As if born to it, you know. And I've only ever had one accident — or one that I regard as entirely my fault — and that was in my first ten minutes, right after I bought my very first car, in nineteen-oh-three."

"What happened?" Leah was beginning to gather her wits.

Mrs Troy bit her lip and grinned. "I ran over a policemen's foot. Even then, you know, it was partly his fault for springing out into the road like that. Fancy thinking he could stop a car at *that* speed! That was a Thorneycroft, too. We've always stuck with them. Wonderful cars! Pity they've stopped making them." She jerked her head toward the vehicle she had so nearly wrecked a dozen times over the previous fifteen minutes. "She was one of the last of the line. Nineteen-eleven. There won't be another so we must try to make her last."

At supper that night Carrington asked his daughter what sort of day she'd had. "Oh, you know ..." she replied vaguely. "We strolled around and chatted about this and that, and ... picked a super-dooper gown for me to wear."

Somehow she didn't think it would please her father to know she had the makings of a pretty good milkmaid, too. Instead, she regaled him with all the if-stones-could-talk stories Mrs Troy had told her — which left him pretty satisfied that the day had not been wasted.

Later, alone in her bedroom, she drew the curtains tight, spread her dressing gown over the cracks in the old oak door, hung her nightcap over the keyhole of the connecting door to her father's room, and than sat down before her looking glass to examine her breasts in the light of today's discoveries. The nipple was like the teat, that was clear enough, but if there were tubes and channels and things like that behind it — like the milk-collecting tubes in the cow — she could not find them.

Then, growing bored at finding so little correspondence, she fell into a more abstract reverie, wondering what it would be like, one day, to have a baby of her own suckling there. Would it pummel at her breast when the flow began to give out? Would its tongue squeeze from the top down, the way she had to squeeze the cow's teat with her fingers?

These questions, too, being unanswerable — at least by her — soon palled. Then she thought of all the steps that must inevitably come between that moment and this — the balls, the picnics, the dinners, the theatre outings, the shy advances, the letters, the first kisses, the first tame intimacies, the Question, the Engagement ... oh, the long *longueur* of the Engagement ... She could not even complete the list in her mind, much less contemplate its application to her life over the years to come.

"There should be an annual lottery and we should make do with whatever we get," she told her image in the mirror.

The image shook her head in fervent agreement.

"Except that one might then end up with ..." She had intended saying 'Nicholas Liddicoat' but the name that popped out — to the obvious surprise of her image — was "Frank Kernow."

16 The weather the Carringtons had expected to find in Cornwall in January finally turned up in March. It lasted most of that week before the welcoming ball. It came not with snow but with subzero temperatures and a dry, biting wind that blew steadily out of the east, day and night. It dried the land as fast as any summer zephyr and what it didn't dry it froze. Even the stems of the grasses seemed frozen for they did not ripple and bend as eddies of wind plucked at them but rather vibrated, like stiff rods on strong springs. Farm labourers wore three potato sacks where normally one would do, and the animals in the fields huddled forlornly in the lee of the nearest hedge. Down in Porthleven the fishermen spat at the ripples and declared the seas too rough for fishing that day. Nobody went abroad who did not have to.

Except the Carringtons, for whom such prolonged spells of cold were annually expected. Only weeks earlier they had laughed at their ignorance in bringing their fine beaver coats and coonskin caps. And as for those skates ...! But now they were the envy of all who saw them, even of Jimmy Troy. Only last year, after a long succession of more typical Cornish winters, he had been persuaded to give away all his fur gear to visiting American cousins. By midweek the Carringtons were not just the envy of Helston, they were the talk of it, too — because of the ice. Before the cold had set in, the River Cober, which runs through the bottom of the town, had followed its usual winter habit and flooded the Lower Green to a depth of several inches, which was shallow enough to freeze right through after several days of subzero wind chill. Then their most laughable imports of all — the ice skates — gave Leah and her father a chance to display skills that most local people had seen only in exhibitions of motion pictures at the cinema. William would have joined in, too, except that he was still going daily to the School of Mines. It would take more than a cold wind to halt the railways.

John Carrington was a skilled skater, if rather dull. Back in his former home he liked to do five steady miles upriver and then five miles back again. Here, with only an acre of frozen pond on which to disport, he just clasped his hands behind his back and did umpteen stolid circuits; people could have checked their clocks by timing his transits. For Leah, by contrast, to be skating again was a bitter-sweet pleasure. She had almost always skated with a beau, and usually with one particular beau, at that. So the air at her side was not just an empty space but an aching void. Her hands would instinctively reach across to clasp his, left to left, right to right, and her body would long for those accidental but exciting touches between parts that otherwise never touched at all.

All in all, though, it was an exhilarating time and when, on the Friday morning — the morning of the ball — a drop in the wind and a rise in the temperature brought hints of a thaw, she realized how much she had missed not just Tom but the company of young men in general. It was a joyous discovery to make, with relief so near at hand! She could hardly contain her impatience for seven o'clock to strike. And when it did, she was standing there with her father and brother, bright-eyed and eager at Elizabeth Troy's side, ready to welcome each new arrival to the old Coinage Hall.

To be honest, when she had first seen the inside of the place, earlier that day, she had been hard put to hide her disappointment. The chamber was so small. She couldn't imagine how more than twenty couples could dance there — two dozen at most, depending on the size of the band. But disappointment turned to bewilderment when Mrs Troy said that she had invited close on a hundred guests. When Leah asked how so many would be able to take the floor, *and* the musicians, *and* a buffet table, she explained that both the dancing and the buffet supper would take place in the much larger Market Hall, just across the way. She had rented the smaller Coinage Hall so as to try out a social innovation that, having crossed the Atlantic from America, was just beginning to take hold in London — a 'cocktail party,' as it was called.

"Oh, I've heard of those," Leah said. "You stand about informally like at a garden party — except that it's indoors — and all you do is talk, while the waiters bring around trays with little glasses of drink and delicacies and things ..."

"And the drinks are all blends of spirits and fruit juices with outlandish names like Harvard Sling and Bushwhacker ..."

"Yale Sling, if you please!" Leah chided.

"Of course, dear." Mrs Troy feigned contrition. "Too insensitive of me! I wonder how Helston will take to this transatlantic innovation? But I couldn't imagine a better occasion on which to introduce it."

She and Leah permitted themselves one secret Yale Sling each (just to be sure it wasn't too, too awful) before the first of the guests arrived. And then, it seemed, they all came at once: Mrs Chinnor, Mr and Mrs Tresidder, Mr Barney Kernow and Miss Pym, Mrs Gilbert, Mr and Mrs Giles Curnow ... soon the names began to merge and then Leah realized she had no hope of remembering them all. Her father, however, had a system and was more sanguine; it let him down only once, when he later addressed Mrs Hastings as Mrs Battle. However, he did not practise it upon everybody there, so the true failure rate might have been a great deal higher.

One name they did not need to memorize: Liddicoat.

Mrs Troy had debated back and forth with the Carringtons about inviting them. They were 'not on her usual list.' Back in 1891, when she had just inherited the Pallas estate and was striving with her late husband's sister, Morwenna Troy, for control of it, Clifford Liddicoat, though not a tenant of the estate, had gone about stirring up people against her. On the other hand, to exclude them when so many others were invited might, in the eyes of some local people, give them carte blanche for the mean little tricks they no doubt planned to carry out against the Carringtons after they settled in at the Old Glebe. To invite them, by contrast, would deprive them of any such justification and, simultaneously, bind them more tightly to the codes of civilized behaviour.

And so here they were, creaking in unaccustomed dance pumps, shining like weather-bronzed pippins: Clifford Liddicoat and his sons Harvey and Nicholas. Also, trying to hide herself behind them, their sister Adelaide, whom none of the Carringtons had so much as glimpsed before, not even through their high-powered binoculars.

"Oh, do call me Adèle, please!" she murmured in agonies of embarrassment as Leah shook her moist, trembling hand. "Adelaide is so fustian, don't you think?"

Her heart went out to the poor girl at once. She was rather short, rather plain, and dressed rather for Sunday chapel than for a Friday-night ball — and she was, obviously, squirmingly aware of these deficiencies.

"I've been *so* looking forward to meeting you," said Leah (who had not until that moment even heard of her existence). "You must keep some time free for me so we can have a nice long chinwag. Don't give every dance away." She tapped her programme and pointed out the table where Adèle could pick up a blank one.

The girl was embarrasingly grateful for the suggestion that she might get more than half a dozen names on her programme. But Harvey's manner was quite different. He was trying to mask his unease behind a cloak of insecure jocularity. "Talking of giving dances away, Miss Carrington," he said, "I hope you have one left for me, you know?" He glanced not at her but at his father, for approval.

"Why, you are the very first to ask it, Mister Liddicoat!" She smiled her most engaging smile at him. "Take your pick." She turned to include his father in her delight.

If Mrs Troy had been right, then the price of keeping old-man Liddicoat from playing any silly tricks on them was now clear: It was to take his obviously gauche young daughter under her more cosmopolitan wing and to fan his elder son's hopes of an alliance. Well, fate had dealt worse hands to better-deserving girls than she. And Harvey was quite handsome. And she could spin out the game for as long as she liked. Also a pointless flirtation with Harvey would be a way to keep Nicholas at more than arm's length. There were advantages all round.

"Oh!" Harvey was now mortified to discover how forward he had been. "Put me down for the first polka, perhaps?" he said, choosing one he hoped would be safely in the middle of the evening — not too conspicuous either way. This lack of spirit did not please his father.

"What a tease you are!" she replied, mainly to wipe the scowl off the old man's face. "The first dance is a two-step and I shall put you down for that — as a reward for honouring me first. I hope you *do* think it a reward?"

"Oh … yes," he replied lamely. "Thank you."

Nicholas, who had been standing impatiently at the end of the Liddicoat queue all this while, smiled apologetically at the next couple in line, as if to say that their delay had not been of his making, nor had it been to his liking, either. Then he shook her hand, once, and briefly, and muttered something indecipherable before moving swiftly away.

As Leah was being introduced to that next couple — a Mr and Mrs Trelawney — she saw in the corner of her eye a suppressed altercation between Nicholas Liddicoat and his father. Then the young man came stamping back to her and, hardly waiting for the Trelawneys to move on, said, "I don't suppose you've got a dance for me, too, then?"

"You don't have to, you know," she told him.

"Oh yes I do." He gazed balefully after his father. "Still" — he turned to her with a smile of relief — "if your programme's full, then ..." He made to withdraw.

"Not at all," she replied before she bit her tongue off. "I mean, I suppose ... if you *insist*, I could *just* squeeze you in."

"It's not me who's insisting. Still, put me down for something near the end. I'll enjoy as much of the evening as I can."

An imp made her say, "I'll put you down for the last waltz, Mister Liddicoat. Since your brother (whom I find much more agreeable, by the way) has the first dance, there's a pleasing symmetry to it, don't you think? And I, too, shall be able to enjoy the evening until we get to its very dregs." Ostentatiously she wrote 'Nark' in the space beside the last waltz.

"Well, Thistle," he said, "on behalf of my father I thank you. Dregs at the bottom. Scum at the top. And nobody knows what's in between, eh?"

"In between?" she echoed. "It will be an otherwise agreeable evening, I trust."

He would have come back with more if others were not waiting to be presented to her. When they, too, had gone in search of cocktails and little things in aspic, Mrs Troy turned to her and said, "I had no idea you and Nicholas Liddicoat got on so well!"

"I can't *bear* him," she said vehemently. "He's quite ruined my evening now."

"Oh ... quite!" The woman beat an amused retreat. "Yes, I quite see that."

Only then did Leah remember that the Mrs Trelawney to whom she had just been introduced was, in fact, the 'Daughter' of the firm whose billboard intrigued her every time she passed it: Kernow & Daughter. So now, having let them go with no more than a polite platitude, she had even more reason to be annoyed with Nark Liddicoat

When the stragglers were arriving at roughly minute intervals, Mrs Troy said they could fend for themselves and so she began circulating her new friends among her old ones. To Leah's delight almost the first people she spoke to were the Trelawneys — Cornwallis and Jessica. He almost immediately plunged into conversation with her father about his plan to create a grand garden at the Old Glebe. Mrs Troy, who had had little chance to talk to William as yet, asked him how he was getting on at the School of Mines — which was a daily topic for Leah and her father and thus of little interest to her. She and Mrs Trelawney exchanged slightly awkward smiles.

"I don't envy you the work that lies ahead at your new home, Miss Carrington," the woman said. "It's a beautiful old house — I do envy you that — but I'd balk at the labour of restoring it to its old glory."

"Oh, Mrs Trelawney!" Leah said fervently. "If you have *any* ideas along those lines, I would so welcome them."

"*My* ideas on home decoration?" She glanced at her husband with some amusement in case he had overheard — which, it seemed, he hadn't. "Well that's something that no one has *ever* thought of consulting *me* upon."

Mrs Troy, who had every good hostess's ability to conduct one intense conversation while eavesdropping on two or three others nearby, laid an apologetic hand briefly on William's arm and put in, "You should know, Miss Carrington, that Jessica Trelawney, it is universally agreed, would prefer to live in a dry, south-facing cave whose one concession to comfort would be glass over the opening."

"And electricity," Mrs Trelawney said equably. "As long as it had electricity, too, I see nothing wrong with that."

"Well," Leah said, "so you think simplicity is the keynote to a successful …"

"I don't know about keynotes, Miss Carrington, but I have one simple rule. If nobody uses a particular item for a week, it goes up into the attic. If it gathers dust there for a month, it goes to an outhouse. If after a year out there, no one has touched it, it goes to the next jumble sale."

"That's three rules," her husband said over his shoulder, with hardly a break in his own conversation.

"It's certainly worth the wages of three housemaids," she replied at once.

Leah tried another tack. "I'd also love to hear how you came to found the Helston Power Company. I've heard a little bit about it from your brother Frank, who is my father's lawyer, as you may know."

She saw the woman's lips tighten at this mention but no comment followed. Leah went on: "It sounds such an exciting thing for a woman to have done. I'm sure you have most interesting views on the suffrage question?"

"What suffrage question?" Mrs Trelawney asked at once. "There *is* no suffrage question. It's a chimæra, a false rainbow, a mare's nest."

"You think so, too?" Leah said.

"Too?" the other echoed, almost as if she were annoyed to find that her views were not unique. "Who else, may I ask ...?"

"Mister Liddicoat the younger — or youngest, I suppose. I mean Nicholas."

Mrs Trelawney relaxed and chuckled. "How gratifying!" she said with more than a tinge of sarcasm. "Last month I spent the best part of an hour convincing him that ..."

Leah interrupted: "... that political power without economic power is useless?"

"My words exactly." A smile of understanding spread across her features. "Why? Have you and he been discussing the same question? And did he put forward those views as his own?"

"He did — most forcefully, too. Most sneeringly. I very nearly hit him, I can tell you."

The two older women — for Mrs Troy had continued speaking in one direction and listening in two — laughed at her vehemence.

"Well, he certainly deserves a lesson, Miss Carrington," Mrs Trelawney said. "He cannot be allowed to go about the district, stealing opinions like that and brazenly passing them off as his own. Perhaps you'll come to tea one day next week and we'll discuss the possibilities? I'm At Home to all the world each Wednesday, so shall we say ... Thursday? Now I mustn't monopolize you tonight, there are so many people here just dying to meet you!"

She did not say 'other people,' as politeness might have suggested. Leah had the impression that Mrs Trelawney would only really be happy at the centre of attention. She had smiled with satisfaction and made little preening movements at the mention of the Helston Power Company and she clearly enjoyed her reputation as a woman whose opinions ran contrary to those of the general herd, whether the subject was domestic decoration or suffrage for women. Still, if she had ideas about taking Nicholas Liddicoat down a peg or two, she was well worth cultivating.

With the help of one more cocktail — which would have been two if Mrs Troy had not caught her eye — the rest of the evening turned into a pleasant, if rather kaleidoscopic blur. If she wanted a good portrait taken, she learned, she should go to Gillot's in Penzance. No, said another, Collett and Trevarton were better. As for medical attendance, Doctor Reeves in Helston was very good. Yes, Reeves was pretty good, but she might find Doctor Moore of Godolphin just as skilled — and quite a bit closer to the Old Glebe. He had a daughter of about eighteen, whom Leah might find it agreeable to know. (Some people, Leah realized, did not appreciate the gulf between eighteen and twenty-two, especially when the twenty-two-year-old was mistress of her own household! But she thanked them for their information.) Had she heard about the ghost of the old rector who had murdered his housekeeper in the tithe barn? She had? Oh, dear — and wouldn't she be afraid to go abroad at night? Did she think the business in Haiti would lead America into war? Martha Richardson had gone on hunger strike in Holloway and had released a splendid (or disgraceful) letter explaining her vandalism in the National Gallery. Would the House of Lords reject the Women's Enfranchisement Bill when it came up in May? Mrs Trevaskis, who kept the milliner's shop up Meneage Street, had a brother in Madras who sent her the most gorgeous silks and calicoes and her prices were very reasonable — don't look too obviously, but that was her over there. If they needed horses for the farm, Johnny Tyacke in Carleen was the man to see. The latest kitchen ranges from Toy's Foundry were really very good — lashings of hot water and a very good pasty oven. The French and Germans were up to their old tricks over the Baghdad Railway. You should never put carrots in a pasty. Did anybody hear the rumour that there was going to be a *coiffeuse* in Penzance (a sort of lady-barber, dear – no, for ladies, of course)? Had she heard about the plague pit beneath the floor of the old tithe barn? The spirits of the poor victims were said to walk abroad when the moon was full ... or was it the new moon?

John Carrington caught Jimmy Troy's eye, toasted him laconically, and said, "Well?"

"One of these things goes a long way," Troy said. "There used to be a swell restaurant near the Blue Island Avenue Station, where the self-styled élite of Chicago liked to dine. Before Lincoln got fashionable. People wondered why they never saw me there, but I'd tell them I met too many stray fools by day to want to hang around the watering hole and catch the main herd at night."

17 At nine-thirty they cleared away most of the tables. Six of the tops were relocated on beer crates to form a stage for the band – Charlie Straws and his Ambrosians. It was a sign of the times that, only a year ago, the same seven men had been known as Karl Strauss and his Vienna Players. Karl or Charlie, his real name was Fred Thomas and he had never been farther east than London; the rest of his band had never been farther east than Plymouth. They still played with the same old Viennese gusto, though.

"They remind me," Elizabeth Troy told Leah, "of a story about the Germoe church choir, who heard a famous adjudicator was staying in the neighbourhood and so put on a special performance for him. And the poor man, who had heard some of the best choirs in England, hardly knew what to say – until inspiration came to his rescue. 'Well,' he told them, 'I've heard sweeter, but never louder!' And they repeated it for years as one of the highest compliments anyone had ever paid them!"

Others around them joined in their laughter, for, though they might have heard but a snippet of the conversation, they knew the rest of the tale well. "Yes," one woman said, "I've heard sweeter, but never louder." And a second, more subdued wave of laughter followed.

"I've just noticed something," Leah told Harvey Liddicoat when he claimed her for the first dance. "Cornish jokes are all about real people being shown up in some way. And when a person tells the joke, they tell it, and everyone laughs, and then they — or someone — repeats the actual funny line, and they laugh all over again but not quite so much as the first time. Also, it doesn't matter if it's a joke they all know already."

He thought it over and then said, "I'd never noticed that, but I suppose we do. Call it good housekeeping — roast meat on Sunday, cold cuts on Monday. Nothing wasted." He laughed and seemed about to tell her more but then thought better of it.

"What?" she urged. He was a good dancer. Not a leg-maniac, as they say, full of brilliant, flashy steps, but an easy mover who made the gyrations seem natural.

"Nothing," he replied. "The words 'nothing wasted' brought another joke to mind but it's not repeatable."

"It can't be a *Cornish* joke, then."

He shook his head. "It is but it's also rather ... what shall I say? Rather agricultural."

Other young men she had known, even Tom O'Leary in the early days, would by now be desperate with embarrassment and looking for any excuse to change the subject. But not Harvey, it seemed. The way he told her it was not suitable was as calm as if he'd said it would take rather too long to tell on this occasion. She was annoyed at being excluded, of course, and yet she also admired his calm manner and sense of authority, which, in a subtle way, did *not* exclude her. She could not say how, but it made her feel a party to his decision.

At any rate, it emboldened her to say, "I'm not as easily shocked as you may suppose, Mister Liddicoat. And we are living in the twentieth century, after all."

"Well," he said jovially, "it's a true story about local people. A couple of farmers living in Sithney parish." She thought he was going to relent and tell her after all, but he went on, "So it won't spoil for keeping and it'll be funnier when you know them. Anyway, we're supposed to be talking about the weather, the season, the last hunt, this wonderful music, and other important things like that."

"Oh — *important* things, eh?" she said. "So tell me about your brother, then." She was pleased to see that this change of subject — or this *particular* change of subject — did not amuse him. "Is he an universal misogynist or has he a particular down on me?"

There was a long, thoughtful pause before he replied, "I've known Nicholas for twenty-three years — naturally — and I still don't understand him."

"Well, that's not much of an answer. In any case, I didn't ask for a complete litany of his character — just whether he's down on all women or only little old me?"

Another pause for thought. "I think he sees women as a threat," he said awkwardly. "All women. I really feel disloyal, talking about him like this. Why don't you ask him directly? Did you put him down for a dance?"

"Yes. Didn't he tell you?"

"No. He seemed pretty indignant to me. I thought you'd probably said no."

"Well, I didn't. I couldn't. Not once he'd made it quite clear how much it cost him and his pride even to ask for it. What *did* he say to you, then — I noticed he said *something?* Or is that also quite unrepeatable?"

He chuckled. "It is, I'm afraid. May I ask — what dance did you give him?"

Rather than answer him, she took up his earlier remark: "He sees women as a threat to *what?*"

"To his life."

"Good heavens!" She stared at him in shocked amazement. He was *very* handsome. It was going to be easy to keep his father contented with the progress of an imagined affaire.

"I don't mean to his physical life, but to his plans. To the way he's planned his own life. He's a great admirer of Jimmy Troy — and of your father, too, I may say."

"Something about Americans?"

"No. Something about self-made men. Nicholas wants to be rich, too, one day — self-made rich."

"But my father *inherited* money from his father. So did Mister Troy, I believe."

"Yes, but they didn't just sit back and spend it. Whatever they inherited, they doubled and doubled and doubled again. Nicholas won't inherit a bean, but he still thinks he can make his fortune. And women offer him nothing but distraction, he believes.

There now! I don't think I'm being disloyal because he makes no secret of that much."

"What's he going to make his fortune *at?*" she asked next.

"Who?"

"Nicholas."

"Good heavens!" He made his surprise seem genuine. "Are we *still* talking about him?"

"Okay!" She laughed, and butted his shoulder with her forehead — an unladylike gesture that did not go unnoticed by others in that assembly.

Especially not by Harvey's father, who had hardly taken his eyes off the young couple since they had stepped onto the floor. William, who had not yet engaged himself for any among the first set of dances, was standing at his side, watching Nicholas, who was dancing with his sister, Adèle. They seemed to be getting on so well together, like true friends, the way a brother and sister ought to get on once they'd passed out of their argumentative teens. Of course, Adèle, being the youngest, had never taken over the role of mother to the family when Mrs Liddicoat died, which was eight years ago now. She'd have been only ten then. Ten or eleven.

"Proper 'ansum couple," Liddicoat said, still watching Leah and his son.

"Yes," William agreed.

"How isn't your old man sending you to farming college, then?" he went on.

"*Farming* college?" The abruptness of the question took William by surprise.

"'Es. Mining won't be no good to 'ee over to the Old Glebe. There's no minerals left under they lands. But I suppose you do already know that?"

"I don't suppose there's much left under Grankum, either, sir," William replied. "But it doesn't seem to impede Nicholas in his studies."

"'Es, but then he isn't going to farm Grankum, is he!" the old man said.

"Ah!" William pretended the point left him baffled, though he knew very well what the other was angling to be told. "Talking of Nicholas, sir — I was wondering ... where does he hope to find employment in mining?"

"Why, anywhere. Australey, Americay, Russia ... there's deep mining all over the world."

"He seems to spend a lot of time much closer to home than that — on the old halvans around Wheal Fortune."

"Oh?" Liddicoat's focus was suddenly vague. "I never noticed."

"Almost every spare moment, I'd say."

The man sniffed. "Studying rocks and that, I s'pose."

"Inside as well as outside!" William laughed.

"Well, what's inside a rock — that's what mining's all about."

"Mmh." William nodded but said nothing.

"Surely they taught you that?"

"Well, the way they *taught* us is to tap the rock with a hammer — not try to get an abandoned set of stamps going again and then use them to crush the rock to dust. That's for mineral extraction, not mineral study."

At that point Liddicoat spotted a man who owed him money, so he said, and went to bend his ear.

William noticed a rather pretty girl, a latecomer he guessed, not dancing, and went to ask her for the next one, a quickstep. Her name was Blanche Curnow. Her mother gave the nod and she accepted. He introduced himself to the woman, expecting her to ask him a few questions, but she merely suggested that he and her daughter should go and stand near the edge of the floor, ready for their dance to begin.

Blanche was eighteen. She lived at Chynoweth Hall, near Culdrose Downs, to the southeast of Helston. Her father was one of Cornwall's biggest wholesalers, mostly in groceries, fresh vegetables, and meat. She was the fourth of five brothers and sisters. Her younger sister, Phillippa, was in disgrace this evening because, being only fifteen, she was too young to attend tonight, and she had kicked a panel out of the door in her anger. Phillippa had the most ferocious temper though she was an awfully sweet girl, really. One shouldn't say 'awfully' ... Was she talking too much? Her elder sister, Gillian, who would be ... well, one shouldn't be too-too exact after twenty-one, should one ... anyway, she'd got married two years ago and was expecting a happy event quite soon. Honestly, you'd think she was the only woman who ever managed it! She'd be furious at missing this ball, which was going to be the event of the season. She *was* talking too much, wasn't she!

William assured her it was not so.

"You go to the Camborne School of Mines, don't you," she said. "My elder brother, Maurice, left there last summer, you know. He did electrical engineering and now he works for the North Cornwall Power Company. How d'you like Cornwall? A bit of a change after America, I should think."

"I like the School of Mines. Cornish mining still leads the world, you know."

Their dance began. They took to the floor at once.

"What about Sithney and the Old Glebe?" Blanche asked.

"I'm fond of that, too," he told her. "It's like a textbook of Cornish geology for me — the landscape at our doorstep. But I can't understand why my father and sister are so keen. The landscape on your side of Helston is much prettier." When she pulled a face he added, "It cuts no ice with you?"

"The scenery's all right but there aren't enough young people there," she said. "Only Meredith Johnson, and I've known him since the nursery. Besides, he's so belligerent."

"Is he here tonight?"

"Yes, worse luck! That's him arguing with your neighbour, old man Liddicoat. Talking of whom — Harvey Liddicoat seemed to be getting on very well with your sister in the first dance. That was your sister, wasn't it?"

"Yes."

"And the *first* dance, too! She must have made a conquest there. He's usually too shy to open his mouth until three sets have gone. I say — you're a good dancer, you know. Are all Americans as good?"

He laughed. "I'm Cornish, really — or trying to be."

"I know. But you know what I mean. You were reared there. Anyway, what d'you think of your neighbours, the Liddicoats? The girl's a bit of a shrinking violet, but what about the boys?"

"I can't understand how a bluff old farmer like him can have such cultivated ..."

"Don't you believe that about 'bluff old farmer.' Old man Liddicoat may talk like one, and act like one most of the time, but ... have you seen his library? He's one of the best read men in Cornwall, so my father says. Always got his nose in a book. And not just religious books, like his fellow ranters. You know he's a Methodist?"

"Yes, and we know the story, too — how my great-uncle, Honourable Carrington, banned his grandfather from buying the Old Glebe backalong. And now here we are, shouldering the Liddicoats aside again. The whole district's talking about it, I suppose?"

She grinned and nodded. "Even I've heard about it — and I make it a point *never* to pry into other people's affairs. I detest gossips, don't you?"

"Only when they stop talking about me."

"You!" She nipped his wrist jovially. She was very pretty when her eyes flashed like that — even in pretend outrage. "I hope you're thinking of asking me for another dance later. It's fun talking with you. Most of these men here — I know *exactly* what they're going to say."

"What d'you think about Nicholas Liddicoat?" he asked. "Rum chap?"

She hesitated — for the first time since they had struck up this conversation. "There's a tale going about Helston," she said at last, "that you saved his life."

"It was hardly as dramatic as all that," he protested. "Though he was well and truly trapped under those stamps. I still don't know what he was doing."

She gave a single, ironic laugh. "That goes for almost everything else he does. No one can fathom him, and no one with any sense would want to. Although ..." She hesitated again.

"He was quite rude to my sister ..."

"Oh, I'd love to meet her. Would you present me to her after this set?"

"Sure. Shall we dance the whole set together, then? It's only two dances after this."

Her expression was both pleased and alarmed. "I think that might cause comment," she said.

"Would that worry you? Do say yes, Miss Curnow. You don't strike me as that sort of worrier. And, besides, I enjoy talking to you, too. And — like you — I detest gossips. I prefer to listen to someone like you, who can dish out good, straightforward, factual information on all my new neighbours, unvarnished and by the bucketful."

She drew a little apart and eyed him warily. "Are you pulling my leg, Mister Carrington?" she asked.

"I wouldn't dream of anything so forward, Miss Curnow. But a little genial rib-tickling, perhaps?"

She pouted. "Then I *do* talk too much. I know I do. My mother always tells me so."

"Not too much for my liking, I assure you. Still, if dancing the whole set with me would cause comment, and comment would cause you distress, then ..."

"All right," she said suddenly. "I'll be killed by looks — and I've never done such a thing before in my life — but if you'll tell me you believe that, I'll put you down for the other two dances as well. There!"

"Good!" he exclaimed. "So now there's no hurry and we can relax ... and so forth."

"No hurry for what?" she asked archly.

"Oh ... to ask you to tea? To suggest we might go to the local movie theatre one evening? Or make up a picnic party of friends if the weather improves a bit? That sort of thing. But now I needn't even mention it for at least ten minutes, need I?"

She laughed and promised to be utterly flabbergasted when he did finally speak of such things.

"And meanwhile," he said evenly, "you can tell me what you know about young Liddicoat. Not gossip, of course, just the simple facts."

Her grip tightened on his wrist. "It'll be the Chinese burns next time," she warned. "Just for that, I'm not going to tell you a thing about anybody."

But her smile challenged him to make something clever out of that.

"I'm sorry." He hung his head penitently and then, brightening, said, "But see here — I won't know how severe a punishment that is unless you let me know what you're intending to withhold."

She frowned. "How can I do that?"

"Just tell me what you're determined to keep back — to rub the salt into the wound. Then I'll know better than to tickle you in the ribs next time."

"How can I refuse?" she asked. He felt that, if they'd known each other ever so slightly better, she'd have stuck out the tip of her tongue at him.

The dance ended but they stood their ground, lke a tennis pair whose opponents were hunting for the ball. William saw that they were, indeed, attracting some attention. Blanche ignored it and continued speaking. "What I think of Master Nicholas Liddicoat" — she mimed rather than spoke the name, because so many people were watching — "could not be properly expressed in polite company. He is a boor. An arrogant, utterly conceited ..." She broke off and stared across the emptying floor. "D'you know who that person is — the man who's about to dance with your sister?"

He followed her gaze. "Frank Kernow," he said. "No relation of yours, I suppose?"

She shook her head. "Different spelling. My father calls them the upstart Kernows — but don't ever tell Frank that. Actually, he has a lot of admiration for Jessica Kernow, as was. She's Mrs Cornwallis Trelawney now."

"Yes. We've mumbled our how-de-dos. She was talking to my sister over in the Coinage Hall earlier."

"I missed that — or, rather, I wasn't allowed to go. My father says I'm too young for cocktails. But I could have just stood there and talked, couldn't I?"

"I'm sure you could have! But you needn't worry about my sister and Frank Kernow. I've heard her say she'd trust him about half as far as she could throw him — and only then in broad daylight."

"He was a much nicer man when he was younger. Of course, I was only just beginning to move into my teens then, so I'd be no judge. But my sister Gillian said so, too. He's become very selfish and scheming, like his father. My father says it happens in all small towns. Big fish in little ponds want to be big fish in big ponds. But they can't be. So they get all frustrated and start nibbling at the edges of the law and good business practice and things like that. Isn't it a pity!"

"It's greed," he said.

The word was a new trigger to her. "You say such sensible things, Mister Carrington! Can I call you William? You can call me Blanche, if you like. I hate greed, don't you? The only thing I'm greedy for is life. I want some life before ... I mean, I don't think Gillian has a life at all. She's ..."

"She has one inside her," William said.

Blanche stopped dead and his momentum almost pushed her over. She picked up the rhythm again quickly enough but the lobes of her ears had turned bright pink. "Oh, dear! I'm so sorry," he said. "I thought from the casual way you spoke about it earlier that you wouldn't ..."

"I just said 'a happy event.' I didn't mean to imply anything so ... so agricultural."

"It offends you?"

She glanced all about them and then murmured, "No. Of course not."

"Why d'you say your sister Gillian's life is nothing to envy?"

"Because she went straight from school into nursing, which is just like school, mostly, and then she married the surgeon — the first man who ever asked her seriously. And that's three different cocoons and no fresh air in between."

"What d'you call 'fresh air'?"

"I want to study art. I want to live in Paris. And travel all over Europe — not staying in posh hotels but in ordinary homes. And" — she smiled archly again — "America, too. What d'you call those flat-top mountains?"

"Mesas? Buttes?"

"I want to sleep on top of one of them, with nothing but the stars above. Does the Oregon Trail still exist? I want to ride that from Council Bluffs to the Pacific, right up over the Continental Divide, like my great uncle did — Byron Curnow. He was a Cousin Jack, too, you know. The family tradition is that Lord Byron was his real father but I don't suppose there's any truth in it, do you? I want to roam the world till I'm too old to walk another mile. Thirty, say."

"You'll be old enough for cocktails then, too."

She laughed dutifully. "But seriously. Wouldn't you love to do something like that?"

"Seriously, Blanche? I think you should ask me the same question — seriously — in about two years' time."

Her face fell. "Why?"

"Because we'll know each other pretty well by then — I hope. Also, you'll be of age and no one could stop you. Also I shall have a profession by then — one of the most transportable professions in the world, as it happens."

"But I didn't mean with ..." she began. Then she paused, looking him first in one eye, then in the other. "Well, come to think of it, maybe I did," she said.

18 A hundred times that evening Leah wished she had not engaged the last dance to Nicholas Liddicoat. What a stupid, *so-there* sort of act it had been — as childish as sticking your tongue out at a neighbour in class. And it did her reputation no good, either. To open the ball with one of her neighbour's bachelor sons and to close it with the other ... well, it was rather blatant. Especially as many people there knew of the ancient hostility between an earlier generation of Liddicoats and Carringtons; and those who hadn't known of it at the beginning of the evening had certainly caught up by its end.

But there it was. The deed was done. The name *Nark* sat four-square in the last box on her programme and to change it now or to plead a fit of nausea (which would not have been too difficult to simulate) would only have increased the attention and interest of the populace.

"Do you think there's anywhere in the world," she asked Mrs Troy as the awful moment drew near, "where one can be truly anonymous — just be *oneself,* you know?"

"It all depends on whether you wish to return, at some future date, to a place where you are known," she replied. "Don't look now but you see that tall lady over there — under the middle window, in the mauve dress?"

"I know who you mean," Leah said. "I've noticed her a couple of times. Once, I'm almost sure, she was going to speak to me. But she didn't. There's something remote about her."

"That's the Honourable Consuela Grenfell. Very well connected. A cousin of Lord Desborough. She's probably the only *real* aristocrat here tonight. She was a débutante back in the eighties but she never finished the season. She was packed home in disgrace. Such a pretty girl — and d'you know what her crime was?"

Leah shook her head.

"She vanished for two hours one afternoon *without her maid!* There now! They tried to hush it up but you know how servants talk and how censorious they are when judging their betters. Word got round and she became completely unmarriageable — not worth spending another penny on. So they packed her off home, and that's where she's been ever since. Languishing in spinsterhood, as they say."

"How awful!" Leah at last dared to look at the woman. The 'something remote' she had seen earlier was now translated into something very sad. To have one's whole life ruined by a mere two hours' indiscretion — what a terrible age to have lived in! "Was it an assignation?" she asked.

"No. That's what made it even worse. It was an act of charity. She'd gone out *with* her maid for some little shopping expedition — all right and proper. And on their way back she noticed a little cripple girl begging and crying. So she stopped to help but the maid told her they had to get home and then there was an argument and she told the maid to go home by herself if it was so important. And she spent those two hours — *alone* — getting the girl into a charity home."

"And couldn't she just explain that?"

"She did, of course. But in a way it only made matters worse. Who wants a wife or a daughter-in-law, no matter how well connected, who gives way to foolish and self-willed impulses like that!"

"But what on earth do they imagine she ought to have done, for heaven's sake?"

"What she ought to have done was to hand the girl a card from the Mendicity Society — to which her parents subscribed — and tell her to apply to them for relief."

Mrs Troy spoke with such uncharacteristic primness that Leah could not tell whether she was being sincere or ironic. "And what has she done with her life since?" she asked.

"Been a good aunt to her sisters' children ... a shoulder for the sisters themselves to cry on ... a grown-up nanny to her brothers-in-law ... a nurse to her dying mother (who has been dying for twenty luxurious years, I may add) ... and a tireless worker for charity. Not what you could call a wasted life by any means — and yet there is that look in her eyes."

Leah stared at the woman openly now, willing her to return the stare. But it did not happen.

"And what does that look in *your* eyes mean, young lady?" a more familiar Mrs Troy asked next.

Leah gave up with a sigh. "I was thinking it must have been a dreadful fate in *those* days but now ..." She broke off and said,

"Don't think me rude but, may I ask — weren't you a débutante in those times, too? Didn't you go through all that?"

"Hardly, dear!" The woman laughed. "I was a working girl. D'you mean no kind neighbour has told you of my humble origins — my rags-to-riches story?"

"No!" Leah rubbed her hands with relish.

"Don't get too excited," Mrs Troy warned. "My father was a horse doctor. A vet. He died when I was eighteen, four years before I got married. He left us with very little money so I went to train as a nurse — at Guy's, which is one of the big London teaching hospitals. My husband-to-be, Captain Bill Troy, was in the army; he was also, of course, the heir to the Pallas estate. I nursed him through an illness. We fell in love and got married. In Brighton. On our way back from the church, immediately after the wedding, he was driving me in a gig, the horses bolted, the gig overturned, and poor Bill died."

"So you didn't …" Leah began hesitantly.

"No, dear. The marriage was never *consumed,* as my maid once put it. It led to a fine old legal argument when his family learned he had left the entire estate to me, I can tell you! The Settled Lands Act of eighteen-eighty-eight will be found engraved on my heart when I die."

"What's that?"

"Don't!" She closed her eyes and shook her head vigorously. "Basically it allows a woman to keep land she has inherited."

"Yes, I had heard he left you the estate. But not the rest of it."

"Really? Well, that is encouraging. People must be changing. After my second husband divorced me — David Troy, the MP — people wouldn't even talk to me. Most of these people here would simply pass me by in the street back in those days. And I sometimes think it wouldn't take much to make them do it all over again."

Leah gazed over the throng of guests and said, "That's hard to believe — looking at them now."

"Aha!" She laughed. "I did two wise things — three, in fact. First I sold the Pallas estate to its tenant farmers, thus creating landowners who were on my side. Second, I married a rich man — Jimmy Troy — too rich to be ignored. Third — we went off round the world and stayed away for ten years, which was time enough to let things settle. Still, I'm surprised they've settled to such an extent that no kind friend of mine has told you the scandal. As I say, people must be changing."

Leah cleared her throat delicately and said, "Bill Troy, David Troy, and now Jimmy Troy ..."

"Oh, you have heard that one, then!" she said with amused weariness. "My supposed motto: If at first you don't succeed ...! Yes, I have to admit that it was quite funny when Jimmy first said it *twenty years ago!*"

"Sorry!" Leah laughed.

"What were you about to say earlier?" Mrs Troy asked.

"When?"

"Oh!" The woman raised her eyes to the ceiling. "Young gels these days — such scatterbrains! You said that the poor Honourable Miss G's fate must have been dreadful *then,* but nowadays ... what? Not so dreadful? Even worse?"

"Oh. Not so dreadful. Perhaps not dreadful at all. I think it would be wonderful if one could just come to a ball like this and enjoy the dancing for dancing's sake — without everybody looking at you with this man or that man and thinking, would she do for him or would he suit her? Dancing still isn't really just for fun, is it. It's still just a way of finding out if a young man has bad breath or is incapable of conversing for three minutes without boring one to death. It's hardly a basis for deciding to marry someone, is it!"

"Well," Mrs Troy replied — being more aware than Leah that the last waltz was almost upon them — "at least you can devote yourself *entirely* to enjoyment of the dance for what remains of the evening!"

"But there's only the ... oh! I see what you mean — I think."

"I mean that, since the question of marriage — or, indeed, of any tender association between you and the younger Liddicoat — is out of the question, there is nothing left for you but to ... how did you put it? 'Enjoy the dancing for dancing's sake'! Go on with you, now — here he comes."

"For this encouragement, much thanks," Leah said grimly. "Well, Nark," she went on, turning to face her opponent for the last waltz, "I'll say it again — you don't *have* to go through with it if you'd rather not. I'd hate to *force* you. There'll be no tears on this side of the house, I promise. We could blame the bruise on your leg."

"Well, Thistle!" He stood with arms ready to hold her body as far away from his as anatomically possible. "*I'll* say it again, too: I do have to go through with it. And that's an end to the matter. My leg is completely better, but thanks for asking."

She joined him to dance in the old style, with one arm at her side and the other just resting on his hand by her fingertips. And a moment later they were off.

She already knew he was a good dancer, from having watched him earlier that evening with other girls. He was even more graceful and confident than his brother — though, lacking his height, he had to put more energy into it. After just a few twiddles and turns she lost a good part of her nervousness — that part which arose from her fear that he might be deliberately wooden and unresponsive.

"Actually," he began, "I have a proposition to put to you. Not a proposal," he added on seeing the alarm in her eyes. "A simple, humble proposition."

"Go on," she replied guardedly.

"It only struck me during the evening, so it may still be a little unpolished around the edges. So kindly bear with me if you will. Hear me out to the end. It starts from the fact that my father, for whom I have very little time — nor he for me, as you may have noticed — intends to make life as difficult for you Carringtons as only he knows how …"

"Then he'd better look to his locks — is all I can say."

"Goodness!" he said wearily. "What a civilized and intelligent response! I'm trembling with fear!"

Her hackles rose. "Are you trying to provoke me into stopping this dance?"

"D'you want to?" he asked. "It's all right by me."

"No," she admitted angrily, annoyed at her cowardice.

"Why not?" he asked in quite a different tone, as if her answer truly interested him.

"Because I don't want a scene," she snapped.

"Oh." His disappointment seemed genuine, too. Against her better judgement it prompted her to add, "Also you don't dance *too* badly, I suppose."

She realized that the distraction of their argument and her annoyance had allowed them to get dangerously close — bodily, that is. Quickly she moved away from him again but, in doing so, wrong-footed him on the turn so that they almost fell. Then, of course, she had to apologize and put herself in the wrong.

"You only needed to ask," he said stiffly, holding her at maximum distance again. Clearly he did not intend any further conversation between them.

But he wasn't tall enough to act in that aloof manner and carry it off. If his head had been above hers, he could have stared directly ahead like that, into empty space, and pretended not to notice she was looking at him; but as things were he had to gaze over her shoulder — or look away so pointedly that he would appear ridiculous.

"All right," she said after the silence had lasted long enough. "What is this proposition of yours? We might as well talk about something. What sort of annoyances has your father in mind?"

"He'll commit every nuisance short of an action that would lay him open to a claim in court. It shouldn't need much imagination to realize that the annoyance could be considerable. Sheep could strip a prize shrub in minutes. Pigs can root up ..."

"But if they were his animals ..." Leah started to object.

"Ah, but what if they weren't! Animals stray all the time. Not everyone can afford wire. One tap with a stick where it wouldn't blind them could be enough to make sure someone else's strays took a wrong turn into the Old Glebe."

"Lord — so childish!"

"Indeed, Miss Carrington. So my proposal is ..."

"Proposition."

"My proposition is equally childish but, for that very reason, it may work."

"Go on then. I meant what I said about your not dancing too badly, by the way."

"Do you think we could dance just eighteen inches apart, then? This chasm between us has become rather tiring."

She did as he asked and then, thinking that rather curmudgeonly, closed the gap to the usual few inches that currently ruled in even the best ballrooms. He passed no comment on it.

"The only thing that would hinder my father is the thought that one of his sons might marry one of your father's daughters."

She frowned. "But there's only ... oh, I see! All right. But even then the son wouldn't automatically get the land."

"Is that American law?"

"No. Well, yes, it is. But it's also English law now. The Settled Lands Act of eighteen-eighty-eight, you know." She had never seen such a self-satisfied smirk on the face of any man. "You *did* know!" she accused.

"Of course I did. But I'm interested that you know, too. You must have looked it up. I wonder why?"

She wasn't going to demean herself by arguing. "Go on," she said tiredly. "You were talking about your father's wish to see one of you waiting for me to walk up the aisle. It'll be a long wait, I can tell you!"

"I know. The longer, the better as far as I'm concerned! However, to get back to him — his dearest wish would be for Harvey to be the chosen one. What d'you think about that?"

She gasped. "I certainly wouldn't tell *you!*"

"Very well," he said calmly. "I'll tell you. There's no hope whatever of any such thing."

"Oh! You know that, do you!"

"Yes." His self-confidence was so infuriating. "I watched you and him dancing this evening. You beguiled Harvey and you duped my father but you didn't deceive me!"

She had to tense her muscles to stop herself from slapping him and walking off the floor. In an insistent whisper, while she forced a smile and tried to look as if they were exchanging the usual pleasantries, she said, "You are just about the most arrogant, insufferable, detestable …"

"Good!" he interrupted. "That's precisely why my proposal — proposition — might work. Because I, for my part, think you are just about the most vain, most smug, least self-critical young lady *I* have ever met. In short, the chances that we might ever fall in love with each other must be close to the minus-infinity side of zero. Therefore there would be no risk whatever in *pretending* to an interest we both know can never develop into anything that might threaten the independence we both cherish."

"That's preposterous!" she said at once. "Do let's talk about something else."

"Very well. I'll talk about my brother. If you have any idea of 'playing him,' as anglers say, forget it! He's interested in you all right. You probably don't need me to tell you he's nuts on you. But he's not a patient man. The Cornish for 'nuts on' is 'hurrisome.' You keep it up with Harvey and you'll soon find out why! And you'll begin to wish you'd paid me more attention here tonight — in every sense of the phrase."

He relapsed again into silence.

Once again it was all she could do to stop herself from striking him, or something equally silly. How dare he call her smug and vain and un-self-critical, when he was all of those things himself, only a hundred times worse!

"Anyway," she said when she could hold her tongue no longer, "it's more risky than you think. Frank Kernow told my brother that his sister made a similar bargain with Cornwallis Trelawney, and just look ..."

"Quite right," he said. "It was at a dance in this very room, so legend has it."

"And just look where it got them!"

"You miss the point entirely," he said.

"Well, I'm sure you'll find a sledgehammer to drive it home."

"The point is that, with them, it was an *amicable* arrangement."

19 On the day the Carringtons moved into the Old Glebe — Monday, 4th May, 1914 — the prophecy Nicholas Liddicoat had uttered came true. Old Man Liddicoat chose that very morning to 'put the land in good heart,' as he waggishly explained it later. He had a contract with the Helston municipal sewage works and he exercised it vigorously, all over the fields he rented and would continue to rent until 21st June, Midsummer Day. Farmyard manure would have been bad enough — and quite adequate to his purpose, which was to fire a warning shot across their bows; but the sludge from the town works was insufferable. The stink of it was, as he intended, almost the only topic of conversation at the Old Glebe.

" 'E done just the same the day 'is sister tied the knot," Dolly Cory, the new kitchen maid, told Leah. " 'I aren't goin' to 'ave none of that old fussin an' fadgin',' 'e said. And 'e went in special-early to the sewage farm. And the whole wedding party had to pass by 'is fields smelling like that."

The new cook, Sarah Gundry, gave an ironic snort. "You aren't hardly old enough to mind the day he got married hisself. Poor Olwen! Olwen Jones, she was. You know they Joneses who do live up Leedstown, by the Horsedowns turn? He's her brother — Billy Jones. Anyway, he wouldn't put up his wedding suit and go to chapel until evening milking was done. The whole family had to argue with him three weeks till he agreed to do it early — three in the afternoon. And then he said the yield was down and Billy Jones had to pay him sixpence compensation."

"But surely the yield was up extra next morning?" Dolly said.

"Course t'was! Course t'was! But that's old man Liddicoat for 'ee. He belong to go on until everyone else do give in, see. He bought a horse once, in Helston market, and when he got 'n home he found two nails missing in one shoe so he put the creature back to the dealer and got fourpence knocked off the price! Cute as a pet crocodile, he is!"

"Can you milk a cow, Dolly?" Leah asked.

The girl laughed at the question. "I shouldn't think there's many round these parts as couldn't, Miss," she said.

"Good," Leah told her.

Maid and cook exchanged puzzled glances.

Leah left them to get on with lighting the range and setting out the kitchen. "I think I'll put on some gumboots and go out and help old man Liddicoat," she said.

"Where are you off to?" her father asked as she passed his library. "Some of these books haven't travelled too well. The damp has got into them."

"Oh, dear. Perhaps if you spread them out on the windowsills? I'm going to help Mister Liddicoat. "

"What?" He was aghast.

"I'm going to show him he doesn't intimidate us. I presume that, as landlord, you have the right to tell him when he's not doing something properly?"

He bit his lip uncertainly. "Don't do anything to antagonize him, dear."

"There's bound to be a clause in the lease that lets us take back the land if he doesn't practise proper husbandry — don't you imagine?"

"Oh, dear!" He set down the book, which was now the least of his problems, he suspected. "What's on your mind now? I know that look in your eye, honey."

"The trouble with old Clifford Liddicoat is that people around him have been saying that sort of thing all his life — don't do anything to antagonize him. He now thinks if you ring a doorbell long enough in an empty house, *someone* will answer it."

She went out to the old barn and pulled on her gumboots; she was already wearing her drabbest, oldest clothes for the moving-in, so there was no need to change them. As a bit of theatre, though, she took an old flour sack and tied it round her waist with baler twine.

"Why don't you go over there and haunt *him?"* she called out loud to the ghosts. On their many visits to the Old Glebe, preparing for this moving-in day, she had taken to addressing them directly in a challenging or truculent fashion — as a way of quelling a fear she was ashamed to acknowledge. "Make yourselves useful for a change!"

On her way out she grabbed a four-tyne yard fork, locally known as an eeval. She had some vague idea of helping them at their work, which would not only make him realize that his shot across their bows was ineffective, but would also encourage him in his hopes of an alliance between her and Harvey. She hadn't done too much encouraging of that sort lately, mainly because the Nark had proved correct in predicting that his elder brother would grow 'hurrisome.'

Walking down over the yard, with the eeval resting on her shoulder and her arm curled comfortably around it, she knew that this, too, should feel more theatrical than genuine. And yet it didn't. In a curious way it felt like something she might have done in another life and could just dimly remember. It felt *right.*

Until then her only agricultural flirtation had been at hay-making on Tom O'Leary's cousin's farm below Sleeping Giant Mountain. And that had been little more than an excuse, a token fee, paid to enjoy horsing around in the hay and not-quite-skinny-dipping in the creek afterward. But this was real. This put a spring in her stride and made her heart sing. Mrs Troy had said, after milking the cows that day, "I sometimes think that if I didn't do this once a week, I'd slowly fade away — like the Cheshire Cat in *Alice.* " It had seemed a charming fancy at the time but now Leah understood what she had meant. There's something of a farmer in everyone.

She kept a watchful eye on the Liddicoats, father and Harvey, as she walked. They had not noticed her yet. The horse and cart stood horizontally across the slope; no brake was needed. The tailgate was down, so that all Harvey had to do was pull a couple of cubic feet of sludge out of the cart with a hooked rake, whereupon his father, who stood at the horse's head, would walk the creature on a yard or so. Then, after covering a few dozen yards in this way, both men would attack the claggy lumps with eevals and attempt to scatter the fragments evenly over several square yards around the track of the cart. Some of the fragments, she noted once she entered the field, were still pretty large.

The old man was the first to spot her, and then only because he looked around as he went to the horse's head. "Well, maid," he called out. "You do look a fright, I must say!"

"What are you doing?" she shouted back. Thoughts of lending a hand were beginning to fade.

That was when he spoke his piece about 'putting fresh heart into the land.' He was, of course, delighted that his disgusting prank had — seemingly — caused enough consternation at the Old Glebe to bring her out here, though the sack round her waist and the eeval over her shoulder were a bit of a puzzler. "You look like some old bal maiden," he added.

She didn't know what he meant but she wasn't going to pass the initiative to him by asking. And that was when thoughts of pitching in with them vanished entirely.

"Never mind that," she snapped. "You say you're putting fresh heart in the land but look at it! The one thing hearts don't like is clots."

"Clots?" he echoed, taken aback.

"Clots! Clods! Lumps! Look at this!" She prodded the largest with her eeval and twisted so that it fell in two. She was relieved to see how easily it did so. "Even those two bits are too large. The sun and the wind will turn them into prairie chips. *Then* how long d'you think it'll take for rain and weather to break them down? Christmas, I shouldn't wonder."

"He won't have no smell by then," he told her.

"The smell doesn't bother us at all. But we have a saying in our family — if you're going to do a job, do it *properly.*" She prodded one of the halves and broke it in two yet again. Then she mashed it with the tynes of her eeval and shook the bits that stuck away again, spreading them over a square yard or two. "Like that," she said.

Recovering from his surprise he laughed at her energetic seriousness. "Why, maid, I've been muckspreading more years than you've got teeth and toes, and if you …"

"Then you've grown slack and careless," she interrupted him. "Come on now. Don't leave it all to me. Do it properly. I want all these clods broken up and scattered." She continued to break up the larger ones as she spoke. "You say the smell will be gone by Christmas. It'll be gone by next week — and all the value will be gone with it. Don't you know *anything* about the *science* of muck and muckspreading?"

"My dear soul!" he exclaimed, breathless now with rage — and a rage that was more than tinged with alarm. He could not remember the last time anyone had dared speak to him in that fashion. And in front of his elder son, too. "Go on, boy!" He rounded on Harvey. "Pull away! Pay no heed to her."

With the eye his father couldn't see Harvey winked at her and pulled another clod off the cart. He started to break it up but the old man clucked the horse forward and called out, "More, boy! Just keep pulling. Never mind she."

The game had turned sour and he wanted to get away as soon as he could.

She ran to a point some five paces in front of the horse and there stood her ground, one hand resting on the top of the eeval handle. He would have gone on, forcing her to leap aside, but the horse jibbed and threatened to put the cart on a potentially disastrous downhill slant.

"What now?" he asked angrily.

"You may not have bothered to read it, Mister Liddicoat, but there is a clause in your lease that allows us immediate repossession of the land if you fail to practise proper husbandry. Leaving huge lumps of sludge to encumber a ploughed field is not good husbandry by anybody's standards. I just don't want you to be in any doubt about our intention to exercise that right if those clods are not broken up by this evening."

If there had been no witnesses, he might have run his eeval through her then and there. As it was, a trapped and frightened animal, he just stood there, breathing furiously, staring at her, and shivering.

"Come!" she laughed. "You tried to play us a trick and it failed. That's all. But you'll think of better ones, Mister Liddicoat.

You'll make us smile on the other sides of our faces yet. Isn't that the idea?"

She stepped aside then and he continued on his way without a word. He also continued to traverse the field at a slow walk while Harvey was obliged to rake great lumps of the sludge out over the tail.

Her spirit sank.

She realized that he had won. He was gambling that, no matter what she might say, her father would not exercise the right to repossess the lands — even if it was in the lease, which he couldn't remember. And even if he should exercise it, the lease was up in seven weeks — long before the law would have lumbered into action.

She changed her tack then. "I'll give you a hand," she called out as they passed her on the return leg. "Just to show there are no hard feelings." And she set to, breaking up the lumps with her eeval.

It proved an even bigger blunder. The old man had probably intended to fetch and spread no more than a single load. The stink off a second and subsequent loads would add little nuisance to that of the first. But when he saw her systematically breaking the clods, beginning with the very first they had dropped that morning, he went directly back to the sewage-farm, down beyond the power station in Helston, and came back with a load of fresher, smellier, even claggier stuff. The journey took about an hour, there and back.

Leah, who had just finished what she imagined would be the entire task, almost broke down and wept when she saw a grinning old man Liddicoat and his desperately apologetic but enforcedly silent son return with the same again.

Except that it was not the same, for by now her hands, unused to the toil, were red to the point of blistering, her arms ached, her shoulders ached, her back ached, and her feet throbbed inside gumboots that were half a size too small for her though they felt fine when worn for only half an hour or so. Not that she allowed any sign of wilting to show while they were in the field. "My father has asked me to tell you how grateful he is," she called out to the old man. "He says this is a fine, neighbourly act and he won't forget it."

But that bravado, too, proved an act of folly for it must have set that cunning little brain to work even harder. As he left the field for a second time he gave her a cheery wave and hollered out, "Leave it if you mind to, maid. Us'll come back and help 'ee tomorrow." Over the other shoulder, after he turned at the gate, he added, "Or the next day." His dying laughter told her how much trust she should put in these promises.

But they did lure her into a false sense of relief — that she had only that second cartload to disperse and then her torment would be over. So she *did* weep when, an hour later, he returned with the third load, for by then the redness had turned to blisters, as yet unbroken, and all her aches were screaming pains. But she turned her face from the Liddicoats and mastered her distress.

"Getting tired, are 'ee, maid?" the old fellow cackled as he and Harvey started raking out the next load. "You haven't done half so much as what you done afore."

She could not trust herself to reply. All she knew was that she would not yield. Every last clod would be broken into the smallest possible pieces. She was resolved that he should not be able to crow over her defeat at the market next Monday — for all the farmers there today would surely have seen him carrying the sludge and the story would soon have spread throughout the district. With grim determination, therefore, she fought her tears, screamed back at every pain, and continued her toil.

She had never battled pain in that way before — never set herself against a challenge so great that, at the outset, she would have given herself no chance at all of winning. And what did 'winning' mean in this context? It no longer meant getting the better of old Liddicoat. She had set a trap for him and walked straight into it herself. Now 'winning' meant getting the better of herself, her own weakness — her bodily frailty on the one hand and, on the other, her almost overwhelming desire to throw her eeval into the nearest hedge and crawl home to her bed. She wondered if she even dared to break for lunch, suspecting that she'd never be able to pick up the eeval again if she did.

But in a curious way it was her hunger — that gnawing emptiness in her vitals — which helped her win. Hunger is allied to pain and yet is different from it. Had it been just one more pain heaped on all the rest, it might have overwhelmed her; but its differences were marked enough for it to push her pain into the background. There came a point, when she reached the farther hedge, at the end of one of those now interminable rows of scraped-out sludge, when she looked back and realized she had been working almost unconsciously for the past twenty minutes. In all that time she had been obsessed by her hunger. Only her hunger. The pains in her back, her shoulders, her neck, her arms — all had ceased to trouble her. Even now, when she was consciously aware of the fact, they did not come crowding back. Gingerly she tested herself, sending careful mental feelers out into those once-screaming joints, and felt — she could hardly believe it — something like exhilaration there.

There is an unsurprising border between pleasure and pain that anyone can explore. Just try scratching an itch harder and longer than its relief requires. No matter what the affliction — from the minor discomfort of the itch to the pain that threatens consciousness itself — that border travels with it, raising the stakes as it goes. Leah had now discovered it at that upper extreme, though her senses moved in the opposite direction, that is, from pain into something curiously like pleasure.

It was doubly curious because her muscles were no less tired, her joints were no less afflicted, and yet they almost sang with joy as they obeyed each new command to perform. She knew then that she could do it. She might pay for it in days of uncomfortable convalescence, tomorrow and beyond, but she could get through *this* day; and that was all that mattered. She could accomplish this task; she could make old Liddicoat's chuckle choke him yet. In other words, she could safely take a break for lunch; she owed that debt of gratitude to her hunger, for showing her how to ignore and overcome pain.

She stabbed her eeval into a particularly large clump of sludge. "Don't go away," she promised it. "I'll be back."

The first person she met, on returning to the yard, was William. "Why aren't you at the School of Mines?" she asked.

"Half day," he replied. "Or practical day, rather. We have to turn up tomorrow with interesting geological samples. Nick Liddicoat and I are going over Wheal Fortune this afternoon."

"Nick?" She was puzzled. "Why should he help you?"

"He's not. He's collecting for himself. We're in the same group. There are places where it'll need two men and a rope."

"Hang on! Same group? What same group? D'you mean he's at the School of Mines, too?"

"Yes!" He applauded her ironically. Then, seeing her continuing puzzlement, he added, "D'you mean you didn't know that?"

"No, William, I didn't know."

She started walking again, toward the old barn, dying to get out of her gumboots.

"You mean I never told you?" he asked, following her.

"William — you never tell us *anything*. Not that I'm the least bit interested in what the Nark does with his days — except that it'll be a relief to know he isn't across the valley most of the time. I can go out safely without the risk of meeting him."

"I'm sure I told you," he grumbled. "Anyway, why were you looking so pleased when you came into the yard just now? If the risk of meeting him was weighing so heavily on you?"

"Was I?" she asked airily. "I don't know, I'm sure."

"You looked as if you'd lost a penny and found a shilling."

"I found shillings all right!" She laughed and proudly showed him her blistered hands. The blisters were large and white as silver. "All alive-oh!"

"Oh God, Leah!" He was appalled. He grasped her upturned hands in his and stared at them in disbelief. "What ever came over you?"

"Nothing came over me — and nothing will overcome me, either. Especially not old man Liddicoat. He thinks he's so smart, spreading this sewage on the day we move in — just to let us know he can make life pretty unpleasant for us every time the west wind blows!" She broke from his grasp. "These gumboots are killing me. I'm going to put on walking boots this afternoon."

"This afternoon?" He followed her into the barn. "You're going back for *more?* What are you doing, anyway? Putting it all back in a cart and dumping it on his side of the valley?"

"No! I'm putting heart into the land." And she explained briefly about breaking it into small, easily incorporated lumps. "And, by jiminy, I'll finish the job today, too, no matter if he brings another load after lunch. Two loads. Let him bring as much as he likes, he won't beat me!"

William cottoned on at once that there must have been more to it than she was saying. Somehow a few heated words had intensified into this battle of wills. "I'd better help you," he said reluctantly. "I can probably find some interesting minerals in any old hedge stone …"

"You'll do no such thing! Oh, blessed relief!" She wiggled her toes in their new freedom.

"You've got blisters there, too," he said.

"I have not. They're just holes in my stockings."

"Pardon me but they are blisters. You're mad."

"I'm mad at the Liddicoats, I can tell you that!" She laughed. "Tell me, William — have you ever felt pain to the point where it stops being painful? Where it's almost pleasure, instead."

"Every Saturday," he replied calmly. "Let me go and get some goose-grease to rub into those toes."

"You can do it when we get indoors. I'll just slip on my shoes and … ouch!" She hobbled a few steps toward the door.

He caught up with her and offered his shoulder to lean on.

"Thanks," she said. "What's special about Saturday? Why d'you get pains then and …"

"That's when I play rugby with the colts."

Again she stopped and stared at him, baffled. "What is the point," she asked, "of living under the same roof as you? What are the colts, anyway?"

"Sort of junior side. I play there because I never played before. Rugby's like American football only not nearly so gentle. They say I may soon be good enough to go into the reserves. Didn't I tell you?"

"Don't keep asking that. You know very well — you never tell us anything."

He sighed but did not speak.

"Do you!" she challenged him.

"Maybe it has something to do with the way you and Dad jump down my throat every time I try."

"We do not!"

"Well, your imitation's perfect."

"Anyway, I thought you spent every Saturday afternoon with Frank Kernow."

"No thank *you!*" he said vehemently.

"Why not? Is this something else you haven't told us?"

"I've told Dad." He held open the back garden gate for her to pass through.

"Well?" she prompted, waiting for him to tell her, too.

He shook his head. "It's not suitable for a young lady's ears."

"Oh?" Now, of course, she was doubly intrigued. She hopped through the gate and turned expectantly to him again.

"It really is unsuitable," he assured her.

"I say!" She grinned knowingly. "Did he make unnatural advances to you?"

He faltered in his stride and his jaw fell open. "He's a *man,*" he said.

"I know all about *that,*" she responded. "Was it that?"

"I'm starving," he said, brushing past her.

"Was it?" she insisted, hobbling after him.

"No," he snapped.

"Worse?"

"I'm not going to tell you."

"Then it was worse. I can see I shall just have to ask Dad."

He spun round and gripped her by the wrist. "No!"

"Or I could ask Mrs Trelawney to ask her brother Frank."

He relaxed and smiled. "Okay — go ahead. I wouldn't object to that."

It forced her to smile, too. "Dear, oh dear," she said amiably as they went indoors. "It seems to be my day for having my bluff called."

20 Fortified by a good farmhouse lunch of bread and cheese and pickles, Leah put on her stoutest walking boots and returned to the sludge-strewn field. Her father was proud of what she was doing but thought her mad for doing it; he understood why she turned down all offers of help, both from himself and from others he might easily have hired. The honour of the Carringtons was at stake and only she could champion it in these circumstances of her own making. And she did not doubt she could do it. The sharp, stabbing pains in her back, neck, and arms had dwindled to a dull, all-over ache. Her blistered hands and toes were soothed and reinforced by goose grease and bandages. She was in good heart.

It lasted until the moment she reached the gate. For there, halfway down the field, with *her* eeval in his hands, stood the

Nark, breaking up the sludge and spreading it with expert little flicks of the arms and wrists, making it look as if a toddler could do it.

"Get out!" she yelled. "Scram! Vamoose! Go home!"

He looked up, gave no sign of seeing her, and continued.

"You're trespassing!" She started down the field in long, loping strides, scattering loose tilth before her. "Give me my eeval," she demanded when she drew close. "You've got no right to come over here and do this."

"You're an idiot," he said quietly.

"Coming from you, that's a compliment."

"Thinking you can tackle my old man head-on!"

A wicked thought crossed her mind. *If I were to burst into tears now, I could really make him squirm!* But, greatly though it would please her to see him reduced to that, the realization that he might try to make it up by *comforting* her was enough to banish the thought.

"Besides," he went on, "you're the one who has no right here. *He* rents these fields."

She realized that just by standing there, saying nothing, she could make him feel uncomfortable, so she continued to stand there, saying nothing for a little while longer.

He said, "I couldn't believe my eyes when I came cycling down the hill to Grankum — seeing you all dressed up like the miller's daughter, making a complete jannacks of it — a simple job like this."

"Oh?" she felt provoked into saying. "I thought I was managing rather well."

"I think you did miracles but so did the saint who baled out Loe Pool with a whelkshell. You must be in agony. Walking *along* a steep slope like this one to spread dung! One leg up, the other down. One shoulder up, the other down. One arm short, the other stretching all the time. I couldn't believe anyone would be so wiffle-headed."

She noticed then that he had been standing facing the slope all this while, walking backwards while breaking up the lumps above and in front of him. She had assumed that was merely to keep his eye on the gate, to mark her approach. But now she saw at once how evenly balanced his body was. And how he didn't have to reach so far down because the slope, as it were, lifted the lumps up nearer him. She could have shot herself for not working out something so elementary on her own. Just because the horse and cart went across the field, she didn't have to follow it.

"That's my eeval," she said rather lamely.

"He's gone in Helston for another load," young Liddicoat replied. "I'll make myself scarce when he comes. We'll hear the wheels on the cobbles, which will give us plenty of warning." When she made no reply, he added, "What I mean is, you can go and get another eeval if you like."

All this time he had not looked at her. It galled her, that.

"Why didn't you bring one of your own?" she asked.

"Oh, the old man would *never* have recognized it, would he!" he replied sarcastically.

"So how am I going to explain bringing two of mine here?" she asked without thinking.

"You could offer one to Harvey — say you brought it for him. Force him to stand up to the old man for once. It'd be interesting to see if he'd take the challenge." He sniffed — and looked at her for the first time. And he even smiled.

She had to admit that he was ... well, not exactly pleasant ... not even tolerable ... but less objectionable when he smiled.

"It'd be even more interesting," he added, "to see if the old man would *allow* him the challenge."

"Oh?" she replied offhandedly. "It would be interesting to some, I suppose. Why?"

"Well, if it's not interesting to you, there's no point in explaining myself, is there."

He had finished to the bottom of their final dung-spreading sweep by now. He slung the eeval easily over his shoulder and set off for the top of the slope again, seemingly not caring whether she followed or not.

"All right — why would it be interesting?" she asked, lifting her skirts and striding up the loose soil after him. "You have broken it up very well," she added. "And you make it look so effortless, too."

"It is effortless," he replied impatiently. "As you'd find out soon enough if you went and fetched another eeval."

She ran, all the way to the barn and back, as if she feared the thread of their conversation might break if she were away too long. "Okay," she said breathlessly as she settled to work at his side, "why would it be interesting — to see if Harvey would challenge your father?"

"And to see if the old man would allow him to do it," he reminded her. "Isn't that easier now?"

"Oh, shut up!" she snapped. Then, after a pause: "Yes."

"A challenge from Harvey would tell you how hurrisome he is. And the degree to which my father accepted it would tell you how hot or cold he still is on the idea of acquiring the Old Glebe by way of marriage."

"Ha!" she exclaimed. "Well, I said it would be interesting to *some.*" When he failed to rise to it she said, "Can I ask why you're helping me, Nark?"

"Because, Thistle, *he* would be insufferable if he won this idiotic challenge you issued."

"D'you really think I wouldn't have gone on till I dropped? Even doing it all the wrong way and suffering the most awful pains — you were quite right about that, of course — but d'you think I should ever have given in and let him win?"

He was silent so long that she had to prompt him. "Well?"

"No," he admitted at last.

"Then the question remains," she said. "Since you knew I would never let your father win anyway, why are you stepping in and helping me?"

Again he was silent.

"You could have sat at home and watched me through your binoculars, suffering the torments of the damned up here, *and* have had the additional satisfaction of knowing I'd still beat your father at this game."

"I couldn't," he grumbled.

"Why not?"

"Because I'm supposed to be out collecting specimens."

"Oh, yes — that's another thing. Why did you never mention you're at the Camborne School of Mines, too?"

He was surprised enough to stop, momentarily, before he remembered he wasn't going to react to anything she might say. Respond, yes — react, no.

"William never tells us anything," she said. "He never told us about rescuing you by the stamps that day, nor about hearing the story of the old tithe-barn murder, nor about having tea with you and the Rogerses at Wheal Fortune. As I say, he never tells us anything."

"Perhaps he's afraid that ..."

"No, don't say anything smart, Nark. He simply *forgets* to tell us. That's all. His favourite phrase is, 'Oh, didn't I tell you that?' He's said it twice to me already today. D'you know why he's fallen out with Frank Kernow?"

He shot her a frightened glance. Or was it something more than simple fright? Alarmed, perhaps — also a touch amused. Ambiguous, anyway.

"I'm a big girl," she said by way of encouragement. "I thought it might be because Kernow tried a touch of the Oscar Wilde."

He coughed and covered it with an explosive laugh. "You're in the right area, anyway."

"I durn well know I am. I could tell by the way he blushed when I asked."

This time the laugh was both explosive and genuine. "I wish you'd waited for me," he said. "I'd love to have seen his face. He didn't answer you, I take it. Or are you just seeking corroboration from me?"

"If you don't tell me, I'll tell him you did. Then he'll challenge you to a fight — which he'll probably win. However, if you *do* tell me, I promise I'll ..."

"You never learn, do you!" he shouted angrily at her. "We Liddicoats do not yield to threats."

His anger excited her as much as ever but this time, for some reason — perhaps because she was desperate to know — she swallowed her pride and apologized. "I should realize that you *are* different from your father," she said.

"I know I am," he replied, softening somewhat. "But how d'you mean it? Not as a compliment, I'm sure."

"I do. Your father never gave me a *second* chance."

He saw how he had allowed her to back him into that one, and he could not help smiling at her cunning. "All right," he said. *"One* second chance coming up."

"Will you please tell me why William has fallen out with Frank Kernow?"

"No," he answered simply, his eyes brimming over with amusement. Then, as she drew breath to argue and tell him he was being unfair, he added, "Yes, of course I will. It seems it all began with your father. He, being uncertain as to how he should go about the business himself — that is, not being a local man, familiar with the local geography, shall we say — he asked Kernow if *he* would kindly undertake the dreaded chore of completing your brother's education. The transition from theory to practice. Am I putting it delicately enough?"

"In other words, he asked Kernow to take William to a sporting house," Leah said.

He laughed. "Admirable." Then he looked at her. "You mean William couldn't tell you that?"

"Could you tell Adèle?"

"She's only nineteen. You're an old woman — almost past it as far as marriage is concerned. Besides ..."

"What?"

"Never mind. Oh, well, why not? The fact is I wouldn't even know where to start *looking* for the nearest 'sporting house.' Good name for it, by the way. I'll bet Kernow knows a hundred. There's something rather" — he shuddered for want of a word — "about that man."

When she said nothing he added, "You agree with me but would just hate to admit it, eh!"

"I'll shake this clump over *you* in a minute," she warned him.

He chuckled and for a while they fell into silence, an easy one surprisingly enough. Then she said, "Can I ask you something?"

"It's a free country," he replied.

"You remember that 'proposition' you made at the ball?"

"Ye-es?" His tone was guarded.

"Why did you make it?"

"I told you at the time."

"Yes, but why did you *really* make it?"

After a brief pause he gave a little sigh and said, "I don't have much time for women."

"Really?" she asked sarcastically. "Are you sure they have any time at all for you?"

"Either way, it doesn't matter. I can have the most wonderful, easy conversations with Adèle, and ..."

"On *most* topics."

"Just shut up and listen. God, you do think you're so smart! Always putting in some smart little ... just listen. You asked a question and I'm answering it. D'you want to hear it or not?"

"Oh, Nark, you're so right. Lordy but I'm so sorry. I'm *awful!* Will you ever be able to …"

"And you can stop *that,* too." He laughed against his will.

"Okay. I will just listen. I promise. You were saying you can have the most wonderful, easy conversations with your sister, and that …?"

"… and I keep thinking why not with other young females? She cannot be unique."

"And have you tried? Sorry, I'm not interrupting or seeking to be provocative …"

"Yes, well, that's it, you see. Provocative! You don't need to *try* to be provocative, Thistle. It's as natural to you as breathing. 'Have I tried'! For heaven's sake! It seems that no association is possible between young males and young females that is not either aimed at holy wedlock or at that disreputable union which has caused William to fall out with Kernow. 'Have I tried'! I try all the time. I try talking to women as I'd talk to any man, and what do they do? They either go all coy and simper and flutter their eyelashes — as if they hope I'm taking the first of ten thousand weary steps to the altar — or, like you, Thistle, they go all prickly and aloof and suffragist, as if I don't really have any right to walk on the same earth where their dainty feet have trod."

"Well!" She plunged her eeval into a large clump of sludge, lifted her skirt three or four inches — enough to reveal her stout walking boots — and exclaimed like a Southern belle, "Well, fan mah brow! Jess look at mah dayunty feet!"

And she went on showing her boots while he stared at them and tried not to laugh. "Wrong foot," he said at last.

"Which one? I'll have it amputated at once."

"No — the one we got off on. I knew it, you see. I had this feeling that you might be the girl of my dreams — the one I could talk to who … I mean, the one I could talk *with*. And there'd be no distant ring of matrimonial bells. And you'd put out no signs saying keep off the grass, beware of mantraps, stick no bills, trespassers will be prosecuted, and all that daw-brained nonsense."

She worked in silence for a while. He did nothing to break it.

"Suppose …" she said at last … and then fell back into silence yet again.

After a while, still with no help from him, she tried again. "Suppose we could start on the right foot? Start again?"

"Why?"

She laughed with astonishment. "God, you are suspicious!"

"D'you wonder?"

Her laughter relapsed into a sigh. "All right. Let it pass. Either you're a most cunning and devious rogue or, just by a million-to-one chance — of a kind I do *not* believe in, really — you would suit me down to the ground. I mean, your *proposition* would suit me down to the ground. Even *this* ground here!"

He sniffed. "At the risk of repetition, I'll ask again: Why?"

"I *was* going to marry ... I mean, I was sort of unofficially engaged ... I mean, nothing was announced or anything but it was always *somewhat* understood that this young man — back in Connecticut — and me ... that we would sort of annexe up to each other one day. So I never had that pressure all round me that makes a girl ... what did you say? Simper and coo and get all desperate about wedding bells. Incidentally, you should try putting yourself in their shoes one day. Not just thinking *about* it and talking *about* it but actually imagine yourself *being* like that. But don't let's get diverted into that argument. I was saying I never felt under those pressures myself — until I came here. But now my father, and Mrs Troy, and Mrs Trelawney, and just about everybody ... they don't necessarily *say* anything — and they certainly don't beat my brains out with it — but there's that insidious idea there all the time. She's got to find a husband. We must find her a partner. They just all *assume* I'll get married. That that's what I'm *for!*"

"And what *are* you for?"

"Me. To just be me. People say poor Miss Grenfell! I say *lucky* Miss Grenfell! *She* may not think so, because she was brought up in a different world ... different expectations ... but I think she's had a pretty good life. I wouldn't mind it. I just wish it was as easy as vanishing for two hours without a chaperone these days!"

"And the alternative is what I proposed?"

"Yes, but not for the reasons you gave — to keep your old man and mine happy."

"But I was lying, of course." He laughed. "If I'd only known you feel like *this* ..."

They had worked their way to the bottom of the hill, or the part that had been spread. They surveyed their work with pride before setting off for the top again. But at that moment they heard the rumble of an iron-tyred cart on the cobblestones of the yard. Nicholas turned at once and made for the cover of Grankum Wood, taking the eeval with him. "Something to think about, eh?" he called back over his shoulder. "See you when they've gone."

She was sure he had taken the eeval deliberately — so that she wouldn't after all be able to offer it to Harvey. Interesting, she thought.

Singing loudly enough to make sure the old man heard her as soon as he came into the field, she strode back to the top and started shaking out another downhill swath. When she 'noticed' him at last, she gave a cheery wave and called out, "I've found a much better way to do it. Come and see."

Old Liddicoat halted the cart in the gateway, where, clearly, he told Harvey to wait. He climbed down and strode toward her, radiating a sort of hesitant suspicion that could turn to anger or scorn, as required.

"See!" she said, demonstrating as she spoke. "You work backwards, downhill. Not back and forth across the field. It's so much easier."

He paid her next to no attention, surveying instead the herculean area she had apparently spread. "I'll bid 'ee good day, Miss Carrington," he said curtly. Then he called out to Harvey to turn the cart round.

"Aren't you going to give us that load, too?" she asked as he walked away. "No, actually, you're probably right. The rain will wash enough of this down to make it unnecessary." As he reached the cart and climbed aboard she added at the top of her voice, "Thanks very much for today, Mister Liddicoat. You couldn't have welcomed us in better style!"

Part Two

Meneage Street

Ghosts of the Past

21 Away from Nicholas's persuasive tongue Leah became less sure that his proposition offered a way out of her dilemma. Two words hovered around it in her mind: deceit and defeat. The element of deceit was obvious. In a curious way it was akin to the deceit in which the two parties to an arranged marriage must connive: to parade before the world a love that has no basis and which, in their heart of hearts, they know does not exist. She did not feel she could do it, or not for long — and nor, she suspected, could he. Sooner or later something would give. She felt sure that had happened with Jessica Kernow and Cornwallis Trelawney when they had hatched up a similar plot; something had given way and, despite her cleverness, she had ended up as Mrs Trelawney. For Leah to end up as Mrs Liddicoat would be a defeat, all right!

But even if she and the Nark avoided such a dreadful fate, the very arrangement itself would represent a kind of defeat for her. The battle was to remain herself. Sure, she wanted to avoid the treadmill on which she saw so many others trapped — marriage, children, and domesticity — but not by subterfuge. Even to pretend to be engaged or, more loosely, spoken for, would be a partial surrender while the guns were still bright and the powder dry. Yet what was her alternative? What did she hanker after? She could not say. She felt great affinity for the suffragists but could not imagine herself a fulltime disciple. For the same reason a life devoted to charities and good works, though equally praiseworthy, did not attract. She was not so singleminded. She craved variety.

The only truly contented woman she knew was Mrs Troy, whose children had grown up and left; well, Trevanion, at twenty-one, was under tutelage in barristers' chambers in London, and Zelah, a year younger, was at a finishing school in Switzerland. "Not off my hands yet," she said, "but out from under my feet!" She was convinced that the best years of her life lay ahead.

But Leah's trouble, she realized, was that she was convinced of nothing so positive. In fact, all her convictions seemed negative; she knew what she did *not* want but was vague as to what she *did* want. It changed from day to day. At the height of planning and rearranging the Old Glebe, she knew she wanted to be an architect. An hour spent helping Walter Blackwell check the stocks at the Angel convinced her that hotels and catering offered the most interesting and varied life of all. Tea and a chat with Mrs Kernow, and playing with the typewriting machine down in her office at St John's, were enough to sweep all that aside and assure her that the hurly-burly of business would be the most satisfying of all. But a summer-evening stroll about the lanes, chaperoning William and Blanche Curnow, provided final proof that the wholesale trade in farm produce offered the richest and most fulfilling life imaginable. It was a merry-go-round.

Blanche Curnow, she discovered, was of a similar mind. Her father had taken her around with him for as long as she could remember. He had invented the system whereby local hoteliers could be supplied with local produce, from fish to french beans, for no greater effort than picking up the telephone. During the early years of the scheme it had involved visits to dozens of hotels and hundreds of farmers. And Blanche, not then in her teens, had often accompanied him. She had thus seen a world that was normally closed to women. But even then she had seen a few farms, and hotels, where a woman ruled the roost. Usually she was a widow; sometimes she'd be an orphan daughter left with a bit of capital, too small for her to simply invest and live off the income.

"But what I think," she said one evening when Leah was driving her back home, "is that any girl should be able to get a bit of capital out of her father — if he can afford it, which mine certainly can — to start her own business. Just like a son can."

"What about your beautiful dream of sleeping on top of a mesa?" Leah asked.

She was shocked. "Did William tell you about that?"

"No. I've heard you say it myself. More than once."

"Oh, dear!" She bit her lip in consternation. "I do seem to prattle on sometimes. Not that I'm aware of it, mind. It's just that once I get going, I seem to ..."

"But what about that dream?"

"Well, I want that, too, of course, but not at the same time as I want a bit of capital. Sometimes I want one thing, sometimes another. Don't you find that?"

Leah chuckled. "Who was it in *Alice* who tried to believe two impossible things before breakfast? You want two impossible dreams before supper!"

"They're not impossible," Blanche protested. "My mother says nothing's impossible if you really try." After a pause she added, "But she also says there's a sting in the tail. Because if you can achieve anything you want by trying hard enough, you'd better be jolly sure you *do* want it. Because by the time you get it, you may have changed your mind completely."

"She sounds a very wise woman, your mother," Leah said. She hammered the rubber bulb on the car horn. Some chickens were taking an evening dust bath in the middle of the main road. "Get out of our way!" she shouted at them, too. The horn protested and emitted no more than a squawk. "Like a dying duck in a thunderstorm," she said and pressed it more gently.

The resulting *parp!* startled the hens into flight and soon the car was mobile once more.

"D'you know what I think she was referring to?" Blanche went on. "Promise you won't tell anyone I told you?"

"Sure. Go ahead."

"Though, actually, I'm sure almost everyone knows the tale," she added.

Considering the girl's facility, both at making public utterances and at forgetting them, Leah thought it highly probable.

"She was very much in love with a young ne'er-do-well," Blanche said. "A 'scape-grace, as they called them then. And her parents refused to let her marry him. So he emigrated to South Africa and died. And then she married my father, even though I don't think she really loved him at that time. He was thoroughly approved of by my grandparents, though."

"Have you ever spoken about it with them?"

"No, they're both dead. Why?"

"Well, my grandfather's dead, too, but my gran is still alive, back in America. I found her much more forthcoming than my own mother. But I'm sorry, I interrupted ..."

"Yes, well, the irony was that her first love *hadn't* died out in the Cape — this was before the Boer War and all that. In fact, he'd made a fortune in gold out there. And he came back to Cornwall, hoping to find Mummy still waiting for him. But of course, by then, she had ..."

"You know that for a fact?"

"What? Mind that haycart. Oh, don't you just *love* the smell of fresh hay?"

"Was he still expecting to find your mother waiting for him?"

"I don't know. He wasn't married — though it later turned out he had been and he'd lost his family in some epidemic. Anyway, does it matter? The point is everyone *thought* he'd come back hoping to claim her."

"And had he? Who is this man, anyway?"

"I'm coming to that. He's our next-door neighbour now, at Culdrose. My Uncle Maurice — Maurice Pettifer."

"Oh, yes, I've met them — at Mrs Troy's. His wife is that big, bony, bonny woman. Mrs Troy said he hitched her to the plough once, for a joke. Sorry! I'm interrupting again. It's a dreadful habit. I can't think *who* I got it from."

Blanche dug her with her elbow. "I shan't tell you if you're just going to insult me. Actually, you've made me forget the point, anyway."

The brakes screeched as Leah negotiated the bottom of Sithney Common Hill, the steepest part of it, by the mill. Frank Trevose, the miller, came to his door and stared after them balefully. It was another lost skirmish in his unending war with what he called the infernal combustion engine.

Leah said, "You were saying something about being careful what you wished for when young because you'd surely get it later. I think I can see the point. Your Uncle Maurice came back and your mother wondered what she ever saw in him. Is that it?"

Blanche screwed up her face, trying to square this gloss with the version she had been about to give. "It wasn't quite that simple," she said at last. "That's the way it is now, I'm sure. But I think it caused a lot of upheaval at the time. Of course, children live in a world of their own. We weren't aware of any of this. I saw Uncle Maurice crying once and I suppose I wondered why for as long as five whole minutes. And I remember an evening when my mother smashed everything in the drawing room."

"Everything?"

"Bookcases. The piano. Little whatnots. Every bit of glass. I don't know why. It was never explained. But I'm sure it had to do with her and Uncle Maurice in some way. But they're all the best of friends now — though when my father beats him at archery you can tell it means more than beating any of the others. There's still a rivalry there."

Leah had to drive carefully among the summer strollers, all along St John's, from the disused toll house below the mill to the weighbridge by the Porthleven turn at the bottom of Coinagehall Street.

"There's rivalry between all men," she said. "They don't need reasons. Even my father and Jimmy Troy. They're both retired from business. They've become bosom pals. They've got no *cause* for rivalry, yet you should see them throwing horseshoes or playing skittles! You'd think they were five, not fifty."

"Isn't it funny to think of our parents having tantrums and emotional storms, just like us. Can you imagine it?"

Leah laughed. "Do you have emotional storms, Blanche?"

"All the time. Don't you?"

"I try not to."

"Oh, so do I. But it doesn't work. Perhaps you've never been in love yet. I tried so hard — I really did — not to be in love with William. But it was no good. Haven't you ever felt like that?"

"Yes," Leah replied.

"And?"

"And what?"

"Well!" Blanche gave a baffled laugh. "You can't just leave it like that. What happened? Is it someone here? Or someone you left behind?"

"Someone I left behind."

"Oh, Leah!" The girl touched her arm. "I feel so dreadful for you. Does it ache all the time? Are you going to be true to him for ever and never look at another? Will he come to Cornwall one day and …"

"Hold it! Hold it!" Leah laughed. "It's not as neat as any of that. Life is messy, full of loose ends that never get tied up."

"Do you write to him? Does he send you the most wonderful letters, full of …"

"Nothing like that. I haven't written to him. He's not written to me."

Understanding dawned on Blanche. Solemnly she said, "You made a pact. No intercourse of any kind for a year and a day — a test of your devotion. How wonderful!"

"I haven't written to him," Leah said wearily, "because ... well, what's there to say? We probably won't ever meet again. He'll start teaching at Yale next September. He'll meet some nice young college girl. They'll marry, settle, and raise a family. If ever we do meet, it'll probably be like your mother and Mister Pettifer — we'll wonder what all the fuss was about. In fact, I already do at times."

"Because of meeting Harvey Liddicoat?"

Leah laughed, sighed, and shook her head, all in one. "For someone who told me, not a month since, that she'd rather be an intrepid lady traveller in a cannibal's cooking pot than the happiest married woman on earth, you've certainly learned to sing a different tune! Why must every important change in one's life and thinking be tied to a man?"

"You're right. I must give up William at once." She glanced nervously at her friend. "Will you tell him?"

Leah shook her head. "I think he'd rather hear it from you, my dear — well, you know what I mean. If he must hear it at all."

The ensuing silence between them was filled by the groaning of gears as the car wound its way up Coinagehall Street. When they turned into Meneague Street, where the uphill slope was much gentler, conversation became possible again.

"D'you miss him already?" Leah asked.

Blanche nodded. "I must break it to him gently," she decided. "And take my time about it. I don't want to get a reputation as a breaker of hearts. I hate those girls who just go around deliberately breaking men's hearts to satisfy their own vanity, don't you?"

Leah nodded. "Scalp-hunters, we used to call them. It always seemed a pointless hobby to me."

"Perhaps William and I could just be the best of friends. D'you think he could accept that? I do enjoy talking to him. He can be very interesting, don't you think? D'you think it's possible just to be friends with a man — the way you and I are friends, for instance, or William and Nicholas Liddicoat? What would be really good would be if you could be friends like that with Nicholas Liddicoat and I could be friends with William. Then we could be a foursome. What fun we could have!"

Leah smiled. "What makes you think Nicholas Liddicoat would welcome such an arrangement?"

"Oh ..." Blanche was airily arch all of a sudden. "Just the way I've seen him looking at you when we've met out walking. And things he's said to William. And I hear he's taken to attending church on Sundays — to the scandal of the whole chapel. The Liddicoats have been elders there for ..."

"What has he been saying to William?" Leah asked.

"You mean William hasn't told you?"

"William never tells us *anything* — as well you know! Come on — stop teasing, or I shall think you just said the whole thing for a tease."

"Nicholas told him you're the only woman he knows — the only woman on earth, probably — whom he'd ever dream of marrying. And even then it would take wild horses to drag him to the altar."

"Oh, how big-hearted of him!" Leah was both pleased and angered at the thought that the Nark was going about the place saying such things. And to William, of all people. Quite why it pleased her, though, she couldn't say.

"I feel sorrry for men, don't you," Blanche was saying.

Leah gave up trying to follow a consistent train of thought — even her own — and said, "Why — in particular? Is this your turning, by the way?"

"No. The next. And mind the potholes in the drive, remember."

"Why d'you feel sorry for men?"

"Because of the way we're changing. Women, I mean. We've been one thing for centuries and now, just when they've got used to it, we're turning into something else. We've been like cats, don't you think? If you read our mothers' diaries — women of that generation — which I do whenever they're foolish enough to leave me alone in the house — and our grandmothers' — you'll find very little faithfulness in them. Only a catlike sort of belongingness. Feed them properly and provide a nice warm home and they'd purr and have huge litters of kittens, et cetera. But they weren't faithful like dogs. If Mummy had felt a real doglike devotion for Uncle Maurice, she wouldn't have behaved like that when he turned up after all those years. This is the drive. Remember ..."

"... the potholes. Okay. And we're no longer like cats?"

"I don't think we are. Do you? *I* don't want to be pampered. *I* don't want a husband at any cost. I don't want to faint with gratitude when a man asks me to have his litters. I want to do the asking — if I feel like it. I want to do things for myself — lots of things. Daddy's going to have tarmac put down in front of one of his warehouses and he's going to order extra to put down on this drive. Won't that be swell?"

"Swell? Now where did you get that word?" Leah laughed as the car swept to a halt before the front door.

And there *was* her father, Giles Curnow, standing on the front steps, staring vacantly across the lawn. Blanche leaped from the car before it stopped rolling. She ran to her father and started pouring out her customary excited account of the day's happenings. But, as Leah noticed when she had parked the car and alighted, he must have said something to silence her.

"Hallo, Mister Curnow," she called out. "What a splendid evening it's turned out to be!"

"Mmm." He nodded and stared back across the lawn, where long fingers of evening sunlight were reaching into the dark beneath the trees at its edge. "We must make the best we can of them," he added. "These days of summer. The news from Europe, I fear, is grave."

"Oh?" She halted a few paces from them.

"Yes. Two days ago, it seems, a member of the Austrian royal family was assassinated by anarchists in Sarajevo."

"Why is that bad?" Blanche asked.

"It's a spark among tinder, my dear. There's no knowing where the conflagration will end."

22 From the moment the Archduke Ferdinand and his wife were shot dead in Sarajevo, on 28th June, everyone knew that war was inevitable. The surprise was that its actual declaration took so long — until 4th August in the case of the British Empire. Throughout that July people expected daily to wake up and find those stark headlines facing them across the breakfast table; but all that the papers contained were tales of increasing tension — hurried conferences here, agreements there (torn up, of course, before the ink was dry), and ultimatums everywhere. And mobilization everywhere. And jingoism everywhere.

The long days of that fretful month gave the Carringtons time — only too much time — to reassess their positions. William was the first to voice the thought that had occurred to all of them: "We're Cornish, of course," he said, "but we're not English. Remember what Coad said when he met us at the station that very first time? About the Cornish and the English? So, if we're not English, we're certainly not British — okay? It's not *our* war."

"Therefore?" his father pressed.

"Therefore we should go back to America until it's over — and we should go now, before they start torpedoing the liners."

"They'll never do that," the old man said. "That's just scaremongering. The papers are full of it. You shouldn't believe a half of what you read. Not even a tenth."

"What about your studies?" Leah asked. She knew she ought to leap at the chance of going back to America and wondered why she didn't. If both his children wanted it, their father would not insist on staying.

William shrugged and spoke to his father, as if he had asked the question. "I can do mineralogy at Yale for a year. It can't last more than a year, surely? Then come back and continue the practical stuff. And Leah could see Tom again." He smiled at her, expecting to recruit her support if, indeed, he did not already have it.

"And Pa's garden project?" she said.

"Right!" her father added.

William stared at them in amazement. "Well, you surely couldn't go ahead with *that,* even if we stayed."

"I couldn't?" The point had not occurred to him.

Leah's heart began to beat a little faster. Some part of her brain comprehended her brother's argument before she knew it consciously.

"You saw it in the papers," William said. "And some things you *can* believe. Island race ... horses and other livestock eat half the cereals we grow here ... grain ships will be sunk ... all the grain in the Empire will be no help at all. Starvation stares the nation in the face, et cetera. We must cultivate every inch of arable land we have. Patriotic duty. They'll pass laws forbidding good farmland to be taken out of use. Your project's canned, sir, until the war's over."

Leah remembered something Mister Curnow had said — which was perhaps why she had seen William's argument before he actually made it. "Blanche's father says they'll set up committees to take over badly farmed land even. They almost did it in the Boer War. They would have done if the Germans had come in on the Boers' side — because of the submarines, you see. Everyone was talking about it."

Carrington was aghast. "You mean they'd push a man off his own land? They'd just expropriate it?"

"No ..." Leah tried desperately to remember what Mr Curnow had said. "They'd force him to rent it to them. They'd pay him market rent but they'd do the ..."

"Who's *they?*"

"The government. Or some official committee — the 'war agricultural committee' or something like that. A committee of local farmers and inspectors from the department of agriculture or whatever they call it here. Something like that. I don't recall the details. But they certainly don't intend to let land lie fallow or go out of production."

"It's no longer a free country, sir," William added, trying not to crow, for, with Leah weighing in with all these depressing facts, it looked as if she were on his side, too.

But she wasn't. She knew now why she was so excited. The Old Glebe would remain a farm for the foreseeable future — a real, live proper farm! And, since the tenants had departed two or three weeks since, it was now wholly and inalienably theirs. At least, it would remain inalienable for as long as they farmed it diligently, wasting no cranny where corn might grow or cow might graze. For her it was the crowning of all her unspoken desires, her unconscious dreams, ever since they had arrived in the old country.

"Leah?" her father said.

Curbing her enthusiasm she tried to sound judicious — on the one hand, on the other, looking at it all round, and so on. "Will's right," she said. He had always hated being called Will in America, because of taunts of 'whip-poor-will!'; but no one said that here and all his new friends thought Will smarter than William. "We're not British and it isn't our fight and it's not going to be too pleasant while it lasts. On the other hand, we are Cornish, and lots of good Cornish boys are going to get caught up in it. And nurses, too, no doubt. I'm just wondering what it'll be like for us if we run back to America now and stay there until it's safe again. How will it be when we come back and ... for instance, face Mister and Mrs Troy with Trevanion buried on some distant battlefield in Europe?"

"Leah!" The two men were scandalized at her frankness.

"God forbid it should happen, of course," she said. "But we'd be fools not to consider the possibility. *All* possibilities. Everyone says the war would be over very swiftly, and they're probably right. But they said that about the Boer War, too. Suppose they're wrong once again? Suppose it goes on and on until both sides have fought each other to exhaustion? Suppose we came back to find that half our new friends were missing at least one of their loved ones? Would they even shake hands with us — the ones who turned tail and ran?"

They were reluctant to admit she had a point but they could think of no effective answer.

"So what are you suggesting?" Will asked. "You say I'm right — which means we should go back. But then you say we can't go back because ..."

"I'm not saying that at all," she said calmly. "I'm saying go back by all means, but face the *possible* consequences. And I only say they're possible, but we have to face them. It may all be over very quickly, with little loss of life — in which case, we can return here with little risk of accusing glances from those who stayed and faced the peril. Or it may drag on for years and lead to the most appalling slaughter — in which case we could not possibly come back and look our friends in the eye. Ever!"

Will looked at their father, saw he was all but won over, and let out a sigh of exasperation. "Now who's scaremongering!" he said bitterly.

"Quiet, son," his father said. "Your sister's right — as she almost always is. This requires some thought."

"We were happy in America," Leah pointed out — knowing she'd won and that she'd have fences to mend with Will before long. "And we can be happy again. You could buy that plot in Hamden, Pa, and create your garden there instead. Maybe some dreams just aren't meant to be. We got close but History had other plans. That's not dishonourable ..."

"You be quiet, too," he growled.

23 In all the negotiations leading up to the purchase of the Old Glebe, Ben Coad had almost always come to the Angel or the farm itself. On the few occasions when some of the business had been conducted at his offices in Coinagehall Street — two doors up from Frank Kernow's office — Leah had, by chance, been engaged elsewhere. So she had never seen the man on his own ground before. Today, however — two days after the official declaration of the war — she had urgent business that could not wait on a visit from him at his convenience. Besides, she was in the town, anyway, taking up a kind offer from Blanche's father to stock up on sugar, rice, flour, and all the tinned foods she could manage. One sight of the Curnows' own larders — and cellars and lofts — had convinced her the situation was grave. If a wholesaler of food felt he had to take such precautions …

She was shown in to Coad's office, which was little larger than a cubbyhole, straight away. He was standing at the open window trying vainly to fan away the cigar smoke and introduce some fresh air.

"Good afternoon, Mister Coad," she said. "Please don't go to that trouble on *my* account. I quite like the manly smell of a good cigar."

"So do I, Miss Carrington," he replied, climbing down off his footstool and coming round his desk to help her into a seat. "But I was dealing with *these.*" He grimaced as he took out a pack of cheap cheroots, no larger than cigarettes. "One step above chewing 'baccy. Ghastly gaspers, I call them, but they're kind to the purse." Then, seeing her eye them curiously, he added, "Care to try one?"

She recoiled with an embarrassed laugh, sat down, had second thoughts, and, reaching forth a hand, said, "Yes, well, why not? As they come so highly recommended!"

He was as surprised as she but he lit hers — and relit his — without comment.

"I do smoke a very occasional cigarette," she admitted as he went back to his side of the desk. "But never one of these things." She held her mouth open and let the blue, acrid smoke curl its way up her face. It stung her tongue and made the saliva pour. But the aroma, once it was diluted with enough air, was pleasantly stimulating to her.

It created the right atmosphere in the metaphorical sense, too, for this was a business call if ever there was one — the most important call of her life, she calculated. "Haven't seen much of you lately," she said, knowing that, in business, one never got directly to the point.

"Well ..." He seemed surprised she should comment on it. "The sale went through some time ago. Your tenants vacated without fuss — I'm surprised old Liddicoat went so quietly, but there it is. Not that I'd set too much store by it." He chuckled. "I heard about the incident with the sewage sludge, by the way. I knew he'd play that card once too often. You trumped him pretty well."

"I simply called his bluff," she said modestly. "He didn't know it, thank heavens, but he should have raised the bid instead of folding. My hand was pretty ..." She took off her gloves, looked at her hands, and changed the sense of what she had started to say. "In fact, my hands weren't at all pretty. They've only just recovered. Feel that callus!"

He looked at her askance.

"Go on!" she urged. "I'm not ashamed of it. I earned it."

Gingerly he felt the hardened circle of skin where blisters had once wept. "Impressive," he said.

"I daresay I'll earn a good many more in the months to come," she added casually.

"Oh?"

"Yes. There's no question of turning the Old Glebe into a garden now. We'll be farming every square inch of it."

"Ah!" Understanding dawned in his eyes. "You want me to draw up new leases for your tenants — or your former tenants. Is that it?"

She shook her head. "We shall be farming it ourselves."

He tried to say something but no words came, except a cautious: "Yes?"

"Yes. We could either put it all under wheat and barley. Or half of it, with store cattle on the other half. Or a small dairy herd — up to a dozen milkers and their followers. Would we need to keep a bull for that number?"

This deluge of possibilities took him aback. He answered the easy one first: "There are lots of bulls all around you. Good ones, too — the ones that are at stud, anyway. There's John Carter down to Gwavas. Or Harold ..."

"So you think dairying is the thing?" she broke in eagerly.

"Ho-back! I didn't say that."

"It would be the *selfish* thing," she mused, as if talking more to herself than to him.

"How so?"

"Well, if we went in for cereals, we'd have to spread fertilizer to keep the land in good heart — because my father does want to create this garden, as soon as we've won the war. Or done our bit to help win it."

He scratched his chin. "Which you wouldn't have to do with cattle on pasture — except for lime. You'd still have to spread lime or the land would turn acidic."

"Quite," she said confidently. "We've still got some left over from the rebuilding."

He laughed, thinking she was joking.

She laughed too, pretending she was joking; she also made a note to look up this 'lime' stuff as soon as possible. It was obviously not the same as what the builders used.

"I thought you might go back to America," he said. "Wouldn't that be the sensible thing to do? You could let the farm again, just until it's over. It'll only last a few months they say."

"It never even crossed our minds," she told him unblinkingly. "How could we look each other in the face if we turned tail and ran like that — let alone all our good friends here once we did return. No — we're Cornish and we'll stand shoulder-to-shoulder with our fellows."

"Is Will going to volunteer?" he asked.

The question floored her. In all the permutations and possibilities she had considered since threats of war had started to loom, that had — truthfully, this time — never even crossed her mind.

"What would he do, I wonder?" she asked — meaning what would be his choice?

Coad took it more literally. "Miners ... sappers," he said. "He could join the Royal Engineers — dig tunnels under enemy strongholds, fill them with explosives, *bang!*" He laughed.

The world was full of overnight military savants.

"I'd go myself," he said, "like a shot — if only my father were well enough to come out of retirement and take up the reins once more. Poor old man!"

The world was also full of people with excellent reasons for doing everything possible to help win the war, except enlist. And now, if she had anything to do with it, Will would be among them, too. Staying here and farming the Old Glebe, when they could so easily go back 'home' to America, was sacrifice enough for the Carringtons to make. But what a coward she would think poor Ben Coad, if she had no brother herself!

"We must keep the home fires burning," he said.

"And the home fields growing," she put in. "And the home herds milking. Wellington said the war against France was won on the playing fields of Eton. Well, I think this war against Germany and Austria will be quite different. It'll be won on the *working* fields of Cornwall!"

"That's good!" he said admiringly and he took up a pencil to write it down.

"So we'll be looking to build up a milking herd at the Old Glebe," she went on. "I hope we can count on your skill as an auctioneer, Mister Coad — your ability to judge a good heifer from a bad one? Perhaps waiving your usual commission?"

He laughed and shook his head. "I'd be the most *un*skilled auctioneer in Cornwall if I did that, Miss Carrington."

"Well ..." She grinned. "Perhaps waiving it altogether *is* asking a bit much."

Still he shook his head. "Tell you what I will do, though," he said, "as long as you'll give me your word you'll never breathe it to a living soul?"

She nodded. "You have it."

"It's in your own interest not to tell, anyway," he added. "If you do as I suggest, you'll start off with a high reputation as a judge of good dairy cattle."

She stubbed out the remaining half-inch of her cheroot and rubbed her hands eagerly. "I can't wait!"

"You'll have to, I'm afraid — till next Wednesday, anyway. You just missed yesterday's auctions. But you come to the market at about eleven next Wednesday. That's when we sell first-and second-calf heifers with their calves still on them. There should be five or six to go in the ring. And I'll tip you the wink if there's anything good coming up in the cow sales after."

"What's before eleven?" she asked.

"Pigs and sheep, mostly for slaughter. You'll probably want a pig or two later, but build the dairy herd first — that's my advice. Anyway, when I'm selling the heifers, I'll ..."

"What about sheep?"

He shook his head. "Not with a neighbour like old Liddicoat. The possibilities for mischief are just too enormous."

"Why not just a few sheep?"

He chuckled. "My old father always said of sheep, 'Keep five and you might just so well keep fifty — or five hundred.' Ever go to a sheepdog trial? They only pit eight or ten sheep against a dog but you should see the mess they can get into sometimes. No, my advice is steer clear of sheep until you're happy with cows, pigs, and chicken."

"Why couldn't old Liddicoat be just as 'ockard' with cows?"

"Because he's got his own herd to think of. If yours go mysteriously straying one dark night, then so can his — and there are a lot more open, unfenced mine shafts on his side of the Grankum than there are on yours!"

"Are there *any* on ours?" she asked in alarm.

He shook his head and chuckled. "That's the beauty of it. But there's at least a couple of dozen on his. He'll think twice before he messes around with cows. Straying sheep are a nuisance without falling down mine shafts. Anyway, as I was about to explain — when you come to the auction on Wednesday, if you see me doing this with my pencil" — he grasped it by the eraser end and dotted it on his blotter, so that his fingertips ran down to the writing end, whereupon he turned it over and did the same again, running his fingers down to the eraser end — "if you see me twiddling like this, it means keep bidding. If you see me tapping it like this" — he demonstrated — "it means make one more bid only. You can bid early on any of them, because we always start ridiculously low, so there's no danger of being landed with one you don't want. And someone just might twig what we're at if you only ever bid when I'm twiddling or tapping. So, bid early on any of them but don't stay in unless I give the signal, right?"

"Okay. How do I know how much to bid?"

"I'll tell you. I do that in any case. I say something like" — he drew breath and spoke in an artificially deep voice to simulate loudness — "Five pounds I'm bid. Do I hear guineas? Will anyone bid me five guineas? Come on now, gentlemen, surely? Half-a-crown, then, for daylight robbery!' and so on. And I'll glance your way when I name a price you should bid. I hope we get away with it!"

She drew on her gloves and rose to go. "I can't tell you how grateful I am, Mister Coad," she said.

"There is just one thing more. I may have to make a joke or two — a mild one — but at your expense. It isn't often we get a lady bidding in the ring, see? The occasional farmer's wife or daughter when the man himself is ill, but even then there's comment. I'll have to do it, I'm afraid, or someone will be sure to shout collusion."

"You don't know me very well, Mister Coad," she replied, "if you think a little thing like that would put me off my stride. There's no harm in names, as they say."

He hesitated, biting his lips, while a slow smile spread across his face. "Well, Miss Carrington," he said hesitantly, "it is true — I do wish I knew you better."

She could hardly complain if he saw an open gate and ran straight through it — especially as she had so unthinkingly opened it for him. "It's a free country," she told him. "And I'm sure you have my address in your files somewhere?"

He grinned again. "Till Wednesday," he said.

"Till Wednesday."

24 Leah arrived home from her highly succesful meeting with Ben Coad, only to find William with a face as long as a dull sermon on a wet Sunday. "You look as if you lost a shilling and found a penny," she told him, reversing a saying he had once used on her.

"Nick's enlisted," he said.

"What?" For a moment the words made no sense ... Nixon listed? Who was Nixon — and who listed him? Then she realized what he'd said. "Nicholas Liddicoat? The Nark?"

"Enlisted. Joined up. Signed up. Gone for a soldier."

"When? I've not seen him for absolutely ages. Well, not for some days, anyway."

"Yesterday. They told us at the school today. I couldn't tell whether they were proud or angry. Bit of both, maybe."

"Well, I know what *I* am," she responded without thought.

"What?" He grinned.

"Relieved!" she snapped. "I wish him well, of course — that is, I wish him no harm — but it'll be easier not having to ..." She gave up trying to patch insincere words over her distress.

Not that she had any reason to resent his enlisting. There was no arrangement between them — not of the kind he had suggested, anyway — nothing to oblige him to tell her he was even thinking of doing it.

"Not having to what?" William asked.

"Oh, shut up! Come and help me and Pansy unload the jingle before it gets dark."

"Didn't you go in the motor? Unload what?"

"We're saving petrol for emergencies. I got twenty two-gallon cans and there won't be any more. Most people are putting theirs up on blocks until the war's over."

"Unload what?" he repeated as he followed her out.

"Pansy!" she shouted as they passed the side door.

A moment later the maid appeared, wiping floury hands into her apron. "Yes, Miss Leah?"

"Bring the two big baskets from the old tack room and come and help us unload the jingle."

Leah watched her brother's eyes as they followed the maid back indoors. She had a most attractive figure; one could not deny it. But Leah believed her stays were laced more for display than for comfort. She made a mental note to have a word with the girl about it. She also wanted to drop a hint to her brother but could not quite think what to say — something light and subtle but not ambiguous.

The body of the jingle was full of the tinned food she had bought from Curnow's — "At wholesale rates, let me add," she told William when his eyes went wide at her apparent extravagance. "Come on! I want to give that horse a rub-down and get on with preparing the store indoors."

When Pansy joined them she, too, gawped at the little mountain of tins.

"This is only part of it," Leah warned her. "Curnow's delivery van is bringing out the rest. We've got a busy week ahead."

"What d'you mean by 'preparing the stores'?" William asked. "Can you solder zinc?"

"I can braze it. Why?"

"We need patches soldered, or brazed, over the holes in the liners to the old bins in the scullery, or the rats will get in. I've got several sacks of flour coming. Plus rolled oats for the hens. Could you get some more zinc sheet from somewhere and make up four or five containers for the sugar? It'll be to take half a hundredweight each."

"Half a *hundredweight?*" he echoed. "You know the English hundredweight is heavier than ours?"

"That's pints and gallons, dear brother," she sneered. "Pounds are the same."

"Pounds are the same but hundredweights aren't."

"A hundred is a hundred wherever you are." She looked at Pansy and said, "Men! They think they know it all!"

"How many pounds in a hundredweight, Pansy?" he asked.

"A hundred and twelve, of course. Eight stone." To Leah she added, "A stone is fourteen pound."

"I did know that, thank you, Pansy," she said wearily. "I might have guessed it. Where else but in England would a hundred and twelve equal a hundred!"

"You can divide their hundredweight by seven — and eight — which is more than you can do to ours," he pointed out.

"Oh, good," she said sarcastically. "That's going to be so useful here."

"We'm seven under this roof, miss," Pansy pointed out as she added the last tin the basket could safely carry. "Where shall us put these?"

"I'll come in with you. We'll clear a space." To William she said, "Can you fill the other basket and follow us?"

"I'll help Pansy if you like," he said, leaping beyond her on the path and taking up the basket.

"I do not like," she said. But she said it under her breath as she watched them wander away.

25 The postponement of his life's dream, the grand garden project, took its toll of John Carrington's spirit. He spoke little; he lost some of his appetite for food; and he took to going on long, solitary walks. The moment Leah had sorted out the stores, a job she completed after their dinner that evening, she went looking for him. She thought it odd that he hadn't come to help her and the maids, or even to see what bounty his money had bought. At the back of her mind, too, was the thought that even if she didn't find him about the farm, she could go on through Grankum Wood to learn whether this rumour about the Nark were true.

She hadn't seen much of that young man recently. Nor had she taken up his suggestion, but her thoughts had turned to him more and more as the days had passed. The idea of knowing a man, not as a beau but just as a friend — a dear, close friend who could talk to her as to a sister, as he clearly talked to Adèle — was becoming increasingly attractive to her. Indeed, by that evening it almost amounted to an obsession — something she simply *had* to talk with him about. So the news that he'd 'gone for a soldier' was doubly disquieting, both for his safety and for her frustrations.

She saw her father as soon as she entered the yard. He was leaning on the gate at the farther end, gazing out over the field that old man Liddicoat, and she, had so liberally fertilized three months earlier. Now the new-sown grass of the ley, which John Carrington had intended to plough in as green manure for his garden, stood tall and lush. A feast for any herd of cows. She knew, just from the hunch of his shoulders, that he was standing there, rehearsing his ancient dream and mourning its death. *She* knew it was not dead, of course, but in the infinite wisdom of her twenty-two years she also knew that anyone at the ripe old age of fifty-two must daily ponder his own mortality and nightly wonder if he would rise to greet the dawn.

"Penny for 'em," she said as she came up close. "Tuppence if they're bright."

"Ha!" he chuckled as he turned to welcome her. "Where did you hear that one?"

"Local saying." She took his arm and turned him back to face the field and the mellow evening sun. "The days are drawing in quite fast."

"Full moon tonight. The rector told me the ghosts of Catherine Geach and John Lidgeycot are supposed to walk at full moon."

"For a man who says he finds it hard, sometimes, to believe in God, he's mighty ready to believe in ghosts! Anyway, it's the soldiers one thinks of when the moon is full nowadays. The snipers have no need for those flares and things. It must be dreadful for them."

She felt his arm go tense. "You heard about Nicholas Liddicoat, I guess?" he ventured.

"I was thinking of going down there to see if it's true."

"That's all, is it?" he asked. "Quite sure?" There was a jocular edge to his tone.

"What d'you mean?"

"I mean it is *Nicholas* you want to hear about?"

"Why — has Harvey volunteered, too?"

"No!" It irritated him that she did not (or would not?) understand his tease. "They'd not take him, anyway — a farmer's eldest boy. If the farm were bigger, they wouldn't take Nicholas, either. I was just thinking — if we rented these fields back to them again, maybe they wouldn't take the boy. Fifty more acres could tip the balance."

The thought tore her in two. On the one hand she could possibly save his life by giving up her own ambitions to farm the Old Glebe; so then there would be *two* thwarted Carringtons moping about the place. On the other, it was the only thing she had ever really wanted in all her life — not just to farm the place but to make a brilliant success of it, too. Just lately her mind had been crowded with exciting images. Herself at the plough with two great shire horses responding to every click and whistle, every tug of the rein. And herself stooping to pick up the rich tilth and let it run through her hand. Herself chopping mangles on a frosty morn. And herself burying her head in the warm flank of a restive cow with an udder full of rich, creamy milk, and relieving her distress. She knew how absurd and romantic those images were, how cussed a draft horse can be in the wind and rain, how her hands would freeze before the third mangle was in the hopper of the chopping machine, and how a restive cow can lash out with one hoof and spill the whole pail before you could blink an eye. But even so it felt so *right* for her. And now, to save the Nark's life, she'd have to give it all up!

"We could run the place ourselves and hire him as farm manager," she suggested on an inspiration born of despair.

"Well now there's a thought," he said gloomily.

"Oh, Pa!" She hugged his arm. "I'm sorry."

"It's not your fault, honey."

"I'm not apologizing. I'm just saying I'm sorry this dream of yours got stopped the wrong side of the grade crossing."

"*Level* crossing they call it here. But you're right. A couple more months and I'd at least have made a start."

"I think you still could."

"Huh?" He stared at her incredulously.

"And I think you might actually end up with an even finer garden, despite the delay."

He reached over and pinched her wrist gently. "Yup!" he said. "You're real enough. But did you really say that?"

She nodded confidently. "You know the long two-acre that stretches from our entrance along the hill to Bose's Burnthouse? It's never been much good for farming. A herd would trample it flat and graze it out inside two days. It's too long and narrow to work easily for cereals. About all it's good for is truck farming — I mean market gardening. If the hedge weren't so stout, I think it would have been incorporated in the ten-acre years back. But that same stout hedge will keep it safe from marauding cattle."

"For a market garden?"

"No. For a nursery. You could plough a patch of it and stick cuttings for your hardiest shrubs up there, where they'd root over winter. And meanwhile you could build a glasshouse 'foreanenst' the end of the tithe barn, as they say, and sow the seeds of your more tender or exotic shrubs and things. They'd be up by next spring, all ready to plant out next summer and harden off in the fall. The war will surely be over by then, but even if it's not, you could still be bringing on every shrub and herbaceous perennial you'll one day move to its permanent site. How about it?"

He went on staring across the valley. The sun bronzed his skin and she was reminded of a redskin chief she'd once met, massive in his silent dignity.

"Well?" she prompted.

"I'm just realizing I ought to have stuck to pork trading, honey. You're so right — why didn't I think of it? I had this picture of teams ploughing the whole farm and setting out paths, building walls, erecting pergolas, designing little temples ... fountains ... sunken gardens with ponds ... the *architecture* of it, you know ..."

"You didn't think of the plants at all? I don't believe that."

"Well, of course I *thought* of them. I saw them as little bushes and saplings that would steadily grow bigger and burgeon into" — he sculpted something massive in the air in front of them — "luxuriance." Then he pointed at the greensward. "It wouldn't take all that long, either. Just look at that! Did you ever see such verdant growth? If only we could have gotten such fertility back in New England!"

"It will be better, won't it?" she asked. "Letting the plants grow sturdy and acclimatize themselves up there? It'll be an even better garden in the end?"

"Sure, sure — I said it. It's a great idea. I'll get to see their habit, too, before I set them out permanently. How can I repay you, honey?"

"Well ..." she began cautiously.

"Talking of which," he went on, "I haven't forgotten it's your birthday the day after tomorrow. What d'you want? More linen for the bottom drawer?"

"Not this time," she said, wondering if she dared.

"What then?"

"Something rather big, rather expensive?"

"Your own automobile? Oh, no — stupid! Okay, I give up. What is your heart's desire?"

"Something to eat this grass."

"Your own horse!"

"No — a herd of cattle?"

He laughed, as if he thought she were joking. Then he stopped abruptly. "By jiminy, you mean it!"

She nodded and held her breath.

He looked away, down across the field again.

"It's a lot of grass," she murmured.

"And then, I suppose, the idea is we'd hire Nicholas to manage the outfit?"

"Well," she said reluctantly, "one thing at a time, eh? Maybe we won't have to go that far. Maybe they'll turn him down. Flat feet or something. I don't know. Let's just wait, huh?"

"A herd of cattle, eh?" He cleared his throat and she knew he was about to tease again. "Well now, honey, I've seen herds in Texas that stretched from ..."

She laughed and dug him with her elbow. "Ten milch cows and followers," she said. "That's the limit of my ambitions. And capabilities, too, come to think of it. If we bought first- and second-calf heifers, we'd get them cheaper than cows."

He looked at her sharply. "You had this all worked out!" he said accusingly. "When they declared war and we had that confab about going back to East Haven or staying here — you already had this in mind!"

She bit her lip and lolled her head submissively. "But then," she murmured, "whose daughter am I? How long have you had your grand gardens in mind?"

"Okay!" He nodded, and now the submission was on his side. "You know what you're doing, I guess. Shall I ask Coad to buy in a good little nucleus of a herd for us?"

She silently blessed him for that 'us' but she said, "I think I can manage the buying, Pa. I know exactly what I'm looking for."

"Yeah ... but how ... I mean, what'll you do? Just go round from farm to farm making offers?"

"No. I'll bid at auction, just like any other farmer."

"They'll walk all over you! They'll bless the day you entered the ring."

"I think not. I think they'll bless the hour I *left* the ring."

He stared into the darks of her eyes and a little shudder ran through him. "It's what you want?" he asked. "Truly?"

She nodded. "There's a cattle market in Helston next Wednesday. Camborne's is on this Saturday. Penzance has one a week today — we've missed today's ..."

"Oh, dear!" he said ironically.

"Let's go to Camborne on Saturday? You could see Will's teachers before term ends and I could at least get a feel for prices and suchlike." She slapped him on the back. "Whaddya say, Pop?"

He laughed and threw his hands in the air. "I say I know when I'm being railroaded!" Then, serious again, "Are you going down to Grankum Farm — see if it's true about Nicholas?"

"Oh, why not?" she answered casually. "There's an hour to go before dark. Just one more thing ..." She put out a hand to stop him for he had already turned to go. "I think we'll have to find some *occupation* for Will during this summer vacation."

"On the farm, I guess," he suggested.

"No. Most decidedly not on the farm."

"You don't think he could work with you as the boss?"

"There's that," she conceded. "But there's more." She bit her lip. "I don't want to fire Pansy just for being so pretty, but ..."

"Oh!" He tugged at his chin. "I see."

"It's not her fault, after all."

"No."

"Nor is she to blame if Will's a little, what shall I say — free and easy with his familiarity."

He nodded again. "So what had you in mind?"

"Jimmy Troy was in the mining industry, wasn't he?"

"He still is. Or his company is. Though he has no part in the day-to-day ..."

"But he would know people in the mining industry?"

"In the States?"

"And here?"

"I guess he would, why?"

"If he could talk someone into getting Will a job as dogsbody to some mine captain in Camborne or Redruth, just for the vacation — with instructions to make sure he's well and truly *exhausted* — and I mean drained of all energy — by the weekend ... it would add a practical dimension to his studies and ... er ..."

"... *remove* all risk of a practical dimension to his leisure pursuits, eh?"

"Quite."

"Leave it with me. I'll see what can be done."

He opened the gate for her. "Shan't be long," she said as she set off down the field. "Hup, Buttercup! Hup, Daisy! Come on — it's milking time!"

To John Carrington it felt as if his heart turned over in his chest. She was so like her mother at times. He missed Hannah now more than ever, more even than in those awful months after her death, when he imagined no man could miss a loved one more.

26 Leah met Adèle in Grankum Wood; the girl had a broad wooden yoke over her shoulders and a bright, galvanized pail swinging at either end. "Gone to fetch water from the well," the girl called out. "The rainwater's all but finished in the tank."

"Can I give you a hand?" Leah shouted back, branching from her path so as to meet her at the well.

"Not really." They were within speaking distance now. "The yoke balances, see?"

At the edge of the well she did a curious kind of corkscrew-curtsey, which dipped the pail in the water, filled it, and lifted it out, all in one. She turned a half-circle and did the same with the other pail, rather more ponderously. Then she smiled at Leah and raised herself a couple of times on tiptoe. "See? 'Tis easy if the balance is right. You coming up our place, are you?" She set off at a sedate walk, picking her way carefully among the trees.

"Just to say hallo."

"They're out after rabbits. Setting snares. There's a plague of them in the top meadow."

"Yes, I noticed some damage in our new grass along the edge of the wood just now. They don't seem to like the new grass as much as the old permanent pasture, though. I wonder if the new varieties of grass aren't as nutritious?"

"Cows with colic," Adèle said over her shoulder, "you put them on old pasture and they'll mend themselves in half the time. Everyone knows that."

Except guess who! Leah thought. "Will the men stay out till it gets dark?" she asked.

"Depends how many runs they find. But I shouldn't hardly think so tonight. They've been gone an hour now. You heard the good news about Nick, did you?"

"About joining the army? Yes."

"No — about *not* joining up. He'll tell you himself, I'm sure."

"You mean … are you saying he's at home now?"

"No. He's out setting snares for rabbits. Like I said."

They reached the edge of the wood, where the path broadened out to the full width of a lane. Adèle paused for a rest, setting the pails down in a gateway to their right. She turned and leaned on the gate, which was tied to its post with baler twine. It seemed to be a rule in Cornwall that you could not talk face-to-face with someone if there happened to be a gate nearby; you both had to lean on it and face out into the field. Leah often thought that if there were such a thing as a gate shaped like a bay window, they'd stand happily at it, talking away at ninety degrees to each other.

"We're going to grub up those anemones and violets, put this field down to winter cabbage," Adèle said. "There'll be more profit in vegetables now than flowers, the old man reckons."

"What does Harvey think?"

"Ha!" was all the answer she gave to that.

"He doesn't agree?" Leah guessed.

"He doesn't even care. All he wants is to go off and fight the beastly Boche."

"But ..." Leah did not quite know how to frame the question.

"They won't take him either, of course. He says he's going to run away to Plymouth and join the navy — lie about being a farmer's son. We can leave the daffodil bulbs in here. They'll hardly interfere with the cabbage, see."

"You could follow with onions," Leah suggested. "Cabbage root fly doesn't care for land where onions grew."

"That's not a bad idea." Adèle broke the rule and actually looked at her — admiringly. "You're becoming quite the farmer's ... girl."

Leah was sure she had been going to say 'wife' — and wondered why she hadn't. "When you say the army turned Harvey down *too* — d'you mean they actually turned Nick down? Rejected him outright?" she asked.

"No." She wouldn't explain any further. "Like I said, he'll probably tell you himself. They said that what he's doing now could be more valuable."

"Studying mining?"

"I don't know. It must be, I suppose. He said he wants a word with your Will."

Leah chuckled. "That shouldn't be too hard to arrange. They see each other every day, just about."

Adèle sniffed and then asked casually, "Is he still couranting with that Blanche Curnow?"

"He sees quite a bit of her," Leah replied guardedly. "Rather less now that he can't just hop in the car and tootle off. A bicycle gives one a different outlook. Coinagehall Street going, and Sithney Common Hill coming back, would make any bicyclist think twice about the absolute necessity for making the journey between us and Chynoweth Hall."

The suggestion that a mere hill could dampen Will's ardour seemed to encourage the girl, Leah noticed. She felt sorry for Adèle if she was harbouring romantic illusions about William — not only because she'd feel sorry for *any* girl who behaved so foolishly, but also because, in her particular case, she knew Adèle would stand no chance. "Can I try your yoke?" she asked.

"There's nothing to it," Adèle replied, helping her fit the thing across her shoulders.

"Hey!" Leah said as she stood to her full height again.

"Straw!" Adèle put in. Then, seing Leah's bewilderment, "You said hay — 'hay, straw, donkey manure' — it's a saying."

"Oh. You're right, anyway — it is wonderfully easy."

They ambled slowly uphill in easeful silence until Clifford Liddicoat's voice rang out on the evening air, crying, "You heller!" It was followed by a bovine bellow and the ringing clang of a gate.

"He's missed her time again, then," Adèle said in disgust.

"Who? What?" Leah asked.

"One of our cows. She was troublesome two days ago and I said we should get her to Johnny Carter's bull, down to Gwavas. Because we missed her three weeks ago, too. She's quick in and out, see. But no. He's fallen out with Carter so he had to go and bring Johnny Meagor's bull from down Scott's. And now he's missed her time again." She shook her head in exasperation.

Leah digested this awhile before she said, hesitantly, "How, actually, do you tell when ... you know ... a cow is, er, troublesome? Does that mean the same as on heat with dogs?"

"Yes. Bitches, we say."

"Yes. I meant bitches."

"You can't tell, not easily. Well, you can if you know what to look for. When you milk them. Of course, if it's a virgin heifer, she won't be in milk ... but with the others. When you wash her tids you grab a-hold of her tail and curl it round on her back ..."

"Yes, I've seen that done at Pallas Home Farm."

"Well, if she stands very still, stiff and still, with a little arch to her back, and pricked-up ears and staring eyes — as if she's looking for the bull to jump aboard … that's it. When you know the way they stand, you can't mistake it. But out in the field the other cows know. They call the bull over."

"How?"

Adèle giggled. "They say, 'Come on, Bully-Boy! There's one here a-waiting for you!'"

Leah laughed dutifully. "No, but seriously?"

"Seriously, they do. Not in words, of course. They jump up as if they were the bull. 'Bulling' we call it. And the bull sees it, of course — if you're running a bull out there with the herd — and he thinks, 'How's this? Someone trying to steal one of my young ladies from me?' and off he charges to do the job properly. The advantage of that is you don't miss the chance to serve a cow or heifer. But the disadvantage is you don't always know the day when he served her, so you don't know the day when she's going to fall due."

"Is that why you don't run a bull with the herd?"

"Yes and no. Why are you asking all this, anyway?"

"I'm thinking of taking up farming myself, actually."

Adèle ran a pace or two to get ahead of her and then, because Leah's head was bowed with the effort, bent forward to look up into her face. "You're not joking," she said.

Leah shook her head. "If there's a war, every acre will count. Whoo! These may be easy to carry but this is quite a hill!"

"Here! I'm used to it." Adèle resumed the yoke. "Are you looking for a cowhand?"

"Don't you call them dairymaids?"

The girl laughed dismissively. "You'll need something more than a dairymaid, Leah."

"Tell me why you don't run a bull with your herd."

"Because a ten-cow herd is too small. The bull doesn't work enough and he eats too much. So that's the advantage of not having one — you don't have to feed him. The disadvantage is you've only got two or three days to notice when a cow is troublesome. If you miss it — like my father's just missed it with Onehorn — that's a cow with one horn, see …"

"I'd never have guessed!"

Adèle pulled a face. "I'll swing one of these pails at you."

"You'd have to go back and refill it."

"Then I'd chuck the other over you, too — it'd be worth it. Anyway, if you miss her time, you've got to wait three weeks till she comes in again. So her next lactation is three weeks late, too — which is three weeks you're feeding her, and no milk to pay for her keep. If you're going to keep cows ..."

"Yes?"

"You're going to need someone who knows things like this. And more — much, much more. What d'you do for bloat? Two hours and the cow will be dead — what d'you do? If the calf scours after the colostrum, how d'you stop it? How d'you make a calf drink from a bucket — head downwards, see — when it's never drunk but head-upwards, from the udder, all its days? If you smell the smell of mice on a cow's breath, how d'you save her life? If a cow gets mastitis in the first flush ..."

"All right, Adèle, the point is taken." She raked the darkling sky with her gaze. "Now I just wonder where I would find a cowhand like that?"

"On your bended knees," Adèle replied haughtily.

They both laughed and nothing more was said on the subject that evening.

They arrived at the farm just as Harvey and Nicholas were coming in from setting their snares. The brothers formed two dark-purple silhouettes against the flaming red of the twilit sky, just minutes after sundown.

"He's missed Onehorn's time again," Adèle said angrily.

"My fault," Harvey admitted ruefully. "I thought I'd told him and ... oh, hallo, Miss Leah, I didn't see you there."

"Head full of tunes of glory!" Adèle said scornfully over Leah's response. "Come-us on in," she said to Leah. "You've not been inside before, have you. Mind your head."

"Hallo, Nark," she said over her shoulder as she followed Adèle indoors.

"Hallo, Thistle." He came in behind her, trying to tread the shoes off her heels.

"You just stop that," she said angrily. "You do that once again and I'll kick."

He laughed. "You know how to stop a horse kicking, don't you? Stallion or mare?"

"Tie her tail to a rafter?" She thought of Mrs Troy's cows.

"No. You do this." He ran to her side and pressed his legs tight against hers — as tight as he could without falling over. "Try and kick me now," he challenged.

"Nick!" Adèle said angrily. "That's no way to behave."

"Go on!" he challenged Leah, ignoring his sister's rebuke.

Leah, trying to think of some way to embarrass him — as he was clearly trying to embarrass her — stood her ground, relaxed, smiled, and said, "Mmm!" It was the sort of noise she'd have made if she'd picked a fruit, expecting it to be sour, and had found it sweet and palatable instead.

And it certainly embarrassed him! He leaped back as if she had stung him — which, in a sense, she had. He turned away from her and called out to Harvey, "Haven't you sorted out those snares yet?"

"Sorry." Harvey came in reading the newspaper. "Mrs Gilbert must have left this in. It says our troops are going to France tomorrow." He looked at the date, which was yesterday's. "So that's today." He glanced up. "They're landing today!"

The light in his eye made Leah shiver. In one way she admired him — his bravery, his burning passion to serve — yet in every other way she wanted him to stay. Not that she loved him but she wanted him to be there. She wanted him not to be killed.

"Will you have a dish of tea, Leah?" Adèle asked. "Or maybe you'd prefer a glass of ale?"

"Oh ..." Leah could not decide. "You have to carry all your water up from Grankum now?"

"It's the same either way, tea or ale, we brew them both."

"Ale, then, please — just a small glass."

Adèle drew glasses for them all, and one for her father, who had not yet returned from dealing with Onehorn. Leah looked around her and saw that what Blanche had told Will about old man Liddicoat being an avid reader was true. There were books everywhere — on shelves, on cupboards and sideboards, and in piles against the wall.

"Nothing exciting," Nicholas said, following her eyes. "No novels or scandalous biographies. Just lives of great men, sermons, philosophers, Milton, Bunyan ... stuff like that. Bowdler's Shakespeare."

"A German officer has killed a French corporal in the Jura," Harvey said. "The German cavalry is out scavenging for horses around Belfort — you see, they're not even *prepared* for war! The French are going to wipe the floor with them. It's going to be all over before we can get there."

"Let us hope so," Leah murmured.

He looked daggers at her. "And America will do nothing — except sell to both sides and take its profit."

"Harvey!" Adèle snapped. She looked angrily at Nicholas for holding back.

"America will do what's right for America," Leah replied, calmly sipping her ale. "And it's nothing to do with me. I live in England now. This is my country and I shall play my part here — whatever I'm called on to do."

Adèle, seeing Harvey's lip curl in a sneer, said, "Careful, you! They're not going to turn the Old Glebe into a garden. Leah's going to farm it and grow food for England. So there!"

Harvey stared at Leah in amazement. Nicholas began to laugh. "Farm it?" he asked. "You?" He laughed again.

"And what will *you* be doing?" she asked him coldly. "I gather the army turned you down?"

He stared at her as if he wondered if she was worth an explanation — and decided she wasn't. "Is Will at home tonight?" was all he said. "I want a word with him."

"Will is one of those immature young men who think it smart to have secrets from those around them," she replied. "You're familiar with the type, I'm sure. So you'll just have to walk over there and take your chance, won't you."

He opened his eyes wide in simulated terror. "Not on the night of a full moon!" he exclaimed.

She turned to Adèle. "Is your father likely to come home soon? I shouldn't like him to think me rude. But I really ought to be ..."

"He'll stay out as long as he dares," she replied. "He knows what I'll say about missing Onehorn's time again."

"The navy's going to engage the German fleet if they attack the French coast," Harvey said bitterly. "They'll pulverize them. It's going to be over at sea before we know it, too."

"I'll go, then." Leah squeezed Adèle's hand. "That thing we were talking about — I'll think it over. Would you like to come to Helston market with me next Wednesday?"

"What's this?" Nicholas asked truculently.

They both rounded on him. "Mind your own business" — "Nothing to do with you," they said simultaneously, uniting in thought if not in their choice of words.

Leah got as far as the lane when she heard someone running behind her. She knew it was the Nark before she turned round. "You don't have to," she said wearily. "I don't believe all that rubbish about ghosts."

"I do. But I also want to see Will rather urgently."

"You could wait ten minutes, surely? You don't have to accompany me."

"Very well." He folded his arms and sat down on a large stone that had fallen out of the hedge.

She walked on ten paces before turning round again. "Oh, come on, then! This is absurd."

"Mine not to reason why," he said lugubriously as he joined her. "Mine but to do and die — or not, as the case may be. Talking of doing and dying — what d'you think of Harvey, eh? Can't wait to get killed or injured!"

"He's your own brother, for heaven's sake!"

"I know. It's even more worrying. Suppose it's infectious!" After a silence he went on, "Still, that's enough about him. What about you? Are you serious about farming?"

She kept her eyes fixed ahead. "I'm not going to provide you with yet more ammo for your quips. What d'you want to see Will about? What's this news that just can't wait?"

He became serious at once. "Actually, Thistle, it's you I want to tell. Then I'd be grateful if you'd advise me."

"About what?"

"About whether I should tell Will anything or not."

She thought a while and then said, "Okay."

"It's confidential," he went on. "I haven't told any of my family and I don't intend to for some time. You'll be the only one who knows, and I'd rather like it to stay that way. So tell me now if you'd rather I kept silent."

"Why me?" she asked.

"Brutal truth?"

"If you must."

"Because your opinion would mean a lot but also — I must admit — because you wouldn't be able to exploit what I'm going to tell you."

They entered the wood, where twilight had already turned to darkness. Over Sithney, no doubt, a full moon was rising, but down here in the valley bottom all was stygian gloom. Somehow that made it easier for her to say, "All right. Go ahead and tell me. I shan't tell anyone."

Now she felt him at her side but saw him only as a darker shade against the dark. "You remember the day Will met me first?" he asked.

"Saved your life?"

He laughed. "If you like. I was trying to crush some rocks for an assay. I was looking specifically for wolframite, which is the ore of tungsten. Does the name mean anything — tungsten?"

"A very hard metal?"

"Good. The thing about it is that it retains its hardness even when white hot — filaments in electric lamps, for instance. Mix it with steel and it still keeps its hardness when red hot. It therefore makes excellent machine tools. Are you beginning to see …"

"Did you find it?" she interrupted. "This wolframite?"

"Yes. What's more, I think there's enough there to make commercial extraction profitable."

"Who has the mineral rights?" she asked.

He emitted something between a gasp and a laugh. "You don't believe in holding back, do you!" he said.

"It's the obvious question."

"Yes, well, I suppose it is. I own them — or I will, shortly — which is why I don't want anyone else to know just yet."

"Not even your own family?"

"If the white-feather fever grips people the way it did in the Boer War, and if people started taunting my family about me not enlisting, they couldn't resist blurting something out. That's all. I'm protecting them — and me. It's nothing underhand."

She laughed. "Whereas you're absolutely sure I'd never blurt out a word in defence of you!"

He fumbled in the dark and nudged her jocularly. "You read my mind, Thistle. Anyway, I've put a down-payment on the surface mineral rights. They're owned by a widow over near Cury. She thinks I'm mad, so I'll be getting them quite cheap — which is another reason for secrecy just at the moment."

"And is that why the army turned you down?"

"Something like that," he said vaguely. "I saw a man at the Ministry of Supply — who arranged for me not to be eligible for enlistment. That's the outline of it, anyway."

After a moment's thought she asked, "What do you want to see Will about?"

"I wondered if he'd like to spend the summer vacation helping me set up the extraction plant."

"Would it be hard work?"

"Backbreaking."

"Take all his energy?"

"Every last ounce. Why this interest in …"

"Then I think you should ask him the very moment you own the rights," she said firmly.

They emerged from the wood into the field where he had helped her put one in the eye of his father. "This grass came on well," he said innocently.

"Yes, I wonder why!"

"Oh, my God!" He stopped dead and stared up the hill in consternation. "Look!"

"What?"

"The moon! The full moon! I said it — and then forgot. I should never have come."

"Don't be so stupid!" She turned on her heel and continued up the slope.

"And yet I can't leave you," he whined. "Oh dear, oh dear, what am I to do?"

"Grow up," she shouted.

He ran to catch up with her. "You really don't believe in ghosts?" he asked.

"Of course not — and nor do you. You're just being very childish and silly."

"Prove it!" he challenged.

"How?" She knew it was a mistake as soon as the word was out of her mouth.

"Go and stand alone in that old tithe barn for one minute. Sixty seconds, that's all. I dare you."

She saw at once that she had but two choices — to weasel her way out of it or to accept. "Okay," she said. "If it amuses you."

But her heart was already beating double — and it had little to do with the exertion of walking up the hill.

27 Leah began dragging her feet the moment the barn door came in sight. She stared at it, hoping against hope to discover a sign saying *Danger! Keep out! Unsafe structure!* But there was no such easy luck. The door had an ethereal quality in the moonlight, as if the wood of which it was made were half dissolved in some kind of mist ... or — the thought struck a chill into her — as if the barn were dissolving away to become a ghost of its mundane self. Perhaps it had been plucked back through the centuries by the ferocity of the passions that had once played themselves out to such a grisly end within its confines. *Confines!* The very word was like a judgement knell. In less than a minute, if she persisted in this tomfoolery, she would be within those *confines.*

"You needn't go through with it, Thistle," Nicholas said with a grin. "No one knows but me, and I shan't tell."

"And me," she replied. "Besides, I'm not going to fail a challenge from *you,* of all people."

"Ooh!" he said, as if she had paid him a compliment.

"I don't mean you're *important,"* she sneered. "I mean that for me to refuse a challenge from you would be like a horse refusing a fence twelve inches high." She peeled a flake from the wood around the locking bar and murmured, "It needs a new coat of paint before winter comes."

He pulled his 'alderman' from his waistcoat pocket. "D'you want me to call out every ten seconds or what?"

"Or nothing!" She spoke with more daring than she felt. "I'll stay in there until I get bored — or until you do. Yes — that's it! You come in and get me when you get bored. Let's see how much *you* dare!"

He backed away from her in horror, putting up his hands to ward off her words as if they had physical weight. "I already told you. No power on earth, or anywhere else for that matter, would get me inside there when the full moon shines. The last person who tried it came out looking like an old man, with hair as white as snow."

"Stop it! Hair is dead. How can it change colour in minutes?"

"It's true. I swear it — an old man with hair like the driven snow. And stark, staring mad. On my honour." He came back to her side. "Please — this joke has gone far enough. Turn your face from this madcap venture."

"Who was it, anyway?" she asked, aware that she was playing for time.

"Reverend Langham."

"But he *is* an old man — and his hair is already as … oh, *you!*" She punched him hard in the chest but he rode with it.

"I didn't say what he looked like *before* he went in," he said.

"Anyway, he's not stark, staring mad."

"You haven't been paying attention to his recent sermons. 'God is in every English bullet and the Devil in every German one' — that's not the talk of a madman?" He looked up at the moon. "All the same — quite seriously — I wouldn't monkey around with the spirits on a night like this. Let's get Will and go for a walk, eh? We might find some lovers to sneer at — safely living ones, I mean."

Annoyed with him, first for challenging her then for making it sound so easy to go back on her acceptance, she put her hand to the bar. "Now don't you dare lock this again," she said — or she would have said it if an eldritch shriek from within had not frozen the last few words on her lips.

Nicholas laughed but swiftly turned it into a whimper of fear. He ran to the far side of the yard, shouting in a stagey rural accent, "Come away, mistress! This be not for mortal eyes."

"I'll come over there and hit you if you don't stop it," she told him. "It was only the spindle thing or whatever you call it — the thing the bar spins round. Probably. It needs oil."

She gave the door a tentative push with one boot. If the spindle of the bar needed oil, the hinges needed a whole oil well. It amazed her that she had never noticed their rusty state by day. The door did not swing far. The hinges were deliberately set at a slight diagonal to ensure that the door would shut by gravity, which it now did, again with a chorus of shrieks.

"Enough to waken the dead," Nicholas said in a sepulchral voice, almost in her ear.

"Oh!" she snapped at him. "You gave me the fright of my life. How d'you move so quietly?"

"You'll never 'ear no footsteps," he said in the same voice, "from the likes of we."

She cried out in frustration, "God give me strength! Now listen, you — just let that door close by itself. Understand?"

He gave up his play-acting. "Look, Thistle," he said, all reasonable again. "If you're determined to see it through, good luck to you. Take my hat off and all that. I shan't touch a thing. But if you think that door is going to close *by itself* on such a night as this ..." He laughed at her naïvety.

She longed to link arms with him and force him to go in there with her, though whether that was out of anger or fear she was not sure. A bit of both, most likely. "If you play any tricks," she said, "I'll come back out and murder you."

"And I, for my part, will come in at the very first scream," he promised with a grin.

It was the grin that finally determined her; it said, 'We both know you're not going through with it so why not give up now?' She pushed open the door again and stepped inside. It closed with a shriek and she was left in total darkness. Her annoyance had been a magnificent spur to action, but the courage it had given her evaporated the moment she was alone ...

... if, indeed, she was alone.

Had the Nark slipped inside with her? No doubt he'd think that very funny — to watch her cope with her terror. She flailed about her in the blackness, hoping to catch him. Part of her longed to catch him, to feel the touch of another human being ... to hold him ...

No! She shook off such weakness. "Nark?" she called out.

His voice came through the door. "Are you giving up already? It's only been fifteen seconds."

"No. I was just checking you hadn't slipped inside with me."

To her surprise his chuckle sent a thrill of pleasure through her. "Curses! I never thought of that. What's it like in there?"

"Oh, it's a blaze of light and they're dancing to a fiddle band and drinking cider ... what d'you *think* it's like?"

"Sorry!" After a pause he said, "Thistle?"

"What now?"

"I think you're pretty good to go through with this. You can come out, if you like. I was lying just now. It's actually coming up to the full minute."

"Not on your life, Nark! The challenge was to stand alone in the middle in the dark — not to play Pyramus and Thisbe through a crack in the door. Start counting again." She stepped out confidently into the dark, hoping to end up somewhere near the middle of the open space between the hay, the straw, and the old farm carts.

The night was suddenly full of sounds — the creaking of ancient timbers, the soughing of a wind that had not even been apparent outside ... the thunderous beating of her heart, the shivering of her breath ... and little rustling noises from living creatures of unknown variety. Never mind spectres and phantasms, this place was filled with *living* terrors — how could she have forgotten it? Mice. Spiders. Rats. *Bats!* Oh, dear God — bats! She could actually hear their squeaks now, and that was no product of a fevered imagination. Those high-pitched explosions of sound, set at the very limits of human hearing, now over there, now over here ... they were unmistakable.

A moment later one brushed her face, or came close enough to fan her cheek with the breath of its wings. Only a superhuman effort on her part, aided by the knowledge that the Nark was out there just waiting for some sign of her weakness, prevented her from shrieking out the horror that now gripped her; for among the many creatures that render the night terrible, bats were the most frightening of all to her. No matter that she was wearing a bonnet and that it was tied tight around her head, there was still plenty of loose hair for a bat to get caught up in. It took little imagination to think how one of those squeaky, furry, flea-ridden creatures would writhe there and scratch her with its sharp little claws and bite her neck with those needle-teeth.

Her flesh crawled. She cringed from the dark, yet the only space into which she might escape was deeper into another dark, full of terrors as yet unimagined. Nothing else but that knowledge could have made her do what she did next, which was to crouch down, catch up the hem of her skirt at the back and draw it up, up around her waist, up over her shoulders, over her bonnet, where at last she pulled it down like a shawl all around her head.

"Two minutes," Nicholas called out but she didn't even hear.

She stayed there, crouching down, flinching from the bats, not comfortable but no longer in abject terror — until she remembered the rats. To say she remembered them is too mild. She actually *saw* one crouching stock still not a yard from her.

For, now that her eyes were growing used to the dark, enough moonlight stole through a myriad small cracks between the roof tiles and around the doors and window shutters to reveal the foul creature. Or the shape of it, at least, if not the texture of hair or the colour of dread. Nor, in this case, the gleam of its beady eyes. In a way that was more horrifying yet — the thought that the brute was watching her through hooded eyes.

Why didn't it move?

Then she thought of it moving ... crawling toward her where she crouched ... disappearing under her petticoats ... Her flesh crawled with loathing for it. But if she stood up again — never mind the bats — it might make a run at her and her petticoats would fall around her ankles and it would be trapped underneath. Sharp little claws making ladders in her stockings and then climbing them ... She froze in an agony of indecision.

There was a stick nearby. It would fall just within her grasp if she stretched to her utmost. Slowly, painfully slowly, she reached out her arm, never for one moment taking her eyes off the malevolent little rodent.

It still did not move.

She almost overbalanced but she got the tips of her fingers beyond the stick and, after resting on them for a moment, managed to tweak it toward her. By and by she manipulated it close enough both to recover her balance and to get her fingers around it. Then she wasted no time but raised it above her head and brought it down with an almighty thwack on the rat.

It did not run. It did not even flinch. It made no sound. Instead it clung to the stick and flew up in the air when she raised it for a possible second strike. It had no weight. It vanished, literally into thin air — into the dark, thin air. She stood there, shoulders hunched, eyes closed, shivering as she waited for it to fall upon her from out of that same thin air.

"Thistle?" Nicholas called from outside, from another world, from a time she had almost forgotten.

She heard a voice call from her throat: "Yes?"

"That's five minutes. I think you've proved your point. Also I'm getting cold."

She laughed, feebly — or sounds she dimly remembered as laughter came out of her.

"May I come in?"

She looked to see if her skirts were back in place — an everyday action that brought her to her everyday self at last.

"No one's stopping you," she called out.

He thrust open the door and kicked a stone in place to hold it ajar. The hinges complained again but the sound evoked no terrors now. The sight of him, however, was enough to rekindle more than a little frisson. He stood there, uncertain of her mood, unwilling to move until more sure of it. With his legs braced apart he looked as if he were carved in anthracite; the moonlight upon him was silver-blue and brilliant enough to burn; his long black shadow reached into the barn, across the silvered floor, all the way to where she stood.

The scene was sinister enough to recall for her, and for the first time since she had stepped inside the barn, the unquiet dead who had been supposed to terrify her. She wondered if Catherine Geach had stood just there, where her feet were now planted, and had seen the black shape of her erstwhile lover, John Lidgeycot, standing there at the door with his long moonshadow reaching out toward her ...

Her fear was rather contrived but it prickled at the back of her neck like the real thing. Then, as her eyes scanned the length of the Nark's shadow, she saw the piece of rag she had mistaken for a rat. She began to laugh.

Relieved, too, he started to walk toward her. Her laughter might even have become a touch hysterical if at that moment a barn owl, annoyed at her intrusion and infuriated at his, had not swept down between them. It swooped as silently as only an owl may swoop, so that it seemed to materialize from nothing, and it hooted as it rose again to its nest.

Without thought she uttered a cry, sprang to him, and flung her arms about him. Instinctively his arms enfolded her. "It's all right, Thistle," he said. "It was only an owl."

She just clung to him and shivered. He began to understand something of the torments she had just endured. "Why should we fear the dead?" she asked. "When the world of the living has terrors enough!"

It really was very pleasant to be held in a man's arms again, even the Nark's.

"It's all right," he said again, patting her awkwardly on the back. "It's over."

"I thought I saw a rat." She looked up at him.

Their eyes dwelled in each other's, unreadable in the moon-light. Slowly, hesitantly he lowered his lips to hers. They met. It was as if she were brushed with something glowing, alive, electrical, unearthly. Her senses ached at it. She vaguely recalled similar feelings, as if in another life, but they had been mere harbingers of this.

It did not last. In the very act of surrender some other part of her, a part that did not welcome this at all, asserted itself and made her pull away. "No," she murmured. "No! It wasn't as ... I didn't mean ... that wasn't the ... Let me go!"

She wriggled free but continued to hold him by the arms.

He pulled himself together with obvious effort. He looked about guiltily, even though he knew that no one else could have been watching. "You're right," he said. His voice was thin and shivery. "Bad mistake. Shouldn't have happened. In fact it didn't happen — right?" He took a different grip on her and began to hop up and down on the spot, dancing to some tune in his head. "The fiddlers are striking up again. What a jolly tune!" He began to sing it: "Oh, I'm a proper country chap, Me family come from Fareham, At 'ome they got some more like I, And they well knows 'ow to rear 'em!" And as he sang he spun her away in a frenzied twostep, round and round and round ...

"What on earth is going on!" Will's cry halted them at last.

They spun down to a halt and turned, breathless and panting, to face him.

He was standing in the doorway just as Nicholas had stood a few minutes earlier. Nick froze, seeing in Will what Leah's imagination had made of him in that same stance. "Why, 'tis John Lidgeycot, mistress!" he whispered in simulated terror.

She shook him and said, "We did all that — remember?"

"Oh, yes." He was chastened.

William laughed. "Are you both mad?"

"No," she replied lightly. "Just dancing. The Nark challenged me to be alone in here, in the dark, with these supposed ghosts."

"And?"

"She stayed in five minutes," Nicholas said.

"And?" William insisted.

Leah smiled at Nicholas. "Nothing happened — did it."

"No," he admitted ruefully. "Nothing happened."

28 The cattle market was within strolling distance of the Camborne School of Mines, so Will escorted his sister there while their father spoke with his tutors. His head was full of the plans to extract tungsten from the wulframite Nicholas had discovered at several sites around Wheal Fortune, for young Liddicoat had told him all about it. He could hardly wait to get started. The little tableau he had interrupted in the barn on the night of the full moon also intrigued him, of course.

"Are you really going to buy cattle today, Sis?" he asked.

"If I see a real bargain, sure," she replied, though in truth she had not the slightest intention of doing so. She just wanted to see how people behaved at cattle auctions so she wouldn't make a complete fool of herself next Wednesday.

"How will you know?" he asked.

"Oh," she said vaguely, "I haven't wasted my time when visiting Mrs Troy, you know."

"Ben Coad is sweet on you."

"So?"

"So make use of it. Get him to help you. He could tip you the wink when to bid and when not to."

She halted and stared at him. For a moment she wondered if Coad had spilled the beans; but Will was so pleased at his own cleverness that it seemed unlikely. "You really have the most devious, underhand spirit, Will," she said. "I wouldn't dream of putting myself under such an obligation to him." But the uncomfortable thought that she had done precisely that now began to nag at her.

"He'd do it anyway. He's been sweet on you since the day we came. He'd do it without expecting anything …" He clapped a hand to his mouth and spun a full circle on one toe. "I shouldn't be telling you this."

"Oh, Will!" She pinched him playfully. "What game is this?" His all-too-accurate analysis of her actions and motives continued to disturb her, though.

"It's no game," he assured her. "Or it's the oldest game of all. It's not a good idea for young females to know what havoc they can wreak with the male psyche. Nor should they know how absurdly monomaniacal — is that the word? Like Ahab and the White Whale? — how monomaniac it ..."

"It doesn't matter. It's all rubbish anyway — what you're trying to say. Can women possess men's minds? Nonsense! Men find it only too easy *not* to think of us for ninety-nine percent of the time. Whether they're hauling fish from the sea or tin from the earth ... or hunting the fox or mauling each other to death in the boxing ring — when do you think of us *then?"*

"Ha!" He raised his hands to the skies, inviting all heaven to bear witness. "About every ten minutes, if you want to know."

Something despairing in his tone made her withhold the scornful reply she had been about to make. "Truly?" she asked.

He nodded glumly. "Maybe not if someone were trying to punch me senseless in the ring. But at all other times — take it from me!"

"You think of Blanche Curnow every ten minutes — is that what you're claiming?"

He hesitated and then said, "Yes."

"How?" she challenged. *"What* d'you think of? Just her face? Or kissing her? Or ... what?"

"You know," he said awkwardly.

"No I don't."

"Well, what do you think about when you think of Nicholas?"

"Nicholas?" She hoped her alarm sounded like surprise. It was true that she had been thinking about him quite a lot these past few days. Not every ten minutes, but more often than she wished. She didn't want to think of him at all but somehow he kept intruding around the edges of her consciousness and then, before she could stop herself, there he was, right in the centre of things. And not just his face, either. She could still feel his lips on hers and the sweet, burning sensation that had filled her ...

But then, within moments, she was usually able to shrug it off again. It had been the merest lapse, a few seconds only ... she had been so emotionally stirred by her ordeal ... and then the surprise of that owl swooping down on them like that ... and the Nark taking advantage of her weakness ... it meant nothing.

So had Will read it in her face?

"I *saw* you," he said when it became clear she was not going to deny it openly.

"Dancing in the barn! So?"

"No, Sis, I saw you kiss him. I didn't deliberately set out to spy but I was crossing the yard and the door was wide open and the moonlight ..."

"Okay, okay — I was there, too, remember. And *I* didn't kiss *him* — just for your information. On the contrary, he kissed me and I stopped him."

"Sure!" he said superciliously.

"I did too!"

He shrugged. "If that's the way you want to gloss it, I won't argue with you."

His attitude annoyed her so much that she blurted out, "Anyway, it's not Blanche Curnow's face that distracts you every ten minutes, is it! It's that Pansy Tregear's. You don't fool me, Jackson!"

She thought he would respond angrily — indeed, she rather hoped for it, so that they could agree to change the subject. But instead he sighed and said, "I know. Isn't it stupid?"

The response took her aback for a moment but she saw it was a chance she could not waste. "Yes, Will, it *is* stupid. It's just about the stupidest thing you could ever embark on. There can be absolutely no question of an alliance between you and her. She's a pleasant enough girl, I grant ..."

"Oh, but she has no idea of marrying. Not me. Not anyone. Not just yet, anyway, she says."

Leah did not know what to say to this; all the arguments she had begun marshalling in her mind evaporated. "You've discussed such things with her?" was all she could ask.

"First thing. I mean it was the first thing *she* said."

"What? You mean to say she just walked up to you and said, out of the blue ..."

"No!" He lolled his head wearily. "If you must know, I tried to steal a kiss — only to have her turn round and hand it me on a plate. On a great big silver chafing dish, in fact. Bowled me over, I can tell you. I've never known such a passionate kiss. So I got embarrassed and started apologizing — but she just laughed and said it was all right but if I wanted more, I should pick my moments more carefully."

The market lay a quarter of a mile beyond the level crossing, which closed as they approached it. So they had to wait for a train to pass through.

"What on earth did she mean by that?" Leah asked with sinking heart.

"Well, without repeating the whole conversation, the upshot was — or is — that she doesn't want marriage or even a steady beau but she's not averse to a little flutter. Or even a big flutter. And she says I'm not to get downhearted if she sparks with other lads, too."

"Indeed!" Leah was astounded, not just at the girl's effrontery, but at her brother's calm acceptance of it. "The baggage will clearly have to go."

"I know." His tone was neutral.

"Well, you seem to take it calmly enough!"

"It won't stop us meeting. She's expecting it, anyway. She thought she'd get her marching orders last Thursday. You saw at once, didn't you — that there was something going on."

'Yes, but I didn't think it was as serious as this."

A big locomotive, all valves closed, went hissing through the crossing and pulled up in the station with a screech of brakes. It was the express from Paddington, Will said. The signalman cranked a wheel up in his box overlooking the crossing and the gate swung open again in a series of lazy jerks. Leah opened and closed her parasol smartly to throw off the smuts. "You've got some on your collar," she said. "Don't move."

She took off her glove and delicately lifted the soot away on her little fingernail. He smiled at her and said, "It's getting harder and harder to play momma, huh?"

"Only because it *ought* to be less and less necessary. Doesn't Pansy mind about losing her place? She was keen enough to get it." She pulled on her glove again and they resumed their stroll.

"She'll be sorry, of course. She thinks the world of you. You're a sort of heroine to her. But she won't have any difficulty getting another place. The naval stores in Plymouth are crying out for hands, male or female. And the munitions factories in London, Birmingham … all over. Girls can easily earn double what they'd get in service."

Leah's heart sank at these words. If the men were going to volunteer all over the place and the women could be enticed away like that by high wages, she could see herself trying to run the farm single-handed — which wasn't at all what she'd had in mind. "And they'd take her? Just like that?"

"They'd take her. And she wouldn't stay down on the workbench for long, either. She's too bright. She can read and write with ease and her mind's as sharp as any blade."

"Hmm." Leah decided that sacking the girl was no answer. Something more subtle, more cooperative, more female, was called for here. "And you're really stuck on her, eh?"

"Seems so." He nodded grimly. "More than she is on me. Maybe that's why. Wounded pride."

After some thought Leah said, "It would be ridiculous to talk of love after so short a while but, er, these feelings you have for her, would they be strong enough to make you *respect* her? You know what I'm referring to, I'm sure."

"On my side, yes. But she doesn't particularly welcome that sort of respect. She says she wakes up each morning and thinks, 'I'll never be as young again as I was yesterday!' She says time is short and we could all be killed in the war, and ..."

"But that's crazy! As if the Germans are ever going to overrun the whole of England!"

"No — we *men*. She thinks all the young men could get killed and then she'd spend the rest of her life thinking of all the chances she missed."

They turned in at the gate of the market.

"Okay," Leah said. "We'll have to talk about this again. But now it's business."

There was no doubting where the cattle were being auctioned. The almost unintelligible singsong — which sounded like *'Hat* four five *hat* four five I'm-bid can-I-hear ten *surely!'* — was coming from a circle of iron stanchions capped by an iron-honeycomb roof clad in lead sheet. The horizontal tubes between the stanchions supported a motley of ragged boys and farmers in leggings and gaiters. Gnarled sticks were everywhere, clutched in equally gnarled hands that prodded the ground or the cattle with indifference. One farmer who passed them as they stood there, uncertain as to how closely they dared approach, brought his stick down with metronome regularity on the back of the cow he was driving. He did not even seem to know he was doing it, for he was engaged in earnest conversation with the man at his side all that while. To Leah's surprise the cow did not seem to notice it, either; he might as well have been swatting flies on her back for all the response she made.

"Want to see a bit closer, do 'ee?" the man's companion called out after he had passed them.

"We wouldn't be in the way?" Leah asked.

With an expansive sweep of his arm he waved them to join him, peeling away from his companion at the same time. "I'll warrant you not," he said. "On holidays, are you? George is the name. Henry George of Copperhouse." He held out a clean but weatherbeaten hand.

When they shook it and introduced themselves he placed them at once. "My wife's aunt had a half-sister who married a nephew to your great-grandfather, William Carrington of Leedstown," he said.

Leah felt awful that she couldn't bring herself to care all that much about such tenuous links, despite their importance to Cornish folk. "Isn't that amazing!" she said brightly.

"Not really," he replied. "Why, I daresay half the people you can see would be able to find *some* connection with you. Hardly so strong as mine, of course, but there'd be something there. So" — he smiled genially at what he considered to be his fairly close if long-lost relations — "you do want to see how we belong to buy and sell bullocks, eh?"

"Oh, is it bullocks today?" Leah was disappointed. "I thought it was milch cows."

"Why, so 'tis, maid. We do call all cattle 'bullocks' down here in Cornwall, see?"

"Except calves and yarlings," a nearby farmer put in.

"Except they," he agreed. "Whoo-up, Tregembo!" He patted a ringside farmer on the shoulder. "There's two Carringtons of Leedstown came all the way from Americay to learn how we do buy and sell bullocks."

Leah, feeling dreadful, started telling the man she had not the faintest wish to deprive him of his place at the ringside. But he grinned and almost pushed her in, saying, " 'Tis nothing but wisht and jealous stock, anyway."

When Leah, rather than William, took the vacant place, Farmer George asked the youth if he wasn't interested in farming. William explained about being at the School of Mines. "Wise man!" was the reply. "There's still more money underground in Cornwall than ever there will be over it, and that's a fact, my son."

Then he noticed how keenly Leah was watching the proceedings and transferred his attention to her.

"You might think she a'n't got much milk," he said of a first-calf heifer in the ring. " 'Cos her bag is so small. But you won't see no bag at all on a mare, yet she'll yield four gallon a day to her foal. That's more'n what that heifer'll give. You can't tell nothing from the size o' the bag, see."

And he went on doling out a nugget for each 'bullock' that entered the ring. He told her what sort of backbone she should look for — straight as a ruler — what arrangement of the hips, what slope of breastbone, what smell on the breath, what thickness of milk-stream ... and half-a-dozen other pointers to a good or bad cow. In between times she watched the farmers and dealers who were actively bidding — how they hardly ever looked at the auctioneer (and yet never let their eyes stray too far from him, either), how they prodded the cattle and, now and then, climbed into the ring to feel their bags. All the cows had been left deliberately unmilked that morning and so they were distended to a painful degree. Many of them spontaneously let down their milk at the slightest touch. The floor of the ring was spotted white and slippery with it.

Above all, she noted how they managed to bid, some by the merest glance up at the auctioneer, some by a diagonal tilt of the head, some by a barely perceptible nod. The most placid of all folded their hands around the knobs of their sticks and lifted one finger in a single wag.

"Blink your eyes at the wrong moment," Farmer George said, "and you could end up on Carey Street!"

She thanked him when the auctions were done and hoped they might meet again at some other market — to which he replied that they surely would.

As they went away another farmer who had been standing nearby, listening to Henry George's good advice, caught up with them and said, "I'll tell 'ee one thing, maid — how *I* do buy a cow. I don't care if she's got five legs of different sizes and horns all down her backbone — if she'll yield ten gallon a day, I'll buy her!" Laughing at his own wit, he went away without waiting for her reply.

"I thought *you* were going to buy something," William said accusingly as they started retracing their steps back into town.

"No," she replied scornfully. " 'Twas nothing but wisht and jealous stock today — or so I'm informed! I wonder what jealous means in that context?"

"Huh!" he exclaimed in a hollow tone. "Jealous is jealous is jealous! Take it from one who knows!"

"Oh, Will!" She rubbed his arm tenderly, anxiously. "I'm sorry — truly, I am."

"Will you sack her?"

"No. That would be too easy. I mean, as you pointed out, it wouldn't solve anything."

"There *is* no solution," he said glumly.

"Don't be so defeatist. There's *always* a solution."

"Yeah! Lock her up in a tall tower!"

She stared at him in bewilderment.

"Well," he said, "it would keep the other fellows at bay."

Leah, catching his drift, laughed at the idea. "She'd only grow her hair long enough for them to climb up."

" She'd do it overnight, too!" he agreed.

"But little changes can achieve big results. Remember what Pa always told us — 'A ten-cent shave and a five-cent shoeshine can turn a thousand-dollar deal'? We've just got to find those little buttons to press that will make Pansy …"

"You don't understand the problem," he complained.

"Okay. You tell me, then."

He checked all about them before he replied: "I love her enough to *respect* her — as you put it. Keep my hands to myself, in other words. Her honour is like my own. Now girls are supposed to swoon with gratitude when they meet such a man. But that's not what Pansy wants at all." He groaned and mimed the tearing-out of hair.

"Go on," she urged.

"In all those penny dreadfuls they read down in the kitchen it's always the young master who has his wicked way with the poor innocent maid. Often, one of his arguments is that if she doesn't yield to his demands, he'll transfer his affections elsewhere and some other lucky girl will get him. I'm looking for the story where it's the maid who tells the master that if he doesn't have *her* wicked way with her, she'll find some other lucky — and willing — man. I want to know how *that* tale ends."

"Mmh," Leah replied. "You're not the only one."

29   The last of the fatstock was sold at ten-thirty. There was a little ritual in which Ben Coad put away one set of books and took out another; it was matched by a ringside ritual, too, in which butchers withdrew and farmers took their place. Butchers wore gumboots; farmers leather and gaiters. Butchers ran their hands along the backs of the cattle and squeezed their flanks; farmers stood back and appraised the shape, or they bent and felt the udder. Butchers hardly ever looked a beast in the eye.

On Adèle's advice Leah had dressed in a plain suit of brown serge with a skirt that finished several inches above the ankle — not that her stout leather boots made for much of a revelation. She wore very little underneath it — a corset and one petticoat — for the day would have been hot even for a naturist. Her father, who came with them to make sure she did not disgrace the family, was the only man dressed for the occasion — in a thin suit of unbleached linen and a straw hat. Farmers in their summer-and-winter tweeds looked at him with envy and wondered if they'd ever dare put up anything so sensible.

Though the old man kept in the background, his presence dampened that spirit which might otherwise have led to many a ribald comment around the ring as his daughter made clear her intention to bid. She saw farmers going up to Coad, one by one, to remind him how they would signal their bids or to tell him of a change to their usual system. The others stayed back a respectful distance meanwhile, like customers in a bank. Leah waited patiently and apart from them. When the last had had his little say, she made her approach.

There was a ripple of surprise, which she affected to ignore.

Coad ignored it, too. "I've thougnt out a tactic," he told her. "There's no time to explain it now. Just trust me. You remember my signal?"

"With the pencil — yes. But how do I signal *my* bids?"

"Just call out yes or put it in plain English. Make every bid obvious. That's part of the tactics. It'll unsettle them — a bit of openness and honesty always does." He chuckled and pretended to be laughing *at* her.

"Is it okay if I feel their bags outside the ring? I can hardly climb over to go into it. Not in this skirt."

He said that would be fine and so, with dry mouth and mounting excitement, she and Adèle went to the gangway leading into the ring, where the first bullock was waiting. She was a second-calf heifer with her calf at her heel, a little bull just ready for weaning. The gangway was about eight feet wide, between posts of cast iron that time and a thousand hands had burnished. The two women made minuscule additions to that polish as they stooped and climbed between the middle and upper bars — to cries of 'Oh my eye!' and 'Here comes the Light Brigade!'

"Do we want a bull calf?" Leah asked Adèle, ignoring the rabble as she stooped to feel the heifer's bag.

"You've got enough grass," she replied. "You could neuter him, bring him on to six months, and then put him back here in the fatstock sale as a yarling store."

"What's this on her bag? High up on this side — can you feel it?" Leah stood back to let Adèle have a go.

"Just a vein," was the verdict.

"Sure it's not mastitis?"

"No. Mastitis feels like a cuttlefish bone under the skin. That's just a vein. A milk vein, they do call it."

"And it's not going to burst or anything horrid?"

Adèle just laughed. "D'you think you're really cut out for this-here farming, maid?" she asked.

"I just want to get everything absolutely right, that's all."

"Ready, gentlemen!" Coad called out, adding as an afterthought, "And *ladies!*"

There was a universal whoop at that and those few who had not noticed the two females craned their necks and followed the pointing sticks and pipestems. With excess gallantry the farmers near the entrance to the ring made way for them.

"Now, first off the mark today," Coad began, "is a fine dairy shorthorn, second-calf heifer. She gave five hundred and thirty gallons in her first lactation. Her mother belongs to give over seven hundred. Look at that conformation! She'd be a credit to any herd so what do I hear for a starter? Twelve pounds? Who'll start me at twelve now surely?"

To Leah's amazement she saw him making the pencil signal.

Panic seized her. Had she got it wrong? Was she to bid when he *wasn't* making the signal? No. She was sure that the signal meant bid. But, even if she had not been at Camborne market the previous Saturday, she'd have known that you *never* accept the auctioneer's opening call — not in any sort of auction.

But she also remembered his final injunction: 'Trust me!'

It was asking the moon of her but she decided to do just that.

"Come on, now. Twelve pounds surely?" Coad asked in long-practised desperation that fooled nobody. "She'll go for double, so you might as well."

"Yes!" Leah called out in a voice twice as shrill as she would have wished. "Twelve pounds!"

"Are you mad?" Adèle whispered at her side.

A stunned silence fell. Coad's mouth dropped. Heads turned between them as if watching a pingpong match. Coad should have been teaching at drama school, Leah thought. His surprise was absolute and his recovery from it a masterpiece. "We have twelve pounds, my lords! Who'll make it guineas?"

The pencil was held quite still in his hand; Leah waited.

One or two farmers began to look more closely at the heifer. They had seen Adèle earlier and now began to suspect she'd seen something they had missed — for twelve pounds was close to the expected finishing price for even a good second-calf heifer. Two of them climbed into the ring and felt her bag. One gave a barely perceptible nod.

"Guineas I'm bid!" Coad crowed. "Do I hear thirteen surely?"

He was fiddling with the pencil again. This time Leah had no hesitation. "Yes," she called out.

"You're mad," Adèle hissed even more furiously.

Leah had not told her of the arrangement. In her pride she wanted her friend to think the day's triumph was — or would be, when it was done — all her own work. "I know what I'm doing," she told her. "Just wait and see."

"Thirteen," Coad announced. "Thirteen on my left. I'll take guineas surely. Will anyone give me thirteen guineas?"

Someone gave a signal. Leah did not see who, but someone had clearly decided he was missing something that others could see. He wasn't going to be left out.

Coad asked for fourteen pounds — and gave Leah the signal. She bid fourteen.

Then guineas. Then fifteen ... sixteen ... until the bid reached an astronomical seventeen pounds − the price of a good, mature cow. And that bid was hers.

At that ridiculous point the rest dropped out. "Will someone give me guineas?" Coad asked with a knowing smile. And once again he gave her the signal.

She was now so committed to following him that she called out her yes without a thought.

Everyone laughed. She looked around in bewilderment, for if Coad could act his head off, so could she. The auctioneer laid down his pencil and smiled at her. With infinite patience and kindliness he said, "The bid is already with you, Miss Carrington. If you *insist* on paying guineas, I'll accept them, of course, but if we're all done" − he surveyed the others with comically raised eyebrows − "she's yours for seventeen pounds. And a bargain at that, if I may say so!" He banged the stone that doubled as gavel and paperweight.

Roars of laughter surrounded her, and her blushes owed nothing to her acting skill, such as it was.

Adèle stared at her miserably and John Carrington came up behind them, trembling with anger. "I think we'll go home now," he hissed in her ear, "and pay Ben Coad to select a good starter herd for us."

For a moment Leah did not move. She knew this was one of those big moments in her life, when a choice in any direction would affect everything she did thereafter. She gathered her feelings, drew a deep breath, and turned to look her father in the eye. "This is my money I'm spending," she reminded him. "My birthday present."

Her sudden calm disconcerted him, but he came back quickly enough. "Squandering," he said. "And it's my pride and self-respect you're squandering along with it."

"You said you'd trust me."

"I said I'd trust you to make a good bargain − which you're clearly incapable of doing. All you seem able to make is monkeys − out of both of us."

"You said you'd trust me to the end and I'm going to hold you to it," she replied, still in that icy-calm voice.

Inside herself, however, she was anything but calm. Her interior voice was shrieking out a prayer that Coad knew what he was doing, or it would be a long time before she'd be able to walk through Helston without giving rise to sniggers all down the street behind her.

The next bullock was in the ring by now, a big friesland in her sixth lactation; her calf had already been weaned from her. Coad knew his clientèle better than they knew themselves. He knew they had scented blood and that, since all Cornish humour is centred on people and their foibles and follies, they saw the chance of a tale that would regale many a bar and hearth down the years. The cow was worth, at most, fifteen pounds but, through signals to her, Coad pushed the bids up beyond that. The farmers cooperated with hearty fervour. When one of them bid eighteen-ten in hope of pushing her higher yet, Coad stopped signalling to her. It did more than leave the poor farmer out on a limb; it did more than ensure that the butt of those jokes round hearth and bar would be him rather than Leah Carrington; most important of all, it cleared the way for Leah's uncrowded bidding for the rest of the auction. From then on, no sensible man was going to risk running her up above a reasonable price for any bullock.

Over the following hour, out of twenty-three put up in the ring, she bought six — for a grand total of eighty-five pounds. All, except the first, were bargains by any measure. And if you looked at the thing in a wider context, that had been a worthwhile bargain, too, in its way.

Leah, with Adèle still in tow, joined her father and the three of them leaned against the railings round the stall she'd hired for her purchases. "Well?" she said.

"A motley lot," he replied.

"I don't care if they've got five legs each of different sizes and horns growing out of their spines, if their yield is good, they'll do me. But that wasn't the point of my asking."

He shifted uneasily and said, "Okay, they look pretty good to me. I grant you that."

"I don't think any farmer here could claim to have done better," Adèle put in.

"That's still not what I asked," Leah insisted.

"I know," he said ruefully. "Tell me, did you *plan* that little coup right at the beginning?"

"Or what?" she asked cautiously.

"Or did you realize you'd dug yourself in a hole and so then you improvised your way out of it?"

Briefly Leah wondered which would reflect more glory. The second, probably. She was just about to confess to it when caution overruled her; after all, Ben Coad just might let something slip one day. "It was sort of planned," she admitted. "You can't map out every little move but you can set up the general shape of the thing."

She hoped that was vague enough.

Carrington shook his head sadly. "I think I retired at just the wrong time," he said. "Never mind Kernow and Daughter — Carrington and Daughter would have made one heck of a team at a pork-belly auction."

Leah grabbed his arm and laughed as she hugged it. "Oh, Pa!" she said, blushing in her confusion.

"Mea culpa! I should have had more faith in my own bloodline." He leaned forward and addressed Adèle past his daughter. "Well, young lady, is your brother going to make a fortune at Wheal Fortune?"

"He thinks so," she said dismissively.

"It's not an idle question," he continued. "If I'm not going to squander a small fortune on my planned garden, I shall have to put that money somewhere. Wars have made lots of men rich but they've never increased the value of idle cash. That was true in Ancient Egypt and it's true today. So is Nicholas Liddicoat a good investment?"

Adèle, realizing at last that he was serious, despite the joking edge to his question, gave an answer whose seeming naïvety surprised him. She said, "Maybe it's just what he needs."

"Everyone needs capital," he remarked.

"Yes, but Nick needs it in a different way. He needs to know that someone believes in him — and believes in him enough to put up the capital."

Now it was Leah's turn to be surprised. It had never occurred to her that the Nark might be lacking in self-confidence.

Carrington made no immediate reply. He stared at Adèle as if seeing her in a new light, then at his daughter — ditto — then at the heavens.

Later, when they had driven the cattle home and baptized the brand new galvanized pails with their milk, he joined Leah at the field gate and said, "Well?" in the precise tone she had used earlier, back at the market.

"Look at them," she said. "They don't know which one is boss. It's more important than food."

"It's all about food, actually. Who gets the lion's share. Nature red in tooth and claw!"

"We're the same — humanity. We're worse, in fact. Cattle fight for a bit of the field. We fight to divide the whole world. And yet ..." She sighed.

"And yet what?"

She leaned her head on his shoulder and said, "I think this is probably the happiest day of my life, Pa."

"It can only go downhill from here on in, eh?"

She chuckled. "You didn't come out here to gloat. When you said 'well?' just now — what are you asking, really?"

"About Adèle?"

"What about her?"

"About what she said this morning. That was pretty astute, don't you think?"

"She is astute. I've never thought her anything else."

"I was watching the new girl — Pansy — while she was running the milk through the cooler. Talking with her about this and that. She's convinced herself that all the young men hereabout are going to be taken by this war. She doesn't think it'll be over by Christmas."

"Has this anything to do with, you know, what we were talking about before?"

"In a way. If Pansy's fears are right — and one can't rule them out — the world is going to need young women who can do what you did to those farmers this morning and what Adèle almost did to me."

"Why?" Leah's laughter was slightly bewildered. "What did she *almost* do to you today?"

"She almost got me signing a cheque there and then, on the spot. She turned a casual, rather vague inquiry into a notion I'm now taking very seriously."

"You could set up a partnership," Leah suggested. "Young Liddicoat's know-how — and mineral rights — plus Will's enthusiasm and muscle power plus your capital."

"Just so," he said.

30 Over the next few weeks there were more bovine skirmishes in the fields of the Old Glebe as Leah brought her herd up to a dozen milkers and the newcomers contended for their place in the pecking order. She became a well-known and ultimately accepted figure in the market and, although she could not go into the pubs, there were plenty of farmers who had signed the pledge and who therefore congregated round the Band of Hope's mobile tea canteen, which toured all the markets to cater for them. 'The cup that cheers but not inebriates!' was its motto, painted in a rainbow arch over the serving hatch.

In sober conversations over many such cups Leah picked up much useful farming lore; but the main thing she learned was that farmers are a maddeningly reticent lot. They'd admit to keeping pigs but if she asked how many, they'd reply, 'a few' or 'quite a few' or 'some' or 'it do vary.' All her particular questions elicited the same sort of response; they were generous with generalities, parsimonious with the particular. She could have asked Mrs Troy and got a direct answer at once, of course — which was what her father had advised when she first thought of building the dairy herd — but pride made her want to go it alone as far as she could.

Eventually, however, she found the answer. She hired a labourer called John Hamden, who came with Ben Coad's recommendation. He was then working as a hedge-trimmer for the county council. Though he wore an old-fashioned frock coat and a battered top hat, both green with age, he looked like a wild man, with his pale blue, staring eyes set deep in their sockets, and his hair like a lion's mane. A bit like old-man Liddicoat, in fact. Because his county-council job took him through many parishes at a time when most husbands were away at work, he was rumoured to have sired a large number of children in the district. But he acknowledged only seven, all by his wife. Because of his reputation the maids giggled when he spoke to them and they treated him with a half-comic, half-serious awe. But he certainly knew about farming and farm animals. If a cow were off her food, he'd know at once if it was a matter for the vet or whether she'd find the right herb and cure her colic by herself. He could tie knots that would never come undone of their own accord, yet they'd fall apart with a single tug at the loose end. He knew when a cow would 'come in troublesome' before her behaviour made it obvious. He taught Leah how to toss a sheaf of corn twice as high for half the effort.

All his help was over little things like that. When she asked general questions — should she get in a few pigs, or some chicken, or what catch crops would be best for this or that field, and so on — he would shrug and say, "That's your caper, missiz." It was so frustrating that, while the farmers would never be specific, and Hamden would never be general, there was still a large area in the middle where neither would tread.

Salvation came when, one day in the market, the stress became too much and she said, "Hamden thinks I should get in a dozen sows and keep my own boar." She chose the figure at random, just to put down a marker somewhere and see if anyone laughed. It was a stroke of accidental genius. For the farmer who would keep his own counsel all the way to the grave if she asked a direct question would feel his own honour imperilled if he let such ridiculous advice from a jumped-up hedge-trimmer pass him by without comment.

"That Hamden," one farmer said, "do know more about breeding and less about pigs than any man west of Plymouth!"

And thus she learned that four to six sows would be a more reasonable number. And since John Carter of Gwavas kept not only a stud bull but two stud boars as well, she could save the expense — and danger — of keeping a boar herself.

Soon Leah was crediting John Hamden with the most surprising opinions across the entire range of twentieth-century agriculture. In response to which she went on to learn that a couple of hundred chicken would bring in a useful weekly income. Also she'd missed the season now but if she could put up a long glasshouse by January, she could get a tomato crop next year; tomatoes were doing very well since it had been proved they weren't poisonous — and she could overwinter the same beds with lettuce and spring onions, which Giles Curnow was always looking for.

She discussed each of these ideas with her father but his attitude was that she'd learn more, and learn it better, if she made her own mistakes. Anyway, he was all fired up again with the idea of a sleeping partnership in Nicholas Liddicoat's tungsten business; he and Jimmy Troy were thinking of putting up the £5,000 jointly.

At last Leah felt she had acquired enough knowledge to try her tentative plans out on Mrs Troy. She drove over to Pallas Home Farm one Saturday in September, when she knew the woman would be doing the milking. By then she could milk as well as any maid who'd been reared to the business, so she took an extra pail and stool and between them they finished the job in record time. Mrs Troy linked arms with her as they drove the cattle back into the field. "I think, dear," she said, "that it's time we dropped the formalities and called each other Elizabeth and Leah, don't you?"

Leah's heart swelled with pride. Nothing could have done more to make her feel she had *arrived* than to be on such terms with one of the leaders of local society. She stammered her thanks and added that, back in America, she'd always been told the English were such stuffed shirts.

"Well, so we are," Elizabeth agreed. "But we do make exceptions for exceptional people. I heard all about your début at the auction ring. Quite a coup."

"And quite undeserved, I'm afraid. I'll tell you what really happened if you promise it won't go further ..." And she explained how Ben Coad had set the whole thing up and guided her every step of the way to 'her' coup. "Don't even tell Mister Troy," she begged. "Because he might let something slip to my pa, and then ..."

"You didn't tell him?"

Leah shook her head. "I ought to have, I know. But he weighed in so proudly, speaking about our bloodline and all, I just couldn't do it."

"Yes," Elizabeth said, tapping the rump of the last yearling through the gate. "Those moments when the moving finger writes ... and you can't go back and cancel half a line! One gathers so many of them on one's journey through life."

"What's your worst?" Leah asked impulsively, spurred on by their new first-name intimacy.

"Oh, my dear girl!" Elizabeth bridled. "That is close to asking the impossible."

"Sorry!" Leah wished the ground would open. Then, to show willing herself, she said, "I'll tell you mine. It's very fresh in my mind so it's easy." And she described the night of the full moon, back in early August, when the Nark had dared her to go alone into the old barn. Her voice broke when she came to the moment of their kiss but she drew a deep breath and, mastering her emotions, said, "And for some reason I pulled away and said no ..."

"Fear?" Elizabeth suggested.

"I don't know? Maybe. Deep down, perhaps, but not on the surface. It was all so sudden, you see. Too much. One minute we were looking in each other's eyes and next minute we were kissing. And everything inside me just screamed out *yes!* It was like, I don't know — coming home? It was like it was the rightest thing I ever did. The whole of my life was a straight arrow zooming toward that one moment. Bullseye! And that just scared me, you know?"

"Why? Don't you trust your certainties?"

"No. I remember in school once saying 'nine nines are seventy-two'! And when I said it I was *absolutely* sure I was right. I mean, I'd have staked my life on it, I was that certain. And then when the teacher frowned and everyone else started laughing and I heard in my mind's ear an echo of what I'd just said ... well, I was so mortified I can't tell you. Look — are my ears turning red now? They feel like they are. And that's how awful I still feel. Not because of the mistake, because anyone can have a slip of the tongue like that, but at my certainty and that shocking, hideous laughter. I'll hear it till I die. And so whenever I get that feeling of *absolute* rightness I just shrivel away from it. I back off. I say no. Go away. Stop!"

"And that's what you said to young Mister Liddicoat that night — stop? Go away?"

"Mmh-hmm. Poor man. His face!" Her tone changed. "Of course, he's too proud and stiff-necked to *do* anything about it. His brother won't take no for an answer — worse luck. I mean, Nicholas could try and push just a *little,* don't you think?"

"I've never heard you call him Nicholas before."

Leah breathed hard a couple of times and then thumped the top bar of the gate with her fist. "He's just so infuriating."

"Many have found him so."

"I mean, I don't want to *marry* him or anything. I don't want to marry anyone just at the moment. I don't want a deep and solemn affair. But what's wrong with a kiss now and then? And a cuddle. And saying sweet nothings in each other's ears. And just having someone who's a little bit more than a friend — why can't he see that?"

"I wonder what he's saying about you?" Elizabeth murmured. "Of course, with your brother working alongside him every day, it wouldn't be impossible for you to find out, would it? How do you and Will get on these days?"

Leah considered this possibility but the pessimist within her rejected it. "Men don't talk like that. Nick could be breaking his heart over what happened, and yet he could work alongside Will for ten years and he'd never breathe a word of it."

Elizabeth took her arm again and turned her homeward. "You're half right, anyway," she said. "He'd never confess to a broken heart, but men aren't as good at hiding their feelings as they'd like to believe. Nicholas might bring you into the conversation rather often. Or there might be a little hesitation when he speaks your name. Or a certain look in his eyes when Will tells of something you've done. The man who even *knows* he's giving himself away in such subtle clues is as rare as hens' teeth. The man who can actually suppress them is twice as rare again. I think Will could be your ally in this — though men have such funny ideas of loyalty. If Nicholas does the usual thing and pokes fun at your efforts to farm the Old Glebe and generally gives the impression he finds you comical and beneath his contempt, Will might easily think he truly means it. And then he would regard it as disloyal to his partner to help you achieve your purpose here."

There was quite a lengthy silence while Leah absorbed all the implications of this advice. "Suppose ..." she said at last. "Just suppose I were to do the same? If I spoke rather too often about Nicholas ..."

"The Nark," Elizabeth reminded her.

"Of course! Suppose I were to speak rather often about him but — in the same breath — make it clear how little I cared about the answer ..." She let the rest of the idea hang; although she could see the general strategy of the thing, she could not grasp its precise tactics.

Elizabeth finished the thought for her: "Then if it just so happens that the Nark is doing the same thing at work all day, your brother would have to be a monster of unheeding … unperceiving … what's the word?"

"He'd have to be a simp, a real punkin-head, not to put two and two together."

"Quite so! And that would make him feel immensely superior. You're both … what? Three or four years older than him but you're behaving like children. It would bring out the altruism in him, don't you think? Having put two and two together he would feel it his duty to do the same with one and one — one Nicholas and one Leah! Oh, I do hope it works, Leah! It's such a pity that men can't be simple and straightforward and honest about these things!"

31   The new farmer at the Old Glebe soon became a fanatical student of the almanac, particularly of the hours of sunrise and sunset. Soon after the first of each month she could reel them off for all its remaining days. They were the hours that ruled her life, especially as the mornings and evenings drew in and each hour of dwindling daylight became correspondingly more precious. "I'll bet there's something you didn't know," she said to Will one evening when she and he were sitting by the fire after supper. "I'll bet you thought that as the days get shorter they lose an equal number of minutes at dawn and dusk. Well, it ain't so! Sunset at the end of this month is fifty-seven minutes earlier than at the beginning. But sunrise is only forty-three minutes later. I wonder why that is?"

"Everyone knows *that!*" he replied scornfully. "The sun likes to lie in of a morning, just like everyone else."

She flung the almanac at his head but missed. Then she said, "Anyway, you've got it the wrong way around — as usual."

To her surprise he picked the book up and returned it to her. She asked if he was feeling quite well.

He grinned, stretched his boots toward the fire, and said, "It's been a pretty good day, one way and another. You know Pa and Mister Troy were having second thoughts about their investment in the …?"

"D'you mean they've now had third thoughts and said yes?" she asked excitedly.

"Wait!" He held up a finger. "It gets better yet. Jimmy Troy came and looked at our samples. He knew the assay was good but he was worried there might not be enough of the stuff just lying around — and he had a very good reason to worry, as you'll hear. He was afraid we'd have to reopen some of the mines — and then, of course, we wouldn't be talking about a measly five grand."

"Ho ho! 'A measly five grand,' indeed!"

"Well, that's picayunish compared with what you'd need to reopen any of those mines. Anyway, the reason he got so cautious is that he once tried to extract tungsten from the halvans around Pallas Home Farm ..."

"*Tried* to?" she interrupted. "When was this?"

"Well, succeeded for a while. Twenty years ago, when he first came here. But the assay wasn't so good and the market fell and ... anyway, it didn't last too long. So it's once-bitten, twice-shy for him."

"That's good, surely?"

"Yes, but it's why he and Pa had second thoughts. Of course, the market is way up now, with the war and all. So, when Nick got a much better assay than he ever had, old Troy fell to thinking. And that's where the men who make money differ from the men who make a living. You or I would simply have thought, 'Oh good — we've got enough without reopening any of the old mines, so now we can go ahead'! But not good ol' Jimmy Troy."

"Nor not me neither," she put in.

"What would you do?" He eyed her suspiciously.

'I'd say to myself, 'If it's just lying around the place at Wheal Fortune, why not at Scott's, too — and Deepwork, Wheal Vor?' I'd look over all the other halvans in the district, too. I'd find out the limit of the mineral ..."

"Okay, okay!" he said with weary disgust.

"... and I'd buy up all the rights to stop anyone else muscling in on the claim."

He heaved a sigh and stared at the flames.

"Sorry if I spoil your tale," she said. "Is that what Pa and Mister Troy have been doing?"

He nodded. "I don't know why you never ran for president, Sis. You'd have been a shoo-in."

"I really am sorry, Will." She rose and came to sit on the sofa next to him. "I honestly didn't mean to spoil your story but" — she rubbed a finger lightly up and down his forearm — "it *is* rather an elementary precaution, don't you think?"

He continued staring at the fire. "I'm never going to be rich, am I."

"Does it matter?"

He laughed at last. "I guess not." Then, as if it were apropos, he added, "I'm going to suspend my tuition at the Camborne School of Mines. Pa agrees. I can go back when LCT no longer need me. That's the firm of Liddicoat, Carrington, and Troy, in case you were wondering."

When she made no reply he said, "You disapprove?"

"No." She stirred. "You and the Nark get on all right together, do you?"

"Of course we do. Otherwise I'd hardly be going to sign ..."

"Oh, well, that's all right then. I just wondered."

"Wondered what? What are you suggesting?"

"Nothing! It's just that some people get on and others don't. Two people working side by side all day ... you obviously *do* get on. So that's fine."

He chuckled. "You mean you and he wouldn't. Well, I can *certainly* believe *that!*"

She said nothing, for fear of giving away her interest.

"Do I ever complain about him?" he asked.

"Do I ever complain about John Hamden? But I find his conversation quite tedious at times. Especially this morning."

"Talking of John Hamden ..." He rose and put another couple of logs in the fire. "What's come over him today? He hardly had a word to say when we passed in the lane."

She sniffed and avoided his eye. "It was something I said."

He returned to his place at her side. "Was it something repeatable?" he asked.

"I guess it is — to you, anyway. Don't tell Pa. It might shock him. One of the sows I bought from John Carter, down Gwavas — which he swore was already in pig — returned this morning. So ..."

"Returned?"

"Came in heat again. So I went down with John Hamden to make sure we wouldn't be charged for another service. And anyway, while it was happening, old Hamden sort of moved closer to me ..."

"You mean you were watching?"

"Will!" she chided gently.

"I mean ..." he said.

"Yes? You mean what? Go on!"

"Nothing. I suppose you have to. Anyway, what did Hamden say? Or do?"

"He sidled up to me and said *he'd* like to be doing that." She laughed to show him she hadn't been shocked.

But it only added to her brother's fury. "The devil he did! I'll punch his head in next time I see him."

"You'll do no such thing. Do grow up!"

"And *he* has the nerve to be shocked at something *you* said!" he exclaimed. Then the implications of her words struck him and, in an altogether more cautious tone, he asked, "What *did* you say to him?"

"I asked him at least to let the boar finish with her first."

She only just managed to keep a straight face. Will tried to recover his anger but the thought of Hamden's response, which he could not help picturing in his mind's eye, carried the day, and once his laughter broke through there was no curbing it. He laughed until the tears ran.

"He spoke not a single word all the way back," Leah added when her brother had calmed down somewhat. "It was a blessèd silence. Somehow I don't think I'll be bothered with smutty remarks and *doubles-entendres* from him in the future. But just think — if I'd blushed and stammered out some embarrassed rebuke, he'd have been cock-a-hoop and he'd never stop insinuating things. You see that, don't you?"

He nodded unhappily. "Guess so."

"But you'd still prefer it if I sat in an ivory tower doing needlework with my maids, eh? Oh, Will!" She laughed. "What d'you think women talk about when we're alone together?"

He stared up at her, mouth agape. "No!"

"Yes. I know, for instance, that you have not heeded my advice in the matter of Pansy Tregear."

He bridled at that. "I don't recall *getting* any advice, actually."

It was a fair point and, for a moment, Leah did not know what to say.

He leaped into the silence. "And what has she been blabbing about me, anyway?"

"Not she. The other maids. Maria Vose and Dolly Cory — they claim to be shocked, of course. I think Dolly is, quite genuinely, but Maria is just jealous."

"I can't think what about. Pansy seems to have cooled off lately. Off *me,* anyway."

His emphasis struck a chord within her. She remembered her father telling her about watching Pansy cooling the milk that time. And on several occasions since then she had come across them together — never in a compromising situation or anything like that. And, to be sure, when two people live under the same roof and one is there to serve the other, it is highly likely that they will find themselves in the same room on numerous occasions, even several times a day. And it was true that Pansy was a bright, nimble-witted girl who learned fast and was not afraid of responsibility; she had made herself indispensable about the house and farm in the few short weeks she had been there. All the same, the old man had taken to singing her praises rather loud and rather often.

"Suits me," Will added. "I find Blanche Curnow more interesting — and more attractive."

The strong whiff of sour grapes in this remark only added to Leah's disquiet. "Has Pa ever spoken to you about marrying again?" she asked.

The sudden fear in his eyes told her he was worried, too, but also that he did not want to talk frankly about it — not yet, anyway. She realized she had to steer toward safer waters. "The reason I ask is that, now the Grand Garden scheme is on ice ... well, you know what energy he has ..."

William bit his lip thoughtfully. "I never looked at it that way," he said.

"Looked at what?" she asked shrewdly.

"Oh ... nothing. Just, you know, the general situation."

"Will!" she challenged.

"What?" He was all hurt innocence.

"You know. It's worried you, too — the reason why Pansy may have put *you* on ice lately."

His head slumped between his shoulders. "I guess so," he said. "But there ain't much we can do — is there?"

"Oh, we can do a lot."

Her blithe confidence heartened him, at least to the point where he'd argue a case. "Such as?" he asked. "If you fire her, first of all he might not let you, and secondly ... well, like I said about me, it wouldn't stop any meetings."

"But that would cause such a scandal. It would even have caused a scandal in East Haven, which is part of a city. Imagine it down here!"

He shook his head stubbornly but did not argue.

She went on. "I know they say there's no fool like an old fool, but Pa's not old. He's only just turned fifty-three."

"Exactly!" He gave a hollow laugh.

"What does *that* mean?" she asked when he volunteered nothing further. "Look — are you going to tell me or not? Surely you're not still trying to shelter my blushing, maiden ears — not after what I've told you tonight! Don't you think I ought to know what you know? Or don't you care?"

He shook his head and stared into the fire at the impossibility of explaining such things to her. But he tried. "What I know?" He echoed her words. "What I know is *me*. I know the absurd, ridiculous things *I* was planning when she knocked me off my feet like that. Even though I knew I hadn't the money ... nor the opportunity ..."

"Ridiculous things like what?"

"It doesn't matter. Use your imagination and stop embarrassing me! The point is, Pa *does* have the money. And the opportunity. And he *is* young, like you say. He still has plenty of that same youth which got me so kiboshed over that girl." He tapped his forehead to show where the affliction had struck him. Then he looked her level in the eye for the first time since this conversation had started. "Do I really need to lay it all out for you?"

"I guess not," she replied wearily.

In silence they stared into the flames for a while, glad of some small distraction.

Then Leah said, "We don't know too many widows, do we! Nice, comfortable, middle-aged, middle-class ladies past childbearing ..."

"… who would share a passion for gardening without having strong ideas of their own …"

"… and who wouldn't object to a stepdaughter who fondly imagines herself a farmer …"

"… nor a stepson who comes home covered in rock dust every evening …"

They relapsed into silence again.

Then he said, "No, we don't know too many like that."

After another, shorter silence, she said, "But we can agree on one thing."

"Such as?"

"Such as: There's no such thing as *too many* widows like that!"

Part Three

Church Street Hill

Shades of the Future

32 Like a wolf on a sheepfold Philomena Liddicoat descended on Helston, all unannounced, on the morning of the last day of September. She was short, slender, pretty, and deadly. Those who knew her and witnessed her grim march from the railway station down to the Angel raised their hats or dipped their heads and held their breath until she had safely passed. She carried with her the aura of an old woodensides man-o'-war under full sail. How one so spare and slight could do so was a mystery, but it was the sort of mystery they would rather observe than investigate.

Sergeant Daws watched her passing from the police station window and murmured, "I've been wondering how long 'twould be afore *she* turned up."

Henry Plum, the town clerk, saw her five minutes later, coming down the steeper part of Wendron Street. He stood well back from his window, to avoid catching her eye, and pointed her out unobtrusively to his assistant, Claude Werry, who murmured, as quietly as if she had been in the room with them, "Poor old Clifford Liddicoat, eh! He must have thought he'd seen the last of her."

Only old Bassett, the tobacconist near the bottom of Wendron Street, had a smiling welcome for her. He spotted her about the same time as Henry Plum, when she was still some thirty grim marching paces away. He dashed back into his little emporium and returned to stand at his threshold proffering one of Miss Philomena's favourite cigars. He was smiling from ear to ear — as well he might, for they were an expensive brand and she had always been an excellent customer. In fact, he still had a whole, unbroken box of them left over from her last visit home, five years earlier.

"Welcome home, Miss Liddicoat," he cried. "Allow me the honour of presenting you with this small token of our delight at seeing you here among us again."

She accepted it with her most radiant smile and he breathed once more. "You may put me down for a box, Bassett," she said. "I think I'm going to need them. If certain reports that have reached me are true."

"By the greatest good fortune, modom," he replied, "I have one that arrived only yesterday."

She puffed the cigar alight. She had nothing but contempt for ladies who smoked cigarettes in the street but cigars were altogether different. Anyway, nobody had ever criticized her for the habit. Not to her face. "You can show me the invoice, of course?" she said casually.

"Ah ..." Bassett was nonplussed. "I had to return it. There were two errors. But they will post me an emended copy." His flat tone signalled his defeat plainly enough and she did not press him further.

"Tell me if these disturbing rumours are true," she said. "About the Old Glebe."

"The Old Glebe?" he asked uncertainly, for there were, of course, many glebes, old and new, in the district. "You mean the one up Sithney?"

"Where else, man? Mrs Kelynack, my cousin in Wadebridge, wrote to tell me it has been sold — and to a Carrington, of all people. I hope it is not so?"

Bassett tilted his head apologetically. "Will you come in and take a seat, Miss Liddicoat?" he asked. "The news on *that* subject is as grim as could be, I fear."

She accepted his invitation and seated herself regally before his counter. "So it's true," she said grimly.

A gentleman entered to make a small purchase, saw her there, recognized her, and beetled off again. She appeared not to notice. "Tell me about these Carringtons," she said in a voice that would ripen green mustard.

Ten minutes later, grimmer than ever, she stomped into the Angel and sought out Walter Blackwell, the proprietor.

Even Walter Blackwell, implacable scourge of those who drank too much or paid too little, quailed at the sight of her.

"Are they still here?" she demanded without preliminary.

"Why, Miss Liddicoat!" he exclaimed with every show of delight. "How very pleasant to see you in Helston again! May I ask whether ..."

"Yes, yes!" She cut him short. "All well and good. You'd better let me have a room until I see the lie of the land. I don't think the atmosphere at Grankum will be too congenial for the time being."

Blackwell, who did not doubt her opinion, was wise enough not to say so.

"Not the room these Carringtons occupied," she added. "If, that is, they have already gone."

"Ah!" He was crestfallen. "All our other rooms are occupied, I fear." It was not true but he was trying to keep the other rooms clear for refurbishment.

"Then move someone," she told him, as one tells a child something utterly obvious. "My bags are at the station."

Blackwell mumbled that he'd see what could be done.

"I shall be staying in the district for a year or so at the very least," she said. "Until this war is over. They have requisitioned my house."

The slight stress she laid on the word 'my' would have alerted an attentive stranger to the possibility that the ownership of the house was, or had recently been, in question. Blackwell noticed it, of course, but then he was no stranger to the story. It had been whispered all over Helston at the time — about a year earlier — when Colonel Jellicoe's family had disputed his will, which left the house and a thousand a year to his 'dearest housekeeper and companion,' Miss Philomena Liddicoat. The most scurrilous inferences had been drawn from that careless use of the word, *dearest* and from the unheard-of generosity of the annual bequest.

Blackwell did a quick calculation. If her house were only half as grand as the descriptions of it that had appeared in the press at the time of the trial, it would easily command a rent of £150 a year, even from a parsimonious war office. Then again, the war was surely going to depress his regular trade as quotas and rationing made travelling salesmen unnecessary. He had only that week decided that a few long-term residents on *en-pension* terms would not come amiss.

"I can offer you full-board *en pension* at one pound, nineteen-and-six a week, Miss Liddicoat," he said, manfully resisting an impulse to duck once the words were out.

It did not take her long to trim three-and-six from the offer.

"I shall start from this minute with breakfast," she said. "And you may sit with me and tell me what you know of this Cousin Jack Carrington who has dared to steal Sithney Old Glebe from under our noses."

Blackwell organized her breakfast while she went for a wash and brush-up. He also sent a pot-boy down to Frank Kernow and Ben Coad with the news that Philomena Liddicoat was back in town, this time for the foreseeable future. He also told Jenny Tregellas, the head barmaid, to rescue him in five minutes with some sort of emergency.

Miss Liddicoat's manner of handling a knife and fork was not in the least inelegant; indeed, objectively observed, she was more ladylike than many who claimed the title of lady would objectively deserve. Yet there was something about it that chilled Blackwell to the marrow as he sat to her table and tried *not* to observe — objectively or in any other way.

"He's a decent sort of fellow," he began.

"Describe him. What's he look like?" She drew her knife across the egg. Euclid himself could not have bisected the yolk more neatly. As the yellow spilled out she stemmed it with equally perfect squares of fried bread. "You still put up the best breakfast in Cornwall," she added.

He wondered why the compliment did not put him more at ease. "Fiftyish," he said. "Indeed, I know for a fact he turned fifty-two this month now gone. He stands about five-foot-nine. Dark hair turning gray. Wavy. Proper handsome. They're a good-looking family, all three."

"Husband, wife, and … son? Or daughter?" She speared a small pyramid on her fork — the firm yolk on top, underpinned by white, bacon, kidney, and fried bread.

It was her eye-teeth, he decided. If Dracula had a daughter, she would have such teeth as that — subtly larger than most but not enough to detract from her general prettiness. "Widower, daughter, and son," he replied, "in order of age. The daughter, Leah, is just turned twenty-two. The son, William, comes of age next January. Will I describe them, too?"

She nodded, swallowed, and said, "Everything."

"Leah would be about five-four, with short, dark, curly hair and dark, piercing sort of eyes …"

"Twenty-two, you said? And pretty? And not yet engaged even?" Philomena listed the facts as if they were contradictory. When Blackwell hesitated she added, "Tell me the worst, man. Something is obviously amiss if *she's* still a miss! If my nephews are both besotted by her, I need to know."

He looked away and shifted uncomfortably. " I hardly ever see them. Your brother's no drinking man, Miss Liddicoat, as well you know. And your niece Adèle, she ..."

"Adelaide! I have no niece called Adèle."

"She brews her own ale, which she and her brothers ..."

"Stop this flannel, man," she interrupted. "I know very well what sort of gossip is exchanged over your public bar of a market day. And I know you're quite able to overhear three conversations at once. So — *are* my nephews besotted by the Carrington creature?"

"William Carrington is said to be sparking with Blanche Curnow of Chynoweth."

"Giles Curnow's daughter? Good heavens is she ... yes," she sighed, "I suppose she is. Last I saw of her she was a spotty little thing in pinafores. I've been away too long." She delivered the last sentiment with an ominous lightness. Few in Helston would have agreed though none would openly disagree.

"And as for Leah Carrington," Blackwell put in before she could goad him, "she is sparking with no one. Instead, she's taken pattern from Roseanne Kitto — remember? Farmed Wheal Fortune on her own before she married Stephen Morvah? Well, Miss Carrington's farming the Old Glebe now."

"Farming?" The toast shattered in two jagged halves under the sudden pressure of her knife. "My cousin, Mrs Kelynack, gave me to understand that this Carrington man intends to turn the whole of the Old Glebe into some kind of ornamental *garden?"* Her question implied she hoped it was not true. Blackwell assumed she was expressing a contempt for gardening that was common among Cornish farming folk, whose motto was, 'If you can't put it either on your own table or on the train to Covent Garden, dig it up by the roots and burn it."

"No. She's farming the place and she's the farmer, too. She bought her herd down Saint John's market backalong in August, or the foundation of it. Turned a neat trick on Sam Hocking, too, when he tried to run her up — she left him with a sour bid."

"And the father's taking no part in this farming nonsense?" She buttered her toast and daubed it with marmalade.

Blackwell eased his collar. "Well," he replied hesitantly, "he's thick as thieves with Jimmy Troy these days — which is hardly surprising. Them both being Cousin Jacks and ..."

"Why should that prevent him from farming? I don't follow. The Troys still have Pallas Home Farm, surely?"

"Why, that's more *Mrs* Troy than her man. The thing is, Troy and Carrington are what you might call venturers now."

"In tin?" she asked incredulously as she popped a sliver of toast and marmalade into her mouth.

Blackwell wondered if any man had ever had the temerity to seek a kiss from those lips. Colonel Thaddeus Jellicoe had, if the rumours were true. The innkeeper took advantage of her eating to get it all out quickly: "They've put up the capital for young Nicholas, your nephew, to extract wolframite from the old halvans round Wheal Fortune."

"Have they, indeed," she said calmly as she prepared another sliver to follow the first. "We shall soon put a stop to that! What sort of capital is involved?"

Blackwell stared unhappily at the door. Where was that Tregellas girl? "I heard tell as the first payment was five thousand pounds, Miss Liddicoat."

She blanched at the sum. *"First* payment?" she echoed. "Are they reopening a mine as well or what?"

"It seems they found wolframite in several old halvans between Wheal Fortune and the Flow at Carleen. So they had to buy up all the surface mineral rights — and word leaked out."

"Even so — five thou' for ... what is it, man? Why d'you keep looking at the door?"

"Oh ... er, I thought I heard a commotion in the kitchen. I'm sorry — you were saying? Five thousand for ... what?"

"For a one-man operation — it seems quite an excessive amount of capital."

"Oh, it's bigger than a one-man operation, Miss Liddicoat." He rose and went to the door. "Jenny? What on earth is going on down there?"

"A lot bigger?"

"No — not a lot. *Jenny?"*

"How much bigger then? Do stop fussing and come back here — I've not done with you yet. There's nothing happening out there, quite obviously."

"It's a two-man operation, in fact," he replied, dithering between obeying her summons and giving Jenny Tregellas one last chance.

"Your reluctance on this point is not inspiring, Blackwell," she said sharply. "I begin to fear the worst. Who is the second person?"

At long last Jenny came running up the passage. "Oh, please, Mister Blackwell, sir, come quick, sir! Cook's been and gone and got her foot caught in the drain and she thinks it's broke."

He stared at her in utter dismay and asked in a fierce whisper, "Is that really the best you can come up with?"

"What is his name?" Philomena thundered.

"No, sir. Honest, sir. 'Tis true, sir. Martha lost a scouring brush down there, see, and ..."

He turned back to his latest guest. "I fear I have to go, Miss Liddicoat," he said, struggling to keep his relief out of his voice. This was a *genuine* emergency! He had never been so glad to hear of one.

"His name?" she insisted.

"Oh — that. His partner is William Carrington."

He ducked from imaginary blows as he beetled off down the passage in Jenny's wake. But no explosion of wrath pursued him. In its way, that was the most spine-chilling feature of all.

33   The stamps at Wheal Fortune and their numerous predecessors back over the years had been crushing ore to a fine sand for the best part of a century before the whole venture was abandoned. The resulting sandy waste, once the heavier tin ore had been vanned out of it, had been left to wash down into the valley until it threatened to choke the stream on which the entire operation depended for motive power. So every few years, teams of mules with drag-shovels had been brought in to scrape the sand into carts and carry it farther up the hillside. There the ever-growing piles eventually formed sandbanks twenty and more feet deep. And now, for Nicholas and Will, those banks had proved to be the richest source of wolframite among all the ready-mined ore.

Certainly it was the most get-at-able and the easiest to load and cart back down to the stamps for a second vanning — this time to separate a lighter fraction than the original cassiterite, or tin ore. Nicholas and Will divided their days between loading a hand cart up at the sandbanks and adjusting the vanning tables to give the maximum yield. The slope of the table, the rate of vibration, and the flow of the water across it all played a part and it was a matter of trial and error — of many trials and many errors — before they got the right combination. They achieved it on the last day of September that year, the day Aunt Philomena arrived in Helston.

They worked till sunset when, weary but happy, they trudged homeward up the path from the bottom Blueborough field. As they went they sang 'Belgium Put the Kibosh on the Kaiser' and dreamed of the patriotic riches their venture was going to bring in. The song petered out when, as they reached the bend by the Blueborough whim shaft, which was part of the old Wheal Fortune deep mine, they saw Adèle hastening toward them.

"You look as if you lost France and found Belgium!" Will called out cheerily. It had become a game among them to think up ever more bizarre variants of the catch phrase.

"Something wrong?" Nicholas shouted more seriously, he being more experienced at reading his sister's expressions, especially at a distance.

"You may well say so," she shouted back.

"Germany won the war?" Will was determined to stay cheerful. It had been too good a day for any little domestic upset over at Grankum to disturb him. Of every hundred shovelfuls he humped from now on, one would be pure tungsten ore!

"Worse!" Adèle replied. They were close enough now not to shout. "Aunt Philomena's house has been requisitioned by the war office."

Was *that* all? Will turned to Nicholas, expecting him to laugh.

Nicholas did not laugh. Indeed, he did not even smile. "And they don't want her to stay on as housekeeper?" he asked.

"Would you?" she replied.

From the very tone of his friend's question Will knew that something serious was afoot. "Who on earth is this Aunt Philomena?" he asked.

"The Eighth Plague of Egypt," was the reply. "The one God never needed to use. The merest hint was enough to make Pharaoh cave in and let the Israelites go." To Adèle he said, "I suppose she's come back here for the duration, then? Is she at Grankum now?"

"She may be. I came to warn you, anyway. She came down on the night sleeper and took breakfast at the Angel. Walter Blackwell got word to Ben Coad, who got word to the Old Glebe and then to us. The old man vanished at once, to buy new moleskins in Truro, he said. We shan't see him until late tonight, I'm sure. I don't know where Harvey is. I've spent the afternoon in fear and trembling but so far there's been neither sight nor smell of her."

"Jee willikins!" Will was impressed at last. "She sounds quite a lady. Is she your late mother's sister or your dad's?"

"Father's sister," Nicholas said. "She's the only person who ever persuaded Arthur Godden, the old station master at Helston, that her watch was more accurate than the Great Western Railway's timepiece."

"She got the train brought all the way back from Pallas Halt," Adèle added.

"And the main-line express was held for her at Gwinear Road." With a tinge of admiration in his voice Nicholas went on to tell his new partner about the aunt's generous inheritance from the late Colonel Thaddeus Jellicoe.

Adèle capped it by adding, "They say he didn't dare *not* leave her the place and the income — otherwise she'd have dug him up and given him a hot enough helping of tongue pie to awaken the dead."

Nicholas cleared his throat.

"They did!" Adèle protested.

"Yes, well, that was *one* of the reasons advanced at the time."

"Tskoh!" Adèle punched him slightly harder than playfully. "That was just scurrilous talk put about by the Jellicoe clan."

"So — have you come out and left the farmhouse empty?" Nicholas asked her.

"Eileen's there, buttering eggs. And Sampson's in the yard."

"Oh! I wonder how much dung will be turned and how many eggs buttered by the time we get back!"

"D'you mean I shouldn't have come to warn you?"

"No." He slipped an arm around her shoulders and gave her a quick hug. "You were absolutely right."

"All the same," she said, "I think we should go back directly over the croft. Not round by the road. You'll have to help me over the hedge."

The hedge in question was on the Grankum side of what they called a 'croft' though it was, in fact, an eleven-acre patch of poisoned land — a dump for ash and waste from the calciner, whose rusting firebox and oven still dominated the hillcrest above Wheal Fortune. Nothing grew there but a feeble carpet of ling and a dry sedge that struggled to turn from yellow to green. It had been walled about to keep the cattle out rather than in. Few birds sang there in winter but in summer it was a haven of skylarks, nightjars, and one ever-returning family of kites. Its near-dead surface offered an easier path than the winding, rutted lanes, but the farther hedge, with a six-foot fall on its Grankum side, was a formidable obstacle. Generations of Liddicoats, of whom Nicholas was the latest, had vowed to build stepping stones into the face of it. He repeated his pledge now, as they approached it. Neither of his listeners bothered to reply.

Will went over first, finding convenient footholds in the furze or among the stone, where the binding earth had been dug out by rabbits or rats. The drop on the far side looked daunting but, with Adèle's eyes upon him, he did not care to hesitate. If he had not been wearing stout boots, he would have turned his ankle on the tussocky grass.

When Adèle stood on the top he could reach no higher than her thighs — which, naturally, he did not even attempt.

"Can you sort of sit and slide off?" he suggested. "Or maybe I could lift you off, if you were sitting."

"I'm quite capable of getting down by myself," she said, contradicting her earlier request for assistance. "So, if you'll just turn your back a mo ..."

"No — come on." He stretched out his hands. "Just sit down. Or squat. As long as I've got hold of you ..."

"Oh, for God's sake!" Nicholas gave her a push from behind and she fell off the wall with a shriek, moving her arms like a swimmer starting a swallow-dive.

Fortunately Will had his hands raised high already and so he caught her round the waist close to the start of her fall, before she had gathered enough momentum to overwhelm him. The effort needed to brake her descent and turn it into a controlled movement was at the very limit of his muscular power but his muscular power had increased greatly since the start of their mining operation and, to his own great surprise, he managed it.

He became the circus strongman to whom she was a mere feather. Showing off at last he set her down among the tussocks in ultra-slow motion, making it look as if her feet were sinking through thick treacle.

"Oh, Will!" she murmured breathlessly, looking up at him with such devoted admiration that he was spellbound by it, unable either to speak or to let go of her waist. It was the very last thing he expected to happen.

She lifted her chin an inch or so. If they had been alone they would have kissed. He knew it. She knew it. Their eyes, dwelling deep in each other's, flashed their knowing back and forth. He had never seen such inner beauty in a face so plain. He did not know what to do about it.

"Come on — she's not hurt!" Nicholas grabbed Will by the arm and hauled him away downhill, past Adèle.

Will pulled himself free and turned back to Adèle, who was still standing as he had left her. She had her back to him so he could not read her expression. "Adèle?" he ventured.

She snapped out of her reverie and turned round. "Yes," she said flatly. "Home."

Before he could stop himself, Will held out his hand to her. "You might still fall," he said solemnly.

She hesitated briefly and then took it with a smile. "So I might," she said.

"Ohmigawd!" Nicholas exclaimed wearily.

They hardly heard him. They were both rather stunned by what had just happened — by what was still happening. For Adèle it was something she had not even permitted herself to daydream about — an impossibility too painful to indulge in, even in moments of fancy. For Will it was something more complex — something he had never remotely imagined and yet, now it had happened, something that did not greatly surprise him, either. It was almost as if some secret part of his mind had been contemplating such a thing without even hinting about it to the rest of him, which went on its merry way, alternately obsessed by Blanche Curnow and Pansy Tregear, whom he had imagined as aspects of sacred and profane love.

He tried to think of them now — one after the other, for he had never been able to think of them both in the same sweep of fantasy — and in both cases the image was of someone receding

— vanishing at the stern of an invisible boat on dimly glimpsed waters in a dark, subterranean lake.

Part of him — the part that had been taken by surprise just now — rebelled at the loss. It would rather have added Adèle to his pantheon of goddesses in some third category, somewhere between sacred and profane. But Adèle was not and never could become a category. She was that warm hand clenched so tight in his — how could mere fingers and knuckles feel so utterly precious? She was that wondering, incredulous smile, provoked by him and him alone — aimed at him and him alone. She was that remembered look of adoration when luck and muscles held just now. In her short, bonny, buxom person she embodied so much sense, such a wealth of good humour, such an abundance of calm judgment that now he wondered that he could ever have thought of another girl.

Nicholas was saying something about building a lockable shed in which to store their wolframite ... and how they must be careful not to undermine the road ... or should they perhaps build a new exit, avoiding the sandbanks altogether? And Will went on saying "Yes" and "Uh-hunh" and "Okay" until Nicholas said, "What d'you mean, 'yes'? I asked shall we or shan't we?"

But the new idyll between Will and Adèle — and the questioning from Nicholas — came to an abrupt end when Adèle, the only one looking directly in front of them at that moment, said, "Well, I'll go to hell! What *does* he think he's doing?"

Nicholas stopped in his tracks and said, "I thought you told us he'd gone to Truro?"

"He did," she asserted. "He must have realized it was only postponing the evil hour."

"But *that's* no answer!"

By 'that' Nicholas was referring to the unbroken shotgun their father was carrying at the slope while he paced up and down the yard like a sentry at the barracks gate. No doubt it was cocked and loaded, too.

"Father!" Nicholas called out reproachfully.

"Never you mind for me, mister!" he shouted back. "I know what I'm about. You go on in and have your supper, all of 'ee. And you — young Carrington — you duck your head down behind the hedge and go on home. This isn't no business of yours. 'Tis family."

They leaned against the yard gate and watched him in dismay. "Really, Father! What good is that gun going to do anybody?" Nicholas asked.

"You'll see," he replied darkly, and would say no more.

A moment later they saw — at least, they saw why he had come out into the yard to pace up and down in that menacing manner. A gig, which he must have spotted the moment it passed Boase's Burnthouse, came down the lane from the junction by Merther Cottage. Without hesitation it turned into the Grankum yard.

No one was more surprised at the sight of the lady at the reins than Will. From what her nephew and niece had said of her, he expected to see a grim, ugly, implacable female, carved in granite and dressed in Bible black. This petite and pretty lady, elegantly and expensively dressed, did not at all accord with those guided preconceptions. He thought they could not possibly have remembered her correctly — or that her inheritance had transformed her beyond recognition.

But the moment she opened her mouth and barked the one word, "Clifford!" at her brother, his doubts fled. It was enough. If old man Liddicoat were the barrack sentry, his sister was the most feared sergeant major who ever paralyzed an entire regiment with a single word. Already Will wished he had obeyed the order to get his head down behind the parapet and, by trench and sap, scurry for the safety of the rear echelon as fast as his legs could carry him.

"Don't 'ee come no closer, woman!" The old man lowered his gun and aimed it at her. "You've no business here. You aren't wanted here. You turn about and go back where you come from, and us'll not fall out."

She flung the reins at Sampson, who had come forward to assist her but who was now skulking behind the horse. "See to him, man," she said as she climbed down. He took the traces and raced the horse and gig over to one side of the yard, well out of the line of fire.

"I'm a-warning of 'ee!" Liddicoat said.

"Oh, Father!" Adèle whispered, beating her forehead gently against the top bar of the gate.

Will slipped an arm around her shoulders but she hissed, "Don't!" at him urgently.

"I'm not afraid of her," he replied with more confidence than he felt. "What can she do?"

"Make life not worth living," she told him grimly.

Aunt Philomena walked straight toward her brother and took the gun from him without even pausing on her royal progress toward the house. "Come on in, you three," she called out, shielding her eyes against the evening twilight sky. "Who's the third fellow? It's not Harvey."

"Ohmigawd!" Nicholas said again — this time with absolutely no comic or satirical overtones.

"Cheer up!" Will clapped him on the back. "You look as if you lost a brother and found an aunt!"

Even at that he did not smile. Then Will, with all the courage of the ignorant — the fools who step in where angels fear even to *look* — vaulted the gate and opened it for the other two to enter. Leaving them to close it, he strode out, smiling, toward the woman, hand outstretched to greet her. "Good evening, ma'am," he said. "Miz Liddicoat — am I right? I am William Carrington, the son of your brother's neighbour ..."

"Are you, indeed!" The slight smile of provisional welcome vanished. "I know my brother's *neighbour!*" She ignored his outstretched hand. "I've heard all about my brother's *neighbour.*" She turned to her brother, who had meanwhile come up from behind, and thrust the gun back into his hand. "*Now* you can shoot," she said.

For an awful moment the old man looked as if he were actually considering the possibility.

Will felt a squirt of fear threaten to sink his empty stomach even as his mind rebelled. It was no longer a tussle between him and this allegedly formidable woman. In fact, there was no 'allegedly' about it. Her steely eye, her coldly belligerent manner, her utter sense of self-possession, even when making the most outrageous proposal — all confirmed that she was, indeed, a most formidable woman. Yet, as he had begun to realize, it was no longer a tussle between him and her but a three-cornered fight in which his body and his mind were at odds with each other: His body wished to yield while his mind rebelled at the very thought of doing so.

Before those juices of terror could fill his veins and render him powerless he laughed and said, "Don't be ridiculous!"

The word, spoken with his American twang, cracked like a whiplash among the other four. A few moments later it stung him that way, too; but by then he was committed.

"Will!" Adèle plucked at his sleeve from behind. "Don't! Honestly, just don't."

It was too late. Aunt Philomena turned to him with a smile. "Ridiculous?" she repeated quietly. It was a long time since anybody had stood up to her — only chaff and riffraff like railway servants and cabmen. Her last real opponents had been poor dear Taddy's relations, who had taken her on without realizing what they were letting themselves in for. Her real opponent would, of course, be the father of this rash and callow youth but if she could send him back to the Old Glebe as a bruised sort of emissary, it would be a good day's work, after all.

"Well now ..." Will said in a tolerant, cajoling tone. "What would you call it, Miz Liddicoat? You'd be appalled if your brother took you at your word."

He looked about him, trying to recruit the other three with a laugh. The father regarded him with anger, Nicholas with apology, Adèle with tender concern. "It *is* ridiculous," he asserted, wishing he sounded more convinced of it himself.

In desperation he even contemplated taking the gun from the old man and thrusting it into the woman's hands, telling her to do the thing herself. But a debater's instinct — something he was hardly aware of possessing as yet — saved him. He saw — or *it* saw — that such a gesture would degrade 'ridiculous' into 'farcical.' And, if he was ever to assuage this lady's anger and bring her to accept the Carringtons in a spirit of surly neutrality (anything warmer was too much to hope for), he would have to avoid pushing her into corners where she would appear farcical. Even to show her up as ridiculous — which she clearly was being — was risky.

But that same instinct then pushed him too far in the opposite direction. Apropos nothing he said, "But what the heck! We've only just met and we haven't even shaken hands." He pointedly did not offer his a second time. Instead he said, "At the risk of annoying you all over again, Miz Liddicoat, may I say that I think that is one of the most strikingly beautiful hats I have ever seen. Do you have them made especially for you?"

"Will!" Adèle cried out in a voice of despair.

He was about to turn and pacify her when Aunt Philomena bridled at his insolence — as she saw it. "How dare you!" she cried. Her nostrils flared. Her entire body trembled with rage. For two farthings, he thought, she'd have grabbed the gun from her brother and done the deed herself. And yet ... and yet ... If he'd turned to Adèle as his new-found feelings for her urged him to do, he'd have missed it — that momentary flicker of fear in the older woman's eyes. Fear and ... something else. Doubt, by golly! Self-doubt. He could tell how rare a moment it was for her by the surprise that soon effaced it.

A brasher young man would have pressed in on this fleeting advantage, would have challenged her to face him — *and* her fear, and her self-doubt — all at once. But he still had that instinct which told him that, in facing him like that, she'd master the fear and uncertainty in passing. And so all future advantage would be gone.

"I'm sorry," he said in his humblest, friendliest manner. "Truly I am. I guess the sort of compliments we learned to pay to beautiful ladies in America don't go down too well over here. But I meant no disrespect, Miz Liddicoat. And I truly do think it is a *gorgeous* hat."

Her doubt, and the fear it brought in its wake, intensified. Her massive armoury of aggression had no weapons against flattery, still less against sincere compliments. The last man to call her beautiful had been her dear, darling Taddy. And now ... this damned little whippersnapper ... She held her peace and put on her grimmest countenance rather than reveal the slightest hint of her confusion.

Or so she imagined.

"I see I am the fly in the ointment here," Will said. "So, by your leave, ladies ..." He bowed at Miss Liddicoat, winked at Adèle and her brother, nodded at their father, and walked past him toward the lower gate.

"Young man!" Aunt Philomena called after him.

He turned round.

"Don't ever come back here to Grankum!"

He laughed. "That will be rather difficult, Miz Liddicoat. But they will be happy to explain it to you, no doubt." He waved generally at the other three as he turned again and resumed his homeward walk.

34 Darkness gathered in the foot of the valley long before it laid its pall over the crests of the surrounding hills. Will was grateful for it, though on any other night he would have been a little wary — especially of that transition from the deep gloom of twilight's final minutes to the stygian night which already filled Grankum Wood. Then the rustle of leaves in the canopy above, the underfoot stirrings of creatures of the dark, and the rising-swooping shrill of bats from the abandoned quarry's cavelets, all combined to people the woodland with phantasms of the mind — on any other night but this.

Now the only image before him, behind him, beside him, was the dear, sweet face of Adèle, forever frozen in his mind in that moment of surprise when their eyes met and dwelled deep in each other's, when her plainness was transfigured for him into something holy and beautiful beyond bearing. Now he went out of his way to walk where she had walked, not diagonally up the long hillside to the Old Glebe but keeping to the valley floor, which was her daily path to the well when their rain tanks dried or turned an unpalatable green.

The enchanted well!

The well of enchantment!

She has been here! his spirit sang. And she was there yet, for the damp earth, the moss, the ferns, the very stones beside her path still caged something of the rare magic of her presence; they joined with him in that ecstatic cry. A line from Oscar Wilde, which had always puzzled him before, puzzled him no longer: *She hardly knew she was a woman, So sweetly did she grow.* That was Adèle. Of all the women on earth that was Adèle — more person than woman.

Pansy was woman. Blanche was woman, or soon would be. They were two fish in the big pool of interchangeable women (as he and other men were interchangeable to them, no doubt). There in that pool all young bachelors, and many a widower, too, could trawl by licence — at dances, chapel picnics, harvest suppers, and At Homes — keeping or returning their catch as head or heart might dictate. But not Adèle. Adèle was suddenly interchangeable with none. Adèle was now unique. Adèle,

Adèle, Adèle ... he thought his heart would burst right out of his breast at the sweet repetition of her name. It had mysterious, magic powers to move him now, and especially here in the dark of her own wood.

And most mysterious and magical of all was the fact that it had taken so long to happen. He had first seen her in March, at the ball where Blanche Curnow had so taken his fancy. He had seen her every week, and latterly every day, since then. Yet the love for her that was in him, and which must have been in him from that very first day, had taken all this time to emerge. Did that not prove how profound it was, how deep it must have lain all these weeks while he worked those other silly infatuations out of his system!

He drank at the well − her well − for its chalybeate waters no longer had their amusingly aperient effect on any of the Carringtons. And he breathed deep draughts of the air that had bathed her and which lingered here, craving, like him, one more brush with her ineffable sweetness. Then, with long, manly strides that she would surely admire if she were truly at his side, he set off up the hill for home. As he wound his way among the trees and across the fields he sang, 'It was a comely young lay-a-dee-eee fair ...' − which tells of a love, unrequited for seven long years, but rewarded at last. Pansy had taught it him but he did not think it disloyal to Adèle, nor, indeed, to Pansy, to sing it now. Love not only conquers all, it sanctifies all, too.

To his dismay, however, his singing of the final lines: 'For a dark-eyed morning, Brings forth a shining day' was joined by an all-too-familiar voice from somewhere up ahead − indeed, by the very voice that had first taught him those words and the accompanying tune.

"Pansy!" he called out; his surprise was genuine enough but the happiness of his delivery was forced.

She was leaning on the lower yard gate, silhouetted for a moment against the rising moon, which was still a couple of days short of full. Her long, fair hair, freed from its everyday coiled plait, framed her in a veil of silver.

"Met her, have 'ee?" she asked gleefully.

He gave a start, thinking she meant Adèle; he had quite forgotten the allegedly fearsome Aunt Philomena, having put her from his mind the moment he left Grankum Farm.

"I'll wager she fell on they other poor Liddicoats like a sky of lead!" she added.

"Oh — Miz Philomena. Yeah. She did."

Her tone became curious. "Of course Miss Philomena. Who did you think I meant, then?"

"Nobody. I couldn't think *who* you meant. I'd forgotten all about her. What are you doing out here?"

"Waiting for a kiss," she replied. Her eyes danced merrily. Her head was resting at a slight angle on her folded arms, which rested on the top bar of the gate. Although the moon was behind her, his night-accustomed eyes could see her features clearly — especially the two full breasts that strained against her blouse as they thrust out beneath that bar. She knew, of course. No woman with her endowments — and attitude — could fail to know what havoc she was wreaking among all his pure and high-minded resolutions.

"Oh, dear!" he exclaimed, disguising the shiver in his voice as lack of breath after his stiff climb. "Am I scaring some young feller off? I'll be gone in a trice."

In a trice she grabbed the hand he intended for the top bar of the gate and carried it to her breast. He felt the firm flesh beneath the cotton of her blouse, the swelling bud of her nipple. She let out a shivery gasp at his touch. He willed his muscles to pluck his hand away; she pressed it even tighter to her. She closed her eyes and lifted her face, reaching her lips toward his. Until then he had not realized how close they were. Nor, until it closed around the full, ripe softness of her other breast, did he realize what his other hand was doing. And then he could not stop it.

Everything within him that was capable of forming words cried out that this was wrong, wrong, wrong! His lips melted in the soft sweetness of hers. They flowed together. *Wrong!* Her nipples swelled like miniature breasts in their own right. *Wrong!* Instincts he did not know he possessed guided his palms, his fingers, his fingertips, his nails, to actions he had never imagined, much less rehearsed. *Wrong!* In all this he was spurred on by the rewards she offered, her feeble moans, her helpless whimpers, her fighting for breath, her hot, delectable tongue as it boldly claimed the freedom of his mouth and shared with him the mint she had been chewing just before she joined his song. *Wrong!*

To his surprise she suddenly broke free from him and laughed. The woman who, a mere second or so earlier, had seemed abandoned beyond all hope of self-control, or any other control, either, broke free and laughed! "That was some mistake," she said gaily.

"Yes!" he agreed eagerly, relief flooding through him. "We must ..."

"Starting with you one side of the gate and me the other," she went on. "Here! I got an idea ..."

His heart fell.

"Put your arms through the gate ... no — *under* the second bar. That's it!"

Then he saw it had been no 'mistake' at all. The bars of the gate could have been made for her purpose there that evening. For the second bar, the one she told him to slip his hands beneath, was so aligned that, if she stood a mere six inches back, the only place he could embrace her was by the hips. If she were pressed tight to the gate, of course, he could hold her more decently round the waist. But, since she seemed unwilling to make that little journey on her own, he had to grope around her hips, get his hands to her buttocks, and pull her to him.

As he did so his nobler self gritted its teeth at such wanton intimacy; the remaining ninety-five percent of him shivered with ecstasy and went weak at the knees as he felt those normally untouchable parts of her anatomy come alive between his eager hands and wriggle snakelike toward him. She was surely wearing no more than a single petticoat (if that, indeed) beneath the loose-gathered folds of her linen skirt.

Reluctantly, yet knowing it was his duty as a gentleman, he lifted his hands to her waist as soon as he physically could.

At once she retreated a few inches, knocking his hands back down to their earlier, more voluptuous hold around the lithe and lively fullness of her bottom. And now it was she who squeezed herself in against the gate, making his hands follow and *appear* to be forcing her do so. He pressed against her, too — which was when he discovered that the third bar down was pressing against the tops of his thighs — and hers — thus forcing those most forbidden and untouchable parts of all into fierce and hungry contact. Her mound was like a darning mushroom in a sock, hard yet delectably supple.

"Here!" she giggled. "You got something for me down there, haven't 'ee! I can feel 'n, so big as a bull."

She massaged her body against his and at once he began to ejaculate. She felt that, too, and wriggled all the more ecstatically, laughing now.

He was more surprised than pleasured by it; indeed, it was the most mechanical, least erotic climax he had ever experienced. Disjointed phrases of shame and apology began assembling in his throat ... and died there, too, as it dawned on him that she was laughing and happy. "Now us'll have to wait a bitty while, eh?" she said, withdrawing slightly and looking up at him with a winsome accusation in her gaze. "Still, we shan't be so hasty then, shall us, my lover. We'll have some sport that lasts."

She opened the gate to let him through. She took his arm as they sauntered back up the yard. "I'll be waiting for 'ee 'bout half-past-lemm tonight," she said matter-of-factly. "In th'ole tithe barn. You bring a blanket and some cigarettes and port wine, can 'ee?"

He composed himself to explain why — or, at least, *that* — he could not honourably comply with her suggestions. But the palms of his hands recalled the adorable fullness of her breasts and the voice that had cried *wrong!* now cautioned him to break it gently to her; it reminded him that hell hath no fury ... et cetera. And the other voice, the one that was incapable of crying *wrong!* — the weasel voice that spoke aloud — now said, "I don't ... you know, Pansy ... I mean, my true feelings ... I ... that is ..."

"You don't love me," she put in gaily. "That's what you're trying to say, innit? Not now. Not ever. You never could. Your heart is engaged to Miss Curnow ... or someone." A wave of her hand consigned the actual object of his true affections to the realms of triviality. "Well, Master Will, if I thought you had *that* much love for me" — her right hand grasped her left little finger and showed him no more than its nail — "I'd no more open up for you than I would for a six-foot quilkin."

"Quilkin?"

She imitated the croaking of a frog. He shuddered at the picture her words now conjured in his mind's eye.

In case he still hadn't grasped the meaning, she freed her hand from his to imitate a frog's leaping, too, all up his arm.

Even that much contact sent a new shiver of lust up his spine, travelling from where lust has its seat to where it is normally controlled. Despairing now of that control, he made one last desperate throw of the die: "Aren't you afraid of ... you know — breaking a leg?"

"Lord!" She gave an inconsequential laugh. "Don't you worry your pretty little head about the likes o' that, boy," she said, parodying advice that must often have made her grit her teeth. "You leave all they worries to them as do understand such things." She took his hand again but then, seeing they were about to come within view from the upstairs windows of the house, she let go and leaned instead against the wall of one of the farrowing sties. "Half-past-lemm, then," she repeated.

Her eyes gleamed at him out of the coal-black moonshadow.

I won't go, he promised himself.

On the other hand, since he'd made it absolutely clear that there was no question of a romantic attachment ...

But it would still be treachery to Adèle. He shrank now from relishing her name. How swiftly had the purity of his love been tarnished! Thoughts of her still filled him with an overwhelming ache of happiness but he now felt even more remote from her than ever. The virtue she had every right to expect of any man who aspired to love her seemed vanishingly unattainable.

For a dozen blissful paces his mind was a blank, void of shame, criticism, self-doubt. He glanced over his shoulder and saw Pansy hasten across the gap in which she would be visible to anyone looking out from the house, trotting toward the kitchen door. He saw her for less than a second but the image burned on when the gap was empty once again. She held her hands to her unsupported breasts to stop them whanging about, and her fine, fair hair streamed out behind her like silvered gossamer.

What was he to do?

If he didn't show at half-past 'lemm,' she'd turn into a hell-cat, spitting fury; she had that spirit, he suspected. She could spread scandal that would hurt Adèle more than one trifling infidelity — of which Adèle would never get to hear, anyway.

So one could almost put one's hand on one's heart and say that keeping this assignation was in Adèle's best interests, too. Of course he ought to have had the presence of mind — and strength of character — to say 'no, no, a thousand times no,' at once. But he hadn't, and now the damage was done, and the only way out was to limit its scope as much as possible.

Also, if there was absolutely no romantic interest on either side, could one brief assignation fairly be called by so portentous a name as 'infidelity'? Surely the word ought to be kept for *important* betrayals? Otherwise its currency was devalued. You could say that he owed it to the very *idea* of fidelity not to relate it in any way to a hasty coupling in the hay. Loyalty and devotion were truly grand elements in the human soul. His loyalty and his devotion to Adèle soared so high above the sordid plane of earth and all things earthy that to measure this night's casual and frivolous encounter by so noble and lofty a yardstick would be ... yes, well, there was no need to argue it to the last dot and comma. Case closed.

He would keep the appointment ... do whatever was required of him to content her ... then ... what?

Well, certainly refuse all future assignations!

Actually, it would be better if he could do something to make sure she'd never even ask for one. Act all clumsy and hurt her? He couldn't do that. Finish so swiftly he'd leave her unsatisfied? Ha ha — she'd already taken care of that disaster! Weep, beat his breast, tear out his hair, indulge in a cataract of remorse and self-vilification? That was the best idea so far but he wasn't sure he was actor enough to carry it off. Or, to put it another way, he *was* sure he wasn't.

Ah, well, something would turn up. He'd find a way to touch her heart and make sure this first time would also be the last.

"Hallo!" Leah greeted him as he crossed the threshold. "You look as if you've lost Blanche and found Pansy!"

"I *beg* your pardon?" He hoped his guilt came out sounding more like astonishment.

"Don't bother trying to pretend." She stepped back to let him pass. "I saw you embrace her at the gate."

But he stood his ground. "You watched?" he asked accusingly.

"That's not what I said. I said I *saw* you — just before she opened the gate for you. But it was quite clear you had been embracing. If the gate had not been between you I should have something much sharper to say."

He pushed past her then, brushing against her with unnecessary brusqueness. "You're not my mother," he grumbled.

She ran two paces and caught him by the arm. "Nor do I speak as your mother. Not even as your sister. I speak as any friend would speak to you, Will. And any *good* friend will tell you it won't do. I'm sure your own conscience is telling you the same — it simply will not *do!*"

He pulled free of her and took a pace or two up the stairs. "Is there hot water for a bath?" he asked.

"Of course." She stood and watched his progress all the way to the landing.

There he turned and asked, "Are you spying on me?"

"Of course," she said again.

35 The moment the Carringtons took their seats at dinner that evening the old man said, "Well, son, don't keep us all on tenterhooks like this. Spit it out! Did you see her?"

Will started guiltily — and only just managed to avoid looking at Pansy, who was passing round the soup plates. "See who?"

"See *who?*" his father echoed. "'Why, Mrs Gundry says she saw something very like a dragon go flying over the hedges with the sparks flashing from …"

"Oh!" Will waved a weary hand, not quite in his direction. "You mean Miz Philomena, I suppose? Well, there's no harm in her at all. People have …"

"No harm?" Leah chimed in scornfully. Then, seeing Pansy hanging around, she thanked her and said she could go back to the kitchen and wait for a ring for the next course.

His father, meanwhile, said to Will, "If you'd seen the gleam in Mrs Gundry's eye earlier, you wouldn't say there was no harm in her."

"Okay." Will, as always, gave up the struggle to tell his father and sister *anything*. Placidly he took a spoonful of soup and said, "Mmmh! It's good. There's nothing like a day's shovelling and vanning to get a man's appetite up."

"Is that what did it?" Leah said lightly.

"Oh? How did that go today?" his father asked — to Leah's annoyance, for the last thing she wanted to discuss was the LCT venture. It was clear that Will had actually seen the dragon-woman and she wanted to hear all about that, instead.

Will droned on, deliberately spinning out the technical detail until even his father, who had money riding on it, grew bored. "So then," he concluded, "just about sunset, we downed tools, opened the sluice, and set off for Sithney, home, and beauty." Then, remembering what Leah had witnessed, he changed it to, "Home and the beauty *cure* of a bath, I mean." He grinned at her as if he had scored a point.

"It didn't work, dear brother," she informed him sadly.

Ignoring her he continued, "But then Adèle came running to meet us and she was in such a bate I thought they must at least have been struck down with cattle plague or something. But it was seemingly worse than that. Apparently, Aunt Philomena — old Clifford Liddicoat's younger sister ..."

"*Younger* sister?" their father asked in amazement. "Are you sure of that? From the descriptions I've been given ..."

"Father!" Leah cried, holding her fingertips to her temples. "Something awful is happening here!"

"What?" he asked in alarm.

"Will is telling us a story. And he's starting at the beginning. And every word of it, so far, is making perfect sense! I don't think I can take much more of it."

"Ha ha!" Will tried not to laugh. "D'you want to know what happened or don't you?"

She hung her head contritely.

"We want to know," the old man said calmly. "Tell us about her. How much younger is she?"

"I guess she's got to be all of forty-five — but she sure doesn't look it. She's a real fashion plate — peaches-and-cream complexion and dressed right out of *Modern Modes*. I complimented her particularly on her hat — which you would have *adored*, Sis."

They could only stare at him. Disbelief was mounting. Either he was unobservant to the point of imbecility or he was pulling their legs. Or, it was beginning to dawn on them, this was a show of perverse bravado — the whole world walks in dread of Miss Philomena, so the bold, brave Will puts his head in her mouth and lives to tell the tale. Meanwhile the tales *they* had been told of the aunt's ferocity coloured everything he said.

"I don't know why they're so scared of her — which they obviously are." He laughed. "The moment old man Liddicoat heard she'd arrived he invented some excuse to go to Truro for the day!"

"So he wasn't there?"

"No — I mean he *was* there. He must have realized that slinking off to Truro was only postponing the evil hour, so he wound his courage to the sticking place and came back to face her." Now his laughter quarrelled with the soup and he had to drink a whole tumbler of water. Even so he had to take several runs at the sentence. "He stood there ... he stood there ... holding ... he stood there in the yard holding a gun — which he actually aimed at her when she arrived."

Now his family did not know what to think. The behaviour of the Liddicoats bore out all they had been told about the old — or, it now appeared, not so old — woman; only Will's responses clashed with the general opinion.

"What did she do?" Leah asked.

"She ignored him, of course. She just walked straight toward him and pushed the barrel aside. Told him not to make such an idiot of himself — and quite right, too. I ask you! He's going to shoot his own sister dead, right there in his own yard, with half a dozen witnesses? Oh, yeah! Of course she called his bluff. What they don't understand is that *she's* all bluff, too. What can she do? Okay, she's all kiln-fired sore at us Carringtons for stealing this place — as she sees it. And I guess she'll foam at the mouth when she hears about Nick and me and LCT — if she hasn't already." He almost mentioned Adèle, too, but wisely held his tongue. "But what can she actually *do?*" he repeated.

"Make life a misery for them?" his father suggested.

"Only if they let her. I don't understand them. They're pretty much in awe of her — and she *is* awesome, I'll grant her that. She's a little spitfire. But she has no real power. Can she stop people calling on us? Stop tradesmen and shopkeepers serving us? Prevent servants from applying for places? Forbid the steel barons to buy our tungsten?"

Father and daughter exchanged glances. This was a 'baby of the family' they had never seen before. It seemed that he was not simply putting on muscle over at Wheal Fortune but the lineaments of manhood at last.

"You're right, son," his father said thoughtfully. "That's quite a list there. However, even without meeting your little spitfire, I get the feeling that she won't let a little thing like impossibility stand in her way. She'll try! Maybe not with the steel barons but the rest will look attainable to her — to some degree, at least. So, while it may be brave and commendable and all that to dismiss her as ultimately powerless, we must also recognize that she could inflict a lot of hurt on us before she acknowledges defeat. There was never any doubt about the fate of hogs on their way to the slaughterhouse but you should have seen the damage one or two rogues could do on their way there!"

"So it's thinking-cap time," Leah said, taking cue from her father. "The first thing to ask ourselves is where she has the greatest influence."

"Leverage — it's always the key to situations like this." Her father rubbed his hands. Memories of commercial and personal skirmishes were stirring — hard fought and enjoyable times. Life had, indeed, been somewhat bland of late. Now he was actually looking forward to meeting this spitfire of a Liddicoat. "She'll fight a woman's war, honey," he said. "With woman's weapons and a woman's guile. So you tell us — where's she gonna strike first?"

"Well, her greatest *leverage*" — she used her father's word with emphasis — "is on her brother and his children. Was Harvey there, by the way?"

"No," Will told her. "He'd gone off without telling anyone. The old man must have been pretty steamed about that, too."

"To try to join the navy, d'you think?"

He shrugged. "No one will say it out loud but you can see that's what they're all afraid of. I didn't say anything."

"So she'll try every which way she can to drive a wedge between us and the Liddicoats, huh?" their father said. "She'll try to unravel LCT, I guess." He scratched his chin thoughtfully and eventually said, "She can't. It's Troy's money and mine. True, young Liddicoat has the Wheal Fortune mineral rights but we own the rest. If she prevailed on him to kick Will out and cut loose from us, we've got the rights to ten times as much wolframite as he does ..."

"A hundred times," Will said. "He wouldn't just be cutting off his *nose* to spite his face ... it'd be like cutting off his whole *head.* The fact is, LCT only works because it's a cartel of three. In effect, you and Troy have agreed to leave your rights unexploited until we've exhausted the Wheal Fortune halvans — and that's how we keep the price up. Cutting loose and going into competition would be suicide for Nick."

"How did he respond to his aunt's sudden appearance among them?" Leah asked.

Will stirred uneasily. "Very quiet ... subdued. Most un-Nick-like. Maybe *she's* why he's got this bee in his bonnet about strident women and suffragists?"

"Okay," his father said. "We put a tick in the worry column for LCT. And someone" — he looked at Leah — "has to put a little backbone into young Nicholas."

"But I never thought he lacked it," she replied defensively — though why she should have to defend him, of all people, she could not say.

"Well, let's just lock this stable door *before* the horse decides to bolt, eh?" He turned to Will. "And as for you, son — I know we've raised you *not* to trifle with the affections of respectable young females, so I wouldn't wish you to do any such thing with poor Adèle. God knows she's a homely little creature but how close a line d'you think you might tread there, *without,* as I say ..." His voice trailed off as he saw the expression on Will's face. "Have I said something wrong?"

Tell them! Will screamed in the silence of his mind. But something stubborn refused to give them that hostage; father and sister had spent too many years putting him down and poo-poohing his hopes and ambitions.

"There's no need for that," he said nervously, slipping his hands beneath the table so that they would not notice the tremor of his excitement. "As a matter of fact, we already get on extremely well."

Leah grinned. "Adèle's nuts on him, Pa. For her, the sun rises and sets with his day." She, too, saw the expression on his face and said, "Didn't you know?"

All he could do was shake his head. "It's not true."

Of course, he desperately wanted it to be true. He longed for Leah to offer a hundred proofs of it, all at once — and still he'd ask for more.

"It is, too," she assured him.

"Has she told you? I'll bet she hasn't said anything. You're just trying to tease."

Leah went on grinning.

"It's cruel to toy with people's affections," he went on. Where was her weak point? Where could he lash out at her? Provoke her into letting something slip? "The way you do with poor Nick, for instance," he blurted out.

"The Nark?" She laughed uncomfortably. "The *poor* Nark? Spare me!"

"Well ..." he said, catching his breath and letting it out in little gasps, as if there were so much he could tell her if only he were not bound by word and loyalty to say nothing at all.

"The Nark?" she asked again; but now she was more incredulous than scornful.

"Forget I said it," he told her uneasily though secretly exultant to have achieved so much for saying so little — indeed, for saying nothing that could be dragged up later.

"Really?" she asked. And now she was more worried than incredulous.

"I said nothing," he reminded her. "I say nothing now. And I'll say nothing in future, no matter how hard you pester. Nothing! I shouldn't have lashed out like that. One day, I'll grow up, I suppose."

"No fear on that score, son," the old man said laconically. "I think you already did. So you reckon you're already friendly enough with young Adèle?"

"Reckon so, Pa." He nodded sagely. " 'Course ... if it's war, I could sort of annexe up to her a bit further. All's fair in ... er, war, they say."

"All's fair in *love* and war," Leah corrected him.

Their eyes met and, hard though he tried to hold her gaze — her cool, penetrating gaze — he had to look away first. He knew that she now suspected him of some duplicity, though whether it was over his attitude toward Adèle or over what he had hinted at between her and Nicholas he could not tell. Already he mourned the days of his innocence, now lost — the days when they thought him too simple for anything like that.

Pansy came flouncing into the room just at that moment. "Mrs Gundry says does anybody want their joint tonight, else she might just so well go on home."

"Sorry!" Leah gave the bell a token ring and made a token effort at stacking their soup plates.

Her father, who had heard from Fenella Compton that 'gentry don't stack,' frowned at her but was soon distracted by Pansy's lithe, provocative young body as she sashayed around the table, making twice as many movements as a factory efficiency manager would recommend for the purpose — at least, for the purpose of clearing the table.

Leah watched her father's eyes as they followed the girl around the room and the problem of Miss Philomena Liddicoat suddenly became quite trivial. The girl did not seem to be wearing a corset; her movements were so lithe and easy. Well, she would simply have to go. It was not, of course, the first time the thought had crossed her mind, nor even the hundred-and-first; but she always came up against the thought that, while Pansy was a servant under their roof, the constraints of society were there to rule him in their most powerful form. Once she was just a girl 'out there,' she was a free agent — and they hardly came more free in their ways than Pansy! She would be open to any sort of arrangement and Leah's father would suffer little in the way of social contumely as long as the business remained discreet. It was more than the hundredth time she'd rehearsed *that* argument, too. Perhaps, she thought, if any Carrington were to be bewitched by the girl, it had better be Will. Maybe she had been a little hasty in her earlier warning.

"Okay," their father said as Pansy placed the joint before him to carve. "The dragon can't break up LCT but she can — or so it would seem — make life pretty nigh intolerable for the other four Liddicoats."

"She do want a *man,*" Pansy said as she waited, holding Leah's plate for the first slices off the joint. "My dear soul — that's some 'ansum beef, that is!"

Leah wanted to tell her to hold her tongue at table but her father had already tolerated — indeed, chuckled at — too many such outbursts for her to be able to do that. Instead she laughed, not at all warmly, and said, "Dear me, Pansy, is that your answer to *every* feminine difficulty? Get a man?"

"She do," Pansy replied calmly as she walked round the table with Leah's plate. "Look at that lovely blood!"

"On what do you base this diagnosis, Pansy?" Will asked. "Is it a general observation on the plight of the female sex or does it relate to Miz Philomena in particular?"

"Stands to reason," Pansy said. She refused to let herself be provoked by his banter.

"Tell us," the old man said, quite serious now, for he suspected she had something significant to say.

" 'Course you wasn't here when 'twas in all the papers — how that Colonel ... what was his name? Jelly bean? Gelatine — something like that."

"Jellicoe," Will said.

The others looked at him in surprise.

"Nick told me," he explained. Then, to Pansy, "I think I know what you're driving at. They said she did more than simply keep house for the old boy."

She nodded and smiled at him saucily. " 'Twas in all the papers. Everyone down here do know it. They do say as she made sure he died smiling."

The old man almost dropped the carving fork in his surprise. "They actually put that into cold print? I mean — in so may words? 'He died smiling'?"

"Well ... no," she admitted grudgingly. "But that's what they meant. 'Cos he wrote about his *dearest* housekeeper in his will. They put that in big black letters at the top of the words — *dearest* housekeeper. 'Twas a nine-day wonder, though, 'cos the suffragettes went and put that time-bomb under the dean of Saint Paul's, to give him a bit of a surprise, like, and everyone forgot the dearest housekeeper — 'cepting down here, of course. Last year sometime it was."

The Carringtons looked at one another. "We never heard about that," Leah said. "Did the suffragettes actually go so far as to blow up the dean?"

"No. A cleaning lady found it and poured water on it. 'Twasn't under him, 'twas under his seat — the one they said was carved by a gibbon. But 'twas lovely carving. Anyway, that's Miss Philomena Liddicoat's trouble, if you ask me. She's missing old jelly — whatsizname."

After she had gone — with the old man's eyes following her to the last flounce of her skirt as the door closed behind her — Leah risked saying, "Well, Paw, you're so keen for me to annexe up to the Nark and for Will to annexe up to Adèle — looks like *this* one's for you!"

He laughed good-naturedly and said, "That'll be the day!"

36 Leah heard Will's bedroom door open and close. She had been expecting it. In fact, she had waited up, fully dressed, glad of the chance to put her household accounts into order. All that evening, whenever Pansy had entered the room — to tend the fire, bring a shawl, or carry out the cups and glasses — she and Will had struggled valiantly to ignore each other, to arouse not a wisp of a suspicion in Leah or the old man. But that in itself was give-away enough, for on any other evening there was plenty of mild flirtation between them, of an amiable or facetious kind. She had to strain her ears to catch the sound of Will's clandestine exit from the house because a strong wind had sprung up during the evening. Indeed, Maria Vose's father had said, when he called to fetch her home, that south cones had been hoisted down in Porthleven and the harbour-master had let down the 'bock,' or bulwark, to close the inner harbour against the approaching storm.

She didn't hear the front door either open or close. She began to wonder if Will had gone up to Pansy's room in the attic, instead. The thought filled her with horror. A little spooning by the light of the moon was something to reprimand, but a furtive visit to a servant girl's bedroom at dead of night would call for instant dismissal. And, despite her earlier thoughts on the subject, Leah did not want to lose Pansy, who was the brightest and most efficient maid she'd ever known. How many other girls could lay a full silver service when called for, wait impeccably at table, invisibly mend the finest lace, milk a cow, and muck out a byre — all with the same infectious, if rather cheeky, good cheer?

Leah would almost turn a blind eye to any shenanigans, rather than lose her. Almost but not quite. She focused her attention upwards, listening out for a creak on the stair, or the complaint of a bedspring from Pansy's room. But then a sudden movement of the air, a rise and fall in its pressure, told her that Will had, in fact, opened and closed an outside door. She gave a sigh of relief and slipped downstairs as swiftly as she could. In the porch she paused only to slip into her galoshes before she followed him out.

The wind, streaming inland off hundreds of miles of ocean, was strong and steady. It was a merciful wind for lovers; there was not a cloud in the sky and, without it, the night would have laid a sharp frost over the land. Indeed, the wind must have been coming up out of Africa. It would have been warm at any time of year but was especially so for the start of October — which it would be in half an hour's time. Despite the warmth, however, there was really only one place for an assignation in such a gale: the tithe barn. Leah reached the back-garden gate just in time to see her brother take the last few paces up to the barn door. He was in his dressing gown, carrying a blanket draped over his arm and a basket, which banged against his leg and made him walk lopsided.

For an absurd moment her childhood memories overcame the grown-up in Leah and she supposed that her brother and Pansy were bent on nothing more reprehensible than a midnight feast. She even thought of calling out to ask if she could join them. The fantasy lasted no longer than the sour laugh it provoked in her as cold good sense returned and, with it, her baleful vigilance.

When Will reached the barn door he leaned toward it, his attitude attentive. He was probably calling out to see if Pansy were already there but not even a shout would carry crosswind to the house in that gale. Fortunately, it cut both ways — Leah heard Pansy coming round from the servants' entrance and was able to dive into a clump of false nutmeg before she might be seen; she made enough noise to rouse the dead, downwind, but did not catch Pansy's attention at all. By the time she emerged from the thicket and returned to her vigil at the gate, Pansy was halfway to the barn. She was wearing a dressing gown, tightly wrapped about her body, and her long fair hair streamed away from her. She was not so much walking as wiggling. Leah stood transfixed, never having seen anything quite like it; she had thought the girl's movements around the house provocative enough but they were the mere gliding of a nun when set beside this coquettish display.

It was so raw, so energetic, so self-enthralled, that it spoke without the need for words. It opened Leah's eyes at last, telling her that her brother and this maid were intent on something much heavier than mere spooning in the moonlight. They were going to do *It* — make the beast with two backs ... go all the way! Her mouth went dry and the blood drained from her limbs. She had to reach out and find a handhold on the gatepost to support herself for a while. Her mind raced as she revised her tactics in the light of this appalling realization. It was worse than simply creeping up to her room — which could, after all, be the impulse of a moment. This was premeditated, planned in detail. The blankets, the prepared basket, the congruence of meeting-place and time — all confirmed it.

And she, Leah, had formed no plan at all to act against this monstrous contingency. She had intended watching them spoon for a while and then she would intervene and play some jape upon them — pretending to be a ghost, say, or a poacher ... make a noise to scare them into giving up and going back home.

But *this!* They must be mad even to think of such a thing. And ten times madder still to carry it through.

She couldn't possibly allow them to start on such madness — no, not even to start.

Not that she had any very clear idea what 'starting' might entail. She had only the vaguest idea of what men and women actually did in those most intimate circumstances. She'd several times seen a boar with a sow but she didn't think it offered much help for understanding humans. The boar butted the sow here and there with his head and foamed a bit at the mouth. A strange corkscrew-thing twisted in and out underneath his belly. And the sow just stood there until he did a piggyback. Then they both grunted a bit, shuddered a bit, and, finally, the boar fell off again, still foaming at the mouth. Leah blushed to think how innocently she had used the term 'piggyback' all her life but she hardly supposed it told her anything about humans. After all humans did not gobble from a trough at dinner time.

As soon as the two lovers had kissed and vanished into the tithe barn she slipped out by the gate and ran across the dusty cobbles to its door. The wind masked any sound she made. Unfortunately it also masked any sound they might be making inside. She was just about to apply her eyes to one of the cracks when she realized that the moon, though almost overhead, was shining inward through that same crack and the sudden darkness would very likely betray her. She stepped hastily backward, a single pace that plucked her shadow off the outer wall, and then she hastened round to the far side of the barn, which was still entirely in shadow.

Even as she ran, though, she knew she was shirking her duty. She ought to go right up to that door, throw it wide, and ... well, a single 'No!' should be enough. She stopped halfway to her new vantage and ordered herself to go back and do the right thing. She would have done it, too, if the most shameful scene had not risen in her mind, even as she hesitated. In it she stood there, having said her 'No!' and Will just replied, 'Go home, Sis. This is none of your business' — leaving her looking the perfect dummy. What would she say to him then? 'I'll go and tell Pa'? Well, she ought to, of course, but she wouldn't. The less Pa got personally involved in any question concerning Pansy, the better — and Will knew it. 'Okay, but don't forget to wipe your feet when you come back indoors' — that would be just about the most authoritative thing she could say if Will got all truculent.

Morally defeated, she resumed her walk round to the back of the barn, though now she had no good reason to prolong this vigil. Unless you counted simple human curiosity. Well, it could hardly be called a *good* reason but it undoubtedly was powerful. At last she was going to witness — in a sense, to share in — the last of life's great mysteries. The compulsion she felt was greater than all the arguments against it.

As she approached the farther corner of the building she heard a regular bang-bang-bang, as if someone were hammering at the wood. Indeed, for a moment, she half expected to find John Hamden out there with a lump hammer in his hand and a mouth full of nails, securing loose planks against the gale. But it was just a loose plank, of course — about twenty feet long, secured at the top but shaken free from about halfway down. The gale continually peeled it back until its own elasticity made it return and slap against its framing again.

It gave her an idea, though, about getting inside rather than simply peeking through a crack in the wood. The bangs were not as regular as a metronome, so a longer-than-average interval would not be especially noticeable. She chose a moment when the wind had pulled it out to the maximum and, praying it would not split if she opened it just a little bit wider — enough for her to squeeze inside — she tugged at its edge and more or less rolled herself vertically through the opening.

She paused in the dark and listened hard, but the resumed banging from the plank would have masked anything quieter than a silver band playing Old Hundred. And the light-dark-light-dark it created, just where she stood, was as if some child were playing with a lampwick, turning it up and down, up and down. However, it allowed her to see that she was standing in a narrow and accidental passage between the outer wall and the stack of hay they had been forced to buy in, since Liddicoat had cut and carried every blade before Midsummer Day. She knew the pile was high, so there was no fear of being observed.

That still left her with the fear of observing. Every decent impulse within her urged her to return now, before it was too late, before she did that most despicable thing — the Peeping Tom. Or Tomasina. But impulses are as chaff in the gales of instinct, and her instincts impelled her onward, to watch, to *know* at last this great and, as yet, unrevealed mystery — unrevealed to her, at least: the mystery of life itself.

She edged cautiously away from the clatter of the loose board, still having no idea precisely where she was in relation to what she remembered of that load of hay — nor where Will and Pansy were, either. They could even have climbed a ladder to lie in one of the lofts, this side of the central open space or that. She froze. They could be above her now, looking down with amusement, having heard her come in. Slowly she raised her gaze to the rafters, ready to call out, 'Good heavens! Did you hear that noise as well?' and spin some yarn about fancying she heard slates peeling off in the gale. But no one looked down. No thing looked down — not even the resident owl. She breathed again, and again sidled toward the centre of the barn. Wherever they were now, they must have started from there.

She edged her way cautiously from the intermittent light toward the dark. But she went slowly enough for the dark to lighten perceptibly as she moved into it; there were plenty of cracks in the walls and the moon was very nearly full. The end of the hay pile (one could not call it a proper stack) appeared as a dark, ragged silhouette against dozens of moonlit dots and dashes — the perforations in the opposite wall. The doorway showed as a recurrent streak of moon-lightning — with appropriately simultaneous thunderclaps as the gale plucked the door open a fraction and slammed it to again.

Between those bangs she heard the two lovers. And then, by that light, she saw them — not eight feet away. They were lying on a blanket spread out on a pile of hay on her side of the open space. She went rigid with terror. Pansy seemed to be looking directly at her. Only the fact that she did not start up with a cry and clutch some shred of clothing about her revealed that Leah was, thus far, invisible. A short while later — fifteen seconds by the clock, perhaps, but an eternity measured by heartbeats — Pansy's continuing lack of response reassured her of her invisibility and she was able to relax. Enough, at least, to begin to take in the extraordinary scene before her.

For a start, they were both naked. The only nakedness of which she had any experience, except when skinny-dipping as a kid, was in statues and paintings. And they were no preparation at all for *this*. Will, who had his back toward her, was a dark triangle with an intermittent silver outline that showed the lithe contours of his muscles and the easy movements of his arms. He was stroking Pansy's body — her thighs, her hips, her tummy, her breasts — and occasionally running his knuckles lightly across her neck and cheeks. She was lying full stretch, staring up into his eyes, smiling placidly, occasionally reaching out a languid hand and stroking him, too — his head, his hair, neck, shoulders, chest, and ... well, lower down. They both laughed with delight when her hand went down there.

Will reached into the dark behind him and his hand returned, bearing a bottle. Port by the look of it. He filled, or refilled, a glass — which both explained the basket and emphasized the adult nature of this particular midnight 'feast.' He took a sip and then put his lips to Pansy's. She gulped and then giggled again; she had a lovely, silvery little giggle.

How did Will know to do things like that? Perhaps this was not their first-ever assignation here, though Leah felt in her bones that it was. These loving gestures had not been polished over many such occasions; they arose spontaneously between them. But how?

To her surprise she discovered that the answer was within herself. She could feel it there — a little knot of understanding which she had only to tweak for it to unravel. Not here. Not as a mere observer of others' passions. But elsewhere, some other time, as partaker herself. Her heart fluttered wildly at the thought. No, it was more than thought. It was a conviction. It *would* be. Her breath shivered. Her whole being shivered, body and soul, at this revelation. She had crept in here, expecting to see a physical act, only to discover that its mere physicality was the least important thing about it. What mattered, what spoke to her directly — and found echoes within her, too — was the tenderness of Will's caresses, the melting light in Pansy's eyes, the spontaneity of their every gesture, the utter ease they obviously felt in each other's nakedness. It was the most beautiful thing she had ever witnessed.

He stretched over Pansy to set down the glass in a beam of moonlight; it sparkled like a ruby. He did not raise his body again but snuggled himself half on top of her. She saw the girl's thighs fall apart to let his knee settle between them. They stretched luxuriously, shivering with the exertion — and with something more. She writhed gently beneath him and he began to move, too.

Leah could watch no more. Nor did she need to. Her own body had taken fire from its empathy with the lovers in their gathering ecstasy. She closed her eyes and pushed her face hard into the hay, savouring the sharp needling of its dry stalks against her cheeks and brow. It was as if she were trying to blot out these new discoveries, though she knew they would never leave her now. They were the new ghosts of the old tithe barn; they would haunt her until she found the means to lay them.

As she edged back toward the loose wallboard, she heard a cry from Pansy that stopped her dead. At first she thought Will must have done something, no doubt unwittingly, to hurt the poor girl. But then she cried out again, this time saying, "Yes! Yes!" as well. Leah stood transfixed and listened. And the final mystery of all was revealed: that this ... this *thing* they were doing, this beautiful, easy, tender thing, was an ecstasy almost too sweet to bear.

Outside again (she hardly remembered getting there) she leaned against the ancient wood and closed her eyes and raised her face to the warmth of the wind and fought to still her racing heart. Everything she had ever heard, or guessed, or read between the lines, about this business was untrue.

Filthy? Furtive? Scandalous? Animal? Gross?

Untrue.

A woman's burden ... grin and bear it ... *his* right ... think of the little baby, instead? Grit your teeth and think of family, nation, race?

Untrue.

The sordid triumph of some 'lower' nature, regrettably necessary, over all that is high and pure and noble in the divine human soul?

Untrue — all untrue!

In a daze she wandered back into the house. In her room she undressed and washed almost without realizing it. Then she lay in bed and wondered how she was going to face Will tomorrow — and tomorrow, and tomorrow. What on earth would she be able to say to reveal her understanding without letting him know what she had seen?

And who was Will, anyway? Certainly not the dull, childish dimwit she and her father had always seen in him. In a way — perhaps in the most important way of all — he was streets ahead of her in the game of life. The game of growing up. Without knowing it he had pulled her down off her high horse, kicked the throne out from underneath her — however you cared to put it. In the past half-hour he had travelled a long odyssey away from her and back again, returning as a voyager who had seen too many strange sights and made too vast a discovery of the wider world to explain to a dull young stay-at-home like her.

She expected dreams that night but had none she could recall the following day. Perhaps dreams were no longer enough.

37 The wind veered westerly during the night and turned several degrees colder. The skies clouded over toward dawn and the rain was falling in big, fat drops by the time Will set out for Grankum Farm, which was now the first stop on his daily walk to Wheal Fortune. In his euphoric mood he hardly noticed the rain, though the wind almost buffeted him to the ground a couple of times on the exposed flank of the hill. To his surprise he met his father emerging from Grankum Wood. When he had gone upstairs to shave after breakfast he had naturally assumed the old man had done likewise. But there he

was, unshaven as the dawn, holding up a large, dead buck rabbit and grinning with triumph.

"Got the bugger!" he said in parody of Hamden. "Set a snare for 'n last night and got the bugger at last." Then he showed why the labourer might have been on his mind. "Hamden told me I'd never do it my way."

"Well done!" Will said, bemused. "Was he giving trouble?"

"Hamden?"

"No, the rabbit."

"He'd have devoured the seedlings I hope to be setting out in the long acre today."

"Are you going to work out in this weather?"

"Sure. You think you're the only *man* in the family?"

His stress on the word, though no doubt innocently jocular, came too soon after Pansy had, in the vulgar phrase, 'made a man of him' for Will to accept it in complete comfort. "We'll probably spend the day indoors," he replied. "Or under cover, anyway — bagging up the ore. It's grown to quite a pile and we've been waiting for weather like this to deal with it. Are you going to stick seedlings alone? Wouldn't Hamden help you once he's finished the chores?"

"Oh," his father said airily, over his shoulder as he resumed his homeward walk, "Pansy said she'd give a hand — if Leah could spare her." Very much as an afterthought he added, "Leah, too, maybe."

Full of foreboding, Will entered the wood by the gap from which his father had left it. Down here in the lee of the hill and the added shelter of the trees, the gale was reduced to a creaking, keening wind. The leaves were showing the first autumnal tints, though none was falling yet, not even on such a day as this. He could not bear to think of Pansy working beside the old man. He could just picture them. His father would stand to one side of the taut-stretched line and stamp the blade of his long-handled shovel into the ploughed and thrice-harrowed earth. He'd change his grip and pull it up three inches, pressing the soil toward him. And Pansy — lithe, supple, slender girl, bent almost double — would pop a seedling into the cleft and hold it there in her delicate fingers while he put his boot behind the blade and withdrew it, tramping the loose soil firm and closing the crack around the baby plant.

True, she'd be swathed in oilskins and a big sou'wester would cover her head, denying him the pleasure of gazing down at her adorable ears and her smooth, slender neck, but even so ... What thickness of clothing was proof against the inner eye of a man when such a nymph is bent double before him?

And what a chatter she'd keep up all the while — what country jokes and reminiscences and infectious giggles would stream out of her, banishing the storm and lightening the day! He almost turned about, to go home and warn Leah, to tell her to stick seedlings with the old man and set Hamden on to do the same with Pansy. He wouldn't object to that. Hamden couldn't stand the girl; to him she was 'that kitey giglet' — the sort of female who would benefit from 'a good fist between the eyes.'

Will knew that Pansy had warned him against falling in love with her, and he didn't think he had. Nor for one moment did he suppose she had fallen for him, not even at the height of last night's frenzy, when she had 'scratched his back to fletters,' as she said when she later bathed the blood away (and showed him the little horseshoe bruises where his teeth had bit into her back!). She relished the freedom to do such things without the constraint or excuse of love — to do them for their own sake, because they were good in and of themselves. All the same, the knowledge that she'd do the same for the old man if he ever lost his wits sufficiently to beg the Favour of her was powerfully discommoding to a fellow.

The only thing that prevented Will from turning about was the thought that, if he were late, he might miss Adèle, who often went to Penzance of a Thursday. Last night, while waiting in his bedroom for 11:30 to strike, he had wondered if he would ever be able to face Adèle again. But now he could hardly wait. His only fear was that, in some rash moment of insane honesty, he'd blurt out what he'd done — merely so that he could tell her that it didn't matter a jot! It meant nothing. It no more impinged on that new, special *thing* between him and her than would ... he tried to think of some other pleasure, just as intense but equally neutral, too. The neutral bit was easy. Eating ice-cream and strawberries ... swimming in the cold of the ocean on a blistering summer day ... Life was rich in neutral pleasures of that kind. But 'equally intense'? Honestly compelled him to admit there was nothing to match it. The first sweet plunge into the coolness of that ocean ... prolonged for an hour or more? The mind could grasp the words but not the reality they sought to convey.

He was out of the wood again before he realized he had passed the well — *her* well — without drinking of its enchantment. He didn't go back for that, either. As he approached the farm gate memories of the tableau he had left behind him last night (was it only last night?) returned. He would not have been surprised to see them all standing there, with Miz Philomena cracking the whip over them still.

But the yard was deserted and, to judge by the 'baling' from the field, as the locals called the bellowing of cattle, the milking had not even started.

"Ho there!" he called out as he swung himself in an athletic arc over the gate, hoping Adèle noticed his strength but not the way the pain from his lacerated back made him flinch.

"Come on in," Nicholas shouted as Will lifted the latch.

He found father and son trying to eat fried bread and bacon that shattered at a touch. "Roll on rationing!" Nicholas said morosely, impaling a fried egg on his fork and waving it about like a pennant.

The old man, still smarting no doubt from yesterday's humiliation, kept his eye on his plate and chewed stolidly.

"Where's Adèle?" Will asked at once.

"Good question," Nicholas replied. "She accompanied the aunt back to Helston last night and was probably sliced into tiny pieces and fed into the Helston River. Anyway, she didn't come home." He popped the egg whole into his mouth, held his nostrils tight together, and chewed as if it were a puncture-patch — which it probably resembled quite closely.

Will decided not to mention the aunt at all. Nor Harvey. He said, "We can bag up some of that stuff today, I suppose."

Nicholas washed the rubber shards down with some tea, pulled a face at its taste, too, and went over to the larder. "No pasty for my croust," he said disgustedly as he helped himself to a bag of sausage rolls and reached for his oilskins. "A fellow's got to marry these days to get a decent household about him."

Will shot a startled glance at the old man. On any other day such a statement would have provoked him to a rage, but he just went on chewing and staring at his *Methodist Weekly* without reading it — probably not even seeing it was there.

"Come on!" Nicholas picked a scabby apple off the tree beside the front door. Out in the yard he twisted a twig off the hawthorn and chewed the end of it to form a makeshift brush. Between them, the apple and the twig, he cleaned his teeth as they walked up the yard and on across the field, among the 'baling' cattle, to the wall where Adèle had fallen into Will's arms — and his heart — some twelve hours earlier.

Standing on its crest, tricing up against the wind, he glanced back, hoping at least for a sight of her returning. Instead he saw her father open the gate and cry, "Cope! Cope! Co-ope!" to cattle who, for once, needed no come-hither cry at all. Normally he swore at them and slashed furiously at the nearby hedgerow with his stick, calling them hellers and devils and every name going. Today he just stood and watched as they hastened past him into the yard.

"It's taken the wind out of his sails, eh?" Will said to Nicholas.

"You got out while the going was good last night," he replied. "What happened? How long did she stay?"

"Too long. Almost three hours. Three hours too long."

They set off across the poisoned croft. Now Will could see that the rain would probably not hold. Great ragged clouds scudded toward them across the sky but in the distance there gleamed a brighter impasto of white and blue — only flecks of blue as yet but even a single fleck was more than dawn had led him to expect.

"I suppose you just sat at home by a nice warm fire reading H.G. Wells or something shocking like that," Nicholas said.

"Something shocking like that," Will agreed. "Tell me — why are you all so scared of the old family dragon? What can she do to you, anyway?"

"I don't know," Nicholas said after a brief, morose silence. "I went to bed last night thinking, why do we let her do this to us? Just like you say — what can she do? But somehow, when she's there in the room with you ..." He sighed and gave up trying to explain it directly. "It's like watching a conjuror — but without the pleasure. You watch him as hard as you can for one false move and yet he still fools you. You *know* there's no such thing as magic — just as we know there's nothing she can really *do* to harm us — but it makes no difference. He beats you all the same. And so does she."

"Did she ever whack you as kids — or what? Did she get a hold over you then?"

"Never! God — the times I've stood there just *wishing* she'd box my ears and let me go ... instead of having to stand there being skinned by her tongue! Last night you could really hear she was Cornish."

"What does that mean?"

"Well, how d'you think she sounds?"

"Lawdydaw? Not Cornish, anyway."

"Exactly. That's what I mean. When she took up with old Jellicoe's circle she forgot every last syllable of her Cornish speech. But not last night. We were edjacks and slummocks and slumps, scadgers and bitter-weeds, eckas, gabbies, gawkuses and ... I don't know what. I didn't know we had so many words for 'idiot'." He laughed. "Of course, we do have more than our share of idiots to start with."

"Did the Old Glebe really mean so much to her?"

The question led to a long silence. They were approaching the old calciner now — or 'calla-siner,' as the dialect has it — the source of all that poison underfoot. Its rusty ribs and the hints they gave of its once-massive bulk made Will wish he were more of an artist than he was; its perverse beauty cried out to be recorded. "Didn't mean to pry," he said at last.

Nicholas spoke as if concluding some internal argument: "What do I owe her, anyway? Her anger has nothing to do with the ancient Liddicoat—Carrington feud — remember? The banning of all nonconformists from acquiring title to the Old Glebe. She *says* it has but she's just picking up any old stick to beat a dog. The *real* trouble arises because her father — my granddad — once promised her that, by hook or by crook, the place would one day be hers. You never knew him, of course. I can only just remember him but it was the sort of extravagant thing he loved to say. He was a lovely man — a local preacher, and very popular because he promised heaven to all and sundry. Very unusual in a Methodist. Anyway, he promised her the Old Glebe one day, and she ..." He hesitated.

"Swallowed it hook, line, and sinker?" Will suggested.

"I reckon so."

They took a little detour to pass by the old Wheal Fortune Number Four Wim shaft, where it was now their daily ritual to throw in a boulder or two. They listened, awestruck, to the huge, hollow roar it gave out as it ricocheted from wall to wall, fetching down loose shale as it went — all of which fell into the water at the adit level with a mighty splash. Or *splooosh,* deep and cavernous, would be more closely onomatopoeic. If they breathed in slowly through a wide-open mouth, they could actually feel the vibrations in the pit of their lungs.

When they resumed their walk down to the stamps, Will said, "In the opinion of the servants at the Old Glebe your aunt is missing the old colonel."

"Could be," Nicholas agreed.

"In every possible way," Will added.

"Ah!" He cottoned on at last. "I wonder?"

He wondered for the best part of a minute and then added, "I don't think so. Women aren't like us in that respect. Females in general. Sows just stand and wait patiently for the boar to be done. Same with cows. Hens just crouch and shudder a bit. Ewes go on eating and staring at the horizon — I've seen them. And ladies don't enjoy it at all, I'm afraid, old chap." He gave Will an apologetic grin and punched his shoulder playfully. "Think again."

Will tugged at his ear, gazed at the sky, and said nothing; after all, he himself could easily have been guilty of those sentiments a mere twenty-four hours earlier.

The rain died back to the occasional flurry as they strode down over the sandbanks and shale of the old halvans.

"We'll still bag up a ton or so, I think," Nicholas said. "Even if it stops raining completely. That pile is getting a bit unmanageable. We'll fill the hoppers first and bag it inside — rather than carry in hundredweight bags of wet ore-sand."

"We could dry it first," Will suggested. "Get a good furze fire going between rows of stones. Lay sheets of that old corrugated iron over the top — the stuff someone dumped in the quarry last month, remember? And spread the sand out on that. We could dry out a hundredweight a minute, I reckon. And then the smelters couldn't tell us we were five pounds light on every bag because it was wet."

"It would never be as much as five pounds," Nicholas said in a dubious tone.

"Try telling them that *after* it's all gone into the furnace!"

Nicholas saw the point and, grudgingly, agreed to the plan.

"I'm not going to sweat inside these oilskins, though," Will said when they arrived at the stamps. "I'll put that old shirt on and keep this one in the dry."

He went into their little toolshed to change. Nicholas followed him, intending to do the same, but the moment he popped his head inside he could only stand and stare. "Dear God!" he exclaimed at last. "Did someone drag you backwards through a bramble hedge or what?"

"Something like that," Will replied casually.

"Go on!" Nicholas laughed and punched him again. "What really happened?"

"That, dear boy, is what one of your passive, bored, unfeeling females can do while granting the Favour — just to express her passivity, boredom, and general lack of feeling, you understand. A *human* female, I hasten to say." He laughed at his friend's gaping incredulity. "Care to revise your opinion of your sainted aunt's frustrations?" he asked.

38   Leah did not help her father stick seedlings and cuttings that day. Nor did she particularly mind when he asked if Pansy could help him. Knowing nothing of her brother's feelings for Adèle, nor of Pansy's unconventional ideas about granting the Favour, she assumed that her brother and the maid now 'belonged' to each other, for at least as long as such casual affairs usually endure. In any case, she was eager to see Elizabeth Troy again, not to tell her about last night but to seek her advice in dealing with Miss Philomena Liddicoat. She arranged the day with the servants, indoor and out, and drove the pony and trap into Helston.

On her way through the cattle market — deserted on a Thursday, of course — she saw Ben Coad standing outside the ring, watching Tony Allet, the local sign-painter, putting the finishing touches to a new nameboard. She turned off the highway and drew up alongside them. "What was wrong with the old sign?" she asked.

"I've got *two* telephone numbers now," he replied with feigned nonchalance. "Anyway, it needed a thorough spring clean — or a fall clean, I suppose. You looking for another couple of milkers, are you?"

She became cagey at once. "I might be. Why?"

"Mrs Pascoe, over to Tregathennan, wants a valuation for probate of her late husband's herd. She might sell, too."

"Tregathennan?" Leah said. "I'm going to Pallas Home Farm, if that's on your way."

"Tregathennan's farther on," he said. "Richard Pascoe used to manage Pallas Home Farm for Mrs Troy — so he didn't breed rubbish."

"You could take this trap and call for me on the way back."

A visit to the Pascoe farm was not particularly convenient to him at that moment but he mentally rearranged his day and gladly accepted the lift, stopping only briefly at his office to pick up some papers and let his clerk know of the change.

"I thought it was set to rain for the day," he said as he climbed back beside her.

"That's the joy of Cornwall — you never can tell. By the way, we are deeply in your debt, Mister Coad, for your warning about Miss Philomena Liddicoat."

"Did she call on you?" he asked in surprise.

"No. Only Will has seen her so far ..." She hesitated, wondering how much more to tell.

"Which way are you taking?" he asked.

"I usually go out on the Wendron road and then cut back in at Coverack Bridges. That's the way Mrs Troy goes."

"Oh, but there's a much quicker way — back through Saint John's to the toll house, then up through Lower Town. It's at least two miles shorter. She only goes the other way because she can pretend she's at the motor races."

When Leah faced the horse back down the hill he added, "When you said you were on your way to the Troys, I wondered why you came in as far as the market. I thought it was to see *me*, of course. How stupid!" He laughed to assure her he was joking.

"Well, I'm glad anyway," she told him. "It's been too long."

"And you've been busy, I expect. We certainly have. The army and the navy have sent in huge requisitions for meat and the cavalry's been round several times looking for remounts. It's wonderful — they just hand you the government cheque book and say, 'Get 'em!' But it's a fearful lot of work, even so."

"I can imagine," she said.

They were repassing the auction ring by now. "A couple of inches higher!" he called out to Tony Allet, who waved cheerily back. "He won't do it, of course," Coad said under his breath to her. "Artistic genius!"

A little farther on he said, "You bought the Old Glebe at exactly the right time, you know. You could sell it for half as much again now — just the land and farm buildings."

"Oh! That will please the Liddicoats," she said glumly. "*Why* are they so obsessed with the Old Glebe, anyway? It can't just be because of what Honourable Carrington did all those years ago, surely?"

"No," he agreed. "It's also got to do with living at Grankum. For three generations they've farmed those acres. Three generations have looked across the valley and coveted your place ..."

"And didn't they have the chance?" Leah interrupted vehemently. "How long was it on the market before we put in our offer?"

"I know, I know," he replied in a placatory tone. "I lost count of the times I warned him that someone would come along and snap it up. But of course, when nobody *did* come along and snap it up, he thought he could laugh up his sleeve until we dropped the price. I'll bet he's kicked himself ever since."

They turned off the old turnpike at the toll house and took the metalled road along the valley toward Lower Town, which was actually no more than a hamlet.

"Especially ever since yesterday evening!" Leah said.

He sighed. "Yes, I missed a trick there. I should have written to her the moment the place came on the market. She wouldn't have hesitated." After a moment's thought he added, "Mind you, that was right after the scandal in the papers. I had no way of knowing what sort of mood she might be in — and no one approaches that woman voluntarily, even when she's in the best of moods."

They drove on in easeful silence under a brightening sky for a while before Leah said, "That colonel fellow ..."

"Jellicoe?"

"Yes. She obviously wasn't all that formidable to him. 'My *dearest* housekeeper' ...?"

"Oh, well, she isn't always in a bate. I've seen her as sweet as Cornish niceys. But I'd say she's even deadlier then than when she's frowning."

"Yes, but that's just being deadly-sweet. I've known people like that. But that's not what I mean. There must have been times when she was genuinely sweet − don't you think? I mean − the sort of woman who won't suffer fools gladly simply isn't capable of *pretending* to be sweet over long periods. She must have been genuinely sweet to old Colonel Jellicoe."

"Well, now!" He coughed awkwardly. "That was the rumour, to be sure."

"As well as *that,* though." Leah refused to share his embarrassment. "I'm not just referring to *that.* There must be a real gentleness in her somewhere."

"In theory," he conceded. "I'd hate to be sent in with a lantern to scout for it, though."

They rounded a corner and the railway viaduct came into view, a mile away at the upper end of the valley. As if it had been waiting for the moment, the sun came out in a single shaft that swept like a spotlight across the tall, slender arches ... and then vanished again as the clouds closed the gap.

"Doesn't it seem an age since that day!" she murmured.

He did not ask what day she meant.

"I think our first impulse to buy the Old Glebe came because *you* showed it to us, Mister Coad."

"I?" he echoed in surprise − delighted surprise.

"Yes. You were so kind to us that morning − assuring us we were almost more Cornish than yourself ... warning us about the ancient feud ... and so on. Tell me one thing − but don't answer if you'd rather not. Did you decide to be so frank before or after you met us?"

"After," he replied without hesitation. "Now, of course, you want to know why!"

She laughed as she obliged: "Why?"

He pinched his brow as if he had to think. "Looking at it all round," he said, "putting two and two together ... taking the rough with the smooth ... at the end of the day ... when all's said and done ..." He glanced slyly at her and chuckled. "I can keep that up a long time."

"I'm quite sure you can," she replied with mock severity.

"All right — penny on the drum," he said briskly. "The long and the short of it is ... I had hopes of a long and happy association with ... you ... people."

She glanced at him hastily, nervously. He had an auctioneer's gift for using pauses. "Not dashed, I trust — those hopes, I mean — not dashed?"

"By no means," he replied. Then, in the same breath, as if it were part of the same thought, he added, "Another reason why Miss Philomena may be particularly aggrieved at the loss of the Old Glebe (as she would see it) is that her father more or less promised it to her."

In her surprise she chucked the pony in the mouth and they came to a dramatic halt. "Sorry," she said, touching the creature with her whip. As they set off again she added, "You'll have to explain that."

"Well, her father, James Liddicoat — who was also Clifford's father, of course ..."

"He was the Liddicoat barred by Honourable's exclusion clause — right?"

"The same. We forget, in these enlightened days — we forget how all-consuming religion was back then. Methodists, Baptists, Christadelphians, Anglicans ... they were different *tribes*. They lived intermingled with one another so they couldn't fight pitched battles, but they fought a war of endless skirmishes with whatever weapon came to hand. The law being one of the most obvious, of course. So, in a curious way, old James Liddicoat *expected* to be excluded from the purchase. Honourable Carrington had the power, so he used it — all according to the rules of war. And when James went to the courts and got the exclusion clause annulled, he was fighting by the same rules."

"So he chalked up the final victory," Leah said.

"I don't think Miss Philomena ever saw it that way, though. The fact was, they had lost the chance to buy the Old Glebe — and that was victory to the Carringtons. She'd be spitting-mad if *anybody*, other than a Liddicoat, had bought the place last spring. But to hear that a *Carrington* had once again snatched it from under her nose — and an almost lineal descendant of old Honourable, too!"

"You were saying that her father promised the place to her?" Leah reminded him.

"Oh, yes. Old James was a preacher on the Helston circuit — but in great demand all over. There are two ways for a circuit preacher to be popular. The commoner way is to preach hellfire and eternal damnation. The more vivid the pictures, the better they like you. The rarer way is to stress God's infinite love, mercy, and forgiveness. Congregations would take seven hellfire sermons — until the children started having nightmares — then they'd send for James Liddicoat to spread a little balm. That was how it worked. The meek always inherited the earth when James was the preacher."

"He sounds a sweet man," Leah said. "Why do such traits die out in a family?"

The comment interested Ben. He stared at her to see if she meant it.

"Go on," she said.

"Well, I suppose that Miss Philomena — growing up in less tribal times — was less willing to accept that it had been a fair fight and that her father had won it in the end. She just saw the practical result — they'd won the legal principle but lost the actual acres. And old James, who promised heavenly bliss to the deepest, dyed-in-the-wool sinner ... well, could he do less than promise his darling daughter that the place would, indeed, be hers one day!"

"But *how?*" Leah was still bemused.

"Lord! James Liddicoat never let a little detail like that interfere. God's infinite love and compassion would do it all. Lean on the arms of the Lord! Leave it to Him. Patience and faith were all we require here below."

They forded the Cober at Lower Town and started a diagonal climb up through Gwavas to Pallas Halt.

Leah said, "It explains a lot about his children — Philomena and Clifford, anyway. Life with such a father must have been hell, not to mince words."

Coad laughed with surprise. "D'you think so?"

" Sure. With someone as insanely optimistic as that — and so blindly trusting in ..." She waved a hand vaguely at the sky.

"You don't believe in any kind of divine intervention then, Miss Carrington?"

"I don't believe in winning prizes without competing. My father says the only things you'll find in a pie — apart from the things you took the trouble to put there yourself — are flies and other feller's fingers. Don't you agree?"

"I do. I do. And I think that's a point on which you and Miss Philomena would wholeheartedly agree." He chuckled at this discovery. "How she would *hate* to be told she has more in common with you Carringtons than with any of her own line!"

When they had laughed at this bizarre conclusion he added, "Except, maybe, Nicholas?" He made a slight question of it to test her response.

"Well," she commented, "as for Nicholas — at last we know where he gets his fear of women from! Fortunately, it does not seem to be infectious. Will has no ..." She hesitated again and then, without completing the thought, said, "Quite the opposite, in fact. Shall we give this pony a rest? It's a stiffish climb. Also, that's part of Mrs Troy's herd in that field, I think?"

He stood and peered over the hedge. "You're right," he said.

The pony stopped rather more abruptly than she intended and he had to grab at her shoulder for support. She dropped the reins and caught his arm.

"I'm so *sorry*, Miss Carrington," he stammered when his footing was again secure. His ears turned pink, too, as he pulled his arm away.

"Don't be," she said, letting her own grip linger a second or so and releasing him with a squeeze.

The pony, still panting heavily, started grazing at the foot of the hedgerow. She set the brake and, leaving the reins loose, leaped nimbly down. A moment later she was leaning on the gate, sizing up Elizabeth's herd with a slightly more experienced eye than the one that had seen them last.

"It shows what you can do if you control the breeding for twenty years and more," Coad said as he joined her.

"You get good-looking cows," she said dismissively. "But not a penny more for their milk. That's another of my father's sayings — you can't taste a hog's pedigree but you can tear it up if the ham is sweet."

"Democracy!" Coad pretended to scorn it. "It has never caught on over here and it never will."

She laughed and dug him with her elbow. "You're good company, Mister Coad," she said. "I'm glad I started off the wrong way. This morning, I mean."

39 Pansy suspected the gig contained the two Misses Liddicoat — Adèle and Philomena — but she said nothing for the moment. Between sticking the seedlings and quicksets in their nursery beds she kept an eye on its progress through the lanes. Only when it turned in at Grankum Farm was she sure. Even then she said nothing. She didn't want to interrupt old man Carrington, who was telling her about his life as a dealer in the Pittsburgh board of trade — a world she would never be able to imagine if he did not bring it so vividly to life. But some fifteen minutes later, when she saw a single female emerge from Grankum, get back into the gig, return along the lanes, and then turn off at Boase's Burnthouse, she could not help crying out, "Oh my gidge! I do believe she's coming here!"

"Who?" John Carrington asked. He was so wrapped up in his memories he had almost forgotten who Pansy was.

"Miss Philomena Liddicoat," she said. "That's her boneshaker coming along the lane now."

Carrington straightened up and, following her pointing hand, saw in silhouette the upper half of a female torso bowling toward them along the lane. She was, indeed, making for the entrance to the Old Glebe. In a moment or two she would pass the gateway into the field where they were working. They stood and watched.

In fact, she did not pass the gateway. When she saw them in the field she reined in her pony and turned toward them. "My good man!" she called out.

He and Pansy exchanged glances. The woman's error gave him an idea. He winked at the maid. "Hold your tongue now," he said. "Us'll 'ave a bit fun wi' she!"

Pansy giggled but he pointed a finger at her and said, in his usual voice, "You'll stay here if you can't control yourself better than that, my lass."

He started to walk over to the gate in a slow, loping, labourer's pace. Pansy, taking pattern from him, slipped into the slovenly gait of a field girl as she followed. It would not deceive Miss Philomena, however, if the woman recognized her, so she didn't exaggerate it.

"I never heard you talk Cornish afore, sir," she said.

"Cut out the sir." He dropped back into dialect. "'E in't too difficult, see. West Country English is faather to American, anyway. I do often hear a man talking and I 'ave to think now is 'e Cornish or American? Hush now or she'll 'ear us."

"My good man," she called again when they were just within talking distance. "I'm looking for Mister Carrington — your master, I presume. D'you happen to know if he's at home today?" There was not a trace of Cornish on her tongue.

He scratched in the stubble of his still-unshaven chin. "Carrington," he said slowly. "Now would that me Maaster William or Maaster John?"

"The father! The father!" she replied angrily. "I know very well where the son is — more's the pity."

Carrington turned to Pansy. "Whurz th'ole bugger got to then?" he asked her in a perfect imitation of John Hamden.

Pansy stared at him in horror and then suffered a coughing fit. He sent her off to drink a 'dish o' tay' from the bottle they'd brought out with them.

"I suppose I shall just have to seek until I find," Philomena said crossly. "What does he look like?"

"Why, 'e's some tall feller," Carrington told her. "Wears a frock coat and top 'at. Fancies 'isself a farmer, 'e do — so you'll like as not find 'n with an eeval in 'is 'and, mucking out the cowshouse or turning the dungheap." He spat contemptuously into a furrow.

But she became interested in the fact that this yokel could string so many words together — and did not seem intimidated by her. "You worked for him long, have you?" she asked, letting a touch of Cornish creep into her voice.

Carrington spat another quid, as if he'd been chewing tobacco. "'E in't a bad ole feller," he replied. "'Course, 'e got 'is funny ways — like anyone, I reckon." If this went on much longer, he'd have to admit that one of his 'funny' ways was to imitate his labourers and pose as one of them.

"Come here," she said.

She descended from the gig and approached the gate. As she walked she took a sixpence from her purse and held it where he could see it. "Tell me about these 'funny' ways," she said. "You, too, girl," she added to Pansy, who had just rejoined them.

"I know you, don't I? Pansy Tregear from over Carleen? Goodness, how you've grown!"

"From Trew, Miss Liddicoat." Pansy corrected her.

"Trew, Carleen ... it's all the same," she said crossly. "What are you doing working on the land?"

"This is gardening, ma'am," the girl replied in a slightly offended tone. "Not field work."

"Hmph!" was all she replied to that. "But *you*" — she frowned at Carrington — "I don't know you."

His heart fell. He had not, of course, planned any part of this practical joke but he had imagined it would run to no more than two or three exchanges. And a good laugh later. He realized, however, that he could not, in all honour, tell her a direct lie. "You aren't gwin to like it, Miss Liddicoat," he said, "but I'm a Carrington, too. Not one o' *they,* though," he added vehemently, waving his hands vaguely toward Sithney, which she could take to include the Old Glebe if she wished.

Another thought was now entering his mind: His unwillingness to give her the lie-direct implied that some part of him assumed there would be a social relationship between them in the future; otherwise, if it was to be outright war, with no social meeting of any kind, he could say what he damn well liked.

He wondered why the woman did not press him on this unlikely assertion — but that was because he did not see Pansy, behind him, gyrating a finger near her temple and pointing to the back of his head.

"I see." Philomena's tone became gentler. She smiled sympathetically at him — which only increased his bewilderment — and turned to the girl instead. "Tell me about your master," she said. "He sounds a great deal more interesting than most of the men hereabouts."

"He *is,* ma'am," Pansy said fervently. "He's the best and kindest master a maid could wish to serve. There's *nothing* what I wouldn't do for him — and I don't mind if he knows it. He can tell tales of his days in America to put all adventures in the shade. I thought Stanley and Livingstone was exciting enough, but ..."

"Yes, yes," Philomena interrupted, curbing her impatience with only moderate success. "But ... er ..." She looked about the field as if she might find there the words to steer her inquiry away from these gushing opinions and more toward hard facts about her enemy.

Carrington, no fool, had meanwhile worked out that Pansy had rescued him earlier by suggesting he was a bit simpleminded. He fidgeted and stared at the sky, as if he could not concentrate on even the simplest topics for very long. Anything now rather than be unmasked.

In a way, Philomena did find her inspiration in her survey of the field. "Gardening, you said?" She echoed the word with more than a hint of disbelief. "What has this to do with gardening? What are you sticking over there? It looks like winter cabbage to me."

Her jaw dropped when the girl replied, *"Sorbus sibirica,* if it please you, ma'am. And *Cornus alba* 'Elegantissima' and *Philadelphus incanus* — that's a rare one, that is."

She mangled the botanical Latin but there was no doubting that the day's work was horti- rather than agri-cultural.

"I see," Philomena said thoughtfully, turning the coin over and over, *almost* as if she had forgotten it was there.

Carrington stared at the maid in amazement, which Philomena took for his simplicity. He knew, of course, that the names were on the labels round the sphagnum-wrapped bundles from the nurseryman but he had never imagined she would read them, much less remember.

"'Course, the war has stopped his plans," Pansy went on, "but 'twill be over soon 'nuff and we shall have this nursery field full of sturdy plants to set out, see?"

Philomena stared toward the Old Glebe. "I still don't quite understand," she said. "The garden is hardly what you'd call large — and is, in any case, filled with well-established ..."

"Lord, ma'am!" Pansy, in her enthusiasm, dared to interrupt. "Didn't Mister Liddicoat tell 'ee? This whole farm — all fifty acres — is to become a garden to rival Trewennack and Skyburriowe and Trengwainton." She waved a hand across the landscape. "There'll be peacocks and fountains and ... and they temple things with columns and bare white ladies in stone ... and a shell grotto ... and a wishing well ... and trees ..." Her invention petered out at that.

During this flight of fancy, Philomena noticed that the maid glanced at her simpleton partner a couple of times. Something about those glances, an edge of nervousness, made her inspect the old boy more closely. She was always on the qui-vive for insults, slights, injuries, shopkeepers' tricks, so she now began to notice his *un*-weatherbeaten skin, his clean ears, his well-tended hair. And when he became aware of her scrutiny he fumbled with his hands, trying to hide them. That was when the penny finally dropped.

Her biggest surprise, though, was not the realization that she was, in fact, in the presence of the man she now most detested in all the world — and a man, moreover, who had just tried to make a fool out of her — but that she was more amused than angry at it. A clumsy attempt at deception, something she would have seen through at once, *would* have infuriated her. But this was well done. It had a certain wit. And, she now recalled, he had, indeed, told her his name was Carrington.

But he was not at all the man she had expected to find ensconced at her beloved Old Glebe. She thought he would be a brash, overbearing man of the mercantile kind, for she had known several Cousin Jacks who had returned 'home' with more money than taste. They were ever-ready to brag about America's vast superiority in every field and their own cleverness at climbing the ladders over there.

This man clearly posed a greater challenge than she had bargained for. She was sorely tempted to linger there and tease them — keeping them in the prison of their imposture while she extracted every last drop of information and advantage. But she was less confident of her acting ability than old Carrington was of his. (And, she admitted grudgingly, with good reason, too; his imitation of Cornish, and specifically of John Hamden, whom, she now realized, she had almost been sent to find, was impeccable.) And so, rather than give away the fact that she had seen through them, she thought it best to beat a tactful, and tactical, retreat.

These rapid musings were not so much thoughts as feelings within her — feelings in her bones, feelings that swept through her mind in far less time than it takes to tell. So Pansy had barely finished her stumbling panegyric to the gardens of the future at the Old Glebe before Philomena said, "How very interesting, Pansy! I had no idea your master had any such thing in mind. As soon as the war is over, you say?"

"Oh, ah." Pansy was nonplussed by this apparent about-turn in the woman's attitude.

"It does rather change things," Philomena said, giving no hint as to whether it changed them for the better or for the worse. "And, talking of change, *you,* my dear, have changed rather a lot from the vain, flighty, empty-headed little giglet you were when last I saw you. You've turned into an observant, nimble-witted, and bright young woman. And a rather pretty one, too. Yes — distinctly pretty."

Pansy blushed, curtseyed, and started to stammer out some vague sort of disclaimer.

But Philomena continued, "So I was all the more surprised to hear you say just now that there was *nothing* you wouldn't do for your master. Surprised and not a little disquieted, let me say. I trust you'll *never* utter such a sentiment in his presence. That would be so foolish, you know." She gave the simpleton an apologetic smile for talking so far above his head and, leaning toward Pansy, lowered her voice confidentially. "We women know what we mean by such words. We use them in their noblest, purest sense. But men are cast from a different clay. I know you won't mind my saying this — as your old Sunday school teacher — but do strive to remember that your master is a widower. He lacks the nightly solace of the marital bed. He is also of that age when men grow desperate at their waning powers. Some feel they must grasp at every fleeting opportunity to exercise them. You do know what I'm driving at, don't you?"

Pansy swallowed heavily and nodded.

Philomena smiled at her affectionately and gave the simpleton another apologetic smile. She was delighted to find him almost beetroot-purple and exophthalmic with rage. "However," she went on briskly, "since you say you would do *anything* for him — in the sense that any dutiful servant girl would mean those words — may I prevail upon you to hand him my card? It is a small but common civility." She fished again in her bag and produced one, passing it over with the sixpence. Then she turned to Carrington and gave him, too, what he thought to be sixpence but later discovered to be half a sovereign. "And as for you, good fellow," she said, "I'm sorry for your affliction, but we cannot all be clever. Nonetheless, we can all strive to be good. Protect this maid to the best of your limited wits, eh? Oh, and buy yourself a good pair of working boots. Keep those for Sundays — they are far too good for field work, even of a horticultural nature."

And, without waiting for his thanks — which were not forthcoming, anyway — she turned about and, smiling to herself, remounted her gig and set off once more.

When John Carrington found he was clutching a half-sovereign, he dropped it in his surprise. "Bitch!" he said bitterly while Pansy picked it up. "She tumbled to me after all."

"Half a sovereign!" Pansy exclaimed, holding it up against her sixpenny piece. They were almost the same size, silver by gold. "You think she made a mistake?"

"No mistake," he said, taking the card from her. "That woman knew exactly what she was doing. The only reason she gave you this is so that I will know where to send my letter of apology: the Angel, Helston. She must have had these printed yesterday." He tried to smudge the ink but it was quite dry. "Or she even brought them from London with her. We start one-down, Pansy — no doubt about that."

"Bloody cheek!" Pansy muttered, staring after the departing gig. "Telling me what to do and what not to do like that." She rounded on him almost belligerently. "Don't you pay no attention to what she said." Belatedly she added, "Sir."

But Philomena's cruel portrait of him — of all men his age — had left an indelible mark, being far too close to the truth for his comfort. He would not even be able to go through the first stumbling motions of a pass at the girl now — not without the clown-like spectre she had raised intervening and mocking him to impotence.

Pansy, who did not mind how long they stood there and chatted, since she was not particularly keen on stooping all morning long, said, in quite a different tone, "She's some bowerly woman, though — don't 'ee think?"

"Bowerly?" he asked. He was not able to hold her eye after the outrageous things that Liddicoat woman had said.

"Eyeable," she explained. "Doxy."

"Good-looking?"

"That's what I said — she's some 'ansum woman."

"So Will said last night. I thought he was exaggerating but he wasn't. Not a bit."

"Still — beauty's only skin deep, they say."

He chuckled. "That's right where any sensible man would want to find it, Pansy." He took the gold coin from her and stared at it pensively.

"You going to send that back, are you?" she asked anxiously, wondering if she dared suggest one or two alternatives.

"No," he said, popping it in his waistcoat pocket, "I'll find some way to rub her nose in it, never fear." He started walking back toward the nursery bed, now with a master's tread again. "A gentleman should never do business with a lady, Pansy," he said. "Remind me if I ever look like forgetting it."

"How?" she asked, meaning 'why'?

"If her position's weak, she'll add in her sex and beat him to the deal. If it's strong, she'll subtract her sex while he's not looking — and *still* beat him to it."

40   Ben Coad was waiting at the gate to Pallas Home Farm when Leah left. Elizabeth Troy caught sight of him when she saw her guest to the door. *"Now* I understand why you refused my offer of a drive into Helston. I thought you'd brought Hamden or someone along as driver."

Leah was about to explain how her picking up of Ben had been pure accident when she saw that the conclusions to which Elizabeth had leaped would happily cover her real reasons for refusing the lift, namely Elizabeth's belief that she could beat Fred Karno on the open road at any time. "He's good company," she agreed.

"They're a very solid, dependable family, the Coads. Ben's father was the Troy family solicitor."

"But not yours?"

"He would have faced a conflict of interest so he very honourably advised me to go elsewhere." She laughed. "So I went to George Ivey and gave him such a horrid time that he got out of law entirely and took to painting instead."

Leah remembered her father's sadness that the Carringtons, as newcomers, would never know all those things that people need to know in order to belong to a community. Even when people told you snippets of their past, they dressed them up in jocular half-truths as Elizabeth had just done.

Ben offered her the whip as she approached but she waved it aside. "It's very kind of you," she said. "But I can look around better and see what everybody else is up to if I'm not also trying to control that creature."

"Well, was Mrs Troy much help in your perplexity?" he asked as they set off.

Leah sighed. "Yes and no. I mean, she repeated all those sensible things we've been telling ourselves since yesterday. Like, what can the woman actually *do?* She's not going to attack us physically. She can't do us much harm socially. There's no legal trouble she could stir up — as far as we can tell. And so on and so forth. But that isn't really the problem."

"What is, then?"

"Just the knowledge that she's somewhere out there, looking for a chance, waiting to pounce. From now on we've got this daily worry. We've got to guard our backs. We've got to think before we do anything — could this give her a chance to poke us in the eye?"

"Strike first?" Ben suggested.

"How? We don't wish to, anyway. My father has spent thirty years on the Chicago and the Pittsburgh boards of trade watching his back like that, guarding himself against *real* sharks — men far more formidable than Miss Philomena Liddicoat. He retired to get away from it, not leap from frying pan to fire."

Ben considered this in silence awhile and then asked, "Did he enjoy it, all that cut and thrust?"

"Of course he did. He was king of that jungle."

"Perhaps he misses it? Perhaps a polite but deadly little war with Miss Philomena is just the sauce his life has been missing — especially now his plans to build a great garden at the Old Glebe have been frustrated."

She slumped. Her head hung dejectedly between her hunched shoulders. "You're right, Ben," she said. She had not intended to use his first name; it just slipped out.

He reacted with surprise.

She smiled wanly. "Don't we know each other well enough by now — Ben?" This time the stress was deliberate.

"Well ..." He flushed. "I certainly hope so ... Leah?"

She put a hand to his arm and squeezed once, briefly. "I'll have to talk him into selling the Old Glebe again before he gets the scent of war in his nostrils. Is that house you once showed us at Gweek still up for sale?"

"No, alas. But there's a farm going at Goonhusband, about three miles the far side of Helston. It's just about to come on the market. Sixty acres facing south, overlooking the Loe Pool and Mount's Bay — breathtaking views. If I'd been able to show it to you last February, you wouldn't even have considered the Old Glebe, I can promise you."

She chuckled. "You could sell a dog kennel to a cat, Ben."

"Shall we go to see it now? We can drive straight up the hill from Lower Town and out along Clodgey Lane."

"No. Another day, perhaps. I'd better get back and start working on the old man — before he decides that a good fight with Miss Philomena will make his life complete." She shook her head and said, "People of their generation, eh! What *are* we going to do with them?"

She arrived home with fifteen minutes to spare before lunch. Her father had planted out all his seedlings and rooted cuttings and Pansy was in the scullery with her arms in hot soapy water up to her elbows, trying to get some life back into her frozen fingers. She was also bubbling over with the excitement of their encounter with Miss Liddicoat. Leah listened until the tale seemed garbled beyond belief — all that bright chatter about pretending John Hamden was the master and being given a half-sovereign in place of a sixpence. Then, halting the girl in mid-flow, she said, "But tell me what she's *like,* Pansy. Master Nicholas says she's quite pretty. Is that so?"

"Yes, miss, she's some bowerly, we do say — a goodly eyeful."

"And was she deceived, d'you think? Did my father's impersonation of John Hamden take her in?"

"Yes, miss. At least to begin with it did. But then, I don't know, she sort of tumbled to us."

"*Sort of* tumbled? She either did or she didn't."

"Well, she did, but she never showed it. Just gave a little knowing sort of smile and ... well ..." She looked away and her manner became evasive.

Leah did not let her go. "A knowing smile? And then parted with ten shillings? It doesn't add up, Pansy. She said something

— or did something — to let you know she'd tumbled to it. So let's have the full story. From the beginning."

Pansy sighed as she took the towel Leah held out for her. "I s'pose it started when the master come out with a thing no gentleman would say — just to convince her, like, that he *was* a field labourer."

"What?" Leah was both shocked and intrigued.

"I couldn't possibly repeat it, miss."

Leah went to the scullery door, looked up and down the passage, then closed it. "You can," she said with a friendly smile as she returned to the interrogation. She did not add, 'And you will,' but her eyes spoke for her.

"When Miss Liddicoat asked for the master, he turned to me and said" — her voice fell to a mumble — "'Where's th'ole bugger got to now, then?' So there — that's what he said." The tips of her ears flushed blood red. "Oh my gidge!" she exclaimed, fanning her face and trying not to laugh.

In the end they both laughed and the tension eased. "He actually said that?" Leah asked.

The girl nodded. "I nearly had a fit. He had to send me to drink a bit tea."

"So that convinced her he was a labourer. I must admit, it would certainly convince me! The question remains, then — what *un*-convinced her? And how did she let you know she was no longer deceived?"

Pansy realized she was not going to be let go short of telling the whole tale. She tried, though. "'Tis a bit embarrassing, miss," she offered.

"Yes? You've already made that quite clear. Go on."

"She read me a little lecture on the wicked ways of masters with pretty servant maids — how I was to keep myself pure and fight him off if he tried anything." She swallowed heavily. "And the master standing there at my side!"

"Good heavens!" Leah could understand the girl's embarrassment now. "But why? Was it just out of the blue like that?"

"Just out of the blue," Pansy affirmed, crossing her fingers behind her back.

"Dear me!" Leah sighed. "Perhaps my father noticed what triggered such an astonishing outburst. I'll ask him. She seems to be a most unpredictable lady."

The threat to quiz the old man had the desired effect on Pansy. "Maybe …" she said hesitantly.

"Yes?"

"It *could* be …" she went on, as if unveiling an extremely remote possibility. "It could be something I said. See — I thought, if the master's going to play tricks on Miss Liddicoat like that, why can't I play a trick on him? So when Miss Liddicoat asked if he was a good master to me, I …" She sniffed. "I praised him to high heaven — to embarrass him like. Made out he was the *best* master who ever trod the face of the earth …"

"And said there was *nothing* you wouldn't do for him?"

Pansy stared at her in open-mouthed dismay.

"Did you say that, Pansy?"

She half turned away. "I don't know, miss. I s'pose I might have done."

Leah grabbed her by the arms and made her face the accusation. "You did, didn't you! And you weren't playing a trick on him, you were taking the chance to tell him that if he tried any *tricks* with you — and you know durn well what I mean, I'm sure — you wouldn't put up too much resistance. Eh? *That's* what Miss Philomena heard in your tone — and *that's* what gave her the idea to read you that astonishing lecture. Eh? You little idiot! You'll have to get up a lot earlier in the morning if you want to pull the wool over *my* eyes. They see a lot more than you think."

The girl's lips were trembling and tears filled her eyes; but Leah knew she had to drive the point home. "For instance, I know very well what's going on between you and my brother," she went on.

Shock momentarily displaced the maid's embarrassment and grief; then she buried her face in her hands and yielded to tears. But after a while she realized that something more than simple contrition was expected of her and she began to mumble words to the effect that it would never happen again.

She stopped when Leah touched her gently on the shoulder. "Don't make promises you cannot possibly keep," she said. "I have to admit that my first thought was to dismiss you at once and without a character. But there are two good reasons why I did not do so."

That stopped Pansy crying between one sob and the next!

"In the first place, you're one of the best maids I've ever known." She raised a warning finger. "But don't let this go to your head. You're not out of the wood yet. And if you think you may now rest on your laurels and let your standards slip, you'll have as much chance as an egg-sucking hen at fricassee time. The second reason is that if I did dismiss you, you'd simply get employment somewhere else nearby and go on meeting my brother anyway — and I'd no longer have any control over you or him. So you'd have the last laugh anyway. There!" She smiled engagingly. "You now understand that I do *not* hold all the cards in this little poker game between us. And the ones I do have I've just laid on the table — except for *this* one." She played an imaginary card in the air between them. "Understand that, while I more or less have to tolerate what is going on between you and my brother, I absolutely will *not* tolerate anything of that kind between you and my father. One kiss ... one tiny cuddle ... and you're ..." She cudgelled her brains for some suitably appalling fate.

"Fricasseed?" Pansy suggested.

"Yes." Leah eyed her coolly. "You bounce back quickly, don't you, Pansy! Will you put all your cards on the table, too? For instance, you do realize what a risk you're running with my brother, I hope? You know there is absolutely no chance of your marrying him — if that's what's on your mind?"

"Marry him?" Pansy echoed. To Leah's surprise there was a touch of pity in her manner now. "That's not what I want, miss — not marriage. Nor yet for a long while, I hope. A bit of fun is all I seek — honest. Besides, Master Will's too much taken with Adèle Liddicoat ..."

"Adèle?" Leah echoed in amazement.

Pansy, seeing now that Leah knew nothing of it, quickly pulled a stupid-me face and said, "I mean that Curnow maid ... Blanche Curnow — that's who."

Leah appeared to accept the correction, though inwardly she was not convinced. A single name — Adèle — might easily have slipped out by accident. But with a surname to validate it ...? Somehow that did not ring true. "So why are you setting your cap at him — even though you know it's hopeless?"

Pansy, not *quite* looking her in the eye, replied, "I wouldn't marry him if he asked me to — and he knows it. So ask him, instead. Why is *he* setting his cap at *me* when he must know 'tis hopeless, just so well as what I do?"

Leah frowned. "But we all know why men …" Her voice trailed off as understanding dawned.

Pansy nodded and said, "What's sauce for the gander is sauce for the goose, you might say. Now I must go and ring the gong for your lunch, if you'll excuse me, miss."

As Leah watched her go she realized that, somehow, the girl had turned the tables on her, leaving her as the one who wanted to ask questions to which she *didn't* already know the answers: Why did Pansy do it? What was it really like? How did she avoid all the usual nasty consequences?

But she swept them to the back of her mind as she joined her father for lunch. A new set of questions took their place at once.

"Well," she said as she took her seat, "I hear you met the Dragon herself this morning. Is she really as beautiful as Helen of Troy and the Queen of Sheba all rolled into one?"

It was a buffet lunch but Pansy stayed to pour out the soup and bring it to table. Leah noticed how her father glanced at the maid, as if to ask how much his daughter had been told; but Pansy's face was a perfect servant's mask.

"She is one handsome woman, right enough," he replied guardedly. "Did you hear how I fooled her I was some local yokel? I tried to fool her into taking John Hamden for me. But it wouldn't have worked because — as I ought to have guessed — she's known him most of her life."

"You say 'wouldn't have' worked — you mean she tumbled to your trick, anyway?"

"No," he said blandly, "she was obviously in haste so she just handed Pansy her card and asked her to give it to her master. In fact — and this'll show you what I mean by *haste* — she slipped me a half-sovereign under the impression it was a sixpence! Too vain to wear eyeglasses, if you ask me."

Leah frowned. "You'll send it back, surely?"

"I?" He was all innocence. "What do I, John Carrington, know of her mistaken gift to one of my labourers! No, I shall not be giving it back. I've thought of the perfect use for it."

"What? Thank you, Pansy. And there's no need to hover just outside the door. We'll ring the bell good and loud if we need anything else."

The girl lingered to see if he would think of something to keep her in the room but he just nodded agreement with his daughter.

"What 'perfect use' have you thought of for it?" Leah asked when the girl had gone.

"Never you mind," he said, relishing his secret. In fact, he relished it too much and had to blurt it out in the end. "Oh, all right!" he exclaimed after she had made some blatant attempts at banal conversation. "I'm going to put a plaque on the fountain saying that funds for its construction grew from an original and most generous donation of half a sovereign from Miss Philomena Liddicoat. And I'll have a quotation there, too — something like 'Great oaks from little acorns grow.' Eh? How about that?"

Leah made a noncommittal gesture.

"Come on!" he said. "You must have some opinion of it."

"My opinion, Father," she replied with a sigh, "is that it's a pity great minds do not from petty actions grow."

"Oh." He was crestfallen. "You think it's petty, then?"

She relented with a smile. "I know how satisfying such thoughts can be. It's not a petty *thought.*"

"As long as it stays right there! Okay, okay."

She said, "I heard some good news from Ben Coad today — two bits of good news, in fact. One is that our farm buildings and land are already worth more than we gave for the whole place. We could sell them off and be left with the house for free, plus a few pounds to spare."

He bristled. "Out of the question! Do you seriously imagine that I'd ..."

"I know, Pa. I'm not suggesting it for one moment. But I'm sure it's not beyond your wit to make sure the fact trickles through to Miss Philomena, eh? *That's* why I call it good news."

He was all smiles again. "And the other — the second bit?"

"Ah, you know the money Granpaw put in trust for me?"

"Yes?" He was guarded now.

"You're now the sole trustee since Uncle Jimmy died, right?"

"Yes?" Guardedness turned to downright suspicion.

"And you're a pretty shrewd investor — or so half the state of Connecticut assured me at various times. I mean, it'd be worth a tidy penny by now?"

"Come to the point," he said. "But I warn you — I'm not going to tell you how much."

"Oh?" she said, as if his words surprised her slightly. "Oh, okay." She pushed her soup plate aside and went to serve herself from the buffet.

"What was this other good news?" he asked as he crossed the room to join her there.

"Oh, it doesn't matter now. It was just a thought." She resumed her seat at the table. "If it doesn't rain again before tomorrow, we'll have to carry a keeve of water out to the long acre and water your nursery beds. Did you mark them?"

"Come on now," he cajoled. "What was this second bit of good news?"

"Nothing — honestly. If my trust fund is absolutely secret and sacrosanct and only to be used as a dowry, then it's not good news at all — nor bad. It's not news of any kind. When I asked if you marked the beds, I meant did you mark them so that even John Hamden couldn't make a mistake?"

"No, I didn't mark them at all. And I've never said the trust fund is *exclusively* for your dowry. It's ..."

"You've always given that impression."

"I just meant it's hard to think of any *other* purpose. In fact, when something worthwhile *does* come along — like your milking herd, for instance — I'm only too happy to release some of the income."

"But not the capital?"

He started to laugh. She asked him why. "Oh, something I said to Pansy while the Dragon was driving away — one of the many pearls I used to cast before the swine on the hog-futures exchange. 'Never transact business with a woman. If her argument's light, she'll throw in her sex and beat you on the deal. If it's heavy, she'll subtract it and beat you anyway.' Words to that effect."

"That's quite a pearl," she said coldly.

"Really, Leah, honey! What d'you want to touch the capital for, anyway?"

"Nothing," she assured him. "I was just asking a general question. *If* some worthwhile project came up, would it be *possible* ... et cetera? That's all. It doesn't matter. I think I'll call on Adèle this afternoon. Ben Coad says that Mrs Pascoe, widow of a farmer at Tregathennan, has some good milkers for sale ..."

"You seem to have stopped for quite a chat with Coad."

"I didn't stop for a chat. We chatted as we drove." She explained how she had come to offer him a lift.

The news did not seem to please him. She asked why.

"I think it's maybe a little tactless just at this particular moment," he replied.

"This moment? Why is this moment any different from ..."

"Because of the Dragon's sudden arrival, that's why. Think of poor Clifford Liddicoat's position."

She set down her knife and fork rather than brandish them. *"His* position?" She waved her hands in annoyance. "What *is* his position — and why *poor* Clifford Liddicoat all of a sudden?"

"You know his position, honey — from that very first day. His hopes of acquiring the Old Glebe without paying a penny on it? Have we any news of Harvey, by the way?"

She shook her head in vexation. "That's another thing I want to hear from Adèle. You mean his absurd dreams of marrying one of his sons to me?"

He closed his eyes in exasperation. "Whether *you* think it absurd or not, honey, is beside the point — which is ..."

"I don't *think* it's absurd. I know it is."

"That's beside the point, too — which is that *he* believes it's the case. So just think of the situation down there at Grankum Farm. In storms his sister Philomena and chews his head off for not buying the Old Glebe — and what excuse is he going to offer? Now d'you see? It doesn't matter — not a jot — whether you or I believe it. What matters is that *he* does. And there's a fighting chance that he'll persuade his sister to the same futile hope. At least it would stop her from going berserk. You're a Carrington, honey — surely I don't have to spell out every little detail? So for you to be seen driving around with Ben Coad — even on the most legitimate sort of business — is going to undermine that whole thing. It's going to bring her down on our necks again."

He expected her to see the point, accept the argument, apologize, and promise to be more circumspect in future. She saw the point well enough but from then on her point of view veered sharply away from his. She picked up her knife and fork and resumed eating in stoic silence.

"Well?" he had to prompt her.

"Well what? I simply can't think what to say, Pa. Maybe it's something your generation just can't see. I've just spent the morning arguing the point with Elizabeth Troy — also to no avail. So I don't see much purpose in repeating the whole thing with you."

"You could try, honey. Am I leaping down your throat? Bawling your head off?"

She shook her head in reluctant agreement. "The point is that both you and Mrs Troy start from this assumption that, since she has no power over us in any direction, she can't do much harm. But *my* point is that she is already harming us, just by being here, by forcing us to wonder what she's up to, by making us ask about every little action — could she use it to our disadvantage? We're living with one eye over our shoulder all the time. She can make our life a misery without lifting a finger."

The implication of her words annoyed him. "We sure as hell aren't giving way to her," he said, adding just in time, "if you'll pardon my language."

"That's that, then," she said with resignation and returned to her meal.

"I can't believe you'd want to give way to her, either, honey."

"I can't believe it would be 'giving way' to sell land and buildings to her for more than we gave for the whole place. Who loses? She can afford it, too, by all accounts. So you've got her by the scruff of the neck — either she buys the land or she shuts up for ever — for *ever* — about us and the way we cheated her family out of it."

"And my garden project?" he asked coldly.

She pursed her lips to hide her triumph. He accepted that selling out to the Liddicoats on such advantageous terms would be no defeat. Or, at least, he did not dispute it. Being his daughter, however, she realized that to produce the farm at Goonhusband at that moment would seem far too pat. It would expose all her manipulations. So, since Ben had assured her it was not yet on the market, she decided to drop the subject for a more propitious moment. "Yes," she agreed. "That would rule it out. Still ... but for that, eh, it would be a fitting way of getting her out of our lives for good."

"No doubt of that," he said easily, thinking there was little harm in such an admission.

41 Leah found Adèle up to her elbows in flour, making a beef pie for their dinner that night. Eileen, whose task it would normally have been, had not turned up that day and inquiries at her home in Carleen revealed she had not spent the previous night there, either. Nobody made the connection with Harvey's simultaneous disappearance — or not to the Liddicoats' faces, anyway — but it was naturally on everybody's mind. Even Adèle hinted at it, obliquely, when she said they'd have to hire another maid but passed none of the expected comments on Eileen's behaviour. She said she was going to Carleen after finishing the pie and asked Leah if she'd like to come along for the walk.

Leah accepted. "You look as if you could do with some cheering up," she said.

"Do I?" Adèle responded.

"Yes, you look as if you lost a lover and found an aunt."

Adèle, far from joining in her laughter, looked at Leah rather sharply. But Leah hoped the little dig would prove enough to provoke her friend into unburdening her fears a little during their walk.

The wind was now a mere half-gale. It had dried out the higher parts of the lane so the two young ladies found it possible, with care, to avoid the wet all the way to the road. Adèle's first question was, "How did Will seem to you this morning?"

Leah, whose mind was still full of last night's caper in the tithe barn, was taken aback. She played for time. "Didn't he call at Grankum for Nicholas this morning? Oh — how silly of me! You weren't there at breakfast, were you. Didn't you find the Angel noisy after the quiet of the countryside?" While she was speaking she recalled Pansy's slip of the tongue; then Adèle's interest was clear.

"I didn't sleep much," she admitted. "But that wasn't on account of the noise from the street."

"And coming up from the bar. That's what used to keep me awake. It was dreadful."

"I was wondering whether strychnine or arsenic or curare would be best — or, indeed, whether any of them would have the slightest effect on my dear, sainted aunt. She's going to ruin everything ... just everything."

Leah was surprised to hear a little catch in her voice, suggesting that her humour was to mask her closeness to tears. "I've been pondering that, too," she said. "It isn't that your aunt can actually *do* anything — or not much — to harm us. My father and Will keep comforting themselves with that thought. But they miss the point — don't you agree? The point is that her reputation and her presence down here are enough to ruin our peace of mind. We now have to watch our backs the whole time. We tell ourselves she can't hurt us but we can't actually guarantee it. All the time we have to think, *could* she do this, *could* she do that?"

"That's fine for your family," Adèle said morosely. "But she *can* actually do things to us."

"For example?"

"She's got the old fellow under her thumb. He'll curse her every way to Christmas but he'll go to heel the moment she snaps her fingers at him."

"But *you* — you and Nicholas — what can she do to you? And Harvey, of course. No news of him, I suppose?"

"I'm sure he's gone to Plymouth to try to join the navy — idiot! She can make our lives so miserable we just give in. Did she see your father this morning? When she left me she said something about a scouting party into enemy territory."

Laughing, Leah told her what had happened — Pansy's version of the tale, not her father's bland, complacent gloss. She omitted, however, the lecture Aunt Philomena had delivered on how servant maids should resist the advances of hurrisome masters, young or old.

Adèle found it amusing, of course, but not for long. Her earlier gloom settled again when she said, "The more you Carringtons triumph over her, the harder it will be for the rest of us Liddicoats. I think I'll run away from home, too. I can manage a household. There must be a nice, retired, elderly clergyman somewhere who wants a capable and energetic young housekeeper ..."

"'To my *dearest* housekeeper ...'," Leah quoted.

"Oh, don't!" Adèle collapsed on her arm. "You see — that's the real danger of having someone like Aunt Philomena around.

She provokes a body to such extreme actions — strychnine ... running away ... anything rather than do her bidding or yield to her will."

"Talking of Will ..." Leah said — having decided to end all this beating about the bush.

"Yes?" Adèle's sudden eagerness was heartrending.

"Penny on the drum — is there anything going on between you and him?"

"No!" she replied at once.

Leah leaned forward and peered into her friend's face. "Look me in the eyes and say that again," she challenged.

Adèle looked away. "It's nothing," she replied. "It's so *tiny* ... you'd only laugh if I told you."

"Try me."

Adèle turned and faced her. "Promise?" The appeal in her eyes was poignant.

For reply, Leah took her arm and held it tight against her as they walked. "I think I may be in a similar quandary," she said. "So which of us goes first?"

Adèle, who had been bursting to tell *someone* ever since last evening, before Nemesis arrived, needed no further prompting. "It's so small," she said. "I told you it's so small. But it's one of those things you just *know* when it happens." She described the way she and the two men had climbed over the hedge from the poisoned croft, how Nicholas had pushed her, how Will had caught her and held her and set her down — light as a feather. "And our eyes met," she said, trembling again at the memory. "That's all. That's the little thing I warned you about. Just — our eyes met. But something happened. It was only a moment, but something happened. He wasn't expecting it, I'm sure of that. But I could see it hit him like a sort of thunderbolt. He couldn't let go my waist. He couldn't look away." She was on the verge of tears.

Leah, to rescue her, said, "And the minutes turned to hours as the evening slowly fell around you, and the stars came out to marvel, and *still* ..."

"No!" She laughed her way out of it. "My dear, darling brother jeered, of course, and that broke the spell. Maybe I'll get *two* doses of arsenic!" They both laughed and the risk of tears subsided.

"So you want to know if Will gave any sign of this … this epiphany — his road-to-Damascus revelation?"

"That was the idea."

Leah was now in a pickle. How do you warn a friend that she has a possible rival in another girl, but without putting it in so many words? Pansy was far prettier than Adèle, who was self-critical enough at the best of times. In present circumstances such news might drive her into the ground. She thought she saw a way — at least, she took a chance on it. "He's said nothing to me directly," she replied. "But then, I was doing my accounts last night" — and that was actually *true* she realized! — "so we hardly said more than two words to each other. And he was out this morning before I came down to breakfast."

"So you can't help," Adèle concluded glumly.

"I do, however, have some slight, indirect, evidence."

Again, the girl hung on every word.

"It's something Pansy said."

"Pansy?" There was alarm in her voice now.

"Yes, there was one thing I left out earlier — something else your aunt said." And she went on to repeat Aunt Philomena's lecture on chastity. "Pansy thought it highly amusing, of course, to be delivered such a lecture in the presence of the man your aunt was warning her against. But when Pansy repeated it all to me, I saw a chance to drive the point home, so I told her it applied equally to Master Will. At which she laughed me to scorn and said there was no fear of that because Master Will was dedicated mind, body, and soul to one Adèle Liddicoat. So there's comfort for you!"

Adèle gave a cry of joy and, slipping her arm out of Leah's, did a dance of joy in the middle of the road. But she stopped in mid-skip and, serious again, said, "You're making it up!"

"Oh, my dear!" Leah put an arm around her shoulder and gave her a quick hug. "You must *trust* yourself more. Stop thinking no man could possibly …"

"That's not it," she replied implacably. "If Will only started feeling like that last night, how can Pansy Tregear tell you all about it this morning?"

This was the dangerous bit.

"Maybe he told her," Leah suggested.

"He discussed *me* with *her?*" Adèle was outraged.

"He discusses lots of things with her — but that's just to annoy *me,* of course."

The suggestion was intriguing enough to make Adèle rein in her anger. "Of course?" she queried.

"Yes, of course. Don't your brothers do things deliberately to annoy you? The day Pansy came to us, I saw Will's eye light up. So I told him — the slightest hint of *that* and she'd be dismissed. I told her, too. So ... you know how, if you tell a little boy he's not to *touch* his brother — when they've been fighting, for instance — and he'll take you absolutely literally? He'll get so close to his brother you couldn't slip a visiting card between them. But he won't actually touch him. D'you know that sort of provocative behaviour?"

"Do I!"

"Well, I should learn to keep my mouth shut. Because now, just to annoy me, Will steers as close a line as he can to intimacy with the girl but, naturally, avoiding any trespass that might make me carry out my threat." She spoke a silent prayer, begging forgiveness for the white lie. "So it's more than possible he said something last night. You know Will! He wears his heart on his sleeve and if that same heart was bursting with a new discovery ... he'd not be able to hide it. I don't imagine he said anything directly, but he must have said enough for a smart girl like Pansy to guess the lot."

"But you weren't actually there," Adèle pointed out. "So you don't really know."

"That's true." Leah bit her lip and looked worried — just enough, she hoped, to put Adèle on her mettle. "Still — it's better to know what we're up against than to live in blissful ignorance. Eh? Cheer up! Forewarned is forearmed. And faint heart never won fair gentleman."

"I just ..." Adèle's lip trembled again. "I just love him so. I can't stop thinking about him day and night. Stupid things. He just fills my thoughts all the time." At last she dared glance at Leah, but what she saw in her friend's eyes surprised her. "Why that look?" she asked.

"Envy," Leah said simply. "I *long* to feel so passionately about someone but somehow I don't think I ever shall. It *almost* happened once — with Nicholas, actually — when he kissed me and I felt ..."

"Nick?" Adèle shrieked in her amazement. "He actually *kissed* you?"

"Just once." Leah explained how it happened and described the feelings that had then started to work within her. "But then I ... I don't know. Perhaps I got frightened of them. I was still trying to keep alive my feelings for ... oh, just someone back in America. And this threatened them, you see. So I pulled away and said no, it was a big mistake, and we were much happier the way we were ..."

"Sparring partners."

"Exactly. And — Nicholas being Nicholas — he couldn't beg me to think again. I could feel he wanted to, but he was too proud. So he agreed with me and promised it would never happen again." She put her hand to her breast. "That cut through me like a knife!"

"So it never has happened again?" Adèle asked.

Leah shook her head. "And then — just when I'd got used to thinking the moment had gone for ever ..."

"What about this person in America?"

They were passing Benny Meagor's fields. He kept a herd of Guernseys and Jerseys, several of which were staring incuriously at them over the hedge. Channel Island milk makes the finest clotted cream. Leah made a mental note to buy some on their way back. Her nearest approach to paradise each day, straight after driving the cattle back into the fields when milking was done, was to devour a slice of bread and butter drowned in golden syrup and clotted cream, and to wash it all down with a mug of hot, sweet tea.

"Eh?" Adèle prompted.

"Oh," she sighed. "I've decided that by holding on to Tom's memory like that — Tom O'Leary was his name — I was just keeping all the *real* possibilities at bay."

"Possibili*ties* — plural?" Adèle asked coyly. "My, my!"

"That's what I was about to say just now. Just when I'd grown to accept the fact that Nicholas is too proud and independent to unbend — and anyway I've got the farm to keep me busy — just when all the dust had settled very nicely, thank you, I went into Helston this morning, on my way to see Elizabeth Troy ... bumped into Ben Coad, who was on his way to Tregathennan, offered him a lift, and ... well ..."

"It hit you like a thunderbolt!" Adèle nudged her delightedly.

"Not really," Leah had to admit. "Thunderbolts don't seem to be part of my make-up. The most I can manage is to go a bit weak at the knees."

"Well, that's *something,*" her friend said encouragingly. "Ben Coad made you go weak at the knees, eh?"

"Not quite. But I realized what wonderful company he is. I feel completely relaxed when I'm with him. I want to touch him, to be sure he's there. I long to feel his arm around me. But it's not like your thunderbolts and ... all that passion. He suggested going on to look at a farm ... Now keep this under your hat because it's not on the market yet — a farm the other side of Helston, over at Goonhusband, whatever that means. What does goon mean?"

"Down or downs — you know, like Carnmeal Downs."

Leah laughed. "Down, husband! Like, 'Down, Rover! Bad dog!' Eh? I'd better not go asking *how* it got its name. Anyway, he offered to take me there to see it and I really had to force myself to say no."

"Why did he want to show it to you? Are you looking for *more* land still? Surely not so far away?"

"Well now, that's the other thing I'd like to talk about. It's only a hazy idea as yet but I'd like to hear your opinion. How would it be if we Carringtons offered your Aunt Philomena the chance to buy the Old Glebe by private treaty? No auction. No public offer. No competing bids. She could have just the land if she prefers. Or the land and the buildings. Or the whole lot. Would she jump at it?"

They walked awhile in silence, Adèle being deep in thought. When they drew near Carleen forge, where Sam Chigwidden, the smith, was shoeing one of Will Tyacke's cart-horses, the acrid reek of burning hoof assailed them. "Poor-man's smelling salts," Leah commented.

They paused on the far side of the road to watch. A small group of loafers was gathered around the door.

"Have you discussed this with your father?" Adèle asked.

"Indirectly. I fired the first shot, anyway. I pointed out that one way to spike your aunt's guns would be to offer her the Old Glebe. The valuation has gone up quite sharply over the past few months — for most unhappy reasons, I admit, but it's a fact of life. And maybe your aunt would jib at giving any Carrington a profit — but at least she couldn't go about the place complaining we're playing dog-in-the-manger with it."

Adèle laughed. "It's brilliant, my dear! She really would have to hold her tongue, then — or buy the place. Either way, the source of all friction between our two families would be removed at a stroke." She did another few skips of happiness. The idlers round the forge watched with amusement.

Leah, who had previously considered Adèle's little displays of her feelings rather childish — something she would soon grow out of — now saw that she was, in her very nature, both demonstrative and passionate. Again she envied her, not simply for the passion but also for the easy spontaneity with which she allowed herself to show it. Will was a lucky man; she just hoped he appreciated it.

"And Downhusband isn't so very far away," she pointed out. "I think I'll call it that."

Adèle stopped dancing. "It's also just half a mile from Chynoweth Hall — and Blanche Curnow."

"Oh, I think that has all died down."

It just so happened that Chigwidden's assistant pumped the bellows at that moment. The fire that had seemed dead was blustered back into life, glowing orange, then yellow, and spitting sparks. "It can happen to any smouldering fire," Adèle commented flatly.

"Well, Blanche Curnow is not the only one with a good bellows," Leah assured her as they resumed their stroll. "But there's something else we ought to think about first, something more immediately important: Are we, the younger generation of Liddicoats and Carringtons, going to play the Martins and the Coys at our parents' sides, or ..."

"Who are the Martins and the Coys?"

"Oh, sorry. Two famous feuding clans in the Appalachian mountains. Like the Montagues and the Capulets, I guess. Are we going to play their game or stay united and play our own? I can certainly answer for Will and me. As far as we're concerned, the feud stops with us."

"With me, too," Adèle said fervently.

"No matter what devilish blandishments your aunt might yet dream up?"

"No matter what."

"And your brothers?"

Adèle hesitated.

"Not so certain, eh?" Leah guessed.

"It's not so much that," was the reply. "It's just that they could promise one thing — and mean it most sincerely — but when Aunt Philomena gets to work on them ... *pfft!*"

After pondering this for a moment Leah said, "So, tell me what you know about strychnine and curare, then."

They laughed and left the discussion there for the moment.

Adèle found a suitable maid at the second attempt; the girl even agreed to come for the normal 12/6*d* a week once she heard Miss Philomena was not to be living at Grankum.

On their return they passed Carleen Flow, a broad piece of sloping scrubland that funnelled down to the Wheal Vor adit, the source of the stream that ran down the Wheal Fortune valley, past the old stop gate, and on to Porthleven, where it emptied into a corner of the inner harbour. Adèle suggested they could follow this watercourse down as far as the stamps and see how their brothers were progressing.

They chatted about this and that, down past Scott's and on between Carnmeal Downs and Trew, where Pansy's parents lived. A little farther on, past Scott's Farm, where another adit drained yet another mine into the valley stream, they came to a neglected and now densely wooded area, which had once quite obviously been a mine halvan. The trees were stunted cork oaks whose hunched, yellowing canopy lent the place an air at once gloomy and sinister.

"We used to climb in there as children," Adèle said. "It's hard to believe there are the ruins of at least two dozen hovels in there. Only the bottoms of the walls are left, but you can see where they were — all higgledy-piggledy. No streets. No plan at all. There's also an old mineshaft."

Leah eyed a gap in the hedge, where some stones had fallen out — or, more likely, been removed by a poacher. "Could we?" she asked. "Just peep in maybe?"

They arrived at the wall to find the gap larger than it had seemed from a distance; they had no difficulty in getting through. The atmosphere inside was quite different from that in Grankum

Wood, where the trees, though slender, were tall and stately. Here the trunks looked as if they had been forced to grow among piled boulders that had since been removed, leaving them all twisted and gnarled. The brightest colour was the intense emerald green of wet moss, which grew on almost every surface and even hung in short, tattered curtains from the branches overhead.

"It's so eerie," Leah murmured. "I'd rather spend a month of nights in our allegedly haunted barn than a single midnight hour out in the open here."

"Actually," Adèle said, "it is a doom-laden place. About forty years ago this shaft was the scene of a triple murder — or what would have been a triple murder if the local people hadn't caught the murderer and saved his victims just in time. He threw them down this shaft and ..."

"But how could they survive that?"

"Have a look over the wall."

Leah obeyed and saw that the shaft, instead of falling vertically like all the others she had so far seen, sloped down at an angle. It was still pretty steep but she could just imagine that, if you dug your heels in, you could stop yourself from sliding down.

"That's the way all mineshafts used to be — before steam," Adèle said. "They followed the angle of the lode down into the ground, digging out the tin as they went. This one goes down at that angle for about half a furlong — until it meets a later shaft, the Blueborough shaft, which goes straight down. And the murderer got them down to the very edge of the vertical bit before he was stopped."

Leah stared into the dark-on-dark of the pit and shuddered. "Are any of them still alive?" she asked.

"I know two of them are. The murderer was hanged, not for that but for another murder — of a woman up Breage who was his common-law wife. One of the people he threw into that shaft was the son of that liaison, still just a little boy. He's now Mister Jake Morvah ..."

"The solicitor in Helston? The one who has chambers in the same building as Frank Kernow? Good heavens!"

"And another near-victim was his adopted mother — Mrs Kitto, who lives in that house on the headland at Rinsey and keeps a watch for German submarines — did you see that in the

West Briton — why she's allowed to keep her binoculars instead of handing them in like the rest of us?"

Leah, still lost in amazement, just shook her head. "It's so quiet and so ... overgrown now. I mean, it could have been dug back in the days of Bonnie Prince Charlie for all one knows ..."

She stopped speaking abruptly. Both girls froze. Somewhere behind them a twig snapped — several twigs, in fact. Someone — or some *thing* — was at liberty behind them. Slowly, fearfully, they turned, half expecting to see some latter-day reincarnation of the hanged man, desperate for revenge.

What they actually saw was Will, who had come through the gap in the hedge and, without bothering to check that he was alone, was desperate to pay a call of nature.

Leah stared in amazement. She had not seen that part of her brother last night. In fact, she had not seen it since they were kids, skinny-dipping out at Tom O'Leary's cousin's farm. How it had grown!

Adèle just stared — until the two girls caught each other's eyes and fought their laughter. They suppressed their giggles pretty well, but not well enough. Will spun round, away from them, leaving a fleeting semicircle of golden beads on the air around him. Then he called out over his shoulder, "Adèle?"

She swallowed heavily and croaked, "Yes?"

"You'll have to marry me now."

Silence.

"What did you say?" he asked as he shook himself and, in the quaint parlance of those notices in men's public lavatories, 'adjusted his dress.'

"She says, 'Yes, please'!" Leah called out, and put up an elbow to ward off the embarrassed blows Adèle tried to rain upon her.

The two girls walked toward him — or, rather, toward the gap, which all three of them reached at the same time. "Why," Leah asked, "with the whole of this secluded valley to make use of, did you have to come in here? I don't suppose you saw us enter by any chance?"

"Good God, no!" he protested as they went back into the bright daylight. "And this valley isn't as secluded as you might suppose. The wife of that farmer up on the hill by Trew ..." He pointed it out on the far side of the valley.

"That's Pansy's Tregear's place," Adèle said. "They're not farmers, they're only smallholders."

"Anyway, she's a small holder of very large field glasses. We should report her, really. She ought to have handed them in."

"You *were* listening to us," Leah accused him. "We've just been talking about that."

"On my honour, not. Anyway, she watches Nick and me with them any time we pay a call of nature — which is okay when we're far away, by the stamps. But up here was, I felt, a bit close. Any *more* questions?"

"You're forgiven," Leah told him.

"Am I?" He leaned forward and peered at Adèle.

"When do we call the banns?" she asked.

He pulled out his watch and said, "Well, I'm afraid we've left it a bit late *today.*"

They all laughed and a dangerously sticky moment was avoided. But his eyes met Adèle's and they both knew that what had been merely glimpsed there yesterday was now confirmed.

Suddenly he struck his forehead. "Of course!" he exclaimed. "You left Grankum before Harvey returned."

"He's come back?" Adèle asked delightedly. "Does that mean he didn't join the navy after all? How d'you know he's back, anyway?"

He shook his head. "They wouldn't have him. He's with Nick now, by the stamps, trying to cheer himself up."

"They must have found out he's a farmer's son," Leah said.

"No such luck," Will replied. "It's rather sad. They rejected him on medical grounds."

"Good heavens! ... No! ... What? ... Why?" The questions and exclamations poured from the girls' lips.

"Something to do with his heart. He's not going to die or anything like that — they told him he could live for sixty years with whatever it is but they can't accept him for fighting service. However, you just try to get *him* to believe it!"

"What did they actually say?" Adèle asked anxiously.

"They said he has a *murmur* — that's what they called it. A murmur and a *thrill*. He has a murmur on one side of his heart and a thrill on the other."

"It sounds like a lot of other hearts one could name!" Leah said quietly.

42 Harvey was just about to help his brother pull the handcart out of a rut when he spotted the others approaching. He let go of the traces and said he'd better not risk it. Will would be there soon. Nicholas reminded him that, only a week earlier, he had been carrying sacks weighing two hundredweight into the barn at Grankum, apparently without strain. Harvey replied that he had — all unwittingly — been risking death at every step.

Will was certainly not hurrying to get back to the digging and hauling — not with Adèle at his side and Leah to act as chaperon. For her part, she was amazed at her brother's apparent devotion to Adèle, when, not eighteen hours earlier, he had been locked in that ultimate intimacy with another. It was all very well for him and Pansy to protest that love played no part in their games — and that questions of fidelity did not, therefore, arise. The very fact that their meeting (or was it meetings?) had been so clandestine, and that Will would surely rather die than have them made known to Adèle, gave such *sophisticated* arguments the lie.

Or did it? No doubt Will would claim he was merely sparing Adèle's feelings. He himself knew beyond all doubt that his frolics with Pansy were mere escapades, pleasant frivolities without substance or meaning. Pansy herself regarded them in that light, so he was certainly not deceiving her. And he was not *really* deceiving Adèle, either — simply acknowledging the fact that she might not be able to see it in the same jovial light. He was merely sparing her feelings as would any decent chap.

And, Leah had to admit, Will was not a heartless man. No wicked deceiver, he; no cold-blooded trifler with Adèle's trust and devotion. Leah could easily believe that he kept Pansy and Adèle in two quite separate compartments in his mind — and, indeed, in his heart, as well — the one labelled profane, the other sacred. She was sure he believed that nothing he did with profane Pansy could impinge upon his love for sacred Adèle.

Watching the pair of them, walking at her side, talking, laughing, renewing the wonder of this strange and sudden thing that had happened between them, Leah could not help thinking of all the other couples she had seen in similar circumstances. The women had been no less radiant than Adèle, the men no less attentive and engrossed than Will. Indeed, if her own suspicions had not been aroused last night and if she had not followed him and Pansy out to the tithe barn and seen it with her own eyes, she would take Will and Adèle as a model couple, for whom the marriage vows of eternal fidelity would be the simple confirmation of ways they had practised (seemingly) from the very start.

One little accident had overturned all her perceptions. She thought back to times when she and Tom had been to each other as Will and Adèle now were. Had been ... or had only seemed to be? Adèle, looking up into Will's eyes with such credulous devotion, and seeing nothing there but a reverence to match her own, could not possibly guess it might be otherwise. So was she, Leah, any smarter? Had there been a Pansy in Tom's life, too — some feather-heeled faloosie who had taken care of him in the profane department? And was there someone like that in Ben Coad's life? Or the Nark's? You could gaze into their eyes as long and as deep as you liked but you'd never find the answer there.

Where, then? By keeping eternal vigil? By mounting watch over the body that had vowed its eternal soul to 'thee and thee only'? You'd make the whole world a jail and yourself a wardress in it.

Her mother, who had told her most things in this area of life, had not told her this. Perhaps she, too, had not known — or, knowing, had chosen to forget? Maybe women of those days, dosed with the bitter but sugar-coated medicine of *their* mothers' times, had not been able to lift the veils of romance entirely from their eyes?

"Penny for 'em, Thistle," the Nark called out as they drew near. He had abandoned his attempts to get the cart out of the rut on his own — though it would have made a splendid show for the two women to admire.

She gazed into his eyes and thought that, of all the men she knew, he was the last and least likely to have that secret faloosie tucked away somewhere. Not that she suspected his passions were weak. Quite the contrary. But his one, singular passion would override all the rest, no matter what their strength — his dread of being beholden to a female for anything. How odd that one of his worst points should also be one of his best!

"D'you really want me to tell you, Nark?" she replied.

"Oh, dear!" He pulled a face. "I should have known better. Only tell me if it's to my own undying credit or glory. You know how one tiny criticism from you can leave me absolutely shattered for days."

"I was wondering if the gift of knowledge about the nature of man is a price worth paying for female emancipation."

"Botheration!" he said. "It wasn't about me at all."

"Well, at the risk of *seeing* to criticize you, Nark, I have to tell you that my musings at the moment you accosted me (and I call them musings because I know only *men* can have actual *thoughts*) were exclusively about you. I'm sure your superior brain can work it all out."

"You've heard my news?" Harvey asked.

"Yes, I'm so sorry, Harvey. But glad, too — that it's not actually going to shorten your life, I mean."

"I just have to be very careful from now on."

Adèle put her arms around him and hugged him tight in wordless commiseration. "What is it, exactly?" she asked as she let go again.

"The heart has these two chambers, you see," he said, putting his hands together in the attitude of a praying mantis. "Called auricles. And there's a kind of wall between them called a septum. And ..."

"You should have seen him carrying two-hundredweight sacks up a dozen steps into the barn last week," Nicholas cut in. "Just because Eileen was out there beating a carpet and watching him with admiring eyes!"

"And there's a defect in the septum. They call it *patent.* I don't know why."

Adèle laughed. "People were beginning to whisper that Eileen ran away *with* you!" she told her brother.

"She did — in a way. The thing is, both auricles pump blood at roughly the same pressure and in the same rhythm."

"Just a mo!" Adèle said. "What d'you mean — 'in a way'?"

"I didn't say 'in a way' — I said, 'in the same rhythm.' So there's no great flow from one auricle to the other. That's why it's not at all ..."

"You said Eileen ran away with you — *in a way*. What does that mean?"

"Oh, I just meant she was on the same train to Plymouth. She's got a job in the naval stores there. Aren't you interested in my illness?" His eyes begged all of them.

They assured him they were. And Nicholas told his sister to let Harvey finish for God's sake or they'd be there all evening.

"Because there's no great flow from one auricle to the other, through this patent hole, the spent blood from the veins doesn't get mixed with the freshened blood from the lungs. It's utterly fascinating once you're in the know. The first thing I did was buy an ox heart at the butcher's and cut it open to see what on earth they were talking about it. This septum thing is about as thin as a good bit of oilcloth, you know."

Nicholas, meanwhile, had taken up a stick and was drawing a traditional Cupid's heart in the sand. He scratched an arrow through it and wrote the initials HL above it — and repeated them below it, too.

Harvey ignored him loftily.

"So where do these thrills and murmurs arise?" Leah asked.

He smiled at her gratefully. "The murmur is from the little bit that leaks across when the auricles are filling and the thrill is what you hear when they're pumping themselves empty again. The doctor put his stethoscope-thing in my ears and let me listen. It was amazing."

Adèle had meanwhile wiped out the two sets of initials with her feet. She scratched NL above the heart and was wondering what to put below it when Leah took the stick from her and scratched a circle there.

Adèle frowned. "O?" she asked.

"Zero," Leah replied. "Nil. Nought. Nothing. Nix." She grinned at the Nark, who smiled magnanimously back at her and said, "I fought with none, for none was worth my strife."

She capped him: "I loved with none, for none would make a worthy wife!"

"Anyway — that's why they turned me down for active service," Harvey said.

Adèle, wanting to end all these cross-currents of aggression, said brightly, "Wouldn't Aunt Philomena absolutely hate to see us here — all being so *friendly* and getting on so *well* together!"

They all laughed — except Nicholas, who was staring up at the rim of the sandbank they had excavated. They had, in effect, created a small, horseshoe-shaped sand quarry with walls about twenty feet high and he was staring up toward the top at the centre of the digging. "Talk of the devil!" he murmured.

They followed his gaze but saw nothing, except the ling and furze that carpeted the whole area. They laughed, thinking he was trying to pull their legs. But he swore he had seen Aunt Philomena, or the living image of her, standing up there not five seconds earlier. To prove it he turned and sprinted up a shallower part of the bank and then around the rim to where he said he had seen her. There he gazed about uncertainly, quartering the landscape like a hawk, using that technique where you gaze at a fixed point but concentrate on everything around it, hoping to spot some telltale movement. But the wind was still too strong; just about everything in view was shivering or swaying in its capricious blast.

"Well?" they shouted up.

He shrugged and launched himself into space over the rim with a cry of "Wheeee!" His heels dug in about halfway down and he braked to an elegant halt at the foot of the sand-cliff.

"Oh!" Leah exclaimed. "I want to do that."

"Me, too!" Adèle chimed in.

Harvey just sighed, implying that it was the sort of thing he'd never be able to do again.

"You were kidding us," Will accused Nicholas.

"If you mean I was jesting," he replied, "I promise you I wasn't. She was standing right there where I was."

"Then how did she vanish?" Harvey asked. "A hare couldn't have got away in that time."

"What would you have done if you'd found her waiting for you?" Adèle asked.

He laughed grimly. "That was exactly the thought that went through my mind when I was standing up there. She's there, all right, hiding behind some bush. But it dawned on me that if I had a choice between facing her and not facing her — well, it wasn't a choice at all."

"It doesn't matter if she was there or not," Leah said bitterly. "This is exactly what I mean — don't you see? Whether she's here or whether she's there, or whether she's in Timbuktoo — it doesn't matter. And whether she's plotting something deep and dark or just puzzling over a knitting pattern — it doesn't matter. She casts a pall over all our lives, *whatever* she's doing and wherever she is. Just by being Aunt Philomena, by being here in Cornwall, she ruins it all for us." She looked around at each in turn and added, *"If* we let her!"

"How do we stop her?" Nicholas asked her morosely.

"Surely there's a way?"

"Just *tell* her," Will said. "Form us a posse and beard her in her den. Tell her we're happy the way things are and she can go take a long walk off a short jetty."

"Or fly to the moon," Nicholas suggested in identical tones to Will. "And paint the same message on the Man in the Moon's face. It would be easier. And safer."

"Hogwash!" Will raised his voice and cupped his hands to his mouth. "Hey! Aunt Philomena! Get your long neck out of our lives! D'you heah?"

Nicholas stuck his fingers in his ears and spun an agonized circle on one heel. Harvey sat down on the handle of the cart, panting slightly, and put his hand to his chest. Adèle plucked nervously at Will's sleeve and murmured that what he had just done was most unwise.

He looked to his sister for support but the most she would say was that they could also try something a bit more subtle.

43 For the first time in her life Philomena Liddicoat felt the lack of an ally. It frightened her, and fear was an emotion she knew little about — from her side of the fence, anyway. She realized that knowing all about it on the *other* side of the fence was of little help. People who did what you wanted them to do, but only because they were to afraid to do otherwise, were not allies. Turn your back and there they were, playing 'cat's in the cupboard and can't see me'! The sight that had met her eyes when she gazed down into that sand quarry had shaken her badly — her own niece and nephews fraternizing with the enemy in broad daylight!

And then there was Nicholas, charging up the banks like that — ready to confront her, which he had never dared do in all his life. And Adelaide, simpering like a mooncalf over the Carrington boy. The *Carrington* boy! Words failed her when she thought of him — shouting disgraceful things like that after her.

She sat in the private lounge of the Angel, nursing a glass of sherry — an indescribably shocking act for a once-staunch Methodist like her. But — like fine claret with dinner — it was a tipple she had learned from the dear colonel, though she had not made it a daily routine until after his passing-on. It had been *his* daily routine, of course; now, for her, it was part pleasure, part act of loving remembrance. On such a day as this, when she could only sit back and wonder what her world was coming to, it was indispensable.

Why should she feel this sudden need for an ally? All her life she had fought her own battles, planned her own campaigns, dictated her own terms for surrender. *Their* surrender, never hers ...

A chilling thought struck her: All that had been in the days before she met the colonel. Or had become his housekeeper. Or — be honest — had become something more than that to him. God, how she missed him — especially now! He was that ally whose lack she felt so keenly. If he were still alive, he would surely understand her bitterness at what her brother had allowed to happen. He would surely help her to undo that harm. What would he advise next?

She took another sip and faced the post mortem with the courage and honesty he always admired in her.

'You charged straight at the enemy flag, old thing,' he'd say. 'You went in with all guns blazing. But you should have done a thorough recce first.'

'But did I do *nothing* right, Colonel, dear?' she'd ask.

'You kept your temper,' he'd reply. 'That was good. When that odious Carrington man saw fit to make you the butt of his practical joke, you rose above it and you smiled. You spoke in well-modulated tones. You embarrassed him in front of his maidservant. And you rubbed salt in the wound with that half-sovereign. Now he must either return it and eat humble pie or keep it and declare himself no gentleman. All that was good. But still I return to my point: To go there like that, all unprepared, on the moment's whim — that's not like my Philly, is it! That was not well done.'

'Something would have come to me, Colonel, dear. It always does. You often admired me for that.'

'Something even better would have come if you had been better informed, my dearest. How often have I said it — one well-prepared regiment can take on the biggest unprepared army in the world and win. You *must* get information.'

'But from whom? Clifford is useless — always was. And the other brother, Frank, is not much better. Besides, he'd see it as Clifford's fight and then he wouldn't lift a finger. Harvey's gone off his chump, if you ask me. Nicholas is in cahoots with the Carrington boy — he won't tell me anything useful. He always was a perverted little liar, anyway. And as for Adelaide — she's just infatuated with that same Carrington boy, though she fondly imagines she has kept it from me. And so she might have done, if I had not met you, my darling, darling man! But now I know every earthly sign of love and loss, love and longing ... love so huge that not even the gift of all the world could requite it. And she imagines she can keep her petty infatuation from *me?* So tell me — where do I turn for this precious information?'

'Are there no servants at the Old Glebe? That Pansy Tregear — you know a thing or two about her people, surely? And what you don't know you can easily discover. She has an elder sister ... what was her name? They were all called after flowers. Violet! You also used to teach her at the Chapel Sunday School. Perhaps she's free at the moment, or would change positions for the right money? And you cannot live here at the Angel for much longer without a maid. Pansy might not be too forthcoming, but Violet would be.'

'I'll look into that tomorrow.'

'See you do, my precious. And while you're about it — does Carrington have no lawyer here in town? And what of Ben Coad, the viper who sold the place without informing you! Has he not a fence to mend with you? Could you not make him feel that obligation? Oh, there is so much you could do before your next assault!'

She closed her eyes and, in her happiness, almost spilled her sherry down her dress. That would be a fine thing to do — the next best thing to reeling down the street! Rather than risk such a spill, she tossed back what was left and breathed out the fire of its afterburn.

A maid knocked hesitantly at the door and poked her head round it. "If it please you, ma'am, your hot water jug is in your room and Mister Blackwell says you may have your dinner served there if you prefer on account of business being so slack today." She heaved a quick sigh as if she were surprised at having got out so many words without interruption.

"Come right in, maid," Philomena said. "I don't know you, do I? Are you new here?"

"No, ma'am. Please, ma'am, I'm Mary Tregear, the scullery-maid here but Mister Blackwell let Nora have the afternoon off, what with there being such little work."

"So will you be serving my dinner in my room?" Her surname, Tregear, had naturally aroused Philomena's interest, though it is not rare in Cornwall.

"Yes, ma'am." She curtseyed.

"Good. I shall be ready for it in half an hour."

Half an hour later, when Mary brought her soup, Philomena asked the maid if she had others to serve. Mary replied that there was only one other resident, a traveller, and he did not wish to dine until eight.

"So tell me," Philomena said pleasantly, "are you, by any chance, a relation to the Tregears of Trew? Take the weight off your feet, my dear."

Mary looked about her nervously.

"Go on," Philomena urged. "I'm sure you do quite enough standing all day. It's not good for a girl. You'll get horrid varicose veins — take it from one who knows."

Mary sat down and said, "My father is cousin to Aaron Tregear of Trew, ma'am."

"Ah, so you must be Noel Tregear's daughter from up Ashton. I taught your elder sister Margaret in Breage Sunday School — before you were born, probably! And your brother Benjamin."

Mary managed a shy smile. This 'old dragon' wasn't as bad as people said. Her nervousness began to subside.

"I also taught Violet and Pansy. They'd be your second cousins — and about the same age as you, if I'm not mistaken? Pansy, anyway."

"Yes, ma'am."

Philomena noticed that the maid's uneasiness returned at the mention of Pansy — because of the Carrington connection, of course. "Well, you must give my special regards to your parents when you see them next. They were the backbone of the chapel — and still are, I trust?"

"Yes, ma'am." She began to relax again.

"D'you see much of Violet, these days? Or Pansy?" She made her tone as casual as possible but even so she saw the maid's fists tighten. "You needn't worry, my dear," she added. "I know only too well where Pansy is working these days — in fact, I met her there this morning and we had quite a chat. She has grown into a very … how can I put it …?"

"Coxy giglet?" Mary suggested impetuously — and instantly regretted her forthrightness. She bit her lip in consternation and waited for the other's famous temper to explode.

"D'you say so?" Philomena leaned forward with interest. "Well, I would never have said this if you had not been so honest with me, Mary, but I'm sorry to admit that I formed the very same impression. We spoke for no more than ten minutes or so but she seemed to me a rather *forthy* maid, as we used to say. In fact, I felt impelled to warn her of the dangers of appearing a mite too *comfortable* — you understand me? — in a house of furriners like those Carringtons. I'm sure she's a good maid at heart …" She watched Mary's expression carefully and saw an incipient sneer. "No?" she added. "Am I wrong?"

Mary shrugged awkwardly; the Tregears were, after all, family. Still, her father had often spoken harshly about his cousin and those preedy daughters of his. "You know what they do call she, ma'am — that there Pansy?"

Philomena shook her head.

"Manhole Tregear!" She blushed and stared at her boots.

"Dear me!" Philomena worked hard to conceal her delight. "People can be so cruel. One little slip and a maid can be branded for life."

"One little slip!" Mary echoed sarcastically. "One every *day,* I s'pose. And she'd never slip without a soft place to fall on." She continued to gaze at the floor until the silence compelled her to look up. Miss Liddicoat seemed lost in thought. "Ma'am?" she prompted tactfully.

The woman gave a little shake of the head and smiled a slightly rueful smile. "God forgive my want of charity," she murmured. "I was thinking that if such infection had to pollute *any* household, then it could not have found ... but no. That would be a disgraceful thing to say. What of the elder sister, Violet? Not tarred with the same brush, I hope?"

"No, ma'am," Mary said — though there had, in fact, been a whisper or two about Violet, as well. But they had amounted to no more than any passable maid could expect when she was rather choosy with her beaux and therefore tended to take up and discard them more swiftly than most. Hell hath no scourge like the tongue of the discarded male.

"I'm extremely glad to hear it. What is she doing these days? Married, I suppose?"

"No, ma'am. She's some pussivanter with men. You want another dole of soup, do 'ee? There's scats in the pot."

"I think I will, thank you, Mary. One needs the extra nourishment now, with the winter drawing on. What an attentive maid you are! I shall certainly commend you to Mister Blackwell."

Mary floated on air all the way down to the kitchen and all the way back again. As far as she was concerned, Miss Philomena Liddicoat was now sun, moon, and stars.

"So!" Philomena went on as she took the first sup of the fresh bowl. "Violet's a picker and chooser among her beaux, is she? I'm glad to hear it — glad for *your* sake, too, Mary. *Two* feather-heeled girls in a family is too many. It begins to look as if it's in the blood, you know. You didn't tell me what Violet's actually doing nowadays? Do sit down again."

"She've got work in the Helston Union, ma'am. Bathing the old cripples and putting on poultices and that."

"Hmm!" Philomena considered the news in silence for several sups. "Not too happy about it, I should think. Still, it's necessary work and Florence Nightingale herself did even less appealing tasks, I'm sure. But tell me a little more about yourself. How long have you worked here?"

While she finished her soup she let the maid prattle on about the various menial jobs she had done and how she hoped soon to go into service in a proper house. When Mary brought her main course — a sumptuous cut of prime beef — she said, "So you were here when Mister Carrington and his son and daughter arrived — before they bought the Old Glebe?"

Mary was no fool. She knew what the woman required of her — and John Carrington's generous sixpence had been spent long ago. She gave out all she knew, which was mostly hearsay, of course, since scullerymaids had little contact with visitors at the front of the house. But there was that night when the visitors had come to the back of the place and she had been there to help. She made the most of that, not just of Master William's inability to hold his drink but also of Frank Kernow's complicity in the affair.

The only other thing she knew was a bit of gossip she'd heard in the kitchen that very afternoon — about Ben Coad and Miss Carrington having been seen driving out Pallas way in her gig. She passed that on, too.

All in all, Philomena thought as she settled her head upon her pillow that night, a disastrous day had been rescued by a much more rewarding evening. Also, to her surprise, she had rather enjoyed being pleasant to the little scullerymaid; at times during their conversation she had felt almost altruistic about it, as if she had forgotten why she was being so amiable and was doing it for its own sake.

44 When Leah heard the back stairs creak that night she knew it was Pansy. She rose and, pulling the quilt around her, stood at her bedroom window. The night was overcast but the cloud was thin enough to let a fair amount of moonlight through. It was certainly enough to reveal her brother, standing at the barn door with one hand on the latch. She would almost swear she could see the grin on his lips. A moment later a movement in the back yard, immediately below her window, caught her eye. It was, of course, Pansy tripping on her way to what was obviously a nightly assignation. The girl glanced up at the window as she passed. Leah froze. Logic told her that the brightness of the cloud, the angle of sight from where Pansy was passing, and the absolute darkness of her bedroom would all combine to make discovery impossible. All the same, she had the uncomfortable feeling that the girl had seen her.

Had seen her — and had not been particularly bothered.

Well, she had her own lecture to the girl that lunchtime to blame for that; she'd as good as given them carte blanche for these clandestine meetings.

As if to rub in the salt, Pansy started wiggling and sashaying in a highly provocative manner the moment she saw Will standing there waiting. Angrily Leah returned to her bed and fell asleep pondering the unfairness of everything.

The following morning, after milking and breakfast, she put on her prettiest hat and went again into Helston, this time to tell Ben that she'd like to see the Goonhusband property, after all. His clerk, Ambrose Bowden, shook his head sadly and said Mr Coad had scats of work ahead of him that day. Ben, hearing her voice, came to the door and said that was nonsense and what did she want?

Two minutes later they left a distraught Bowden rearranging files, writing messages, and changing his master's appointments diary — yet again.

"The poor man must curse the very sight of me," Leah commented. "I ought to learn about your appointments system."

"It's extremely simple," he replied. "It rearranges itself automatically whenever you call."

"You drive," she said, handing him the reins. "You're so much better at it than me."

He looked at her askance as they set off up Coinagehall Street. "Apart from the fact that that's just not true," he said, "it's also not a sentiment one expects to hear falling from your suffragist lips."

"You know the way, then," she said. "Is that better?"

"It's the literal truth, anyway. People are still going to talk. Tongues are already wagging about our driving out together yesterday. I hope you don't mind that?"

They were nearing the Angel at that moment and, before she could reply, Walter Blackwell, having noticed their approach, hastened out to warn them that Miss Philomena had gone out not five minutes since and was walking up Meneage Street — if they were thinking of going that way. They said they were, thanked him, and drove on.

"I've not actually seen her yet," Leah said and went on to describe her father's encounter with the woman yesterday morning. Also Nicholas's conviction he had seen her on the halvans at Wheal Fortune.

"That means she hasn't seen you yet, either," Ben mused.

"Why d'you say it in that tone?"

"Because that's her on the right, looking into Pascoe's window. She's bound to see me."

"Good!" Leah exclaimed. "Will you introduce us?"

He shook his head and kept his eye on their quarry.

"Scared?" Leah asked.

"No, it would just be very irregular. People in trade do not have leave to introduce ladies and gentlemen to one another unless asked. She's spotted me!"

"Coad!" Miss Philomena called out. "The very man! I wish to call on you today."

"In what connection, Miss Liddicoat? I have a very full day, as it happens." He slowed the trap but did not quite halt it. She began to walk, to keep pace.

"Not too full to see me, I'm sure," she said. "And I think you know very well what I wish to see you about. I have a crow to pluck with you."

She stared curiously at Leah, clearly not recognizing her from that brief glimpse on the halvans.

"I'm just off to show this young lady a property over Culdrose way," he said. "I'm sorry not to stop, this pony doesn't like to start again on a hill — especially with two up."

"What property?" she asked sharply.

"A cottage near Higher Pentire." That was true, for there was such a cottage on the Goonhusband farm. Over his shoulder he added, "See my clerk, Ambrose Bowden. Tell him I said to move heaven and earth to find time for you this afternoon."

"Stop at this little flat bit up ahead," Leah said quietly.

"You want to risk it?" he asked, equally softly.

"Yes. It's not much of a risk. She's hardly likely to think we Carringtons are looking at properties again so soon. And if what you say about tradesmen is true, she won't expect an introduction, either."

"He can start again here," Ben said to Miss Philomena as she caught up with them. "It's more level. I'm sorry we can't offer you a lift."

"Not at all," she replied. "I'm only going as far as the Union." She nodded toward the entrance, which was only a hundred or so paces away. "Tell me, Coad, what reports have you of Violet Tregear, from Trew? I used to teach her at Sunday School and I hear she's working at the Union now."

"You mean Pansy's sister?" Ben said, in case Leah didn't already know it.

"Of course that's who I mean. I don't know any other Tregear girls all named after flowers, do you? Have you heard anything to Violet's discredit?"

"On the contrary, Miss Liddicoat. The complaint is that she's mighty purnick, as they say. Are you seeking a replacement for that Eileen Bersey, who ran away from Grankum?"

"My brother's family can look after themselves. *I* need a maid — someone I know and can trust."

Coad chuckled. She asked if he'd kindly share the joke. He said, "Someone with a sister at the Old Glebe, too — now that might come in handy, ma'am!"

She bridled. "You're very impertinent today, Coad."

He dipped his head in apology.

She went on, "But don't talk to me about that Pansy Tregear — what a baggage!" As she spoke a broad smile spread across her features. "But she'll wreak havoc in that household before too long — you mark my words. Haven't we all seen it happen? She's a fireship. That Carrington fellow thinks he's the cleverest creature since Plato. But she'll ..."

"You've met him?" Coad mingled surprise with admiration in his question.

"I've *met* him," she replied. "Round One — ten points to me, none to him! That's what I wish to talk to you about. But don't let me hold you up now." She turned toward the Union entrance and waved them on. "He's not at all the sort of man I expected him to be."

"He has surprised quite a few people hereabouts," Ben said as he took up the reins.

"Yes," she called out as they set off again. "He's going to be a more worthy adversary than I dared hope for."

"I'll tell him that, ma'am," he called back at her.

"Tell him anything you like," she said.

Ben waited until they were so far away than not even a bat could have heard him before he said, "Well, I'm in trouble now and no mistake — letting her go on like that with you sitting beside me."

"Yes, Ben," she said. "That occurred to me, too. Why did you do it?"

"Because I want *you* to know whose side I'm on, Leah." He laughed grimly. "I'm certainly committed now!"

She reached out and stroked his arm a time or two. "It is greatly appreciated, Ben. Tell me more about Goonhusband."

"Tell me what you make of Miss Philomena, first. Is *she* what *you* expected?"

"If Will hadn't told me how good-looking she is, I'd have been more surprised. In fact, she's almost exactly what I expected her to be. And ... I don't know if one can have intuitions about a person one has never met — just from hearsay, you know — but I think mine about her are correct. Especially now I've met her, even for just a moment like that."

"And what are your intuitions, if a mere male is permitted ..."

"She's tough and rude and belligerent because there's a chink in her armour somewhere — a soft spot she doesn't want anyone to know about."

He laughed dismissively. "No one down here has ever seen it," he assured her.

"I can believe that. In fact, I think only one person *has* ever seen it — the man whose house she shared for so many years. You'd have to be that close for that long to manage it — back in those days, at least."

"But not now?"

"Maybe not. It's possible she had as much affection for the colonel as he obviously had for her. And once a woman yields to the luxury of being adored, it's hard to go back to the old diet."

He drew a deep breath and swallowed hard. "You speak from experience, do you?"

"Yes." She slipped her arm through his and said, "Let's give them something to talk *about*, eh, Ben?"

He looked down at her hand, then into her eyes, and said, "Are you suggesting I should ask your father if I may call upon you, Miss Carrington?"

"I'll kill you if you do, Mister Coad," she replied.

He laughed and pretended to collapse for a moment or two. "Why d'you do that?" She joined his laughter.

"For months I've dreamed of this moment," he said. "I've tried to imagine every possible way we might arrive at it — but I never remotely imagined it would be so simple. Is that really you? Am I here?"

"And are we by any chance going to a nice empty farmhouse?" she asked archly.

His face fell. "It's not empty," he said. "That's why it's not quite on the market yet."

"Oh," she said with resignation.

"But there is an empty cottage — at Higher Pentire, just as I told the old girl back there." He grinned at her.

She reached up and gave him a quick kiss on the cheek. He smelled of shaving soap. It was wonderful to have a beau again. It was even more wonderful that the beau was Ben Coad and that it *hadn't* been love at first sight — on her side, anyway. "Have you really been thinking about it for months?" she asked. "Why didn't you say?"

"What would you have done if I had?"

She hesitated.

"See!" he said. "A man doesn't get two shots at that sort of thing. He dreams and dreams ... and he waits for the right sort of smile."

"And when did I give it you?"

"Yesterday."

"Good heavens!"

"Why? Did you imagine you'd been flashing it earlier?"

"It's been sort of on my mind," she replied vaguely. "But so have lots of other things — other responsibilities, I mean, not other people. Oh, dear — life was so much easier when we were young and fancy free, wasn't it!"

She glanced over her shoulder. The entrance to the Union was just about to pass out of sight. Miss Liddicoat was still standing there, obviously watching them until they were no longer visible. It gave Leah yet another intuition — that the woman had tumbled to what she had just done.

He was still wondering how to reply to her when she went on, "Also, I have to confess, I ... well, I have to confess two things, really. I left behind the love of my life in America, my head-over-heels, drowned-deep-in-love, only-ever-man for me ... and I had to come three thousand miles and wait several months before I discovered he was none of those things at all."

His arm, which had tensed almost unbearably when she started this confession, relaxed again — but incompletely. "And the other 'confession'?" he prompted her.

"Oh, that's a bagatelle. I did, for a week or two, imagine I might be falling for the Nark — Nicholas Liddicoat."

"But not now?"

She was silent awhile — too long a while.

"A bagatelle?" he murmured.

"It's not easy to explain. I do still feel a certain attraction to him, even though I know it's, one, absurd and, two, impossible. I mean — he *is* an impossible man. I suppose that 'growing up' means you get to recognize the existence of attractions like that but you also realize you don't have to do anything about them. If you don't plant them and water them, they don't grow."

"But you're still friends?"

"That's the only reason I'm telling you this, Ben. The Nark and I are as close as two friends could be and I don't want to have to turn it all off. At the same time I don't want to have to contend with any fits of jealousy. Oh, dear! That sounds dreadful. I don't even know if you're a jealous man or not. Are you?"

He shrugged awkwardly. "I'm not sure."

"Really? Haven't there been other girls?"

"Not like you. I've never felt like this in my life."

She gave his arm another squeeze. "Nor have I, my darling — which is why I know that my friendship with the Nark, and even the attraction I feel for him, *is* the merest bagatelle. Could we have a look at this empty cottage *before* we look at the farm? I'm absolutely *dying* to kiss you."

45 Ben Coad's eyes upon her were as caressing as any hands. Leah felt his adoration like a physical warmth, a fire, like a pressure on her skin. He trembled when his hands went lightly to her waist and pulled her to him. Too late she realized they were standing by the window, where any passing ship's officer with a good spyglass could see them from five miles away — or any sparrow in the overgrown hedge outside. It was her day for recklessness, her week ... her year.

Her lips went up to seek his as his loomed down to find hers. She rose on tiptoe, holding him tight, pressing her body firmly against his and relishing the lean hardness of his muscle and bones through the linen and tweed that separated them now.

One day, she knew, it would not be so. One day they would lie together as she had seen Will and Pansy lie together the night before last, and it would be just as beautiful and just as easy. Ben was the first man she had ever considered in that light. Even with Tom, something inside her had always shied away from the thought. Was that because she had not been ready — as she was now? Or because he had he not been right — as, she knew, Ben was now?

Their lips met, melted ... fused together. She lost all sensation of weight, and even of up and down. The breath that keened in her nostrils, and his, was to keep alive not them but their earthbound carcases; they were now two ethereal beings, twin souls who floated at liberty in and near their physical selves, held to them by the most tenuous threads yet bound to each other with ties that nothing material could now sever.

"Just every now and then ..." she murmured as their lips finally parted.

"More often than that, I hope," he said as he kissed her again.

Another timeless while later she said, "No, I mean that just every now and again life behaves as it should."

"I see," he replied slowly, in a tone that implied he didn't see at all but he wasn't going to spoil the thought by asking her to explain it.

She explained it, anyway. "I mean, one reads those descriptions of love in books — and those lurid things the servants read, which we all pretend never to look at ourselves — and it sounds absolutely wonderful and you think, why can't it *be* like that? Ever? Why is there also the milking to do and brass to clean and cows to buy and sell and bills to pay ...? And then, just occasionally, life *is* like that — the way it ought to be. Like now. Do we squander the moment luxuriously, Ben, or try to cling on to it with ever-increasing desperation until we've completely clutched it to death?"

"We squander it," he decided. "But how?"

"By telling ourselves we don't *need* to hold on to each moment, each time. By behaving as if ... Oh, I don't know!" She laughed and hugged herself tight in against his chest again, wondering if he enjoyed the pressure of her bosom as much as she did. "I'm talking garbage. What I mean is that I feel as if I've just walked through a door and closed it behind me and shut out all the hubbub and bustle ... all those cares and cautions ... and here we are, alone with each other, where no one can see us or reach us. And it's all snug and warm and dry in here. And everything is now up to us. We decide for us. No one else says yes or no, do or don't. D'you know what I mean?"

"Nothing like this has ever happened to me before," he said. "What about you?"

"I've had intimations of it," she admitted. "Like when you start a car and it fires once or twice and then splutters and dies. It's a genuine fire in there — the real thing — but it doesn't last. Something else was missing. And whatever it was, it just came along — just now. You brought it. It's something you've got that no other man ever had for me. So, now that the engine's ticking over as sweet as a mountain stream" — she changed her embrace and held him as if for a waltz — "where shall we let it take us, Ben? Now we've got her running nice and smooth?"

Laughing, he obliged her with a few steps, making them as flamboyant as the cramped little room would allow. "You're amazing, Leah," he told her. "I've never met another woman who gets within a mile of you."

"And what am I bid for this unique little article!" She laughed, for his tone had been so like the one he used in his ringside patter, down in the market.

"The reserve alone would break the Bank of England," he assured her with reproving solemnity. "Shall we go and look at the farmhouse itself?"

As they climbed back into the gig she said, "Do you ever get that feeling where you want to tear everything up, burn all your boats, do something so outrageous that no one you know will ever want to know you again, and then go off and start afresh? *Be* someone new."

He shook his head. "Sometimes, in the middle of an auction, there's a bit of me that sort of breaks loose and watches me — and asks what on earth I think I'm doing there."

"That's the start of it," she said.

"And the end of it," he said fervently. "D'you know George Ivey, over to Mousehole — the artist? You've seen his work, I'm sure. He's quite well known."

"Elizabeth Troy told me he was her solicitor once — oh! Talking of solicitors, by the way — my father has decided to bid farewell to Frank Kernow. I'm glad. I never quite trusted that man. Do you?"

Ben shrugged. "It takes all sorts," he replied diplomatically. "Who are you going to instead?"

"Jake Morvah. I just heard his astonishing story yesterday afternoon ..."

"He told you?" Ben asked in amazement. "It's the one thing he never speaks about."

"No. Adèle told me. We were walking near the mineshaft where it happened and she showed me. Anyway, what were you saying about George Ivey?"

"Oh, yes — he was a fine solicitor ..."

"Your father was solicitor to the Pallas estate but he pleaded a conflict of interest to Elizabeth and advised her to go to George Ivey — very honourably, she says."

"You'll find it runs in our family," he said loftily. "Anyway, young George started asking himself that sort of question — what on earth am I doing this for? — and decided to chuck it in and take up painting instead. He married Lilian Rodda, a beautiful dark-haired girl with the most amazing green eyes. She could have had her pick of Cornwall's eligible bachelors but she chose him and has stuck to him through thick and thin. And they had a *very* thin time of it for many years. If Elizabeth Troy hadn't bought some of his work, they'd have gone under. But only certain people are as singleminded as that. I don't know whether to pity them or envy them."

"You're warning me you're going to remain an auctioneer for life, eh?" She hugged his arm tight to show him she didn't mind.

"I could give it up for farming," he admitted. "For the right sort of farm."

"Or combine the two — farming and the auctioneering," she said. *With the right sort of wife,* she added mentally, though she thought it would sound too precipitate to say such things out loud just yet.

"Could be." *With the right sort of wife,* he thought, though he knew it would sound too brazen to drop hints like that just yet.

46 They both longed to make something of the name Goonhusband, as well, but again it seemed far too audacious a thing to do; one giant leap was sufficient unto the day. Leah loved the farm, of course, with its fine views over southward-sloping fields to the Loe Pool and the massive sandy bar that isolated it from the sea, but, for the moment, they both maintained the fiction that she wanted to persuade her father to move over this side of Helston and sell the Old Glebe to the Liddicoats, with or without the house.

"Back in the middle ages," he said, "that sandbar wasn't there and seagoing ships could sail right up the creek to the foot of Helston. I often think of that when I'm standing in my box above the ring. If a time machine were to transport me back seven hundred years all of a sudden, I'd be standing in the rigging of some coastal lugger. I don't know who'd be more surprised — me or half a dozen medieval peasants watching a lunatic in funny clothes asking twenty-four pounds for a cow worth fourpence!"

Meanwhile Leah was thinking that this would be *their* bedroom, with the nursery just across there, and they'd have to get rid of that wallpaper ... and *she* didn't know which of them would be more surprised if her thoughts suddenly decided to speak themselves aloud. "Damp," she said, pointing to a patch above the mantelpiece.

"Chimney needs repointing," he said. "Make a note of that — and anything else. We'll try to get the cost of it all taken off the eventual purchase price."

"*Purchase* price, Ben?" She dug him playfully in the ribs. "Don't you mean *selling* price? Which side of the fence are you squatting on now?"

"Hmm!" He sniffed. "There may be a slight conflict of interest here — I can't deny it. Mind you — looking at it as impartially as possible — even if nothing got knocked off it, today's fair price is tomorrow's bargain. As long as this war lasts, anyway. I might even buy it myself."

"And becoming a farmer would be a capital way of staying beyond the reach of snipers and dysentery!"

He shook his head. "Being able to find good remounts for the cavalry and commissariat is even better. But you're right in one way — I've no taste for guns." He eyed her evenly. "D'you think that's cowardice?"

She shook her head, implying that it was sad he should even feel it necessary to ask. "I danced all round the room when I heard that the wolfram business would keep Will safe."

He suspected she had meant to say Nicholas. "But Will would be safe anyway, surely?" he asked. "As an American?"

"Altruism knows no frontiers," she told him. "Young second-generation British-Americans are remembering their roots every day and signing up in their droves. Surely you've read about it?"

He said nothing — merely continued staring out of the window. She touched his arm, ran one finger up and down it gently. "Penny for 'em?"

He shook himself, smiled at her, and became brisk again. "A new intimacy is such a fragile thing," he replied. "You said it's like entering a room and shutting the door behind you — and so it is. But then you notice, in my case, that the room is full of beautiful and fragile-looking things. And so, although you've been longing for months to go through that door and close it behind you, you still daren't move. I mean, even to touch you like this" — he slipped his fingers into the hair behind her ear and scratched her scalp, making her shiver all over — "even that would have been *unthinkable* yesterday. Now I may do it without alarms and excursions."

"Anytime!"

"And to say the words I've longed to say to you from the day we met — 'I love you, Leah Carrington. You are all the world to me' — would have given me a heart attack yesterday. Today I can say them with impunity."

"Anytime!" she said again.

"So the summit and utmost pinnacle of yesterday's ambitions is merely the ground on which today's are stood."

Leah thought this over and said, "My mother always told us at Thanksgiving and Christmas and other times when we were set to eat more than our fill at one time ... she would say, 'Always rise from the table feeling you could eat a little bit more'." She looked at him to see if he took the point.

He chuckled. "Mine always said that, too — and no doubt *we'll* be saying it one day to ... er, the next generation ... er ..." He subsided in confusion.

She laughed and took his arm. "Come on, Ben. Back to the world of cows and counting frames."

They chatted happily about nothing in particular, the way new lovers love to do, all the way back to town. As they passed the entrance to Chynoweth, Blanche Curnow appeared, taking one of their dogs for a walk.

"I haven't seen much of Will lately," she called out to Leah. "Tell him he's a heartless wretch and it will be many minutes before I forgive him, even if he does pay us a call."

"He is a heartless wretch, too," Leah said to Ben when they were out of earshot. "There's only one woman for him in all the world now, and that's Adèle Liddicoat."

"Oh, there's a come-up! Does Miss Philomena know?"

"I'm sure she doesn't. Actually, there's something I want to ask you, to do with Will and Adèle."

"Ask away."

They were passing the Union by now. She had little time left but it might be an advantage to limit this particular conversation. "It's actually about Will and Pansy," she said. "Adèle is the love of his life but Pansy is his little bit of fluff on the side — is that the right expression?"

"Oh, dear."

"Yes, it's not exactly a pleasant thing to contemplate — still less to try and deal with. But that's my question, really — should I deal with it at all? Or shall I just let the pair of them go to hell in a handcart?"

After a moment's thought he said, "You are Pansy Tregear's mistress. Have you spoken to her about it?"

"I have — and I went completely off on the wrong trail. I thought she was setting her cap at Will. I told her there was no chance of any such union. She said she wouldn't go near him if there was. She just wants a bit of fun and no permanent ties. I can't fire her because it wouldn't stop her assignations with Will and I'd lose what minuscule control I have over her now. Besides, she's one of the best workers I've ever known. Intelligent, reliable, thorough ... a dream."

"Have you spoken to your pa about it?"

"Don't!" she answered heavily. "She's flirting with him, too, and would be quite capable of going further, just to thumb her nose at me. But I've warned her about that — one slip and she's out without a character. Not that the factories look for characters when they offer our maidservants twice what we pay them! In a way, I tolerate what's going on with Will just to stop her trying anything with Pa — isn't that awful?"

"When you say she's capable of 'going further' ... how far ... with Will, I mean?"

"All the way, Ben. And practically every night as far as I can tell. I feel just *awful* about it every time I meet Adèle, who's my best friend." She stroked his arm. "Girl friend, anyway. And then there's poor Blanche back there whom I'm also very fond of. Isn't love ruthless!"

"Blanche Curnow's young yet," he said. "Learning how to put a cheery face on rejection is valuable, too."

"I hope the young man I left behind me in America has forgotten me by now, but if he hasn't, I'd do nothing to cheer him up if it threatened our love in the smallest degree. I know I ought to feel heartless to be saying such a thing, but I don't."

They turned down into Coinagehall Street and she asked to be put off at the Angel — leaving their conversation unresolved but simmering. Ben offered to take her into the hôtel for lunch but she declined. "I want to see Miss Philomena," she said. "Alone, if you don't mind. I want to put matters straight between us and recover your good standing with her."

He laughed — a bluff, hearty laugh. "I don't give a fig for her now," he said.

"That's as maybe, but there's no point in making enemies needlessly. Besides, we may yet need her. Don't ask me to explain it — but I just have this feeling, somewhere in my bones, that she's going to play a part in solving our present difficulties. And even if I'm wrong, she and I cannot stare at each other in naked hostility for ever."

She shook his hand, giving it a squeeze that no one else would notice. She could see his eyes begging her to tell him when they'd meet next. "Don't let's start that sort of desperate caper, Ben," she said. "I'll be with you every *possible* moment — which is exactly when you want to be with me, too. Isn't that enough? That and the telephone."

"Toute à l'heure, then," he said jovially. "I'll put your pony in our stables. No sense in paying a day's livery at the Angel. He'll be in the end stall."

"That's right," she said solemnly. "We've got to start saving every penny now."

Walter Blackwell greeted her like a favourite niece but he was clearly anxious to shepherd her toward some part of his establishment that Philomena Liddicoat was unlikely to visit. She, however, amazed him by sending him up to her family's sworn enemy, carrying her father's card. First she scribbled her own name in pencil beneath his: Miss Carrington. The British left out the 'Leah' since she was the only daughter.

The woman kept her waiting almost twenty minutes and then greeted her coldly and without any attempt at an apology. But Leah made an oblique reference to this rudeness in her opening words: "I owe you an apology, *too,* Miss Liddicoat," she said, offering her hand — which Philomena ignored. "I regretted the little subterfuge I induced Mister Coad to play upon you the moment we met."

"It is no less than I expected of any Carrington," the older woman put in frostily. "Especially after my extraordinary encounter with your father."

"Quite! I do see your point, Miss Liddicoat. If I were less of a coward than I am, I should have owned up at once and saved myself this shameful and humiliating scene."

"Hmm!" Philomena pursed her lips and stared at the girl speculatively through narrowed eyes.

"I should have realized you are much too astute to have been deceived for long."

"Enough flattery," Philomena said severely. "Tell me what you really want."

"Your acceptance of my apology is the most I could hope for, I think."

Philomena did not believe it for one moment but, by way of a test, she snapped, "I accept, Miss Carrington," and turned on her heel to go.

"Also ..." Leah said before she reached the door.

"Also," Philomena said, "I commend your courage in coming so swiftly to make it." Again she made to leave the room.

"Also there are other matters we should discuss, I believe."

"*Should* discuss? I cannot think of one, Miss Carrington."

"But that is what I am here to tell you, Miss Liddicoat."

Still with one hand on the opened door, Philomena said, "Name one."

Leah took a deep breath and said, "For example, we both have an interest in seeing the Carringtons leave the Old Glebe — I think?"

The woman's hand fell to her side. After a moment of complete immobility she came back into the room, to where Leah was standing, and peered deep into her eyes — a chilling, raptorial scrutiny that almost put Leah to flight. "Is this some joke — another of your father's childish pranks?"

"He knows nothing of this. Indeed, he'd have a fit if he knew I was here now. He's looking forward to a battle-royal with you, which he's quite sure he'll win, of course — though, mind you, he also says you're the first opponent who's truly worthy of him — the first one he's met since leaving the old shark pond in Pittsburgh, Pennsylvania."

"Ha!" Philomena pretended to be severe though she could not entirely hide her delight at the backhanded compliment. "He has a high opinion of himself, I must say!"

"And of *you,* Miss Liddicoat. I know him when he talks like this. He's afraid he might not win, you see — even though he seems to hold all the important cards. He's already preparing the grounds on which he'll excuse his defeat at your hands."

Philomena went over to the window and stared out at the passing scene for a while, taking in nothing. Nothing in her planning could have prepared her for this. Her cautious self advised her to send the girl away, setting an appointment for another day, by which time she could have made inquiries, imagined all the things the girl might have to say, and prepared herself to answer them. But her cautious self was a midget beside the leviathan of her self-confident and pugnacious alter-ego. "Tell me, Miss Carrington," she said at length, "have you eaten luncheon yet?"

"As a matter of fact, I have not, Miss Liddicoat."

"I have taken the room next to mine for use as my private sitting room. We could have a light repast sent up there?"

When she saw that Leah still hesitated she added, "Or what had you in mind?"

"If we eat together privately, word will still get out, and eventually it will reach my father. Then the fact that we tried to conceal our meeting — or gave that appearance, anyway — will not be helpful."

"But if we dine in public, you've been here long enough, I'm sure, to realize that word will get to your father at once — and then the fur will fly, surely?"

"I hope I shall be ready for it in either case. Besides — as you will see, I hope — we do not have the luxury of time."

They were the first to arrive in the dining room. Blackwell stared at them in amazement, which the professional in him quickly suppressed. "A table for two, Miss Liddicoat — certainly. This way."

Leah watching his departing back, said, "The message is already on its way."

"Tell me, Miss Carrington," Philomena said as she spread her napkin and peered at the chalked menu on the blackboard, "why is Ben Coad showing you a property out by Helston Downs? If it's not an impertinent question?"

"Not in the least," Leah assured her. "It's the farm called Goonhusband, which I'm sure you know? Sixty-odd acres, slightly larger than the Old Glebe, and all of them facing south and with superb views of the Loe Pool and the bay. My father could make a much more spectacular garden there than ever he could in Sithney. And now, perhaps, you see the way my thoughts are running?"

The maid took their orders. Both chose leek soup and steak pudding and smiled, slightly surprised to find themselves in agreement on anything.

"The house is nothing like so impressive as the Old Glebe, though," Philomena pointed out.

"It's adequate. It could even be grandified in time. My father will put up with a lot for the sake of his beloved garden project. On the other hand ..." She sighed.

"Yes?"

"On the other hand, he also loves a challenge. The fact that a quarter of the Old Glebe faces north of west and gets less sun than the rest is just the sort of thing to set his blood racing. He's got to whip the world into line with *his* thinking. Ignorant people might gawp in wonder at an easy-to-make garden facing south on those sunny slopes at Goonhusband. But *real* gardeners, the cognoscenti whom he'd invite to the Old Glebe, would look at his verdant, flourishing north-facing acres and ask how on earth he managed it. And *that* would be worth more to him than all the ignorant praise in the world."

Watching Miss Philomena carefully during this little speech, Leah saw that she had guessed correctly; the woman was much more in sympathy with John Carrington's love of a challenge than with his daughter's preference for the easy road. Naturally, she would rather die than admit it — especially to that same daughter — but the seeds of the internal conflict were sown within her.

"Goonhusband has hazards of its own," Philomena warned. "There is a frost that forms up on the downs on windless nights under clear skies, and it spills down into all the surrounding valleys. I have seen it with my own eyes. The frosty air is perfectly clear up on the downs but as it descends, a mist forms upon it even as you watch. And soon the whole valley is like a vast lake of mist. And a cold, clammy mist it is, too, which shrivels the buds off many a shrub and blights many a garden flower. Maurice Pettifer planted a belt of cypresses to shelter his land at Culdrose from it."

"It sounds quite spectacular," Leah said. "And you describe it so vividly. I should love to witness it myself."

The maid brought their soup and some white-bread rolls.

"You'll get your chance soon enough," Philomena told her as they began their meal. "In the calm days that follow the autumn gales the same thing happens up on Carnmeal Downs — on a much smaller scale, of course. It just pours down into the Grankum valley."

"And does it affect the Old Glebe?"

"No." Philomena stared at her coldly. "Why d'you think *we* always wanted to farm on *your* side of the valley!"

Leah dipped her head as if accepting a rebuke. Then, smiling again, she said, "However, if we can only put our thinking caps on — you and I, Miss Liddicoat — we may arrive at a solution congenial to all parties, don't you think? And without a single shot being fired!"

47 John Carrington had taken to dropping in at the Angel of a Saturday, around lunchtime, to moan about English beer with Jimmy Troy and otherwise chew the fat about this and that. They called it the weekly board meeting of LCT. On that first Saturday in October, however — the day after Miss Carrington joined Miss Liddicoat for luncheon in the public dining room — there was only one topic of conversation. Poor Carrington had a hard time keeping a civil tongue after the first half dozen good-natured friends had broken the news to him, each hoping to be the first to bend his ear.

"What I can't fathom," he said to Jimmy as they retired to their usual alcove near the fire, "is why Leah didn't breathe a word of it to me. Did she think I'd never get to hear of it? She's never so naive. What's her game, anyway? What business could she and the Liddicoat woman possibly have in common? Sometimes she just baffles me."

"Wa-al," Jimmy drawled, "let's lookit this-hyar thang in a calm and collected manner …"

"It's no laughing matter, Jimmy."

"And it's not the end of the world, either."

"The *independence* of the girl! A year ago she'd never have done such a thing — nor even dreamed of it."

"That's what growing older usually entails, John."

"Does she really think she can wave some wand behind my back and make all smooth?"

Troy merely cleared his throat in response to that.

"Well?" Carrington prompted him.

"Well, in my limited experience of these matters, when a woman starts behaving like that, she's exercising something a mite more substantial than a wand."

"For instance?"

"Intellect? A cussed propensity to be more right than wrong, more times than not? An ability to skin away mere cleverness and expose the flesh and bone of the thing — which is otherwise known as intuition? I'd say she has some intuition about Miz Philomena and she's acting on it — for your ultimate good, I'm sure. Or do you doubt even that?"

"No," Carrington conceded reluctantly. "I'm sure she *thinks* she's acting in our best interest all round. That doesn't mean she *is* so acting."

"Well, the Yankee *calculates* his conclusions, the Missurian *opinions* them, the Southerner *suspicions* them, the Hoosier *allows,* and the Buckey *reckons.* It doesn't mean they don't all agree in the end."

Carrington stared at him balefully. "Take my hat, Jimmy, if you aren't hard to follow sometimes. Speak plain, man!"

Troy sipped his warm beer with relish, though he pulled the ritual face of disgust. "Plainly spoken, John, Leah is your daughter. You raised her. You launched her. You've got to let her sail a piece on her own."

"It augurs badly, that's all," Carrington said morosely.

"Augurs?" The word surprised Troy.

"I don't think I ever told you this, Jimmy, but under the terms of her granmaw's will, Leah is all set to come into full possession of her trust at the age of twenty-three — which, heaven help us, is only ten months off now."

"No, John, you never told me that before. More to the point — did you ever tell the girl herself?"

"I was about to. Now ... I don't know. This news has fair taken the wind out of *my* sails, I can tell you. Never mind her sailing a piece on her own."

"Without mentioning any figures now — as the Irishman said — what exactly does it amount to?"

"It's enough to let her do any damfool thing she wants."

After a further ruminative silence Troy said, "Okay, but that doesn't really *change* the problem of her independent action, does it. It simply makes it more acute. The question we have to address is: What is Leah likely to have discussed with Miz Philomena? Did she attempt to apologize for your little practical joke, for instance?"

"Why should she do that?"

"To gauge how mad the lady really was? I'm only canvassing possibilities here. Did she talk of LCT at all? Probably not. Is there any spark kindling between her and one of the Liddicoat boys, I wonder? A woman in love would go into the lion's den to size up the lion's ferocity. Or lioness in this case. Now that's a sharp possibility."

"Harvey maybe," Carrington agreed. "But not Nicholas. She wouldn't let him walk where she walked last year — that's how much she likes that young man."

Troy grinned. "That's how much she *says* she likes that young man." He punched his friend playfully. "You're mighty trusting when it comes to the *word* of a female, John. Or maybe there's some little preemption between your boy and the Liddicoat girl — Adelaide."

"She likes to be called Adèle now. Yes, there may be at that."

Troy chuckled. "Of course, Leah might simply have been asking Miz Philomena how much she'd offer for the Old Glebe!"

Carrington despaired of all this speculation. "Or they were discussing quilting patterns or how to put new life into old velvet! In short, Jimmy, reasonableness ain't gonna get us out of *this* forest. I'm minded to go home and put it to her, direct. It's the only way."

He half rose to go but then, seeing his friend staring past him toward the door, he hesitated.

"I wonder?" Troy mused. "There could be an even more direct way. Are you in a mood to apologize? You'd better be or this won't work, either."

And before Carrington could say a word, he had leaped from his seat and was striding across the lounge bar to the door, where, a moment earlier, he had briefly glimpsed Miss Philomena Liddicoat. Carrington himself did not make the connection until he saw Jimmy Troy returning with the lady — who, like Carrington himself, seemed none too happy at the prospect of this meeting.

It was just as well the surprise was sprung on him like that, for a moment's thought would have confirmed his determination never to apologize to *that* woman. With no time for reflection, however, he was at the mercy of half a century's training in etiquette, in which apologies to women were *de rigueur,* no matter who was right and who was wrong.

"Miss Liddicoat," he said with a somewhat glassy smile, "can you forgive me? I was so ashamed to be found in working man's rags — which is idiotic of me, I confess — that, on the spur of the moment, I pretended to be one of my own labourers ..."

His voice trailed off when he saw the woman smiling broadly. He had expected any reaction but that. "Say not another word,

Mister Carrington," she replied. "I was annoyed for an hour or so, I admit, but I hope I can see a joke as well as the next person, even when it is at my expense."

"May I offer you something to drink, Miss Liddicoat?" Troy asked. "A cordial or some lime …"

"A pint of Rosewarne's export ale, Mister Troy. Thank you." She took the seat he held for her and offered cigars all round.

The barmaid asked would two half-pints do as Mr Blackwell never let them serve a lady with a pint glass.

She laughed and said it would have to do, wouldn't it!

The laugh surprised John Carrington, it was so rich and warm. It also filled him with distrust. 'Beware of Greeks bearing gifts,' he cautioned himself — though he was quite prepared to play the civilized game on the surface, if that was what the lady wanted. He lit her cigar and Troy's and then, obeying a new superstition, lit his own with a fresh match.

"Well, Mister Carrington," she said as soon as they were all seated, "I presume your daughter told you of our meeting yesterday? Such a charming girl! And so full of good sense." She looked him up and down as if wondering where the girl could have got it from.

"Er …" Carrington eyed Troy nervously. "More or less. In outline — yes. The bare bones of the thing. I wish she'd spoken to me first, though."

She was not deceived for a moment, of course. "Oh?" Her tone implied that his reply surprised her beyond words. "You mean you *don't* think it's a good idea? Well, well, well — you do astonish me. The whole … what can one call it? Contretemps? Fracas? The whole thing is to be solved at one fell swoop — and not a shot fired in anger, as she said — and yet you don't think that's a good idea at all?"

Having taken a position, however tentative, Carrington now felt he had to defend it. He stared balefully at Jimmy Troy, silently willing him to step in. Troy could say all those things he himself could not — that they seemed to be talking about different things and perhaps Miss Liddicoat could summarize Miss Carrington's notions so that they could all agree on what was at issue.

Troy beamed at him and toasted him with a silent lift of his glass.

"Say?" Carrington challenged him directly.

"Me?" Troy asked innocently, puffing his cigar again. "I say what I always say — when a feller's done flummoxed, he's flummoxed, and salt won't save him!"

"You were *relishing* a fight!" Miss Liddicoat said suddenly, as if it were a revelation.

Carrington, his back to the wall, said, "I'll fight for any principle that's worth defending, ma'am."

"Good for you!" she replied. "I understand perfectly for I feel exactly the same way myself."

The maid brought her ale. The sight of the two glasses made Carrington aware of something the mere idea of them had failed to drive home — that the woman was going to be sitting there for another twenty minutes at the very least. He was either going to have to temper his words or leave in a huff. That was no real choice.

He was so preoccupied with these thoughts that he did not notice she was setting her drink down at the same moment as he decided to set down his. Their knuckles touched briefly. Their eyes met. A fire burned and did not die. With something of a thrill he realized that the accidental contact was a symbolic enactment of the touch between boxers' gloves before the first round begins. She had thrown down a gauntlet and he had picked it up.

But their contest was not to be a public row that divided (or entertained) the whole community; it was to be a polite, smiling affair — intimate, decorous, and deadly. So be it. They were damn fine cigars.

"My brother tells me that, before this war put paid to your plans, you intended to turn the Old Glebe into a magnificent garden, Mister Carrington — something to rival Trengwainton, he said."

He nodded gravely. "That was my plan, ma'am. Indeed, it still is — when these hostilities have ended."

"Ah, yes," she said. "These wretched hostilities! I don't wish to sound unpatriotic, but I do miss my garden. I think the only reason they requisitioned my house was that the officer in charge of that sort of thing at the war office was in the colonel's old regiment and had dined with us quite frequently before the war. He never liked me. There were many more suitable houses in the same area. And I know the garden will be a ruin by the time they hand the house back to me."

"One garden returning to a state of nature and another that cannot rise out of it!" Troy mused aloud. "Is that not an astonishing symmetry!"

Miss Liddicoat ignored him. Speaking directly to Carrington she said, "That girl, Pansy Tregear — was she inventing those names she reeled off? I can hardly think so. It sounds as if you are cultivating some interesting plants, Mister Carrington. You know that roses never do well down here? It's too wet. They succumb to mildew, black spot, rust ... everything. Though some of the species roses are quite resistant."

"Yes," Carrington said cautiously. "I've seen them thriving over at Trevivian ..."

"Jane Scawen's garden. What a woman, eh! The first person to use dynamite in Cornwall! Did she show you around?"

"She's my chief inspiration. I've always wanted to lay out a substantial garden, mind, but when I saw Trevivian ... well!"

"Quite — I do understand. And I know something of that same urge, too — though on a far more modest scale, I hasten to say. I laid out the colonel's garden in Cheam. It was five acres of grass and trees when I came to him. And I left it a ..." She closed her eyes and shook her head. "Forget it. What's done is done." She brightened and smiled again. "All the hebes thrive down here. And so does ceanothus. And I wonder about the himalayan laburnum ...?"

"Piptanthus nepalensis?" he said.

"You know it! It's quite a new subject."

"I've seen pictures."

"The yellow is quite astonishing, like burning sulphur. I had one in Cheam. A pod of seeds came away in my hands on a visit to Kew! They do very well from seed. Ah, me!" She sighed. "This is the time of year to be in Kew. Hardly anything's in flower so there aren't many visitors to observe one ... and *everything's* in seed!"

They all laughed at this pleasant fantasy but Carrington himself, she noticed, had a thoughtful look all the same.

She risked it. "D'you know, Mister Carrington," she said, "I would consider it the *greatest* favour if you would show me over your fields and explain to me your plans for their transformation."

"Well, ma'am ..." He scratched his head diffidently, trying to think of a way to refuse without giving offence — and then, suddenly, realizing he actually *wanted* to boast of his plans to someone — anyone — and that she would do very well indeed. Rub her nose in it. Also learn more of what she *really* intended.

"You are far too busy?" she offered. "I quite understand."

"Not at all, ma'am. I was wondering if I might invite you this afternoon — if you have nothing better to do?"

"You'll take luncheon here?" She addressed the question to both men.

"Not me," Troy said, fishing out his watch. "I'm expected back home." He smiled at Carrington.

She turned to him, too.

He had meanwhile decided it would be a fitting revenge for Leah's secrecy *not* to go home for lunch, and then to spring a 'friendly' visit from Miss Liddicoat upon her. "Indeed," he said. "May I invite you to join me?"

"The invitation is already mine, Mister Carrington," she replied firmly. "Your daughter yesterday, you today ... I wonder? Shall I book the table for your son tomorrow, in hope of completing the hat-trick?"

48 It was a pleasant lunch, considering they were sworn enemies. Philomena talked of the harshness of her early life at Grankum Farm, of the liberating power of books, of ambition, of setting oneself goals and never losing sight of them, of the virtues of hard work and persistence. John Carrington found himself in the curious position of agreeing with almost every word, even though he knew she was firing salvo after salvo across his bows, warning him that she would not yield. The goal she never mentioned was that of driving the Carringtons out of the Old Glebe for ever. The persistence she extolled was her own, in pursuing that goal.

His feelings were thus a close match to his behaviour. At a shallow level he felt warm and well disposed; he actually enjoyed her company. But deep down he knew she was deliberately fostering his delusion. Her smile was that of a tigress. The things he enjoyed in her were, in reality, the strands of a spider's web.

He had lived in conflict, surrounded by duplicity, all his adult life; yet this situation was new to him. His battles had been against the unknown — the future, the movements of the market, the success or failure of crops. Or they had been masculine conflicts, as when men of business jostle for advantage, political favours, a commercial edge. They slapped each other's backs and said things like, 'I'll lick you on this one, John — durn me if I don't!' And when it was over, they'd shake hands and swear there were no hard feelings, even if there were. It was all so open and above-board and manly and beautiful.

But this corrosively sweet warfare with Miz Philomena was something so far removed from his experience that even the most innocuous remark would leave him feeling profoundly uneasy. He felt as Gulliver must have felt when tied down upon the Lilliputian strand by a thousand flimsy threads, any one of which he could have snapped with ease but which, combined together, could hold him powerless and at their mercy. In his case those insubstantial threads were the ties of polite convention — that a smile should be answered with a smile, and a pleasing remark should not be rebuffed with a curse or a growl. And so, each time he smiled, each time he met a pleasantry from her with one of his own, he felt she was casting yet another Lilliputian thread over his supine carcase and that soon he would have lost the power of free and independent movement.

Something had to be done. Either he would bring this warfare back to those masculine levels where he could manage it, or he would be rendered powerless. 'Masculate or be emasculated,' you could say — or, in the terse language of his former commerce: 'Git or get got!'

"Civilization is a powerful thing, Miss Liddicoat," he said as he helped her into the gig. Even her physical charms — for she was still a fine figure of a woman — appeared as a threat to him, all of a piece with the seductive charm of her conversation. The elemental male within him found it hard to keep his eyes off her as she climbed aboard, but the wise man-of-the-world forced him to avert his gaze at last.

"In what way, Mister Carrington?" she asked as he leaped nimbly aboard and took his place beside her — which was also odd, because he had given up all his nimble leaping quite a few years ago.

Stretching his back to ease the twinge this particular nimble leap had caused, he reached for the reins, let off the brake, and clucked the pony to a careful walk out into the bustle of Coinagehall Street. "In that it enables a Liddicoat and a Carrington to sup at the same table, talk with amiable pleasure for the best part of an hour, and fix to spend the next hour in each other's company, walking over the very piece of land that has for so long ... I mean for which they would ..." All the images that occurred to him were either crassly belligerent or laughably feeble.

While he struggled to find something in between, she said, "I know what you're about to say, Mister Carrington, but believe me, it is not so. Not any longer."

He had to haul on the brake all the way down the hill — as well as steer the gig around street-traders' stalls, children with hoops, and two dogs and a bitch. He wished he had not started this conversation until they were down on level ground in St John's. "Of course I believe you, ma'am, since you assure me it is so. Yet I still wonder at it."

"So much has happened since last Wednesday," she said. "Was it only last Wednesday I arrived? Dear me! I was *seething* with anger that day. I have been seething with anger ever since they commandeered my house. We do not realize how intimately we are bound up with property — with land and buildings — until it is seized and taken from us."

Now that he had steered her into the one area — indeed, the only area — of legitimate debate between them he decided to play along with the line she had taken. "A house is especially important to a woman, I know," he said.

"Do you mean domesticity? Nest-building? No, I am talking about something much more profound than that. I mean the *uniqueness* of a place. Even people who live at number one-hundred-and-one in a terrace of identical homes know that their house is different from all the others. But five acres of garden that you've created yourself from nothing but grass and trees — the winding paths among borders of shrubs, the broad, lily-padded pool you enlarged from a tiny dew-pond, the rustic pergola ..." Her voice caught.

She did it very well, he thought. But to show her he was not fooled he said, "Not to mention, of course, fifty acres of prime arable land and pasture that you've coveted for as long as you can remember!"

She swallowed heavily and said, "We're still talking about last Wednesday? Yes, I admit that, having lost what was so precious to me in London, it was the last straw to discover that the Old Glebe was now in the hands of those hated Carringtons. I had indeed coveted it for as long as I can remember. And at last I had the means to acquire it, too. But instead there are those *Carringtons!*" She said the name as if it were of some third party whom they both detested. "He was an American pork whole-saler, I learned. No doubt he would be some brash, loud-mouthed, tub-thumping Yankee with more money than taste. And as for his daughter — the things I heard about her! Or, rather, the things I made out of the things I heard about her: a brazen, freethinking hussy, rising twenty-three, never been engaged, walking into Helston market and buying cattle as cool as any farmer who's been at it all his life! Well!" She smiled engagingly at him once again. "So much has happened since then, as I say."

They were down in St John's by now and he could relax a little, concentrate less on his driving. She had been so explicit about all the bad qualities she had imagined in him that he wanted to be told what pleasant surprises she had found there instead. But he also suspected that she *wanted* him to ask about it; so he held his tongue. Instead he said, "So now you wish me to believe you don't mind at all? Or you mind much less than before? Or what?"

She chuckled. "I'll tell you how much I mind — or how little — Mister Carrington, when you've told me your plans for the place. I love it still, the Old Glebe, and I always shall. But I wouldn't be the first lover in history to console herself with the knowledge that, though her love belongs to another, he could not be in better hands."

It was clever, he had to admit. Devilish clever. She was in a fortress whose walls were encased in sheer, unbreakable glass that offered him not the smallest toehold. She was frankness itself where any lie would be so obvious as to be untenable anyway; and in all other places she masked her hatred of all Carringtons and her undying ambition to own the Old Glebe behind a veneer of that same disarming frankness. Well, he was not disarmed — though perhaps it would now be wiser to appear to capitulate, to *seem* won over, to lull her into standing down the guard atop that fortress wall.

"The half-sovereign you gave me," he said.

"Yes?" She chuckled at the memory.

"You had me beaten fair and square, there," he allowed.

"But you have hit upon some way to even the honours, I make no doubt?"

"Well ... to regain a little lost ground," he admitted. "I don't know about getting even, though. I planned to have one of the stones beside my water-garden engraved with a dedication, saying that funds for the garden were begun with a generous subscription from Miss Philomena Liddicoat."

It pleased him to see the smile fade from her lips. And though she said, "I hope you still do," the words lacked the sweetness she had ladled over everything else she had said. *Yes,* he thought, *the claws are still there, underneath all this soft velvet.* And he complimented himself on his ability to make them visible whenever he needed the reminder.

She showed something of her true nature in other ways, too. As they passed one of the poorer houses near the foot of Sithney Common Hill, she called out to one of the urchins by its front door, telling her to mend that hole in her stocking before it got any bigger. To John Carrington she said, "I know the mother there — a slut from birth." She glanced back and shouted, "Now, girl! Now!" as the poor little creature tumbled over the threshold in her haste to be gone.

As they started up the long haul of the hill she became all sweetness again. "Were you always a keen gardener, Mister Carrington?" she asked.

He tapped his forehead. "In here, ma'am. But the soil in our part of Connecticut was pretty thin. Six inches down you hit stone. I had a hothouse where I grew orchids and cacti — that was my outlet then."

"Orchids?" she asked excitedly. "Did you have any of the *Cattleya* hybrids? They were first crossed in England, you know. I had a little fernery where I ..." Again her voice caught. "Never mind. Never mind," she said.

Trying to sound quite casual he said, "I had several specimens of the *Odiontioda* cross. The first cross between two genera!"

"Vuylstekeæ?" she asked in even greater excitement — and taking him completely aback. "I've seen it at Kew. Quite superb! But aren't they *terribly* difficult to grow?"

"That's what I was working on — and hope to work on again, once I have a proper place: a safe growing medium for orchids. It's so heartbreaking to lose them just when they seem to be full-grown and thriving."

"I know, I know!"

"I almost had it, too — an extract of seaweed, with the salt removed, of course. I'll lick it one day. I still have plans for a hothouse at the Old Glebe. Trouble is, the ideal location is right where that old tithe barn stands."

"Oh, I'd demolish that at once," she said. "And no regrets. It's been an eyesore for more than five hundred years — high time it went."

He stared at her in amazement. "But I was warned off doing any such thing. Ben Coad said I'd become that cultureless Yankee vandal you were talking about back there."

"Well ... yes." She nodded thoughtfully. "Perhaps *you* couldn't do it after all. It would start people talking like that — they all get so sentimental about preserving *other people's* property! I could, though. I'd like to see the person who tried to stop me."

"The Liddicoat Demolition Company ..." he mused. "I'll hire you right now."

"Ah, yes!" she replied sadly. "Anything unpleasant or unpopular — send for Philomena Liddicoat!"

"Oh, come!" He spluttered with embarrassment. "I didn't mean *that.*"

"Of course you didn't!" She patted his arm a couple of times and laughed. "I was only joking."

Yes — only probing for my vulnerable points, he thought. *Only seeing how quickly and easily I bend.* He was angry with himself — but not, curiously enough, with her. Indeed, as a seasoned warrior in this particular field of battle, he rather admired her skill. And, in the end, his admiration overcame his anger as he braced himself not to fall for the same trick twice. She was going to prove the most worthy opponent he had ever faced. Faced *down,* that is. It was going to be a real pleasure, whether he won or merely fought her to an exhausted standstill.

The remaining possibility was, of course, merely theoretical.

49 Leah was filled with consternation when, just after luncheon, Pansy came running indoors in great excitement to announce that the master and the Dragon were strolling about the fields like a pair of turtle doves. After her meeting with that same Dragon the previous day she had developed the most acute case of cold feet and had intended going back into Helston that afternoon for a further meeting with the woman, just to make sure that she had appraised her character correctly. To discover that her father — entirely without consulting her — had struck up some independent association with Philomena Liddicoat was unsettling to say the least.

How had it happened? It must have been during the weekly 'board meeting' of LCT in the bar at the Angel. She really should have foreseen that possibility. Not that she could have done anything about it — except, of course, own up honestly to what she had done.

Well, it was too late to worry about that now. The harm was done — and even more serious worries now pressed upon her: How much had Miss Liddicoat blurted out? For she, naturally, would assume that the daughter had gone straight home and told the father all. Had she mentioned Goonhusband? The outing there with Ben Coad? Had she started some campaign of her own, setting aside their common interest? Leah realized she would be riding a stormy current or two when her father and Miz Philomena came in for tea.

But they did not come in for tea, and that turned her consternation into something more like anger. The pair of them climbed back into the gig and drove straight out into the yard — presumably back to Helston. And presumably he stayed to enjoy tea with her at the Angel or in one of the town's little cafés, for it was almost dark by the time he returned. She was busy milking by then. He came laughing into the cowshouse, saying, "Guess what I was told. I was driving up past the mill at the bottom of Sithney Common Hill and the miller fellow ..."

"Frank Trevose," she said.

"That's the man. He warned me it was getting a little dark to be driving without lights — and that the cops often lurk in that side lane halfway up the hill. But, he said, if I pointed out that the pony was white, I might get away with it."

Leah's laugh was more dutiful than amused. "What were you doing, anyway, staying all that time — and with Miz Philomena of all people?"

"I'm amazed *you* should ask that," he replied coldly. But his ebullient humour broke through again. "Oh, she thinks she's so *smart!* She thinks she's got me eating out of the palm of her hand! Won't I just show her!"

"Go in and bathe, Pa," she said, nodding her head significantly toward where John Hamden was milking another cow. "We've only two more to do and then I'll come in and put some liniment on your back."

"How d'you know my back needs liniment?"

"Because of the way you're standing. You always stand like that when you've strained it."

"Oh!" he exclaimed. "If you ain't just about the cantankarest female ...!"

Later, while Hamden drove the cattle out to their field and came back to muck out the cowshouse, she gave her father the promised massage. It restored his humour. The question he had intended asking quite sharply came out rather mildly instead: "What the dickens were you doing taking luncheon with that woman yesterday, honey, and why didn't you tell me?"

By now Leah was prepared with her answer: "Because I wasn't sure of her. I would have told you once I was sure. Honest, I would. Anyway, I didn't go in there to see her in the first place, I went to see Ben Coad. I just bumped into her after I'd said goodbye to him. And *she* invited *me* to lunch. I could hardly say no, could I. Did she say anything to you about Violet Tregear — Pansy's sister?"

"No?" He frowned. Mention of Pansy always put him slightly on the defensive.

"She went specially up to the Union to hire Violet yesterday, as her maid."

"Oh, I get it!" He laughed again. "She thinks she's so smart! As if Pansy's going to tell Violet anything! They've hardly spoken for years."

"Ah — you knew about this already, then?" Leah asked. "You've already spoken to Pansy?"

"Er ... no." He was defensive again. "I just knew it — already, I mean. She talked about her family when we were sticking those quicksets last Thursday. Oh, thank you. That feels so much better. I can't think how I ricked it like that. But I'll tell you one thing, honey" — he stood up, rubbing his hands gleefully — "we're going to walk small circles round that lady, who thinks she can get the better of us."

"Does she?" Leah wiped the liniment off her hands while he struggled back into his shirt. "I thought Will was right for once. Her bark is much worse than her bite. In fact, I ended up feeling rather sorry for her. Poor, lonely old woman — except that she isn't at all old, is she! She's still quite young — and pretty good-looking, too, don't you think? And desperately lonely, I'd say — since the colonel's death."

Her father was silent awhile. Then he said, "She's not as smart as she fancies she is."

"Yes, you said that before. Isn't it strange — she *loved* that house of hers in Cheam. The one the colonel left her. And the garden ..."

"She designed it and created it herself," he put in, almost as if he were proud of her. "Supervised its creation, that is — though, from the way she talks, I'll bet she got plenty of dirt under her fingernails, too."

"If the war hadn't come along, she'd be there now, happy as the day is long. I'll bet she'd almost forgotten the Old Glebe and our ancient feud. That only rekindled itself when she came back here — especially when she heard who'd bought it."

"I expect you're right, honey," he said. A lot of his earlier ebullience had gone.

"She needs another interest," Leah mused aloud. "A love affair, perhaps. Or even a husband. D'you think Ben Coad's father is too old for her? Yes, I guess so. Who else do we know? We don't want a middle-aged bachelor. He'd be too set in his ways for a strong-minded woman like her. We want a widower — a little senior to her in years and one who doesn't need her money ..." She ended with a sigh. "We just don't know enough people yet."

"I'd volunteer myself," he said, pretending to be quite serious, "except for two small impediments."

"Namely?"

"For one thing, she wouldn't have me and, for another, I'd rather marry just about any other woman in Cornwall before I'd even think of her."

He was trying to knot his bow tie but was no more successful than usual; at this point each evening he usually called for her to come and rescue him. She did it unbidden on this particular evening. "Besides," she said placatingly, "don't take offence, now, but you are just a teeny bit *old* for her — don't you think?"

He let out his breath explosively and stared at her in outrage. "I beg your pardon?" he almost roared. "Too old? Too old, d'you say?"

"I'm sorry, Pa! You don't think you are too old? Well, obviously not." She looked at him as if she hadn't conducted an inspection for quite some time. "No, I guess you're not at that," she added, as if the finding surprised her. "Still, as you say, it's entirely academic, since she probably feels just as negative about you. She'd sooner emigrate to northern Greenland than marry *you* — probably."

Again he bridled at her tone. "She could do a lot worse than me, let me tell you," he said. Then, recollecting himself, he added, "However — as you say — it *is* pretty academic."

Half an hour later, when Will had joined them for dinner, she said, as if mere seconds had intervened, "She *is* good company, though, Pa — didn't you think?"

"When she wants to be," he agreed — showing that the woman had not been out of his thoughts much during that time. "She can put herself out, all right. But so can the trapdoor spider, come to think of it."

"Who is this?" Will asked.

"That Philomena Liddicoat," Pansy told him.

"Thank you, Pansy," Leah snapped. "This is *our* conversation."

"Sorry, I'm sure," she replied, shaking her head huffily. "I just thought as you might be interested to know as she've asked our Violet to be her lady's maid at the Angel. That's all."

"Violet, eh?" Leah responded. "The sister you never talk to."

"'Cepting when there's things to say ... and things to tell."

"I see. Are we now going to be blackmailed by the Tregear sisters? Is that what this is all about? You want a rise in wages, eh? You're about to tell us how much Miss Liddicoat is paying your sister, I suppose?"

"No!" Pansy protested vehemently. "It never even crossed my mind. But — if you *must* know — 'tis twelve-and-six a week. Plus keep, pinafores, cap, and half her shoe leather. Will that be all, miss?" She tossed her head and even managed to turn a half-inch curtsey into a threat.

"It's more than enough, anyway," Leah replied. "But I don't suppose it is all."

"I say, Sis — go easy, eh?" Will murmured at her side.

"And you'll keep right out of this," she said, pointing a finger and sticking it an inch under his nose. "If you know what's good for you."

"That's right," said the unsinkable Pansy.

Will — and his father — stared at the two women in amazement. "I think we should eat this soup before it goes cold," John Carrington said at last.

They supped in silence a while. When neither of the men was looking, Leah winked at Pansy — who did not know what to make of it, of course, except to understand that she had not been reprimanded as severely as it had seemed.

"Whenever people try to be clever," John Carrington said, "they always give something away."

"For instance?" Leah answered.

"And the cleverer they try to be, the more they give away."

"You're referring to Miz Philomena?"

"Thinking it over, I don't believe this story about her magnificent garden in Cheam — not for one minute. She may have had a fernery — I accept that. And even some kind of small hothouse. She certainly knows her orchids and it's not all book learning. But everything she said about gardens was all Kew, Kew, Kew. *That's* all she knows about gardens in my opinion. See! They give themselves away."

"What can you do about it, though?" Leah asked. "You've never been to Kew. She can tell you anything she likes and you'd still have to accept it. She's still got the edge on you."

"Ha, ha!" He shook his head craftily. "If that's her game, I'll soon wipe the smile off her face!"

Leah shrugged and appeared to lose interest. "I don't see how — still, that's your ..."

"Because I intend going to Kew — that's how!"

"You?" Will asked.

"When?" Leah put in simultaneously. "This is very sudden, isn't it?"

"You bet! I decided it this very afternoon, when she let slip she's going to Wadebridge for a week's visit, starting tomorrow."

"That'd be to Mrs Kelynack, her cousin," Pansy told them. Airily she added, "There's another two females who never talk to each other, 'cepting when there's summat to say."

"Now listen! Nobody's to tell her I'm going," Carrington said. "And when I'm back, nobody's to tell her I've been. Is that understood? Pansy — you understand?"

"Yessir."

"It's rather drastic, isn't it, Pa?" Will asked. "Unless you're interested in going anyway, of course."

"I just don't like being one-down to that woman any department. Let her try talking about Kew when she comes back!" He chuckled.

"She *has* got under your skin!" Leah said, almost admiringly.

He shook his head and grinned, not rising to it. "Besides," he added, "it's that time of year."

"What time of year?"

"Oh — you know — when hardly anything's in blossom and there aren't too many visitors to see what you're doing, and seeds and seed pods and capsules just somehow seem to stick to your hands as you pass by ... Do we have an up-to-date *Bradshaw* in the house? Or a Great Western timetable? And what was the name of that hotel in Saint James's — the one the Troys said was so good?"

50 Earl's Hôtel was the one the Troys recommended; it stood in St James's, close to the corner of Jermyn Street. Indeed, despite the fact that the manager there had once been rather rude to him, Jimmy Troy recommended it so heartily that, before he had finished listing its superior features, he decided to come along, too. They travelled up by train on the Monday, intending to stay a week. Elizabeth at first planned to accompany her husband but then she met Sibylla Petifer after evensong, who told her that Laura Curnow had told her that Leah Carrington had been seen twice recently in the company of Ben Coad and that he had shown her over the farm at Goonhusband. Laura's daughter Blanche, who was sweet on Leah's brother, Will, had seen Coad driving Leah back into town. But Goonhusband wasn't even on the market yet — so what could it all mean? Elizabeth told Sibylla what she had seen of Leah and Ben Coad, the previous week, and they agreed that there must be a romance in the air and that that was when it had begun. So, remembering what mice do when cats depart, Elizabeth decided to stay.

The day after the men had slipped their leashes and departed, however, Jessie Trelawney brought further amusing news, which made her wish she had gone after all.

"It was the most extraordinary thing," she said. "After church on Sunday I went to tend my grandparents' grave, which is up in the top corner, by the big, straggly laurel, you know? Anyway, I've never paid much attention to the other graves around there. And even if I had, I doubt I'd have been particularly struck by the name of Jones. But I suppose you know — or maybe you don't — Clifford Liddicoat of Grankum Farm married an Olwen Jones. She was C of E, which caused a big brouhaha at the time. Even I can remember people talking about it, though I was just a child. But that's why she's buried there, with her family, rather than with the Liddicoats and the other Methodists. And who should be standing there, saying a little prayer, but ... I'm sure you've already guessed — Olwen's sister-in-law, Philomena Liddicoat!"

"On Sunday?" Elizabeth asked. "But I understood from John Carrington that she was going to her cousin in Wadebridge on Sunday."

"Ah!" Jessie's eyes promised a full budget of fun. "You're jumping the story a little. She *was* going to her cousin but an old friend telephoned her at the Angel on Saturday night ..."

"You spoke to her — obviously."

"Yes. Not at once. I said a prayer and uprooted a few weeds. The cleaver up in that corner is dreadful. I shall have words with the sexton about that. Anyway, we chatted a bit on our way back to the gate. We've known each other — distantly — for years. And she was obviously bursting with this news she'd had from this friend in Cheam."

"Where her house is? The one there was all that fuss ..."

"The very house — 'my dearest housekeeper's' house!"

"Which was requisitioned by the army."

Jessie held up a monitory finger. "Requisitioned but not yet occupied! That was the exciting news. She said it proved what she'd always said about it. One of the colonel's old regimental comrades, who had always resented her ... her ... how may one put it delicately? Her *influence* over the colonel. He'd always resented it and so used his newly granted emergency powers at the war office to commandeer the place. It was a purely dog-in-the-manger act, she says. The army actually has no need for it and their failure to take up occupation proves it. Anyway, she asked her friend if they'd posted sentries or anything like that — and it seems they have not. So she intends going up to London this week, where she will hire a gang of big, burly plug-uglies and dig up every shrub and bush and baby tree she can manage. She'll wrap their roots in hessian and wet moss, or whatever they use, and bring them back here. She says she's spent five years creating that garden and she's not going to let one man's spite ruin it. What a woman, eh!"

"Indeed! But where's she going to replant them? Surely not on Grankum Farm?"

"That was the first thing I asked her, of course, but she just waved her hand and said she'd find somewhere. The main thing was to rescue them. She'd worry about replanting them later. I suppose she'd get away with two or three weeks out of the ground at this time of year."

Her eyes were still brimming with merriment. "Come on!" Elizabeth urged. "There's more, isn't there. You're still holding something back."

"The best is yet to come," Jessie promised. "She said she had only ever *lived* in London, never just visited it, you know. And she asked me if I could recommend a good little family hôtel."

"You didn't!" Elizabeth could see what was coming now. "Oh, Jessie! Jessie! Why did you not tell me this yesterday? Wild horses wouldn't have kept me back. It's too late now. They'll have met and she'll have moved out."

"It was Whittaker's Hôtel in Jermyn Street, wasn't it — the one you always recommended?"

Elizabeth slumped. "No. Earl's in Saint James's, just round the corner. Oh!" She clenched her fists and shook them in frustration. "Now we'll be on tenterhooks all week — will they, won't they meet?"

"I'm sorry!" Jessie pretended to weep. "I thought you always stayed at Whittaker's."

"Yes, dear, it's not your fault. We do — usually."

"Ever since I've known you."

"Yes. But before that we always stayed at Earl's. We stopped because the manager was rather rude to us once. But this time Jimmy just took it into his head to give them another chance. It is quite a bit more comfortable. And much more expensive. I suppose he didn't want to seem a cheapskate in Carrington's eyes — you know the petty way they compete with each other, those two! Oh, what do I *do* now? Do I go up to London and give Fate a little push? Or do we leave it all to chance?"

After a pause Jessie, speaking carefully, said, "Actually, Elizabeth, d'you think she *would* have left the hôtel the moment she discovered she was sharing it with Mister Carrington?"

Elizabeth eyed her warily. "Why d'you ask it in that tone? What else d'you know?"

The other waved a hand expansively. "I know what everyone else knows — that the Liddicoats have had their eyes on the Old Glebe lands for the best part of a century now. And that Philomena Liddicoat is the most covetous of them all. One wonders what she would *not* do to acquire them." She licked her lips daintily and stared at a fingernail. "One way or another."

"No!" Elizabeth said excitedly. "Although …"

"What?"

"They did take luncheon together — Carrington and Miss Liddicoat — at the Angel last Saturday."

"Really? I heard that Leah had been seen dining with her. But that was on the Friday. Are you sure the story hasn't got garbled in the telling?"

Elizabeth was delighted to reverse their rôles and to impart news her friend had not yet heard. "Absolutely sure. Jimmy was there, so I got it straight from the horse's mouth. In fact, he rather pushed them into it. I don't think either was particularly keen. Also, Leah hadn't told her father about that Friday meeting — so I'd love to have been a house-martin under the eaves of the Old Glebe dining room that evening! Oh, why does everything have to happen at once? I know — why don't *you* go up to London and I'll stay here and we'll telephone each other every evening, so we'll get the best of both worlds!"

It was a pleasant fantasy but no more than that. They laughed at it and turned to other matters.

That afternoon, however, Elizabeth drove over to the Old Glebe, doing the hedge-cutter's work for him most of the way as usual. Leah heard her and came out of the dairy to greet her. As the car screeched to a halt she pulled a small branch from the bumper bar and shook her head at Elizabeth in pretend despair.

Elizabeth peered at it and said, "Sloe. Or sloan, as they call it in Cornwall. Naughty me! One shouldn't really pick the berries until after the first frost, you know."

They kissed and Leah threw the branch over the hedge. "Have you heard from Mister Troy?" she asked.

"I was about to ask the same of you and your father. Out of sight, out of mind, eh!" Elizabeth nodded toward the field at the end of the yard. "Isn't that one of Mrs Pascoe's heifers?" They started walking toward the gate.

"Yes. I bought three yesterday. Herded them over this morning. Just as well we didn't wait until this afternoon. We must have walked the same road as you've just driven!" She leaped aside with a little shriek of laughter as Elizabeth tried to pinch her arm.

"Just for that," she said, "I've a good mind not to tell you what I heard from Jessie Trelawney this morning. Did you say you bought three? Aren't you a little overstocked?"

"I'm putting two others back into Helston tomorrow."

"Where Ben Coad will get you the best price, I'm sure!"

Their eyes dwelled in each other's and Leah broke into a huge smile. "Oh, very well! You were right, Elizabeth, as usual. The Coads are a very good family and Ben is one of the best ..."

"And is the name Goon*husband* significant at all?"

Leah stopped dead and hung her head low. "One can't do a damn thing!" she said wearily.

"Is there?" Elizabeth insisted.

"Not yet." They resumed their stroll.

"But maybe?"

"I'm not saying. I'm superstitious that way." Their eyes met again and she added, "Okay — maybe. What is it you've decided not to tell me?"

They had reached the gate. She stared proudly at her three new heifers and waited for Elizabeth to compliment her on her choice. "I'm not mixing them with the rest of the herd yet. There's already been too much fighting and I want them to settle down."

"Good idea," Elizabeth said abstractedly. "Good choice, too. Tell me — I take it you knew your father and Philomena Liddicoat had luncheon together at the Angel last Saturday?"

Leah nodded. "*And* spent the rest of the afternoon walking over *my* fields, talking gardening, gardening, gardening. *And* he drove her back into town and stayed for tea."

"D'you think there's something going on between them?" She saw Leah's smile and added, "You do! Is it some plot you and she cooked up between you ..." Her voice trailed off as Leah shook her head.

"I did start out with a plan — I don't mind admitting it. At least, I don't mind admitting it to *you*, though I'd be grateful if it didn't go further."

"Of course not."

"Anyway, it's been swept away by events. The reason Ben showed me Goonhusband was that I'd asked him — last Thursday, in fact, when I came out to see you. I asked him if there was another suitable bit of land where my father could make this garden-dream of his come true."

"Well, he's right. Goonhusband is perfect. Much better than this place."

"Except that the moment I saw it, I wanted it for myself."

"Or yourself and ...?"

"Stop it, Elizabeth!" Leah laughed.

"Will your father buy it for you?"

Leah grinned. "He won't need to. You're not the only heiress in these parts, you know! I'll come into my inheritance next August, so I could easily borrow against it anytime between now and then."

"But you're not supposed to know about that — or so Jimmy told me."

"Sure. But my grandmother told me all about it, of course — when I was sixteen. She just told me not to tell Pa I knew and to act real surprised whenever he deigned to tell me, finally. Anyway — to get back to last Friday — I didn't know *what* to think when I went back into Helston." She described their meeting with Philomena on her way to the Union, which explained why she had to seek the woman out and apologize to her. "But the apology was all I intended. The notion of having lunch with her never crossed my mind. I *had* wanted to tell her about my plan — my original plan — which was to talk Pa into selling her the Old Glebe and moving to Goonhusband instead. He'd make a good profit, too, which is always a compelling reason to get him to do anything."

"Don't tell me," Elizabeth said. "I married one of them, too. So what *did* you tell her instead?"

"Well, I didn't have time to think up any other rigmarole so I stuck to my story — about persuading Pa to buy Goonhusband. I mean, we can find him *another* place over on that side of Helston. Near Goonhusband. He'll want to be near me, anyway, if ... well, never mind about that."

"If you marry and have grandchildren for him to spoil! You might as well say it, Leah!"

The girl took her arm, as if for support, and leaned her head briefly on Elizabeth's shoulder. "Oh, it's so beautiful when you say it!" she murmured. "God! How I *long* for it to be!"

Elizabeth gave her hand a squeeze and said, "Anyway ...?"

"Yes." Leah straightened herself and sighed. "Anyway, when we got talking about Pa's ambitions to create this grand garden, she seemed to take a different ... I mean, her whole attitude changed. She'd been a bit prickly before that but then she *seemed* to be genuinely interested."

"Only seemed?"

"How can you tell? Pa thinks her gardening interest is limited to orchids and houseplants. The rest is fake — to ingratiate herself with him. He thinks she's going to lull his suspicions, get his guard down low, and then ... bam!"

"Bam? What's that?"

"Exactly," Leah said scornfully. "He won't be specific — because he *can't,* of course. We keep coming back to that unanswerable question: What harm can she actually *do?* Apart from being a pest and making our lives uncomfortable from time to time. She can't *do* anything. *Bam* is just meaningless. But that's his theory, anyway. I hope Jimmy will talk some sense into him this week."

"I doubt it," Elizabeth said heavily. "He thinks the whole thing is one great sport. He agrees with you — the woman can't *do* anything, so why not milk the situation for all the fun it holds? Tell me — why does your father think her interest in gardening is all put on?"

"Because she *talks* about this magnificent garden she created in Cheam, but whenever he asks for details, she just gets close to tears and says it's all too painful to think about. The one garden she talks about forever and a day, however, is Kew. So that's why he's gone up there this week, while she's in Wadebridge. Next time she mentions Kew, he'll be able to trump her! What does that enigmatic little smile mean?"

Elizabeth told her at last.

Leah heard the tale out with mounting frustration. When she learned that Philomena was staying not a hundred yards from the two men, it was the last straw. She thumped the top bar of the gate hard enough to hurt herself slightly. While she jumped up and down, nursing it under her arm, she said, "And I *have* to take those two cows into Helston tomorrow." She turned her big, dark eyes on Elizabeth. "I don't suppose you would take them in for me? Please? Hamden would make sure he took the whole day over it. And if we don't get the cabbage hoed ..."

"Say no more," Elizabeth assured her. "Of course I will. Gladly. But just answer me this — what will you do when you get to London?"

Leah thought awhile and had to admit that she didn't know. "I just want to be *there,*" she said.

"In case they go and do something foolish?"

"I suppose so."

"And you'll be able to wave a magic wand and stop them?"

Leah looked around her, for help or inspiration from any quarter. Finding none, she said, "At least I might be able to do *something.* As long as I'm stuck away down here there's absolutely nothing I can do."

"There is, you know," Elizabeth assured her calmly.

"What?"

"You can do what every son and daughter has to do sooner or later — admit that you've done the best job you can in bringing your parents up and concede that they must make their own way in life sooner or later."

51 London was exciting but Kew Gardens was, frankly, a disappointment. It was not so much a garden as a vast park with specimens of this or that liberally sprinkled about the place. It was also inhibitingly open from the point of view of any clandestine seed harvester. Time and again John Carrington would find himself standing at the edge of some bosky dell (the most interesting specimens were always planted at the edge, somehow), and the most desirable seeds would be a mere up-on-tiptoe arm's-length away, and there would be no uniformed keeper in sight ... and still he could not banish from his conscience the thought that someone was following his every move through a powerful telescope. Moreover, that unseen watcher could immediately semaphore his description to an attendant hidden in the bushes nearby. It stood to reason that, at this time of year, they were all lying in wait for people like him.

Two damp, drizzly days passed in that sort of misery. If it had not been for the theatres, the Café Royal, and the night clubs — and Jimmy Troy's determination to make him, John Carrington, seem five years the senior when he was, in fact, five years the junior — he would have returned home on Thursday. As it was, he had no further wish to explore Kew. Instead, he intended visiting the public library and going through the back numbers of the newspapers to read up on the scandal surrounding Philomena Liddicoat and the 'dearest housekeeper' bequest. He might also get the address of the place and go out there on Friday, just to see what sort of 'wonderful garden' she'd actually made there.

He awoke that morning with the sort of head that instantly made him ask what he had done the previous night; it also left him disinclined to seek the answer too assiduously. He paused at Jimmy's door on his way back from the bathroom at the end of the corridor. Loud snores were all he heard. He considered going in and waking him up with some hearty greeting but then he had a better idea. It would be much more telling to go out for a brisk walk around St James's Park and return in the pink of health, rubbing his hands, eating a hearty breakfast, and telling Jimmy what he'd missed in his senile sloth.

The hall porter told him that Green Park was nearer, if he just wanted a quick, brisk walk. Also, if he didn't want to go out and come back by the same path, he could go down to the bottom of St James's and wander through the alleys behind the palace to a little gate between Bridgewater House and the London Museum. He could then stroll through the park to Piccadilly and so come back directly to the hôtel.

He thanked the man for this information, but he was somewhat less grateful when, on arriving at the gate by the museum, he found it padlocked. What jumped-up pipsqueak of a pen-pushing civil servant had decided to do that? he fumed to himself. Then he, the man who had flinched from plucking a pod of seed from a tree at Kew, drew out his pocket-knife and selected the long, thin prong designed for piercing the butt-end of a cigar. After a little fiddling, he sprang the lock, lifted it from its hole, drew back the bolt, slipped through the gateway, and then reassembled it all, leaving the padlock looking as if no one had touched it.

As he stepped back to admire his handiwork, an oddly familiar voice behind him said, "And what, pray, are *you* doing here, Mister Carrington?"

He had been vaguely aware of a female walking down the path through the thin mist that hung over the wet grass but it took a second or two before he identified the voice.

"Miss Liddicoat!" He spun round in amazement. "Well! I think I could ask the same of you. Have you followed me to London? If so, I may tell you at once ..."

"*I* followed *you!*" Her nostrils flared with anger. "How dare you even suggest ...!"

"I cannot imagine what *else* you are doing here. You *told* me — or at least you told Leah — that you'd be in Wadebridge all this week. Are you surprised that I am ..."

"If I change *my* mind, it is none of *your* business. As a matter of fact, I came up to carry out certain work at my house in Cheam before the army actually moves in and wrecks it. I had no idea you were in London. You said nothing about it. Your daughter said nothing about it. You must have made a very *sudden* decision to come."

"It was no more sudden than yours, ma'am. Can you wonder at my suspicions?"

His effrontery made her gasp. "And can you wonder at mine? I have given you my reasons for being here. You have given me none." She raised both hands briefly. "Judge O ye gods!"

"I came up to visit Kew Gardens," he said quietly.

It took her aback.

"Kew," he repeated.

"Yes, I know — I heard you. Why did you do that?"

He glanced at the skies. The sun was beginning to paint the clouds pink. "D'you really need to ask?" he replied.

For the first time she smiled; that was something of a sunrise, too. "Good hunting?" she asked.

He shook his head. "Miserable. I even contemplated returning to Cornwall today."

After a pause she said, "Were you out here to take a morning constitutional, may I ask?"

"Yes. We're staying at Earl's in Saint James's. Earl's Hôtel."

"We? Is Leah with you, then?"

"No. Jimmy Troy. He's the one who recommended Earl's."

"Oh, I'm at Whittaker's, just round the corner. I was going to stay the week but we made excellent progress these last two days. One more day and we'll be done."

"Are you taking a constitutional, too, Miss Liddicoat?"

"I am. I was going to do a circuit, down to The Mall, but I'll go back with you along Picadilly, if you like. I want to hear why you found Kew so disappointing."

He told her as they set off up the hill.

She said it surprised her that a man who could pick a padlock like that would balk at picking seeds that were going to fall the the ground anyway — and be chewed up by some lawnmower.

"It's just the fact that the gate is *there*," he explained. "It's there and yet some petty clerk has decided we, the public, aren't to be allowed to use it. Seeds are different. Those people have a right to protect their trees and shrubs from marauders like me."

"Isn't that odd?" she said. "I have absolutely no qualms about raiding the plants at Kew but I would never pick a padlock the way you just did."

They walked in thoughtful silence a while and then she said, "I still cannot accept that this meeting is entirely a coincidence. I believe you when you say you had no idea I was here. I hope you believe me, too?"

"I do, ma'am — though I hope you'll understand why, at first, I leaped to ..."

"Yes, yes — same here. But tell me — if your purpose was to visit Kew, why did you not choose some hôtel out Richmond way? Why here in central London? Mister Troy *steered you* toward this hôtel, you say?"

"Yes," he agreed warily. "Why? Did he also suggest it to you? Or the hôtel next door?"

"No. It was ..."

"Because — pardon me for pointing this out — it's not exactly adjacent to Cheam, either."

"Oh?" She was suddenly interested. "You actually know where Cheam is, do you? Not many Americans would." She smiled sweetly.

"I looked it up," he admitted, unabashed. "To tell the truth, I had thought of going out there today and having a look at this garden of yours — having heard so much about it!"

She laughed. "Allow me to conduct you there — and Mister Troy, too, if he's interested."

"I'll make quite sure he is not! You think that steering us toward adjacent hôtels was a prank on somebody's part? In particular, Jimmy Troy?"

She shook her head. "I was recommended to Whittaker's by Mrs Trelawney — the electricity woman, you know."

"She's a friend of the Troys."

"Yes, but they didn't know I'd changed my plans. They couldn't have put her up to suggesting Whittaker's to me because they didn't know I was going to London at all. So it's still a mystery."

"How did she come to advise you at all, then?"

Philomena explained the circumstances.

"By morning service on Sunday," he pointed out, "she could quite easily have known that Jimmy Troy and I were coming to London. The prank could have been hers — on the spur of the moment — when you asked her."

"Then why didn't she direct me to Earl's? If you had not taken your walk this morning — which was the merest fluke — we'd never have met here at all."

"Yes," John Carrington had to concede with reluctance. "That bit doesn't fit."

There was a further silence before Philomena said, "What did she expect to happen, I wonder? Or they? Because if it was a prank, I'm sure she went directly to Pallas and told Elizabeth Troy all about it. Has she telephoned him?"

"Yes. The first morning." He had to admit it — she was not only a quick thinker but a thorough one, too. She covered all the possibilities and she went after them like a terrier. It was useful to know these things about one's opponent. He was grateful to the prankster, if prank it was.

"And has he mentioned Whittaker's at all ... suggested you pop round for a drink there or anything?"

"No. Maybe he's saving it. Come to think of it, he did mention Whittaker's on the night we arrived. We were just strolling round the West End and he pointed it out. He said he and Elizabeth used to stay there, for many years. Before that they always stayed at Earl's, but the manager was offensive to them once so they switched. There's a new manager now and he's giving the place another chance."

"You see — the little pieces are falling into place," she said, rubbing her hands gleefully. "Jessie Trelawney's too young to have known the Troys when they first used Earl's. She only knew about Whittaker's. The whole thing is *her* idea, then. She assumed you'd both be staying there and thought it would be the greatest joke to send me there, too — all unawares. Well, well, well, Jessie! We must think up some nice little surprise for *you* before too long."

"I have to raise my hat to you, ma'am," he said. "The way you ran that down — I declare, a Dalmatian bloodhound couldn't have done better."

But she had not quite done. "It also means that she didn't tell Elizabeth Troy at once. You're sure she hasn't telephoned him since that first morning?"

"I can check with the porter when we ... when I return."

He glanced at her for more questions but she was now deep in thought. The rumble of iron tyres and the muted roar of engines told them that Piccadilly would soon loom out of the mist. "The porter said the gate's in the corner there," he said, changing direction slightly. "What are you thinking now?"

"I was thinking that I do, after all, feel the same impulse that led you to pick that lock — the impulse to do the opposite of what someone else has decided *for* me. Jessie Trelawney has decided to force us under the same roof, to make us both feel uncomfortable ..."

Gallantry alone compelled him to interrupt. "Well now, see here — I don't allow as I'd have been so very uncomfortable about that. How about you, ma'am?"

"Well, that was quite a little shouting match we had back there at that gate — I wouldn't have enjoyed holding it in one of the public rooms at Whittaker's! And I wouldn't have enjoyed bottling it up, either! However — it's very kind of you, Mister Carrington, to say you wouldn't have felt uncomfortable to find yourself in the same hôtel as me — because I'm thinking of moving to Earl's this very day."

"Ah ..." Carrington said uncertainly.

"And I shall pay particular attention to Mister Troy's expression when he sees me there. I put you on your word of honour to say nothing to him in the meantime. Now — you'd better call for me at Whittaker's, so that he doesn't see me before I wish him to. Ten o'clock?"

52   They went by the Epsom & Leatherhead branch line as far as Ewell, where they took a cab the remaining mile to that part of Cheam where Philomena's house lay, waiting its military occupiers. The gang of hired stevedores, bummarees, and porters had been at work since sun-up, so that, by the time the cab halted at the foot of the drive, they had one dray almost loaded with bandaged and insulated shrubs, and a few small trees, as well, bare-rooted but moistened with sphagnum and thickly padded where they were most likely to abrade their tender bark.

She had said nothing of all this to John Carrington on their way to Cheam, so, for a long moment, he could only stand and stare while she prodded and pulled and directed that this be loosened or that be made a little tighter. "Cotoneasters," she said to him, pointing at one group. "That's *franchetii* and that's *hupehensis* — very graceful. And *Escallonia bifida* — that should grow against a wall somewhere. It won a medal this year. And that's *rosea* — quite common but hard to kill. It goes well with pittosporum ... there should be a dwarf red one here somewhere ..."

"Pardon me, ma'am." He found his voice at last. "What is going on here?"

"Isn't it obvious, man? I'm making sure the army doesn't ruin my garden."

"You're saving them the trouble?"

"Oh, no! They could wish they had as few casualties as we'll have with these plants!"

"But where are you taking them? Not that it's any of my business, mind."

She laughed. "Oh, but it *is* your business, Mister Carrington. They are going — immediately — to Paddington Station and thence in an enclosed wagon by passenger train to Gwinear Road and Helston."

"And then?" He broke into a grin. "Are you intending to start a rival garden across the valley?"

"Not a bit! They're all for you. I had intended it as a surprise, but dear Jessie Trelawney put paid to that. I still haven't thought of an appropriate way of thanking her. But now, perhaps, you understand why I was so angry this morning?"

He took a step back from her. "But I ... I mean, I could not possibly accept such a ..."

"Nonsense, man! Of course you can. You're a gardener, aren't you? Some gardeners I know would sell their immortal souls for a collection like this."

She turned to the men on the dray, which was just about to depart. "Remember, now — keep them as upright as possible. Plants use up a lot of energy trying to get themselves properly aligned with gravity, and these fellows don't have too much to spare." Speaking to Carrington again she added, "At least take a look at the whole thing before you turn it down." Then, without waiting for him, she turned on her heel and walked up the drive.

Shrubs and trees in various stages of readiness were lined up on each side. More were being brought from distant parts of the garden every minute. A lot of the deciduous ones had already lost their leaves, or they wore their autumnal russet and gold and were not easily identifiable. Even so, a gardener of next to no experience could have told that the variety was amazing.

Miss Philomena spouted *officinalis*-this and *variegatum*-that and *lanceolata*-the-other as they walked but it was, of course, too much for him to take in all at once.

"Well?" she asked when they had reached the top of the drive and he could see the devastation her workers had left behind them. The house was pretty splendid but he gave it not a second glance. She went on: "I believe our military friends will feel quite at home here, don't you? Certainly if the recent pictures from Picardy are anything to go by! What d'you think?"

"I think I want to kill you, of course," he replied.

She laughed. "Why?"

"Because how can I possibly turn your gift down, woman? And yet how can I possibly accept it, either?"

"Listen," she said quite seriously. "*You* will be doing *me* a favour in accepting it. My beloved plants will live and the army won't get them. Also ..." She hesitated.

"Also what?"

"Well ... John — may I call you that? We may not have known each other for long but we're old enough enemies for it, surely? In accepting this gift you'll also have to accept that I have well and truly buried the hatchet between us — and not in your skull, either. Dear man! I don't think you do believe that even now, do you?"

"If I refuse them ...?" he asked.

"I'll just abandon them in the lane outside the Old Glebe — alongside that field where you and Pansy were working. Try watching them die, then!"

He shook his head. "You couldn't do that."

"And you couldn't risk my doing it. They're going to Helston, anyway, whether you like it or not."

He turned about and looked at the plants. He sighed. Every worried atom in his body shouted that it was a big mistake but he knew he was going to accept the gift. "How will I ever thank you?" he asked morosely.

She touched his arm briefly. "Merely in accepting them you thank me enough. In giving them a second life you do more than thank me."

They filled five drays in all. It could have been cut to three if Philomena had been willing to stack the plants on top of each other. The last of them set off for Paddington just after midday.

John and Philomena went by hackney to New Malden, where they had a pie and a glass of ale at an inn before going on by train through Kingston to Kew.

On the way Philomena pointed out Hampton Court, Strawberry Hill, Sion Park, and the Old Deer Park, just south of Kew Gardens itself. "So many beautiful gardens," she said. "You could almost walk all day through one after the other."

"*You* couldn't, I'm sure," he said.

She stared at him pugnaciously. "Is that a challenge?"

"I mean your pockets would be bulging before you reached the exit of the first of them."

"Oh, that!" She laughed. "I don't only acquire seeds and little slips of twigs, you know. I also steal *ideas.*" She spoke as if that were not simply virtuous but so *very* virtuous that it made up for all her material thefts. "There's a little group of shrubs near the end of the tulip tree avenue which I duplicated perfectly at Cheam. You should see it, because you could do the same."

It was the first thing she took him to see, past the Temple of Aeolus, past the museum, the pond, the great Palm House ... right out into the centre of the gardens. On the way he was amazed to see how little bits of this and that just seemed to spirit themselves into her hands — and then, with lightning rapidity, into one or other of her voluminous pockets.

"Now *this* you *must* have," she said at one point, waving a conjuror's hand in great arcs toward a firewheel tree, distracting his eye from what the other hand was doing. *"Stenocarpus sinuatus.* It can flower at any time. And look! See? Two flowers up there actually growing out of the trunk!"

They were brilliant red and yellow tubes, three inches long, and radiating like the spokes of a wheel. "I *want* it," he murmured, captivated by its beauty.

"We have it," she said.

"On its way to Paddington?"

She patted one of her pockets. "Not just yet."

And so they passed the afternoon in happy piracy, taking nothing that Nature, in her profligate fashion, would not have wasted anyway.

"Well, that was fun, wasn't it?" she said as they passed safely beyond the last attendant who might have challenged them. Several had looked as if they intended doing so but, for some reason, they had changed their minds at the last moment. On one of those occasions John, himself burning with preparatory embarrassment, had glanced at her and understood why. There was something so solidly menacing, so implacable about her very walk. It helped him remember that, although today had, of course, been fun — indeed, he couldn't remember a more enjoyable day, certainly not in the past half-dozen years — she was still the most menacing element in his life. She was playing some highly devious game here and he had little choice but to play along until her purpose became clear. He must constantly bear in mind that she was the spider who whispers, 'Come into my parlour!'

"Yes," he replied. "Great fun. But I hope we have enough in the way of seeds and cuttings by now?"

"For this year, anyway," she assured him.

And it was 'great fun' to play along with her plotting and scheming. It produced a curious kind of intimacy between them. She was — not to mince words — throwing herself at him. In normal circumstances he would have run a mile rather than get involved — even with a woman as physically attractive and as mentally companionable as Philomena. But he knew that was not her real purpose. One day this mask of sweetness would be cast aside and the claws would be unsheathed. He knew all that very well and never ceased reminding himself of it, most particularly when he found himself wanting to touch her, take her in his arms, kiss her … and more. It had been a long time, after all. And so, with those reminders constantly whispering away at the back of his mind, he had a licence to be as forward with her as she was with him, to match each of her advances with one of his own. Strangers, observing them, would have guessed that they were childhood sweethearts who had lately met each other after a long separation and were just beginning to rediscover all that had once held them together so dearly.

"They have a very good hothouse over at Trewennack," she said. "It's the wrong side of Helston from us, but in every other way it would be ideal. I wonder if we might beg a dozen square yards for our seeds — and share their heating bill, of course?"

"When you say it's the wrong side …?"

"I mean it's over Goonhilly way, beyond Culdrose Farm. Incidentally, Ben Coad was showing your daughter over

Goonhusband last week. Do you know why? It isn't even on the market yet."

They boarded the bus for Piccadilly and took seats outside at the top.

"I knew nothing of this," he said slowly.

She laughed and dug him with her elbow. "Then she *didn't* discuss her plan with you — the plan I asked you about at the Angel last Saturday. I thought not."

As the bus set off he held out his hands, wrists together, as if for cuffing. "You done caught me fair and square, ma'am," he replied. "Guilty's all I can plead. So tell me."

"I think I'd better, John. Your daughter has some idea of wheedling and scheming you into accepting the notion. But she's young and idealistic still. She doesn't realize that when people reach *our* age, we've had enough of duplicity ... saying one thing and meaning another. We can take it on the chin. D'you know Goonhusband at all?"

He shook his head. "Is it an estate or what?"

"No, just a farm. It *ought* to have been an estate. The Penroses were mad to build where they did, facing north over the Loe Pool. Goonhusband is more-or-less opposite, on the farther shore and facing south."

"It must be near Giles Curnow's place — Chynoweth."

"About a mile farther south — no, less than a mile."

"I know it, then. I know the country. When we were looking for a property we all said it was a pity none was going on the shores of that lake."

"Ha — the irony of it, eh! Still, Goonhusband's going now — or it soon will be. And Leah's idea is to persuade you to sell the Old Glebe to me — since you can't do much more than build a plant nursery until the war's ended — and move over to Goonhusband. Shake the dust of the Liddicoats off your coattails for ever! That was how she outlined it to me."

"Well!" he said and, clasping his hands in an attitude of prayer, sank deep in thought. At length he asked, "Is that a roundabout way of making me an offer?"

"Not any longer," she replied. "Why d'you think I came out to the Old Glebe with you last Saturday? Do you imagine I relished the prospect of hearing *you* tell *me*, of all people, what you were going to do with the place?" She laughed.

He stirred uncomfortably. "I guess, at that ..." he mumbled.

"I intended making you an offer sometime that afternoon, of course. But then, as you unfolded your plans, as I listened to you describing the lily pond, the pergola walk, the bromeliad grove, the azalea banks ... I realized I couldn't."

"Why not? You could do all those things yourself. Much better, I'm sure."

"But I wanted *you* to do them. Did you never covet something as a child — covet it for years and years — and then, when at last you got it, you found it wasn't at all what you wanted? When I was a girl I absolutely doted on a certain man in Helston. He's dead these twenty years and more so there's no harm in telling you his name. Barry Moore. He had a one-man haulage business down in Saint John's but he drank himself to death. But when I was fourteen and he was in his prime ... oh! I trembled if I just saw him a hundred yards away. I hankered after him for years even though he had children only a few years younger than me. And then, just before my twentieth birthday, he carried some kibbled wheat out to us from Trevose's mill and he made an indelicate proposal to me. I'm sure he knew of my feelings. And, d'you know, they suddenly evaporated! Just like that."

"Waal," he drawled laconically, "thar's a warnin'!"

She looked at him sharply, as if she had never expected him to make a joke of that nature. Then she smiled, rather enigmatically, and went on, "Perhaps it's different with you? You're probably the sort who doesn't blow hot and cold once you've made up your mind to a certain course ..."

"What will you offer for the Old Glebe?" he asked.

"I told you — nothing. I *want* you to carry out your plans there — why else d'you think I've given you all my shrubs and trees, man?"

He could think of plenty of reasons but he didn't say so.

"Besides ..." she ventured when he made no reply.

"What?"

"Call me sentimental — tell me I'm that sort of twittering old maid who sees romance behind every bush — but I found myself wondering, even while Leah was telling me of her plans for getting you to move to Goonhusband, if that was what she really wanted."

"Ah!" He tugged at his lower lip.

"You follow my drift?" she asked.

"I've been aware that she has taken to dairy farming as if it's been in her blood from birth. She has a feeling for cattle that just can't be taught. So I've also been aware that, when the war's over, she's going to need a spread of her own. I just didn't think she'd be on the lookout that quickly."

Philomena smiled even more broadly. "And you can't think of anything *else* that might just possibly have tilted her thoughts in that direction?"

He frowned and waited for her to explain.

"I knew it as soon as I saw her and Ben Coad in the trap on their way out to Goonhusband — last Friday. Of course, I didn't know it was Leah Carrington then, but I said to myself at once — 'This girl's in love with this man.' She had the look in her eye that I must have had when poor old Barry Moore was around."

"My God!"

It amused her to see how pale he had become. She did not doubt that he was a shrewd man of business, that few competitors had ever been able to pull the wool over his eyes. So his blindness in matters like this, especially when it touched his nearest and dearest, was all the more remarkable. She wondered if he had the faintest inkling of what was going on between his son and Pansy Tregear — which a rather breathless Violet had told her all about.

"Leah and Ben, eh?" he mused.

"Do you approve?" she asked.

"I guess I do — though it shows how wrong a man can be when he sets himself to guess a woman's heart. She and your Nicholas were like two cats in a sack. I always thought they'd end up getting spliced."

She made no reply to that.

"You'd have put a stop to it, though," he said, to prompt her.

"Nicholas has lost his chance now," she replied. "It'll be a good lesson to him, not to be so arrogant. Not to take a woman's feelings for granted. Ben must learn the same, too — or Nicholas could become a threat to him once again."

A sudden pang seized John Carrington. Everything the woman said seemed so utterly right the moment she said it. He had never set himself up as any kind of expert on the vagaries of human emotions, especially on the distaff side, but he had never felt his ignorance as keenly as now. Leah should have someone like Philomena to tell her these things. "Would you ..." He hesitated. "I mean, could you ... find some way to tell her that? She'd laugh if I tried, but she'd listen to another woman — especially, I think, to you."

"Why me?" she asked in delighted surprise.

"You make it sound so ... I don't know. Like a *fact*. Like a law of nature. I mean, you don't make it sound like your own opinion which you're trying to foist on her."

"Well," she said sadly, "that's very flattering — and I'm honoured you should ask. But it's hardly my place. I think she might resent it."

He sighed. She was right, of course. It was hardly her place.

When they arrived back at Earl's she came in with him to see if her bags had been moved across from Whittaker's yet. To his consternation, the desk clerk told him that Mr Troy had booked them both out. He handed John a letter that would explain all.

Jimmy Troy did not know it, of course, but it explained more than all. It revealed that Elizabeth must at last have got word to him that Philomena was staying at Whittaker's, and what a jolly jape it would be if he, Jimmy, moved the pair of them there.

He handed the letter to Philomena and, while she read it, he said to the clerk, "Well, Mister Troy may book himself into Whittaker's if he wishes. But I'm booking myself back into Earl's, right here and now."

Philomena, having read the letter, burst out laughing.

John reached for the registration book but the clerk stopped him taking up the pen. "I'm sorry, sir, but we are now full."

John's eyes narrowed. "How much did Troy pay you to tell me that? What's happened to the room I was in last night?"

"It went almost the minute Mister Troy booked you out, sir. Just after breakfast. He had a phone call from his wife and then he booked you both out. And almost immediately we received a note from a lady, who, funnily enough, was staying at Whittaker's until today."

He said more but it was drowned in their laughter.

John was selecting a banknote of a denomination which, he felt sure, would shake one more room out of the tree at Earl's when Philomena put a hand out to stop him. "Leave it this way, John. Don't you see — it's perfect! They won't *dare* say a word!"

53 One week later to the day John and Philomena ceremonially replanted the last of the uprooted trees from Cheam, a Prince Albert's Yew, in the long field at the Old Glebe. Even though John had seen the care with which Philomena prepared them for their long journey, he found it hard to believe they had survived so well. To be sure, there was still a long and possibly hard winter ahead, so they would not know the final toll until the spring, but even the most damaged of them, the ones whose roots had been impossible to separate from among the roots of established trees, still felt supple and alive. Even the clerk of the weather seemed to conspire with them, withholding the sun by day and sending a good soaking of rain almost every night.

"All that remains to do now," Philomena said as she ran a satisfied eye over the ranks of her rescued plants, "is to keep down the weeds. They hate competition early in life, you know."

"Don't we all!" John said, slipping his arm through hers. "Let's go in and talk with those two youngsters — and remember: I'm going to sell this place to you and buy Goonhusband. Watch their faces!"

Two hundred yards away, standing a little way back from the window of Will's room, Leah said to Ben, "There! See! D'you believe me now?"

"I suppose I have to," he replied. "Seeing's believing. D'you think she's playing tricks?"

Leah shrugged. "I honestly don't know. Pa thinks she is — and something more serious than tricks, maybe. At least, that's what he said when he came back. These last few days he's been more ambiguous."

"How did he come to tell you? I mean, how did the conversation come about?"

"After the first day — watching them together — I said I thought he was getting dangerously pally with her. And he just chuckled and said she'd soon find out just how pally he really was — the moment she tried anything on with him. But he forgets his own advice."

"Which is …?"

"About doing business with a female."

"Oh, yes."

"And if she's still out to get the Old Glebe, house and land, by hook or by crook, then it *is* still business. Not ... what it looks like out there."

"It *looks* like the real thing," he said.

"Oh, yes?" She laughed. "How would *you* know?"

"Oh?" He bridled. "You think only a woman can tell the real from the fake?"

"*She* could." Leah nodded toward the field, where her father and Philomena were now gathering up their shovels and twine and strips of dirty hessian. "She knew about us. The moment she saw us going out to Goonhusband that day."

"Well?" he asked. "What of it? *I* knew about us then, too."

She butted him with her head. There was a brief tussle, which ended in a passionate kiss. Or two. Or three. Or ... until the sneck on the back door clicked.

"This will not do," she said, pulling away from him and straightening her dress, her hair, her collar, her hair, her dress, her hair ...

"D'you think he'll ask me about buying Goonhusband?" Ben said as they made their way down to the drawing room.

"I can't think why else he'd have sent for you."

"He might want to ask if my intentions are honourable."

"I hope he knows better than that," she replied menacingly.

"When you told him about Goonhusband ... I mean, did he say about getting in touch with me?"

"We didn't talk about it in much detail. He tried to seem surprised, which he obviously wasn't. It's funny. He's good at pretending in commercial situations but he's utterly hopeless in anything personal. I'm sure Philomena told him. The thing is — will he now try to play little jokes on us? Will he pretend that he thinks my original idea is still going strong? I mean, the idea that we should sell the whole of the Old Glebe to Philomena and all of us move to Goonhusband."

He chuckled. "Two can play at that. We'll just pretend to go along with it."

Philomena and John came through from the scullery; she still had a towel in her hands. "We made this rather dirty, I'm afraid," she said. "Where d'you want it?"

"Oh, just throw it at the bottom of the stairs," Leah told her — which, rather reluctantly, she did. When she returned, the line of her jaw said that in her house such things would be done very differently.

"Well, Ben," John said when they were all seated, "Leah has told me of your great kindness to us."

"Sir?" he replied warily.

"Letting us know about Goonhusband before the rest of the pack. We certainly appreciate it. It probably won't affect the price but it gives us longer to think about it." He chuckled. "I guess there won't be objections if I pull down that monstrosity of a barn at Goonhusband to make way for my hothouse!"

"No, sir!" Ben replied eagerly. "I know three of your new neighbours who will be only too delighted."

"Pa!" Leah cried excitedly. "D'you mean you've decided to sell to Miss Liddicoat and buy Goonhusband? How marvellous — and wasn't I clever to have thought of it!"

He glanced uncertainly at Philomena, who just laughed and said, "It's not going to work, John." To Leah she said, "Your father's going to stay on here, my dear."

"Stay *on?*" Leah echoed. This was not part of any little joke; it sounded ominous. Servants stay *on;* masters simply stay.

Philomena shrugged. "Hark at me! This is none of my business. I should just learn to hold my tongue. *You* tell them, John."

"I'm buying Goonhusband for you," he said to Leah. "That is, I'm using some of the money in your gran'maw's trust to buy it. The residue will be yours next August, anyway."

"What?" she asked, almost shouting the word. Her eyes were like saucers. You'd swear it was news to her.

She is good! thought Philomena, watching her closely.

"So there's little point in holding it back now." He turned to Ben. "Will you be farming it, young man, until after the wedding? I assume the idea is for Leah to take over once she's Mrs Coad?"

Ben scratched his head diffidently. "Well, that's something I hoped to talk to *you* about, sir."

His stress on the word caused Philomena to spring to her feet, muttering something about having things to do.

"No, stay," Leah urged. "Ben's only going to say that we want to get married in a month or two's time — as soon as the banns are called. Or as soon as we know the purchase will go through."

She looked from one to the other, slightly surprised. "Isn't anybody going to say anything?"

Her father just stared at his boots.

She tried again: "Like — 'Isn't that rather hasty, dear?' Or, 'Marry in haste, repent at leisure?' No? Nothing like that?"

Philomena rose again. "I will go, dears, if you don't mind. I do have rather a lot of things to see to." To John she added, "Don't worry, I'll be back tomorrow to look over my treasures."

He saw her to the door and returned, wiping his lips.

"I must say, I expected an explosion," Leah told him. "If any daughter of mine ever comes to me and announces her nuptials like that, she'll get a piece of my tongue."

Her father shook his head and said, "It's awkward."

Ben now rose to his feet again. "Perhaps it's my turn to go," he said diffidently.

"Stay!" Leah commanded. "This concerns you, too."

"I don't think it does," he told her. "Does it, sir?"

"You see, honey, I'm kind of in the same boat as you."

"Meaning?" she asked. Then, to Ben: "Do sit down, darling."

Ben obeyed, saying, "I think your dad's telling us he's asked Miss Philomena to marry him."

Leah laughed until she saw her father's face. Then she said, "No!"

He nodded miserably.

"But you hardly know her."

"Oh! Who's talking? Isn't that rather hasty, dear? Marry in haste, repent at leisure?"

"Well, at least I've known Ben for the best part of a year. Not two or three weeks."

"Some people you can know at once. I don't know how. It's just like that. And knowing them for *twenty* years more may add things but it won't change them."

"But you *don't* know her, Pa. She *seems* all sweetness and reason, but you don't know."

"I do now — if you'll hear me out."

"It's not a wedding ring she's after. It's the Old Glebe. Marriage is just a step for her. It gets her the title to this place without having to risk a penny."

He nodded. "That's what I thought, honey. So I set about testing her. I didn't exactly propose, I sort of ..."

"Why did you broach the subject at all?" she asked, still appalled, still taking it in.

"Because," he replied unhappily. "Because I felt myself ..." He glanced at Ben, then at the ceiling. "I was falling in love with her if you must know — and yet I needed to test her. To test someone you love! I felt awful."

"You weren't falling in love with *her*. I'll say it again — you don't know *her*. You were falling in love with the Philomena she wanted you to see. The Philomena she *wanted* you to fall in love with! Didn't I say as much when you came back from London, all full of it? Didn't I say at the time that *that* was the danger? And didn't you agree?"

"That's *why* I broached the subject — to answer your question, if you'll permit me? You seem much more interested in making your own points than in listening to mine."

She raised her hands. "Sorry. I won't say another word."

He gave a hollow laugh and said to Ben, "Just see how she keeps *that* promise!" To her he went on, "I didn't propose to her. I just raised the general idea of marrying. I asked her what she thought of it. And what d'you think she replied?"

"I'm sure she said what any sensible woman would have said, Pa — to a vague sort of question like that. She told you that she wasn't *implacably* against it — and then she waited for you to add something more substantive."

"Oh," he said.

"Why? Did you really expect her to leap about the room and smother you with hugs and kisses and say she could never thank you enough?"

Ben laughed and changed it into a cough.

Her father said in a wounded tone, "Nothing as exaggerated as that. But her lukewarm answer was a bit of a ..."

"And *did* you say something a little more specific then?" she interrupted. "I'll just bet you did!"

He stirred uneasily. "I might have. I think I said something about ... you know ... I made a joke about being mistress of the Old Glebe at last. But — and this is the point I keep trying to make — what d'you think she said to that?"

"Well, I don't know about her but I know what I would have said in her position. I'd say it was out of the question. I wouldn't even consider it."

"Exactly!" he crowed, breaking into a broad smile. "That's precisely what she did say, too. Now doesn't that *prove* she's not simply after the Old Glebe?"

"Not to me, it doesn't! At the risk of sounding brutal — which I don't intend — it shows only that she doesn't want *you,* even if the Old Glebe comes free with the gold ring."

"Ha!" He rubbed his hands as if she had fallen into his trap. "Well, that's just where you're wrong, Miss Cleverpuss! She's perfectly willing to live here as my housekeeper ... even" — he cleared his throat — "as my 'dearest housekeeper,' if you follow. But not as the second Mrs Carrington."

At last Leah was nonplussed. "Is it just the name?"

"That's what I asked her. I told her I'd change it to anything she liked — Liddicoat, even. But she said that wasn't it."

"What was it, then?"

"I don't know — and she won't say." He smiled thinly at her. "And it's obviously not some reason that 'any woman would give' — or you, daughter dear, would be reeling it off by now."

In a tone more like thinking aloud than actually speaking, Leah said, "Why would she be willing to live in sin with you — which is what it amounts to ..."

"Because she loves me," he responded awkwardly. "Or so she says."

"No." She shook her head. "I wasn't really asking *that* question. I meant why would she risk all the wagging tongues ... social ostracism ... all that ... when she could have the same life with honour? And the Old Glebe, which she admits to coveting all her life? It just doesn't make sense."

54 About two weeks after her father returned from London, Leah received a letter from America:

Weds., Oct 21, 1914

Dear Leah:

I hope this doesn't come as too much of a shock. I must have written you a hundred times, mostly in my head, of course, but this is the first I've mailed. The reason? I'm coming over to Europe! In fact, by the time you get this, I may already have arrived. Your brother wrote Willa Henderson to say he was now a mining magnate, set to make five fortunes out of some wolfram the miners of old left lying around for anyone to pick up, so that's how I got your address.

My boat is due in Southampton on Monday, November 2nd, and I will be spending some days in London. Then, at a date yet to be determined, I'll be going to Dublin via Liverpool, after which I will not be a free agent. I would be so much happier in my mind if I could see you some time after the 2nd. According to Bradshaw, it looks pretty easy to get from London to Cornwall and go from there via Bristol to Liverpool. So, if you are tied to the homestead and William to his wolfram, I could do that. I'll try to 'phone you from Southampton, otherwise from London, where I'll be staying with Father Cassidy, c/o the Night Refuge for Catholic Girls of Good Character at 9, Lower Seymour-street (I kid you never!).

Oh, there is so much to tell you. Not only the things in all those unmailed letters but the things that have been happening in my life this year. I'm bursting with them now. My heart runs over. But it would be impolitic to commit them to paper. So, till the day when we meet again — let it be soon!

Thine ever,

Tom

The arrival of this curious letter threw Leah into confusion and put her father's problems almost entirely from her mind.

'My heart runs over'? He had written a hundred letters? Then he was still in love with her. But, 'impolitic to commit them to paper'? They were rather the words of a lawyer than of a lover. And, 'Thine ever'! Could he have forgotten that those words came from a song sung by a blackface minstrel with a grating, adenoidal voice and that they had mocked him on campus all one summer? Or was Tom making a deliberate hint at something — at the childish amusements of gilded youth, for instance? She must have a clearer idea before she invited him down to Cornwall.

Lloyd's Register, which carried sailing details of neutral vessels only — to warn the belligerents not to go doing anything stupid — told her that the America Line's *Tallahassee,* which sailed from New York City on 25th October, was due in Southampton at midday on 2nd November — the only American liner scheduled for that day. There was no call from Southampton on that noon.

At three o'clock she telephoned the night refuge and spoke to a (presumably Catholic) Girl of Good Character, who volunteered the information that she had just changed the warming pan in the bed they were airing for Mr O'Leary; then she went off to find Father Cassidy. Her feet rang on a marble floor; the place sounded cold and echoey.

The priest agreed, reluctantly, to let Tom have her telephone number but he seemed to think it an impertinence that old friends from America should seek to get in touch with Tom, here in England. He didn't believe Tom would have much time for a social life from now on. When Leah asked why not, he said he had to go and rang off abruptly.

Leah was so perturbed by this that, although she hung up the earpiece, she forgot to ring off, and so the next call from London to Helston came straight through to her. It was from a woman in Hampstead who was giving a party the day after tomorrow and desperately wanted a barrel of live lobsters from a particular fisherman in Porthleven, who was to put it on the six-o'clock up train that evening. Leah turned the magneto handle desperately but could not get back to the knitting circle that ran the exchange. So she felt honour-bound to convey the message herself.

"And they say the telephone's a blessing!" she remarked to Pansy as she set off to find this man in Porthleven. And when she at last ran him down in the bar of the Commercial Inn, he merely said, "Well, my lover, you tell she to pay I for the last two barrels I sent 'er — and return they barrels to us — and I'll think about it. Maybe."

She fairly exhausted the pony in racing back by the direct, but hilly, road through Ventonvedna and St Elvan; but it was worth it. Five minutes after her return, the call from London came through and she heard Tom O'Leary's voice for the first time in ten months.

She said it was wonderful and he replied that it was pretty good. She asked what sort of crossing it had been and he said the first day had been awful but the rest had been fair for the time of year. Now the durned land wouldn't hold still beneath him. She laughed and said yes, she remembered that feeling. And, talking of feelings ...

There was a pause before he said, cagily, "Yes?"

"Well, Tom ..." She knew she had to get this in before her courage failed her and before the palpitations in her heart and the constriction in her breathing prevented it. "Things have changed, you know."

"They certainly have!" He almost crowed the words.

"I mean they haven't stood still."

"No, they've gone back! And I'm just *sick* about it all. I can't talk on the phone — obviously — but I could if I could just see you, even for a day, I'm sure I could tell you everything. So you'd understand the importance of it from my point of view."

Her heart fell. There was nothing for it but to tell him straight. "I'd love to see you again, Tom. And it's true — there is so much to talk about. I have a lot to tell you, too. I would have written and let you know about it anyway but it'll be so much ... well, 'nicer' is hardly the right word! It'll be so much more honest and honourable to tell you in person."

"Tell me what?" he asked in a slightly bewildered tone. "I'm the one with news I'm bursting to tell you."

"Well ..." She was more than a little miffed at this. "I have my own share of that commodity, you know. The thing is" — she swallowed heavily — "I'm unofficially engaged to a Helston man and it's about to become official any day now. And it won't be a long engagement, either."

"Oh!" he exclaimed, but more as if it were the change of topic, rather than the news itself, that surprised him.

Meanwhile Leah, hearing the echo of her last words, realized how they might be misconstrued and added, "Not that there's any particular *reason* to rush things — other than that Ben and I are buying a farm together and, well, Nature won't wait."

"Yeah ... sure!" he said, still sounding quite bewildered.

And now Leah saw that she had dug herself even deeper into the mire. "I mean ploughing and sowing and reaping and mowing — *that* sort of Nature, Tom. Not ... you know ..."

"Well, that's just swell!" he exclaimed.

"Are you being ironic, Tom?"

"How d'you mean?"

"You know — swell ... swelling ... and me saying Nature can't wait. You're not by any chance making snide remarks along those lines?"

"In a home for young females of upright character — I should hope not!'"

She laughed. *"Now* I remember you, Tom! I was just beginning to wonder."

"Well, like I said, things *have* changed. So — you're going up the primrose path to the altar. Will I like him? Will I approve? Does William approve — that's the real question? He's a better judge of people than any of us. If he approves, then so do I. Shoot — I'm longing to see you all again! I just hope my schedule allows it."

"Father Cassidy didn't seem to think it would."

Tom laughed. "You know the Irish. They have to pop half a dozen corks and remember The Invincibles before anything gets going. I'll *make* time — never fear. Just tell me what days over the next two weeks you won't be free."

"Golly! In a way I'm already tied up *every* day. I mean I'm already running a farm here."

"Yeah — William said that to Willa — who sends her regards, by the way."

"Oh, thank you. But farming and free time don't exactly go hand in hand, you know. However, the chores can be rearranged and relief workers can be engaged. All it takes is a little notice. You let me know the day before you're coming down — two days would be even better, if you can manage it — and I'll make sure I'm free. Take the branch line from Gwinear Road to Helston. I'll meet you there. Did you get that?"

"It's already written down, honey."

"My! Things really have changed. You're getting organized! When did you last wear odd stockings?"

Silence.

"Well?" she prompted.

"I've just checked," he said. "And I'm going to plead the Fifth Amendment on that one. Listen — there's the Angelus. I have to go. But I *will* let you know."

"But, Tom — your folks are Baptists!" she objected — to an already silent line.

This time she remembered to ring off.

55 In the event, Tom gave the Carringtons two days' notice. On 10th November, a Tuesday, he phoned to say he would arrive at Helston early in the evening of that coming Thursday and would like to stay until the following Monday morning. He asked Leah to book him in at a good local hostelry. She told him not to be so stupid; he'd stay at the Old Glebe, of course. But at least he made the offer, she thought — which showed he understood the new situation.

The day after he phoned, Leah had a serious argument with Will. All that day she'd had the feeling that Pansy was avoiding her. When Pansy's sister Violet called by to collect an earring that Philomena had dropped into the lining of an armchair the previous week, she learned why. Violet could not be more different from her sister. Where Pansy was blonde and willowy, Violet was stocky and dark; and where Pansy was feather-heeled and carefree, Violet was intense and serious.

Leah told Violet she thought Pansy was avoiding her and asked if she could find out why. Violet had words with her sister (they had not had conversations for years) and, on her way out, told Leah that Ben Coad had given Will a lecture on the folly of dalliance with the household servants. Indeed, he had given him more than that, namely the addresses of certain houses in Constantine, Goldsithney, and Leedstown where those needs could be 'tooken care of' for a small outlay in silver. And — according to Pansy — Will was now 'so maggoty as a big ferret in a small sack.'

That evening, as usual, Leah hung around when Pansy brought the hot bathwater up to Will's room. And later that evening, *not* as usual, Will hit out at her for it. He said she must have a mind like a sewer to suspect him and the girl, and what tales she'd been carrying to Ben Coad he couldn't imagine, but he'd thank her to hold her tongue in future because he'd never been so humiliated and embarrassed in all his life.

It was much too long a speech, not only because he 'did protest too much' but also because it gave Leah time to recover from her shock at the onslaught and face her brother calmly — once he had finished speaking. Or, rather, once he paused to draw breath. "It doesn't wash, Will," she said calmly. "Pansy's with child and the game's up."

He sat down abruptly, his face drained of all colour. "She's not!" he said. "Oh, my God!" He closed his eyes and shook his head. "Why did she tell *you*, of all people? Why didn't she come to me?"

"She's done quite enough of *that*, don't you think?" she asked severely. "It was bad enough when you both went out to the old barn each night, but now …"

He rose again and made for the door. "I must go and see her," he said.

"Will!" she snapped.

He hesitated, poised on one foot. "What?"

"Let me give you *some* good …"

"I didn't need any advice, thanks, good or bad. Especially not from you or your precious Ben!"

".. good *news*, I was going to say. Very good news, in fact."

"What?" Now he was merely testy.

"She's not."

He just stared at her blankly.

"Pansy," she went on. "She's not with child."

"You …! You …" he spluttered.

"Careful!" She rose and came to him. "I might have been only rehearsing."

"Well, are you or aren't you?" he roared.

"Keep your voice down! The truth is I don't know whether or not she's in that interesting condition. And nor do you. And nor does she. A woman doesn't, you know, until it's almost two months too late. You've been going at it like rabbits for the past six weeks, so what I pretended was a certainty could well be a possibility. Are you going to sit down now and discuss it calmly?"

He just stared at her. She had never seen such anger in his eyes before. "I'll thank you not to meddle in my affairs in future …" he began icily.

But she behaved as if he were not speaking at all. "Have you promised to marry Pansy if anything like that should happen?" she asked. "Does she have some sort of understanding with you along those lines?"

"Whether any such understanding may exist between us or not is none of your …"

"Because, if not, then your affairs are not *her* affairs — and I shall certainly meddle in her affairs."

"She has come of age and she is a free woman who may make her own ... oh, hell!" He was furious that she had seduced him into a discussion he had set his mind against entering at all. He turned on his heel and made for the front door. But there he found it was lashing with rain, so he had to come back and put up his oilskins. It ruined the grandeur of his intended gesture — flinging out into the night.

Leah stood at his elbow and said, "The title 'free woman' has a certain irony in this situation, don't you think? You'd be better off with the kind that charge for it."

"I'm not saying another word," he replied.

"Good! That gives me time to tell you more. I have been aware of your shenanigans — yours and hers — from the very beginning. And I warned her at the time that the one thing I would *not* tolerate would be if she tried to do the same thing with the old man. I also warned her against expecting any help or consideration if she broke her leg with you. So she's under no illusions about that."

He opened the front door again, still with several buttons undone and, at last, flung out into the night, leaving the door swinging behind him.

"Oh, Will, you are such a fool!" she called out into the dark.

She slammed the door and turned round to see Philomena coming up the passage from the kitchen end of the house. "I hope you don't mind, Leah, dear," she said. "It's such a filthy night I came directly from the yard in through the scullery. Was that Will?"

Leah nodded. "We've just had words, I'm afraid. Come into the sitting room."

Philomena did not move. "So I gathered. I suppose he's going down to Grankum to complain about you to Adelaide. Has he eaten anything?"

"No." Leah was hardly listening. She was wondering if she should go and play a variant of the same trick on Pansy, so as to drive the dangers home to her: 'My dear girl — from the way you've been behaving lately, you remind me of a friend of mine at around the time she conceived her first baby. And look at the texture of your skin! Are you *absolutely sure* you're not ...'

Philomena said, "Nor have they, yet. So he won't go hungry — unless he's off to a certain house in Goldsithney! Or the other one in Leedstown!"

That got Leah's attention at last!

First the hostess resumed control. "Have *you* eaten, Miss Liddicoat?" she asked. "Do take pot luck with us."

"I haven't as a matter of fact, my dear. How kind of you — and all unprompted! But see here — hadn't we agreed you'd call me Philomena?"

"Yes. I'm sorry. I intended no … I'm just rather *distrait* at the moment — what with Tom O'Leary coming tomorrow and now this quarrel with Will …"

Had the woman hung back at the far end of the passage until Will had gone? Had she heard that bit about Pansy setting her cap at the old man? Leah groaned inwardly.

"Come into the drawing room," she said again, leading the way this time. "Put your shoes to dry out near the fire. We won't be dressing for dinner tonight — much to my father's delight. I try to keep up the old standards but it's hard to do that *and* run a farm as well."

"The colonel always dressed for dinner," Philomena said, but in such a neutral tone that Leah could not tell whether she approved or disapproved. In the beginning she had always spoken of her former employer with such admiration, but not nowadays. "Thank you for finding my earring," she added.

They sat down and reached their hands eagerly toward the flames. "It was easy once you were able to say where you had probably lost it," Leah replied. "I take it Violet told you about her discussions with Pansy, then? It's very *kind* of Ben to be so liberal with his directions to Will of houses of that sort. He seems to be a walking vade-mecum! I just wonder how he's able to reel them off so pat?"

Philomena chuckled. "Oh, my dear, everyone knows about them down here. It doesn't mean anything special in his case. I remember the time I passed the one in Leedstown and saw all the sheets hanging out in the garden to dry and I dropped some remark about it's being rather a grand house for a washerwoman — and everybody laughed. Nobody told me but I guessed. That's how one picks things up, of course." She smiled at Leah. "So don't go bending Ben's ear, eh?"

"Thank heavens I spoke to you first." Leah glanced at the clock. "Fifteen minutes. D'you want to go up and wash?"

She shook her head. "That won't take a moment. Actually, Leah, there's something I wish to speak to you about."

"My father."

"What else! I'm afraid I overheard what you said to Will just now, but I had intended asking you about it before — in fact, ever since the very first time I met him — met *them* — when he pretended to be John Hamden. Do you object to speaking bluntly about it with me? I take it there is nothing actually going on there?"

Leah shook her head. "Only with Will — which is bad enough. But there's no point in dismissing her because it would only continue between the pair of them. And then I'd have absolutely no control over her at all."

"Yes. I'd already worked that out for myself. I think you've done quite the right thing."

"Have I? Surely there was a time when shame and moral sense would have made such behaviour unthinkable? Among people like us, anyway."

"People like us!" Philomena gave a hollow laugh. "Perhaps there was, but it was before Adam delved and Eve span — I mean, before Adam *needed* to delve or Eve to spin. Ever since then we've each had to find our own accommodation. Tell me — is there any likelihood your father will overhear us?"

"None whatsoever. We'll hear him coming downstairs before he even reaches the landing. Why?"

"Because I think there are one or two things I ought to tell you — and one thing I ought to ask you, too. The main thing to tell you is ..." She sighed and, with a wave of her hands, sculpted something huge in the air between them. "It's as big as a whale. But what it comes down to is that the 'moral sense' you spoke of is a general prescription for the generality of people. It makes us promise never to tell lies even though we know we're going to tell Mrs so-and-so she's looking radiant and that colour suits her to a tee. Or that we'll never steal even though we know we'll reuse the next uncancelled stamp we find among our morning's post. Or that we'll never be slothful again — a resolution I found impossible to maintain in the bath at Earl's last month, even with people hammering on the door."

"Yes," Leah responded uncertainly. "But these are all trivial lapses ..."

"Are they? We send Mrs so-and-so forth into the world, a laughing stock. We make the posting of letters more expensive for those who honestly pay for it. And so on. But if Pansy slips between Will's sheets at night — or I between the colonel's (which, I confess to *you*, I did) — who is harmed thereby? That's what it comes down to — who is *harmed* by it?"

Leah could only stare at her. Her heart dropped a beat and then raced. "How can you say that?" she murmured.

"Well — answer me? Who is harmed?"

"But ... I mean, everybody *knows* ..."

"Never mind what *everybody* knows. Tell me what *you* know. Tell me who is harmed?"

"Well — Pansy is for one. I mean, she could so easily become ... did you hear what I said to Will earlier? The thing that started our argument?"

Philomena shook her head.

"I pretended that Pansy had told me she was expecting — just to shock him. To show him it *could* happen."

Again the woman shook her head, this time with a pitying smile. "Not if he's a gentleman — and she's cautious. There are ways to avoid it, you know. I don't want to go off on that track now. Just accept it from one who knows. It is a very small possibility when you go about it in the right way. And when you set it against the pleasure of the thing — a pleasure of which you cannot have the faintest ..."

"Philomena!"

"What?" Her big, questioning eyes were all innocence.

"You know what! I mean, what you're advocating is against all common ... I mean, what would become of society if we all ..." Words failed her.

"I'm not advocating, dear. Nor seeking to promote some new and outlandish form of behaviour. I'm simply explaining the way things already are. As to what would become of society — look about you! The society in which you live is not one that would fall to bits if half its members engaged in clandestine encounters between the sheets, it is one that has already been shaped by such behaviour — all down the centuries. The pendulum has swung between periods of licence and periods of prudery, but that has merely led to greater or smaller discretion in the business."

Leah put her hands to her temples and pressed hard, as if to dislodge some obstruction. "Are you saying you wouldn't mind … I mean, the question you asked earlier about my father and, you know, Pansy, and so forth — are you saying you wouldn't really mind if …"

"Ah!" Philomena exclaimed, holding up a finger and smiling savagely. "Whether *I* would mind is a totally different matter. I was talking about whether society as a whole should mind particularly what we do in that sphere of life. But of course *I* should mind. I'd be beside myself with fury, let me tell you. I'd tear her eyes out. I'd dismiss her from this life, never mind from this house!" Her eyes glowed at the prospect, making Leah shiver. "And as for your father — oh, what torments would I *not* prepare for him?"

"But why? To quote you back at yourself — who would actually be harmed?"

"*I* would be harmed. My *amour propre* would be shattered. To know that he'd choose her when he could have me!"

"But he's asked you to marry him and you've said …"

"I'm not talking about marriage. I'm talking about It. Doing It. I'll gladly come here as his housekeeper — and keep his bed warm — I've told him that."

"But you won't marry him! I don't understand."

Philomena smiled sympathetically. "You don't need to understand. Just accept that I have my reasons."

"Do you lose your inheritance from the colonel if you remarry — is that it?"

She laughed. "That proves you haven't sent for a copy of his will. It has gone through probate, you know. It's a public document. Anyone can purchase a copy. But I'll save you the money. That is not the reason. My inheritance was absolute and inalienable."

"Pa doesn't understand, either. He does love you, you know. It's driving him almost out of his mind."

"There's no need for him to torment himself a moment longer. He can have me at his side day and night. I'm growing to love him, too. It started in London. I never thought there would be another man for me — not after the colonel. But, against all the odds, your pa has crept in under my armour and ... well, 'nuff said. I'll move in tomorrow if he'll only say the word."

Leah sank her head between her hands. "But he never will, Philomena. He loves you too honourably simply to take you in as a housekeeper by day and a mistress by night."

"What a perfect description of a wife! Granted that the parties love each other, too, of course — which it seems we do."

"He'd never see it like that. He wants to take you round, show you off. He wants to swell with pride when he says, 'And this is my wife' — and people see how beautiful you are."

Just for a moment she thought she, too, had slipped a rapier-word beneath Philomena's armour. If so, the woman ignored the wound and riposted: "The great John Carrington, eh — who subdued the dragon in Philomena Liddicoat and put a band of gold on that finger! No, sirree — as he says! It might as well be a ring of gold through my nose, with an invisible chain to his key-ring! No, sirree again! One of us must yield and it won't be me."

"And *that's* the reason?" a shocked Leah asked.

"No," Philomena replied. "That's *not* the reason. Suffice it to say I have my pride. That's all. And I care for his reputation, also. You keep on telling him that — I have my pride and he must yield to it."

56 Tom's train was due at the Helston terminus at 6:02 that Thursday evening. Leah was there in good time but she need not have bothered; the main-line train had been delayed by troop movements at Exeter and, though it had made up for lost time since, the connecting train from Gwinear Road would be at least a quarter of an hour late. At six o'clock, just after Leah had found someone with sufficient authority to let her know these details, she was surprised to see Nicholas Liddicoat come sauntering onto the platform. And a curiously nervous kind of saunter it was, too. Perhaps it had something to do with the fact that he was still dressed in his working clothes. Claggy man-made clay hung like strips of cracked elephant hide around the bottoms of his trousers and his dark hair was grizzled with dust.

"Oh, it's you! Hallo," he said, making a half-hearted attempt at surprise. Meanwhile, his eyes roved up and down the ill-lit platform — the sun having set an hour earlier. "But where is your baggage?" he asked.

Something in his attitude made her decide to volunteer as little as possible. "I didn't bring any," she told him.

He nodded grimly, as if he had expected as much. "A bit of a rush decision, eh?" he said.

"At least I dressed for the occasion," she replied.

He looked down at his clothes, as if seeing them for the first time. "And to think I almost broke my neck coming down Sithney Common Hill."

"On your bicycle?"

He nodded. "All the way I kept praying it wasn't true, that Will was pulling my leg. I actually hoped he was, even though I'd smash his face in for it. I honestly didn't think I'd find you here. But I had to be sure."

This was such an absurd over-reaction to her present errand that, she realized, Will must have spun the poor Nark some quite different yarn. It was his revenge for her interference in his night-life, of course. That was why he had searched for her luggage. Will must have told him she was leaving by the next up-train, for some spurious reason.

So, how to break the truth to the Nark gently — but not so gently that he didn't go back and carry out some part of his threat to deal with the dear boy?

"I can't imagine why you should be so perturbed at a simple act of courtesy, Nark," she said. "It's terribly sweet of you to show such concern in my behalf but Tom is a civilized person, a graduate of Yale and a doctor of jurisprudence. I do not need a bodyguard just to meet him off the train."

"Tom?" He cleared his throat awkwardly.

"Tom O'Leary. Have I never mentioned him to you? Surely I have? Anyway, he's visiting us for the weekend, before going on to Dublin. And I'm meeting him here."

"Yes, well, I knew that, of course," Nicholas said, sticking his hands in his pockets and trying to seem nonchalant. Then, staring out into the dark across the tracks, he muttered, "I'll kill the fellow!"

Leah smiled. "Did he tell you I was going away, then?"

He nodded tersely. "Something like that. God, I could have killed myself coming down that hill without lights."

"But *why,* Nick?"

She so rarely used his name that he was astonished into silence; he just stared at her.

She went on: "Suppose I *had* been doing a moonlight flit — or whatever cock-and-bull nonsense Will gave you — what would you have done?"

He returned his gaze to the darkness that faced them. "Dunno," he said. "Waved goodbye, I suppose."

"Tell that to the horse-marines!"

"All right," he cried angrily. "I'd have somehow tried to talk you into staying."

"But why?"

"That's none of your business."

"Ah!" After a pause she began humming a little tune.

"I need someone to argue with," he said. "You're the best I know. All right?"

"Not that we have argued much lately," she remarked airily.

"Well, whose fault is that? You have been rather ... how shall I put it? Preoccupied?"

She could smell tigers in the country up ahead. "Before you say something you might regret ..." she began.

But he interrupted her. "Don't do it, Thistle."

"Do what?"

"That's what I came in here to say — don't do it. I meant don't run off, then, but I still mean it now. Don't ..."

"Will told you I was running away — and you *believed* him?"

"He made it sound very convincing. How you can't abide Aunt Philomena — it's not hard to make *that* sound convincing! How you ..."

"But I *like* Philomena. I didn't at first. None of us did. But we all do now. We can't understand why she refuses to marry my father though she seems perfectly willing to live in sin with him. D'you understand it?"

"Never mind that." He waved her question aside. "When I thought you were just running away from it all, I thought that included Ben Coad. So I came in here to tell you not to." He licked his lips nervously and drew a deep breath. "I still say it — don't! Not Ben Coad. You can do a lot better."

"Meaning?" she asked quietly.

"You're besotted with farming now. All right — it's new, it's exciting, it satisfies something deep within everyone. Lording it over land and livestock. Forcing Nature to our will. But it's not *you*, Thistle. You belong on a wider stage."

"All on my ownio?" she asked.

"That's a later question. Just think what's right for you now."

She sighed. "I don't seem to be very good at that. Whenever I try to imagine the future, it's always *with* someone."

"All right. Here's a picture for you. Imagine yourself twenty-five years from now. The children grown up and gone. Just you and Ben Coad. And he's still cracking the same feeble jokes in Helston market every Wednesday. And you're still looking out on the same fifty acres at Goonhusband, thinking we'll plough that field and put that one down to oats and cabbage in that one and return that one to pasture. And it'll hit you that you did exactly the same five years earlier, and six years before that, and four years before that for two years running ..." He gripped her arm fiercely and stared deep into her eyes. "And you'll remember this conversation then. And you'll say to yourself, 'The Nark was right. I *do* belong on a wider stage than this'! But it'll be too late. You think you're choosing to *do* something in marrying Coad. But I tell you now — you're really choosing *not* to do something." He smiled at her, rather desperately, and added, "Here endeth the first and only lesson."

She shook her head. "You have a much higher opinion of me and my capabilities than I do of myself," she said.

"Much higher than Coad's — if he really sees you as a happy farmer's wife till death do you part."

"Well, Nick, I'm afraid that's the way I see myself, too. That's why I think he's the man for me. Tell me why your aunt won't marry my father."

"Oh, go to hell!" he said quietly — and walked away, out of the station.

A moment later, however, he was back at the gate. "Pride!" he shouted at her. "It runs in *some* families, you know."

This encounter did nothing to dent her love for Ben nor her resolve to marry him and live the happy, contented life Nick had just sneered at. But it filled her with a great sadness for him. He had obviously felt much more for her than he had ever admitted to feeling. And now, with her apparently dramatic flight from home, he had seen his last chance to declare it to her. But the sadness did not soften her heart to the point where she might humour him, tell him she'd think it over, go along with him a little and hope to let him down gently over the coming weeks.

And that was fitting, in a way, because — as she suddenly realized — if Tom felt the same about her, she would be just as blunt and firm with him, too. People talk of being cruel to be kind; but there is also its counterpart, especially in matters of the heart — being kind to be cruel.

Also, his final taunt about the pride that ran in the Liddicoat family gave her something else to think about.

57 Outwardly Tom hadn't changed a bit. He stuck his head out of his compartment window as soon as the train had cleared the bridge, some hundred yards down the line. The light from within picked him out against the darkness — and he was still the golden-haired son of Yale with stars in his eyes. And he opened the door and leaped out onto the platform before the train pulled to a halt. "Leah!" he cried, throwing his arms around her and lifting her off the ground to swing her around in a great circle. But his quick, cheerful kiss on her cheek was in marked contrast to the long orgies of kissing that had attended her tearful departure at the beginning of that year in Connecticut.

"No husband-to-be?" he asked as he set her down again. "He trusts you with me?"

The bluntness of the question, even though he intended it jokingly, left her nonplussed. She could not think of a quick reply that did not belittle one or other of them. Then it came to her: "*I* trust me with you, Tom."

"Ah! There's that independent Yankee streak! How does it play in Helston?"

"Pretty well. Where are your bags?"

"Just the carpet bag." He paused to retrieve it from the luggage van. "I sent everything else on from London to Dublin. They have this wonderful system called 'luggage in advance' and they swear it's infallible."

All the way down into Helston he enthused about aspects of England's novelties that she had forgotten by now. Most of all he had been impressed by the varieties of landscape he had passed through on the three hundred miles between London and Cornwall — the rolling beechwoods of the Thames valley, the picture-postcard farmlands of Berkshire (so unlike the mountainous 'Berkshires' of Massachusetts) and Somerset, the seascapes after Exeter, where the line is built on the tidal rocks and penetrates the cliff headlands in short tunnels ... the wild fringes of Dartmoor ... Brunel's magnificent bridge, soaring over the Tamar at Plymouth, and then the lush, damp, closed-in valleys of Cornwall itself. He had viewed them, appropriately, in the gathering dusk, as the train sped on into the dark, Celtic west. His final view, before night fell and the sparks and glow from the engine gave the line an infernal cast, was of the broad, treeless hills of the far west, like a school of black dolphins frozen against a burnished leaden sky.

"And all those familiar names!" he said. "Plymouth. Truro. Falmouth. Portland. Weymouth. Bideford — they have only one 'd' here, I noticed. And there are dozens more."

"You have to keep reminding yourself that they got them first. We borrowed the names from them."

"Yeah," he said. "Except that when we did it, we *were* them, too. The same people. We're not any more, thank God!"

She thought that a rather odd remark but she let it pass. "What's all this about going to Ireland?" she asked.

"Hey!" he exclaimed as they entered Coinagehall Street. "What a quaint little burg! What does it remind me of? If there was ocean down there at the bottom, instead of that green, it'd be like New Bedford in *Moby Dick,* don't you think? All these hunched houses leaning against one another as they march down the hill."

"Except they're built of granite, if you notice." She tried not to let his slightly patronizing admiration annoy her; but the fact that she had forgotten the time when her feelings were almost identical showed her how much she now belonged here.

"That's the Angel Hôtel." She pointed it out. "It was once the town house of the earls of Godolphin, who were ministers of state to Queen Elizabeth back in the days of the Virginia plantation. Doesn't it make you thrill to think of all that history?

I mean, it's our history, too — only back home it was just like the backdrop to the *Mayflower* settlement. It's as if a backdrop on the stage suddenly turned into real landscape. D'you know what I mean, Tom?"

After a pause he said, "Only too well, honey." He took her hand, briefly. "We'll always be friends, won't we?" he asked.

"Of course!" She laughed, slightly embarrassed by his intensity.

"No matter what I ... I mean, what you may hear of me?"

"Good heavens, Tom!" Now her laugh was wholeheartedly embarrassed. "What are you intending to do in Dublin? Stage another Phoenix Park murder?"

"No," he replied vehemently. "That's the whole point. I'll tell you at dinner. I want your father to hear it, too."

"Ben will be there, too."

"Oh."

"Why d'you say it like that?"

"Well, I mean, he's English, isn't he?"

She chuckled. "He wouldn't thank you for the description. Practically his first words to us, when he met us on that same platform at the station, were to the effect that *he* was Cornish and *we* were Cornish — or that local people would consider us more Cornish than American."

"Good salesman!"

"No, it's true. Total strangers come up to us and say things like, 'My wife's aunt had a half-sister who got married to a nephew of your great-grandfather, William Carrington of Leedstown'! That actually happened to me — more or less those very words. We used to think the Irish were like that, over in America — always sorting out their genealogy before they can ask for a light. But the Cornish are just the same."

"Interesting," Tom said. "And your Mister Coad has no love for the English, either?"

"Oh, I wouldn't go as far as that. He sneers at a certain class of English tripper and insists that he's Cornish. But he wouldn't blow up the bridges and dig the Tamar clear through to the Bristol Channel."

Tom laughed at her imagery and said, "No. I guess God was kinder to the Irish in that respect."

At dinner that night he told them more. He had been offered a teaching post in jurisprudence at University College, Dublin;

there was a detour there while they sorted out that Trinity was for Protestants and UCD for Roman Catholics.

"But your people were always Protestants," John pointed out, repeating the objection Leah had tried to make on the telephone. "Weren't they?"

"We were Irish before we were either," Tom replied. Then, turning to Ben, he added, "I gather, sir, that you will understand the sentiment. We Celts are of our own nation before we sign up to any other."

"We are clannish," Ben agreed. "But I'm not sure the English don't favour us by posing as the common enemy. You Irish converted us Cornish to Christianity, you know — blithely ignoring the fact that we had been quietly practising the faith for three hundred years already. You came ashore from your little *curraghs,* with the wild fire of the new convert in your eyes, and with sword and dagger you did it. The carnage was appalling."

It was clearly not the message Tom wished to hear but, lawyer that he was, he found something in Ben's words on which he could build. "It is to help prevent such appalling carnage that I have accepted this post. You should have heard the murmurings in Boston, and other Irish communities over there, when the English suspended the Home Rule Act until the end of this war. Carnage isn't the word. And the same hotheads will take over the struggle in Ireland, too, unless we can have some movement on the legal front. If the English just dig in their heels and say no, no, no to all the peaceful, legal moves, then the blood will run through every street in Ireland."

Any worries Ben harboured — that Leah's former beau might still feel some lingering desire for her — evaporated during this speech. Looking into the man's eyes he saw the light of a new love shining there — the sort that leaves no room for others. He smiled and said, "I don't think you'd find echoes of such sentiments down here, old chap."

And so it continued the whole weekend. She proudly showed him a field of oats she had drilled herself; he remembered the Great Famine and the way groaning shiploads of cereals were exported from Ireland while millions starved to death. The stamps at Wheal Fortune were a metaphor for Anglo-Irish landlordism. The poisoned croft was the face of Irish nationalism, poisoned with ideas of physical force.

Tom O'Leary had turned into a zealot, consumed by one idea: that Ireland should be free and a nation once again. It left no room for any other. Leah could remember how his eyes, once upon a time, would follow any pretty girl who came into view, never realizing how much it pained her to see it. But now, when Pansy was around, even when she flirted with him in those ways she could not help, she might just as well have been a machine for all the notice he paid her. Indeed, if she had been a machine, he might have been more interested — wondering how cheaply she might be duplicated and put into the service of Erin the Brave.

Leah hated to admit it but, when he finally left them on the Monday morning, she had never been more glad to see the back of anyone. "It was the longest weekend of my life," she told Ben when she called by on her way back from the station.

"Poor you!" he said sympathetically, though he could hardly conceal his relief at the way things had turned out.

"Did my father give you a letter of authorization to retrieve the deeds to the Old Glebe from Frank Kernow?" she went on.

He made a guilty grimace and nodded.

"Which means you haven't done so yet?"

" 'Fraid so. Things have just been so ..."

"It doesn't matter, Ben. It's rather good that you haven't, because, if you do it this afternoon, it'll mean ..."

"Not this afternoon!" he groaned.

"Please," she insisted. "It must be. You must bring them to the Old Glebe tonight. You're coming to dinner, by the way. And you'll call at the Angel and bring Philomena with you. Everything hinges on three conditions: the presence of my father, the presence of Philomena, and the presence of those deeds. So don't fail me! Eight o'clock."

"And if I tell you it will mean postponing yet again the final act of the Goonhusband purchase?"

"Then it just has to be postponed, Ben. I'm sorry. I cannot marry you until I'm sure my father is properly fixed up. And I think that means being *married* to Philomena, not just living under the same roof."

He sank his head between his hands. "Not all that again!" he begged. "I thought we'd agreed to give up trying. Let them stew in their own juice — isn't that what you said?"

"That was before the Nark let drop an amazing revelation about his dear aunt."

"What?"

Leah's eyes brimmed with merriment as she said, slowly and portentously, "Aunt Philomena has *pride!*"

He waited for more and then said, "And that's it?"

"That's it."

"Well, I'm blowed!" he exclaimed. "Who ever would have guessed it!"

"You think about it," Leah advised, unshaken by his sarcasm. "What particular point of pride would prevent her from marrying my father?"

And away she went to invite Philomena to join them for dinner that night — equally determined to take nothing but yes for an answer.

58 John Carrington had developed a taste for Rosewarne's export ale. Tom O'Leary had found that difficult to believe, even after — or, perhaps, especially after — he had tasted it, but John said it showed he had truly crossed the Atlantic and was now a Cornishman, through and through. There was a flagon of Rosewarne's export ale before him on the table that night. Philomena, by contrast, had confided once to Leah that a particular Saint Emilion claret called Château Clos des Jacobins was her favourite of favourites. When the merchant told Leah that it cost seven shillings a bottle she had turned pale. Nonetheless a decanter of the precious fluid, properly *chambré,* was at the woman's right hand that evening. Leah was leaving nothing to chance.

"I hear your American friend was a rather *intense* young man," Philomena said as soon as grace was over and they took their seats.

"You may say so," John responded. "He left me wondering why the British ever went into Ireland in the first place — and why they didn't march back out again singing hallelujahs the moment someone asked them nicely. No!" He put his hands over his ears. "I never even want to hear the country named again." He grinned at Philomena. "Please?"

"That's that, then," she said, a little miffed that she was to be told no more. "What shall we talk about instead?"

Will put up a finger, like a schoolboy.

"Behave!" Leah told him.

"May I introduce a topic, please?" he insisted.

"Has it any connection with the pan-Celtic nation?" his father asked warily.

Will shook his head. "Not as far as I know. It's to do with marriage ..."

"Whose?" Leah asked at once, trying to warn him with her eyes that he was trespassing and to back off.

"Mine," he said. "My engagement, anyway."

"Well now," his father said judiciously, "an engagement usually involves *two* parties. I realize that times are changing, but ..."

"It's your niece, Philomena," he said. "Adèle. I've asked her to marry me and she is thinking it over."

As soon as he spoke Adèle's name Leah looked up at Pansy, who was handing round the soup as she, Leah, filled each bowl. The girl grinned and winked back at her. The message behind that wink was much more than a 'see if I care!' it was more like 'don't imagine that's the end of what's going on between him and *me!*'

"When did this happen?" Philomena asked.

"About an hour ago. I asked her on my way home from Wheal Fortune this evening."

"And did it come as a complete shock to her? I'm sorry — perhaps 'surprise' would be a better word."

"Hardly. I've been dropping huge hints for weeks now."

"For instance?" Philomena leaned forward eagerly. "I long to know how you youngsters manage these things nowadays." She sipped her wine idly — then froze, made dainty connoisseur's smacks of her lips ... peered at the wine again, sniffed it, sipped it once more, and then — her question to Will forgotten — turned ecstatically to Leah and said, "You angel!"

Leah dipped her head modestly. "I was only testing you, actually, Philomena," she said. "Just to see if you could recognize it from a decanter, with no label to guide you."

"That was an expensive test, my dear. But you have my leave to conduct it as often as you wish!"

"We would talk, Adèle and I ..." Will began.

But another thought had crossed Philomena's mind, for she did not believe Leah would go to such trouble and expense for nothing. "Have you devised any other tests for me tonight, Leah?" she asked.

"Ah!" Leah held up a finger. "Now that would be telling, wouldn't it! There's no point in a test if you know it's coming."

"And am I left out of it?" her father asked.

"And me?" Ben put in.

"We are all being tested all the time," Leah replied in a pious tone. "Will — you were telling us how you littered the ground at Adèle's feet with hints as high as Olympus?"

Will glanced wearily at Ben, who told him, "I think marriage is the only way, old son."

Leah asked him what he meant by that.

"I mean," he explained, "that perhaps when Will is married, the rest of you will stop treating him as the baby of the family. You've all done it in the last five minutes — even Miss Liddicoat has caught the family habit."

Leah and her father were about to protest when Philomena said, "He's right. You're right, Mister Coad. We shall cease this cross-examination forthwith. Will — my humble apologies. There is no need to answer my question. I know very well how one drops such hints. One talks of one's taste in wallpapers, one's preferences among breakfast dishes ..." She hesitated a moment and then added, "... and how one would like this or that specimen placed in the garden."

John cleared his throat significantly and said, "Not in front of the children, my dear."

Philomena looked at Leah as if to say, 'Have I given you the opening you want?' And, had she actually spoken those words, she might have added, " — before your father's head is fuddled with ale and mine with the wine!' She clearly knew something was afoot and wanted to take over the agenda.

But Leah thought it much too early in the evening and so she demurely accepted her father's rebuke.

Will, seeing his chance, leaped in again. "It won't necessarily be a long engagement," he said. "If she accepts me, that is."

"*If* she accepts you?" Leah asked. "Don't you know she's had her heart set on you from the moment you met?" Glancing warily at Philomena she added, "And once a Liddicoat female has her heart set on one of you Carrington men, all the will-power and determination in the universe isn't going to help you! It's *pfft!*"

"I just wanted to say that, well, the fact that we're making so much money at Wheal Fortune has nothing whatsoever to do with her feelings," Will protested.

They all stared at him blankly. "Who said anything about that?" Leah asked him.

"I was about to," he explained. "That's why it won't necessarily be a long engagement. I just wondered if anybody here has any objections? If so, speak now or forever hold your peace." He looked at his father and Philomena in turn.

Leah stared again at Pansy, provoking her into asking: "Will that be all, miss?"

"For the moment, yes," Leah replied. "We'll ring if we need you. And just let me remind you — the bell rings quite loudly enough in the kitchen. You don't need to press your ear against this door to hear it."

Pansy flounced out. Leah noticed that Ben's eyes followed every wiggle and bounce — which annoyed her, just as Tom had annoyed her back in Connecticut with the same sort of behaviour. But then she saw that her father and brother did not so much as glance at the girl; indeed, their avoidance of her parade was studious. It made Ben's behaviour easier to tolerate.

"Are you asking me or your father?" Philomena said to Will.

"Either," he replied. "Or both, actually, since you each have some sort of interest."

His eyes, still darting between the pair of them, came to rest finally upon his father, who said, "I'm delighted enough to know you will no longer require an allowance, my boy. To learn that you may persuade someone to take control of all other aspects of your life is the cup that runneth over as far as I'm concerned." Then, glancing uneasily at Philomena, whose frown revealed that she considered his reply somewhat flippant, he added, "Of course, we'll have a serious sit-down before anything official is announced — going through your finances and prospects and so forth. And we must also address the question of your resumed education at the School of Mines when the war is over." He glanced again at Philomena to see if she approved.

She said, "I admit that I have — very occasionally — passed the odd critical remark about my niece Adelaide. This news, dear William, gives me the first vestige of a hope that she might buckle to and make something of her life after all. I, for my part, hope you and Adelaide will be very happy. Or" — this with a glance at Leah and Ben — "as happy as most people have any right to be."

The rest of the meal passed in light, inconsequential conversation — the sort of verbal grooming in which all well-knit families indulge. Leah did not return to her little scheme until they retired to the drawing room for coffee, by which time the claret and ale had done their mellowing work.

Her chance came when her father said, "Well, Ben, you've been rather quiet this evening. Does all this talk of marriage make you feel nervous?"

Ben shook his head. "I'd just like to be able to set the date, sir. That's all."

"Oh?" Philomena was suddenly alert. "Why so? Is the purchase of the property at Goonhusband not progressing as you had hoped, then?"

"On the contrary, Miss Liddicoat," he replied. "It has progressed with exemplary speed, In fact, apart from one small signature, it *is* completed." He smiled at Leah. "We could marry and move in tomorrow."

"So what in tarnation's name is stopping you?" John asked. "Certainly not any objection on *our* side."

Ben shrugged awkwardly and looked at Leah.

She could have hugged him there and then; he had obviously thought over their last conversation and was now improvising what assistance he could give her. "It's *deeds,* not words, that count," she replied vaguely.

He caught on at once. "Ah!" he cried, rapping his knuckles against his brow. "Is there anyone at home in here? Talking of deeds, I almost forgot. I've brought the ones you asked me to retrieve from Frank Kernow. They're in my briefcase." He rose as he spoke and went to the door. He popped out into the passage and returned a moment later with a large manila envelope, sealed and spattered with hard red wax. "I think you ought to cast an eye over them, sir, before they go to Jake Morvah. I'll put them on the bureau, shall I?"

John nodded and then, with a chuckle, said, "Neatly done, young fellow!"

Ben stared back in alarm, thinking he had given Leah's game away — whatever it was. "Sir?"

"You neatly avoided answering my question — why not set a date? And do it right now?"

"Pa!" Leah objected. Her tone suggested he was deliberately trying to embarrass them. "You know very well why."

"Do I?" he asked belligerently. "You may imagine I do, but I assure you ..."

"Think!" She squirmed with embarrassment and looked apologetically at Philomena. 'Men!' said her eyes.

But Philomena took John's part. "It may be crystal clear to you, my dear," she said. "But let me say that I, too ..."

"Well, it involves you, too, of course," Leah said, still embarrassed but now with a tinge of annoyance at their obtuseness. "It very much involves you — as I would have thought you, of all people ..."

"Me?" she asked in a slightly wounded tone. "My dear young lady — I fail to see how your wedding and Ben's could have the remotest connection with ..."

Leah interrupted her again, in the tones of one cornered and absolutely forced to speak out against her will. "How can I possibly leave the Old Glebe. Surely you can see my difficulty ... things being as they are? "

"As they are? What d'you mean — 'as they are'?"

Leah gave a bitter little laugh. "Actually, I mean 'as they *aren't*'! And you know very well what I mean."

"Oh, well ..." Philomena tossed her head. "*That* little matter is entirely up to your father."

"Now then, let's just everybody take it easy and calm down," John said. "This conversation has gone quite far enough. *Too* far, in fact. We'll talk of other things."

"He knows I won't budge — on a matter of principle," Philomena told Leah quietly. "But he refuses to draw the obvious conclusion from it."

"I said that's enough," John warned her.

Leah's eyes caught Ben's. He raised one eyebrow a fraction of an inch. They had rehearsed nothing, of course. Philomena would have seen through them at once if they had. She realized she had to trust him now — trust not only that he had divined her purpose but knew how to promote it, too. Fearing that Philomena might already have noticed this briefest of glances, she just sighed, and lowered her head, as if accepting her father's ordinance.

"Your pardon, sir," Ben said, "but I feel I should point out that I'm not quite as patient as my composure tonight may have led you to believe ..."

"Young man," John warned him in an ominous tone. "I said 'enough' and I meant it."

But Leah, as if Ben's intervention had fired her own courage, now leaped back into the contest. "No, Pa," she said quietly. "You've been so caught up in your own difficulties that you haven't appreciated how the ripples of misery have spread. Nor have you, Philomena. This business has festered long enough. If we do not lance it tonight, we'll be throwing away the best opportunity that's ever likely to come our way."

"Talk your heads off! I shan't say a word," he replied curtly.

Leah turned her appeal toward Philomena.

The woman hesitated. She knew very well that Leah had been driving toward this point all evening — had even arranged the evening for that very purpose. But she had no idea what the girl might have in mind. So it came down to a question of trust. Could she trust Leah to further any interests but her own — and, to a lesser degree, her father's? Nothing within her leaped up and cried, 'Yes!' On the other hand, matters could not be allowed to drift much longer. Temporary stalemates had a pernicious tendency to set into permanence. Whatever Leah had in mind, it would almost certainly break the logjam. She would just have to stay astute enough to make sure the logs rolled the way she wished, that was all.

So, taking her courage in both hands, she said, in the same quiet tone as Leah's, "I think your daughter's right, John. We'll never have a better occasion than this."

He looked daggers at her. "In front of my own children?" he asked. "Are you mad?"

"When those same 'children' are talking of their own marriages, my dear, it's time to stop thinking like that."

"Talk away," he said again. "But don't expect me to take any part whatsoever."

Leah winked gratefully at Philomena and said, "Have you ever explained to him exactly why you refuse even to contemplate the idea of ..."

"Him?" her father exploded. "Who's 'him'? *He* has a name, you know."

Leah repeated her question in exactly the same tone: "Have you ever explained to John Carrington why you refuse" — her father snorted angrily — "to marry him?"

"He does not require an explanation," Philomena said irritably.

"You mean because any person with just a bit of common sense could work it out for himself?"

"Just so!"

Leah looked at her father, who folded his arms and stared intently at the fire, half turning his head away from his two female tormentors.

"It's a matter of pride, after all," Leah went on, as if she were now explaining Philomena to herself. "It may be a silly, distorted sort of pride but John Carrington, of all people, should understand that!"

"Yes ..." Philomena agreed warily.

"I mean, one might think that nothing could be worse for a lady than to have everyone in the neighbourhood treat her as a scarlet woman. But there *is* something worse than that, isn't there! Much worse!"

Philomena did not respond. They were both watching John Carrington, who was now as tense as a steel spring and seemed hardly to be breathing. At last he became aware of their scrutiny and snapped, "Well?"

"Well, what?" Leah responded.

"Well, tell me — since you seem determined to bend my ear on this utterly distasteful subject — what could possibly be worse than to have every female tongue in Cornwall wagging away with talk of your moral turpitude?"

Leah and Philomena looked at each other. Leah said, "You tell him, then."

"Oh, no!" Philomena laughed. "You don't catch me so easily! If he *still* can't work it out, then ..."

Leah cut across her and said to her father, "The thing that could be worse — and I can't honestly *believe* the thought has never once crossed your mind — would be to have those same tongues saying that she only married you to get the Old Glebe — the way the Liddicoats always wanted to get it."

John turned pale and stared at Philomena. "Tell me it isn't so," he said, barely above a whisper.

Her lips compressed to a thin, bloodless line.

"You mean you won't marry me because people would say a thing like that?"

"Yes!" she snapped.

"My God!" He stared at her, at his hands ... the fire ... the ceiling. "That does it, then," he said miserably.

"In what way?" Leah asked.

"Well, she'll never marry me as long as she's possessed by a crazy idea like that."

"I don't think it's crazy," Leah replied. "Nor would any woman with a streak of pride in herself — *and* more than a streak of love for the man in question."

John turned to Philomena. "This is turning into something completely unreal. I don't understand — *why* are you willing to live with me — in every sense of the word?"

"Because she *loves* you, you ... you big palooka! Aargh!" Leah stood up and strode impatiently about the room. "Don't you understand anything?"

"When it comes to the ways of a woman, I've never staked the smallest claim to ..."

"She loves you enough to sacrifice her honour in order to be at your side — because your own honour won't be touched by it. Men's honour never is besmirched in *that* situation, is it! In fact, the world would think you no end of a fellow. But it's *your* honour would be blackened if everyone thought she'd only married you to get her hands on this place. They'd say she hornswaggled you — or whatever the Cornish for 'hornswaggled' is. She'd be the smart skirt then, the wisenheimer of West Penwith, and you'd be the jackass. She didn't want to do that to you — don't you see? So tell her! Tell her she really ought to have explained all that to you!"

He questioned Philomena with his eyebrows.

She nodded.

He hung his head. "What a fool I am," he murmured. Then, glancing up at Philomena again, he added more robustly, "But you weren't much better — if I may speak quite frankly. D'you honestly mean to tell me that's really all that was holding you back? A little thing like ..."

"*All*, he says!" Philomena appealed to Leah.

Leah turned again to her father and said, "So?"

"So?" he responded. "What d'you expect me to do? Tell her she's been a fool as well?"

"No."

"What then?" he asked in exasperation.

"Do something that will make it completely impossible for people ever to say such a thing."

"Oh! Now why didn't I think of that?" he asked sarcastically. "I'll take a whole page in the *Helston Vindicator*. I'll tell the whole gossiping world that I am freely marrying ..."

"It wouldn't work," Leah interrupted. "Besides, there's a cheaper way."

He stared at her blankly.

"You could do it right now." She waved toward the bureau.

He followed her gesture, saw the deeds to the Old Glebe ... and turned even paler than before. "Oh, no ..." he whispered.

Slowly he turned his gaze on Philomena.

She knew exactly what he was thinking for it was what would be going through her own nasty, suspicious mind in his circumstances: Was this the culmination of a plan she had laid down in those days after their first brush with each other — when she realized that a frontal assault would never dislodge the Carringtons? And that marriage would bring her only half a loaf? And that for her, Philomena Liddicoat, half a loaf was *not* better than no bread, for she was an all-or-nothing woman. Would she now get the all and he get the nothing?

Her heart was racing so fast she was sure it could not actually be pumping any blood at all. Her whole body felt drained, weak, and shivery.

"Greater love hath no man than this ..." Leah murmured, fighting an urge to push her father ... guide his hand ...

He did not take his eyes off Philomena. "Greater love hath no man than I," he told her.

She nodded and tried not to blink, for fear that the tears in her eyes would roll. It was a futile struggle. Soon two juicy drops made tracks down her cheeks and gathered at her jawline, where she wiped them angrily away.

He rose and went across the room to the window, where he opened the curtain and peered out into the dark. A rather fitful moonlight gleamed on the fields and buildings — showing him all that he owned. Would he risk it all on what was no more than an intuition? The man of business flinched from the decision but the man in love continued to wonder. How great *was* his love? Did it measure up to this?

"By God, I'll do it!" he said, crossing the room again, this time to the bureau. "And I'll do it properly, too." He went to the door and bellowed, "Pansy!" just before he opened it.

She almost fell into the room, recovered her balance, and stood there looking sheepish.

"No need to explain it all to you, I guess," he said crisply. "I'm going to need your witness-signature. Yours, too, Ben." To Leah he added, "Honey, get pen and paper, I'm suddenly in a dictating mood."

He returned to the sofa, where he stooped and kissed Philomena on the brow. "My father is turning in his grave at this moment," he murmured.

"And so is old Honourable Carrington, too, I make no doubt," she replied.

"Tell me I won't regret it."

She shook her head. "I can't do that. It's your judgement, John. It has to be."

He sat beside her, placed the deeds symbolically in her lap, and took her hand. "I, John Carrington, being of sound mind and sober," he said to Leah, who was writing furiously at the bureau, "do hereby give in its entirety all those lands, dwellings, and outhouses known as the Old Glebe to Miss Philomena Liddicoat of Cheam. This gift I make with no consideration whatsoever in return." He drew a deep breath and closed his eyes as if in pain. And there was a hint of pain in his voice, too, as he added: "It is hers absolutely and inalienably, no matter what course she might hereafter pursue with regard to any other arrangements or understanding that may or may not presently obtain between us."

Philomena collapsed on his shoulder and whispered, "I do!" The deeds fell to the floor. Neither of them stooped to pick the envelope up.

"Wait till it's signed," he warned her.

"I don't need to …" she began but they were both startled by a cry of anguish from Pansy: "Oh, sir! Oh, sir!" she repeated again and again. She was panting as if she'd run a mile and the tears were streaming down her cheeks.

"What is it, maid?" he asked in alarm.

"That was the most beautiful thing I ever heard. I can't bear it! I can't bear it!" And, burying her face in her pinafore, she fled from the room.

"We need you to witness!" Leah called after her, but she did not return.

John Carrington signed the document with a flourish and Ben witnessed it. "The mere fact that she saw it would stand up in a court of law," he said.

"We'll still make sure," Leah told him.

She found Pansy out in the garden, holding on to the gate as if wondering which way to run next. It was a mild night with a waning moon holding its place among streets of high, swift-moving clouds — though, curiously, there was hardly a breeze at ground level. "Quick, before the nib dries," she said, handing pen and jotting pad to the maid while she turned to 'make a back' for her. Pansy had stopped crying by now and was sniffing her salt-laden nostrils clear once more. "Why did the master do that, miss?" she asked in a jerky, bewildered tone.

"Risk *everything,* you mean?"

"Yes, miss."

"It's called love, Pansy. And I think it made you cry because you suddenly realized it's what you've been missing in your life. Am I right?" She turned and took pen and jotter back from her. "Am I?" she insisted.

Pansy nodded and stared at the ground.

"And as long as you persist in your present ways, you're not likely to, either — eh?"

The girl sniffed and said she ' 'spected not.'

Ben came out at that moment and put his hands on Leah's shoulders from behind. She handed the things back to Pansy. "Take these indoors," she said. "And if my brother hasn't the nous to leave the drawing room on some excuse, you find some way to get him out."

Pansy started, none too willingly, back up the path. "An excuse? Me? Like what?" she asked.

"Oh ... I'm sure you'll think of *something*," Leah said heavily. Then she added, "And — remembering what we were just saying — take him anywhere except the tithe barn!"

Pansy turned round angrily and stuck her tongue out, thinking it would not be observed in the dark; but the moon and clouds betrayed her.

To avoid having to make a scene, Leah said, "And wipe that self-satisfied grin off your face!"

The offensive tongue was immediately replaced by a self-satisfied grin.

"That's better," Leah said.

When they were alone, Ben asked why she had been so specific about the tithe barn.

Leah looked at him sharply, wondering if he was being facetious. But when she saw he was not, she gave him a quick kiss on the nose and said, "Come along — I'll show you!"